Wildfires

N. KAY

Cover Art: Reginald Van Langenhove

This is a work of fiction. Names, characters, places, and incidents are either the product of the author's imagination or are used fictitiously. Any resemblance to actual persons, living or dead, events, or locales is entirely coincidental.

This book is an erotic romance, intended for adult audiences only.
It contains sexually explicit scenes.

DEDICATION

To Nora Ann and Adonna Lyn

In Memory of Stephen Nicole

ACKNOWLEDGMENTS

I thank my many family, friends, and colleagues whose support and patience helped make this book possible. First, I must thank Joyce for her wonderful counsel, encouragement, and lack of censorship which allowed me the sense of freedom to create an erotic novel. Next, I must express sincere appreciation to my editor, Janice, whose professional expertise, standards, and love of the written word contributed to a better-crafted story.

Also, I pay tribute to my wonderful writing and research consultants, Antonia, Barbara, Colbert, David, Josh, Kevin, Kimberly, Lyn, Phyllis, and Tim. Their candid comments and insightful critiques provided a solid foundation for rewriting and storytelling.

Finally, I must convey my gratitude to Ava, Debora, Karen, and Susan for their unceasing inspiration.

Wishing all my readers a pleasurable romp through the pages.

PROLOGUE

The young stripper screamed and threw a temper tantrum. The fire captain in the orange helmet rushed over to calm her. Fire trucks surrounded them, and flashing lights streaked through the inky blue sky. Police and fire radios buzzed. Water seeped outside the strip club, slickened the streets, and formed rancid puddles. The smell of smoke filled the air, but the flames had been extinguished and no longer licked the sky.

Everybody was accounted for, and the fire captain had everything under control, except for the young blond stripper. It was New Year's Eve, and she was obviously high. He wished he had taken the night off and had a few drinks himself, but duty called, and he had to cover for some of his crew that he had permitted the night off.

"Rae's still in there!" the young stripper exclaimed. "The manager's still in there."

"You don't see him out here?" the captain asked in alarm.

"It's she! She's not out here. I've been calling her cell phone. She's not answering."

The fire captain looked doubtful. "We checked the club thoroughly. I don't see how we could have missed her."

The young stripper jumped up and down. She shouted at the top of her lungs. "She's in there! Our manager's still inside!"

The captain exchanged glances with one of his rookies. They both wondered if the young woman was lucid, but other strippers started crowding around her in support. "You gotta find Rae," they insisted. "The owner's outta town. Rae's in charge. She probably went to that office behind the stage."

"Alright, alright," the captain said reassuringly. "If she's in there, we'll find her. But we need you to calm down so we can do our jobs," he said in warning to the blond stripper as a couple of police officers on the scene headed over. "You want to be here when we bring her out, right?"

The young stripper quieted down and stared into the handsome, brown-skinned face of the captain. His manner relaxed and reassured her. "Please go get her," the young woman said.

The captain nodded and tugged on his breathing apparatus. He signaled to a few other firefighters to follow, including the young rookie.

Inside the strip club, the floors were water-soaked and messy. Chairs, tables, and booths sagged from the drenching of fire hoses. The club was in shambles, but the captain and his crew had extinguished the fire in record time.

After one of the air-monitoring crew gave the signal, the captain removed his breathing apparatus. The small group behind him followed suit. Then they pushed and shoved all obstructions aside and went behind the stage. They searched the office, dressing rooms, and bathrooms, but still saw no sign of anyone. The captain called out, but no one answered.

"You think she's in here, Captain?" the rookie asked. "I mean, that girl outside is high as a kite."

The captain nodded in agreement. "She is, but the rest of those women think the manager's still in here too. Keep checking," he ordered.

If the manager was back here, the captain thought, she was damned lucky that they squelched the fire before it spread to the stage. The captain went back inside the office and looked around again. A couple of his men followed. The captain stood in the middle of the floor and scrutinized every wall, crack, and crevice. Then he noticed a pile of debris shoved against a faux brick wall. The remnants of a heavy desk had also been pushed against the wall. The captain pushed the desk aside and some damaged stereo speakers. He tapped the wall with the back of his gloved hand for heat. Then he tapped for density.

"Soundproof," the captain muttered to his men. Then he noticed a latch in the wall. He shoved more debris aside and clicked the latch. It appeared jammed. The captain used a pry bar and forced the latch to unlock. A door suddenly opened outward. The captain stepped into a room the size of a large walk-in closet. Then he saw her trying to rise to her feet.

She was a beautiful chocolate brown woman in one of the tightest, shortest dresses he had ever seen. Water had seeped into the room and plastered her dress around her hips. Her thighs glistened from the water. The captain stared. He couldn't help himself. He immediately squelched a hardening in his loins.

A trickle of blood ran down her temple, and he assumed the portable metal fan at her feet was the culprit. It must have fallen off one of the shelves. She appeared disoriented. Her wig had fallen off. But she didn't seem badly hurt. Maybe, a minor concussion.

"I couldn't get out the door," she explained. Then she pointed to a wall safe and shook her head. "I don't remember the combination. I need to get some papers out."

In a few strides, the fire captain reached her. He picked her up. "We need to get you out of here."

The young rookie suppressed a wicked smile. "Aye, aye, Captain."

"No," she protested weakly. "I gotta get my papers, my wig. I need my handbag."

The captain didn't see the handbag. He determined the wig and the papers could wait. "Let's go, young lady." He lifted her up higher in his arms.

"You swept me off my feet," she said dazedly.

CHAPTER 1

Carla Rae Hepburn thought she had died and gone to heaven. She half-opened her eyes and stared into the face of the handsome firefighter carrying her. His skin was a warm brown complexion, and he had light brown eyes and full, kissable lips beneath his mustache. Carla knew she was in heaven as she snuggled against him.

For the moment, she let everything go, all her worries about the safe, the money, her handbag. She sank deeper against him, but she couldn't feel him the way she wanted to because he wore a tan turnout jacket with yellow stripes, layered to insulate him from the fire. Carla tried to push against him to feel his chest against her face. Despite his jacket, she guessed accurately that he was broad-chested and buff. She wanted to feel more of him and pressed with even more abandon against his chest. She still couldn't feel as much of him as she wanted.

Carla closed her eyes groggily, but knew that she had to remain awake to fully savor the moment of being carried by this handsome, muscled hunk. Carla heard his boots thudding on the cement of the strip club floor. *Please don't wake me up,* she prayed, *whether I'm in heaven or not.* She reached for his arms and tried to feel his biceps through the jacket. But she didn't have the strength to grip the way she wanted. Her grip must have been strong enough though because he reacted.

Baxter Rose stifled an amused smile. His triple-layered pants and jacket protected him from one fire, but apparently not from the "hot momma" he was carrying. She had an incredible body on her. He guessed she was in her late thirties, possibly forties, close to his age. But it was hard to tell because her ass was so nice and firm. No way was he going to let that ass burn. He had felt the need to scoop her up immediately in case of a rekindle, though he doubted that the fire would start up again. He didn't allow rekindles on his watch. He intended to rake somebody over the coals for not finding her in the first place.

She was a dark chocolate girl with a deep, exotic cleft in her chin. She was a beauty with long eyelashes and very dark eyes when she opened them. Her features were a bit rough around the edges from the club life, but she was still lovely. Yet she had very little hair. Her wig had fallen off, but not the wig cap. He could see through the netting of the cap. Her short, natural hair was thin in a number of spots and almost non-existent in the crown. He understood why she wanted to retrieve her wig. But no time for wigs, he had decided. Her wig could have been a fire hazard. That's when he scooped her up and carried her. She could always buy another wig.

What a shame. She was gorgeous, but he preferred women with a full head of hair. It could be relaxed, it could be an afro, maybe even a short afro like hers, but not so sparse. No matter, he was here to rescue her, not date her. He wished she would stop snuggling against him. He was at work, on the job, proud to be a firefighter, but he was still human. Damn, she had a nice body. She might be a manager now, but he guessed she was a stripper in her younger days. She still had the curves, and hardly any gray hair.

Baxter advanced down the hallway with a somewhat dazed Carla in his arms. They were close to the exit. The air was fresher even though the door opened onto a sleazy Los Angeles street. Baxter could hear the commotion outside—the hum of the fire trucks, the buzz of police radios, and the haggle of reporters, jockeying for the best coverage. Beyond the exit, lights swirled from the fire trucks and police cars on the scene. The police had put up barricades to keep the public back.

Through a haze, Carla heard all the commotion too, but she wanted none of it. She just wanted to never leave heaven nor wake up from her dream of being carried by the handsome fireman.

Baxter stifled a slight quickening in his groin as Carla nestled deeper into his jacket. The moment they crossed over the safety threshold outside, strippers, reporters, and his crew clapped and cheered for Baxter. He nodded humbly in thanks. Since it was New Year's Eve, the cheering crowd raised imaginary glasses in toast. Baxter suspected some of the crowd had real glasses and other stimulants, but in the spirit of the moment, he lifted the woman in his arms higher and returned the toast. "Happy New Year," he grinned. Then he reluctantly handed over "sleeping beauty" to the paramedics.

Carla tried to hold onto Baxter, but her grip was too weak. "No," she said.

One of the paramedics laughed as they placed her on the stretcher. "Somebody's in love."

Baxter shook his head in amusement. Carla simply sighed in dismay. The young blond stripper flew immediately to her side.

CHAPTER 2

"It's okay for you to go home now," the doctor said. He was a young ruddy-faced intern, very matter-of-fact and serious for his age. "Your x-rays are good. Everything looks fine. You're lucky."

Indeed, she was, Carla decided. The cut at her temple was only superficial and required no stitches. She'd dab some Aloe Vera on it to make sure it didn't scar.

Carla's feet hung over the side of the bed in one of the partitioned cubicles in the hospital emergency room. She didn't quite know what to do with herself. Was she dreaming? Where was the fireman, her knight in yellow armor? she wondered.

The young doctor's face softened. "Do you have somebody to pick you up? We can call somebody for you if you'd like?"

Mimi, the blond stripper, who had accompanied Carla to the hospital, had gone home at Carla's insistence. Mimi had partied from sunup to sundown on New Year's Eve. One of the other dancers had taken her home. Carla was afraid that the emergency room staff might forcibly keep Mimi if she didn't go home. That would have been the ultimate injustice against Mimi for saving Carla's life. She was eternally grateful to Mimi.

Carla finally responded to the young doctor. "No, my sister will be here soon. I'm just glad I memorized her number. I lost my cell phone back there." Carla waved her hand in the air and shuddered at the memory of the fire. The doctor nodded in understanding. He finally succumbed to the urge to stare at her legs under the short, tight dress. Then he tore his eyes away and politely excused himself to the next emergency.

Carla smiled and shook her head tolerantly. "Thanks for everything, doctor," she said. *Men,* Carla thought. They were all alike. Well, not her rescuer. She kept thinking about him and wondering if she would ever see him again.

"Doctor," she said, stopping him before he left. "Do you know the fireman who brought me in? I wanted to thank—"

"Paramedics brought you in," the doctor said, puzzled.

"Just wondered," Carla said sheepishly. *How silly,* she thought. Of course, her rescuer didn't bring her here. "Nothing, doctor . . .," her voice trailed off. She felt like a schoolgirl with an awkward crush.

Get over the handsome fireman, she told herself. *He's too young.*

"You'll be fifty soon?" the young doctor had asked in surprise when he reviewed her chart earlier. He had nodded at her, impressed.

Carla had tried to stifle a pleasant smile. Yep, she still looked good for her age, despite being an aging stripper—no, manager, she corrected herself. In her younger days, stripping had thrown her into a hard life of late-night partying and fending off jerks who wanted to paw all over her. Then there were the drugs, although she was more of a pothead than anything else when she was younger.

She had done some coke every now and then, but fortunately, coke never affected her. As for uppers, she didn't feel anything from them either, and if she did, she hadn't recognized the feeling. Maybe, she couldn't let go enough for the high to take effect. Some subconscious restraint always reigned in her partying so that she could never totally let go. She knew she always had to be careful. She hung with some shady characters, guys who would call her "ho" in a minute, and co-workers who would allow scumbags to call them "hos" to keep the coke, heroin, and meth flowing.

But a lot of that was behind Carla now. Or so she thought—until the fire in Wendell's club. In her earlier days as a stripper, she had gone to work for Wendell Jones. His club was sleazy, but had a little more class than others. At first, he treated her like any other dancer in his club. He demanded that she start her shows on time, pay to dance at his club, and give him fifteen percent of her tips. He also demanded that she mingle with the guests and make them feel that she would fuck every one of them. Yet Wendell didn't allow you to mess around with the clients unless he got a cut.

Wendell's rules were easy enough to follow. Of course, she did screw around every now and then with a customer, but not for pay. After all, she was only human and at that time, in her partying stage. But she wasn't a whore, and she only screwed the men who showed her some respect, as much respect as they would show a stripper. As for sex-crazed, disrespectful, arrogant bastards, she told them to kiss her ass whenever she could get away with it, but they got no coochie from her.

Some of the "clients" could be so disgusting with their drooling, clawing, and pawing that a lot of the dancers wanted nothing to do with men. These dancers only dated and had sex with other women who showed them some tenderness. Carla couldn't fault them for it either, but she herself screwed men.

By the time Carla started working with Wendell, she was in her thirties. She had gone to him because Wendell hired some of the "older" strippers and exotic dancers to work in his club as long as they kept themselves in good shape. But he only messed around with his young dancers. However, he made an exception for Carla—not that she gave a damn at first.

Wendell liked the way she handled herself professionally. He admired how she could fend off most guys who wanted to slap that round, firm ass of hers. Wendell said her ass shook enough to be sexy, but not flabby. So Wendell had to tap that ass, and the fact that Carla didn't look up to him the way some of the younger dancers did, intrigued him. She and Wendell started dating—well actually, fucking—and their relationship surprisingly grew into one of friendship along with hot, crazy sex.

As Carla got older, Wendell started fucking her less and sampling the younger dancers more. Carla didn't care. Wendell was becoming addicted to porn. At first, she thought it was okay that he wanted to watch dirty movies while they screwed, but he had gotten to the point that porno movies, orgies in particular, seemed to be the only thing that got him off while they had sex. Wendell's losing interest in her sexually was a welcome relief. He was getting fat and out of shape, and he sweated a lot more, though he was still a handsome man. In his and Carla's heydays, the dancers and the patrons referred to the couple as "coffee and cocoa." Carla never figured out who was the coffee and who was the cocoa. The references varied. She and Wendell both had smooth dark skin.

These days, Wendell hung around several young strippers at a time. Carla figured he was probably acting out his orgy fantasies with the young dancers.

Wendell's declining sexual interest in her coincided with Carla's meeting a "nice" guy outside the club. He held the car door open for her and took her out to dinner until he happened into the club one night and found out that she was a stripper—the headliner. The next time they got together, he tried to shove his dick down her throat until she bit down hard. Then she delivered a swift kick to his groin and split.

Eventually, she and Wendell developed a business relationship. She started managing the club for Wendell after his previous manager got hooked on heroin. They renamed the place, "The TiTi Bar," and Carla served as the hostess-manager. They had problems at first with the name of the club. She and Wendell got a kick out of insisting that patrons pronounce it "TeeTee," not "Titty Bar." After a while, people caught on and called the club by its proper name.

As she entered her forties, Carla was glad to get away from the grind of performing so many nights a week. She was more detail-oriented than she realized and good at managing. The TiTi Bar started picking up even more clients because of the way Carla managed the club. She was still in good shape and wore some of the most provocative clothing to turn the men on. Between her skimpy dresses and the exotic dancing on stage, the guys spent freely. Even though she wore skimpy attire, Carla did so with class. She wore short clingy dresses, sometimes with glitter or lace, sometimes in an animal print. Though she always wished for bigger boobs, the ones she had filled out her dresses and push-up bras well enough.

Her butt was her best asset. Nice and round. And her legs were long and shapely. Sometimes she wore her dresses just below the panty line, and her necklines just above the nipples. Yet, she purchased good fabrics that weren't cheesy so she didn't come off as tasteless. She was still toned and firm with perhaps a wrinkle and some cellulite here and there, but this simply gave her character.

While she wore high heels to show off her legs, she refused to wear stilettos since she had to move about and circulate. She had to titillate the men so that they would hoot and holler, and above all, tip the dancers and buy plenty of drinks from the bar. She always sported a sexy manicure and pedicure and a nice collection of wigs. She wore heavy makeup too. She liked wearing the heavier perfumes, just a dash so that the men barely got a whiff of it as she sauntered by them. And lest any man reach out for a feel and mistake Carla for a hooker, Wendell's henchmen would not hesitate to bounce the offender out of the club.

She used her middle name, "Rae," as a stage name. To maintain some privacy, she had tried using the name, "Linda," but it never worked. People would address her as Linda, and she'd look around for Linda. It simply became easier for her to use her middle name in the club arena. She liked her middle name. Very few people knew her first name, and though Wendell did, he stuck with calling her "Rae."

Sometimes, Carla stripped at the TiTi. Wendell would have posters made for an older crowd. He'd use social media, too, at Carla's insistence. Mimi, the young blond stripper, had a knack for social media. She'd reach the younger guys and lure them to the show. Between the flyers and social media, Carla's striptease act drew a large crowd, which meant more money for the other dancers too. All the clients got revved up for the show. The younger patrons weren't always impressed until they saw Carla perform. Then they became a nuisance after being titillated out of their minds by her show. She had to fend them off more than the older guys. The older guys used her steamy show to get their dicks hard so they could grope the younger strippers and dancers.

When Carla stripped, she gave her all. She taunted and tantalized the men to the point that some of them went to the bathroom and jerked off. She would start off in front of a gauzy curtain that amplified her beauty and her curves and downplayed any signs of age. One of the favorite shows the men liked was when she wore a black satin tuxedo that graced her curves. The fabric didn't wrinkle or appear tacky, but it clung to every part of her body. She would dance around the stage slowly and provocatively.

The men would hold their breaths waiting for her to remove the first item of clothing. Somebody would holler, "Work that ass, baby. Work that ass."

And that's exactly what Carla did. She would gyrate that ass a little more, but still play coy with her performance. Then she would open up the jacket to reveal a sheer, loose blouse over a sequined push-up bra that showed lots of cleavage. She would open up her pants and slowly unzip them and stand with her legs wide open, shaking and twerking. Then she would start peeling down her pants, but zip them back up teasingly. Of course, she always turned around and gave the crowd a bumping and grinding view of her butt.

Then the pants fell to the floor, and she'd be wearing sheer boy shorts over a sequined G-string. Next, she'd remove the sheer, loose blouse to reveal the sequined bra. She'd follow that display by removing the push-up bra that covered the pasties over her nipples. After a lot of teasing, she'd finally pull the boy shorts down and uncover the glittery G-string.

By the time she had stripped down to pasties over her nipples and a G-string that showed almost all of her goodies, the men were whipped up into a frenzy, all the while throwing money on the stage. Horny breathing was the only thing you could hear in the place. Patrons loved Carla's show. Every one of them wanted to fuck her. And she reveled in it, gave them the performance of their lives. When she was up on stage, she turned stripping into an erotic art form. In her twenties and thirties, Carla could make a few thousand a night between tips, lap dances, and a cut from her shows.

Even in her later years, the TiTi Bar provided a decent

enough place to work, until that stinking Joe Cook started coming to the club. She and the girls at the club named him "Gutter Joe." In fact, some of the clients who frequented the club adopted the name, but nobody called him Gutter Joe to his face. He was tall, slim, and lanky. You couldn't tell whether he was White or Black. His skin was very fair, and he had reddish-brown hair and hazel eyes. He could have been a handsome man if his eyes weren't so cold. He skulked around and walked like trouble.

Nobody knew what race he was, and he never spoke of it. Was he a White man who mingled with Blacks or a Black man who could pass for White? Nobody could really tell, but it didn't matter. He was pure evil incarnate.

Wendell always warned the young dancers in the club to stay away from Gutter Joe. Several of the dancers had been lured by Joe's seeming good looks and manner. They couldn't see through his slick, cold veneer. They just wanted to party with Joe and his money. Then he'd hook them on heavy drugs, anything from crack, to heroin, to meth. They'd try to come back to the club and work, but Gutter Joe had used them up, and he let his slimy hangers-on use up the young dancers too. So Carla issued what Wendell called a dictum, "Don't fuck with Gutter Joe—literally." Still, Joe would flash his money around, and some young, dumb dancer would fall into the trap.

Carla wanted to bar Gutter Joe from coming to the club, but Wendell always stopped short of backing her up. Joe brought in a big entourage with him. In the club, they acted like perfect gentlemen, showed more manners than most patrons. They bought plenty of liquor, top shelf. They tipped everybody well. Gutter Joe was into everything, from drugs to prostitution, and for some reason, he started becoming a fixture at the TiTi Bar.

Joe made Carla's skin crawl. His eyes always raked her over with his stare. He tried to intimidate her when once he told her, "Let me put my dick in that hole in your chin. Come all over the place. I'll give you so much money."

"Ain't that much money in the world," Carla had responded and walked away. She deliberately shook her ass at him and dared him to come near her. She knew he was a force to be reckoned with, and she would never underestimate him. But because he was such a vile, low-life coward, she wasn't afraid of him. He might get the best of her in a fight if he ever tried to subdue her, but he'd be one injured mother fucker when the fight was over.

Though evil, sneaky, and despicable, Joe could be surprisingly kind on occasion. He'd plucked one of Wendell's dancers from the club and sent her off to college.

When the girl hesitated at first, Joe asked her, "This where you wanna hang out for the rest of your days? Don't throw your life away." Joe made it sound like more of a demand than a concern. Nobody at the club understood it. Perhaps, the young woman reminded him of somebody. Gutter Joe wouldn't say. He also wouldn't admit that he was the one behind the fire.

Carla knew Joe was starting to frequent the club for a reason. He wanted Wendell to start distributing drugs at the club. Wendell had a policy at the TiTi Bar. He didn't care what you did outside the club—blocks away from the club, that is. But on his premises, you could not do drugs. Wendell didn't do drugs. He only drank—hard liquor. So nobody was allowed to do drugs, let alone deal or distribute. Carla loved the policy. While the TiTi attracted some shady characters, Wendell's policy kept a lot of riff-raff away. His policy made the TiTi a more stable place to work for all the girls, including Carla.

Gutter Joe had told Wendell, "Man, you'll be balling all over the place. You can buy as many clubs as you want."

Wendell's mouth had formed a hard line. "No drugs in my club. Case closed. Not up for discussion." Wendell turned his back on Gutter Joe and walked away.

Carla had seen the smoldering fury in Joe's eyes, but he maintained his composure. He waited until Wendell left town for a funeral to enact his vengeance. He set the fire. Carla couldn't prove it, but she knew he was involved, and he did it on her guard, when she was in charge of the club. Her New Year's Eve had been great until the fire. She served as the consummate hostess for the night. The liquor flowed freely, and the bar raked in plenty of money. The dancers and the waitresses collected wads of cash in tips. But then, the fire had shut down everything. She and Wendell's most trusted henchmen had managed to salvage most of the bar money, but everything else was in shambles.

She owed Gutter Joe—big time. Somehow, she would pay him back.

CHAPTER 3

Carla sat in the waiting room. The doctor had departed to other patients. Fortunately, the room was no longer crowded with victims of New Year's Eve mishaps. Carla was tempted to get up and walk out. But she had no keys, no cell phone, no handbag. She hadn't been able to hang onto anything because of the fire.

Moving to an innocuous corner of the room, she reached up and lifted her wig cap. She tried to pull some of the edges of her hair over her balding crown. She shifted the cap back in place just as her sister, Natalie, rushed in and hugged her.

"You okay?" Natalie asked.

"A little tired, but I'm okay."

Carla was pleased by her younger sister's concern since Natalie didn't approve of Carla's lifestyle. Now that Natalie saw for herself that Carla was fine, Natalie found it difficult to mask her disapproval.

"You've got to get out of there, Carla. It's not a decent place to work, and you're . . . ." Natalie stopped.

"What?" Carla asked.

"You're too old. It's a sleazy place to work, and you're too old now," Natalie said without flinching.

"And you're thirty-eight going on sixty," Carla retorted.

Carla didn't feel like listening to another lecture from her younger sister. Instead, she wished she were back in the arms of the handsome fireman. Yes, she knew she didn't work in the most wholesome environment, but she didn't need Natalie to keep chastising her.

Natalie pulled out a light jacket for Carla to wear over her dress. The dress barely hung below the jacket. Natalie shook her head and frowned.

"Well, you brought the jacket," Carla snapped.

"I had no idea your dress would be so short." Natalie sighed. "What do you think mom would say?"

Stone-faced, Carla refused to answer.

Natalie's features softened when she noted Carla's hair. She dug into her tote bag and produced a colorful scarf. Carla accepted it graciously, and tied it around her head. Together, they walked down the long antiseptic hallway out of the hospital.

When Carla and Natalie stepped outside, the sunlight was dazzling. Carla lifted her face towards the sky and smiled. It was a beautiful Los Angeles day—New Year's Day to be exact. She was glad to be out of the hospital and glad Natalie had parked on the street. It gave Carla a chance to walk and reflect. She had gone from one extreme to the next—from the dark shoddiness of the club to the stark cleanliness of the hospital. And now she basked in brilliant sunlight.

Carla laughed excitedly when they reached the car. Her New Year was turning out to be good. Natalie had brought Carla's nieces along. As Carla opened the door and slid into the front passenger seat, her nieces, Stephanie, Brittany, and Tiffany, ages eleven, six, and five, greeted her with big eyes and smiles. Their names all ended with the "ny" sound. Carla had asked Natalie about it once, and Natalie shrugged and said she liked the sound.

"Hi, girls," Carla gushed. "Happy New Year!"

"Happy New Year! Aunt Carla," they chimed in chorus. Their eyes devoured her curiously. Stephanie and Tiffany tittered and raised their eyebrows at the skimpiness of Carla's dress under the jacket that Natalie had given her. The eyes of six-year-old Brittany, however, only gleamed in admiration. Carla noted that Brittany was wearing lipstick. Carla stifled a smile. Brittany was a pistol already—like her aunt. She also had Carla's rich, dark coloring.

"I didn't have time to fight with her about the lipstick,"

Natalie said. "We were in a hurry to get you. You talk to her," Natalie urged.

Carla turned around and winked. "Girls, you've got plenty of time for makeup."

They grinned in response.

Stephanie, the oldest at eleven, was a fashionista—tall, lanky, and beautiful. Five-year-old Tiffany acted like the crystal princess of the bunch. Stephanie and Tiffany resembled their mom and possessed her honey brown features. Brittany resembled Carla.

"See, that's what I'm talking about," Natalie said, miffed. "Sounds like you're encouraging them to wear makeup. They're kids."

"Okay, okay," Carla responded. "Girls," her eyes fixed on Brittany, "watch the makeup." She didn't feel like getting into an argument with her sister, but she was tired of Natalie's self-righteous attitude. "Why'd you leave them in the car by themselves?" Carla asked accusingly.

Natalie defended herself. "They wanted to stay in the car—listen to music, play their games. Besides, they all have cells. I parked on the street in broad daylight. I would never—"

"Now you see how it feels to have somebody nagging you," Carla said.

Natalie was quiet for a moment.

"I know you're a good mother," Carla said, softening. "A good sister too. Thanks for coming to pick me up."

Tiffany, the five-year-old princess, spoke up clearly. "Auntie, we're so happy you're safe." Her sisters nodded, their faces showing concern.

Carla choked up for a moment, but didn't want to break down in front of her nieces.

Brittany, the "pistol" looked at the scarf Carla had wrapped around her head and said, "Mom, can we stop and get a scarf? I want one like Aunt Carla's."

"You've seen that scarf before. It's mine," Natalie said, surprised.

"Oh," was all Brittany could respond.

All of the girls realized that their aunt had given the scarf a kind of pizazz. The beautiful colors contrasted well with Carla's skin. Carla had forgotten about the scarf. She smiled at the compliment.

"See how you influence them," Natalie said.

Carla sighed. She didn't want to get into a fight with her younger sister in front of her nieces. She was so grateful that Natalie brought them along. She seldom saw her nieces because Natalie used them as leverage to force Carla away from the club life.

Carla squelched her irritation with Natalie. She turned around to her nieces, excited. "Girls, I may have found you an uncle."

"Really?" Stephanie, the oldest, asked. Her eyes sparkled with the curiosity of a young woman who's starting to discover boys.

The girls waited wide-eyed for Carla to continue. Even Natalie was curious.

Carla suddenly wished she hadn't backed herself into a corner over a fantasy. "Hopefully, I found you an uncle."

The girls stared, waiting for an answer. Natalie waited too.

"Oh, I don't know," Carla shrugged. "Probably, nothing's going to come out of it, but . . . ." She had to say something positive. She didn't have the heart to disappoint her nieces. "This wonderful fireman rescued me. He carried me out of that burning building."

Natalie frowned, disappointed. "That's his job, Carla."

Natalie's daughters were still caught up in the aura of romance and the thought of an uncle.

"Was he cute?" Brittany asked.

"Was he handsome?" Tiffany, the princess, asked more formally.

Stephanie, the oldest, still waited for an answer about the possibility of an uncle.

Carla realized that even if she had to make up something, she couldn't turn back now. "Yes, ladies, he was very handsome, with a gorgeous mustache and the most kissable lips." Encouraged by the dreamy looks of her nieces, she added, "His chest and arms—they were so strong. I wanted him to carry me forever."

She held the girls' rapt attention. They giggled and grinned.

"You felt his chest and arms through that heavy raincoat they wear?" Natalie was determined to poke a hole in Carla's balloon.

"That's not all I felt," Carla goaded.

The girls tittered louder now.

"Alright, Carla, that's enough," Natalie said.

Carla grinned. "Okay, okay." Then, she turned to the girls again. "He was really handsome, and somehow, I know I'll see him again. I know it. So get ready for a new uncle. I know I've said that before, but this guy rescued me. He lifted me up and carried me in his arms."

Natalie couldn't resist. "You mean he did his job. He's a good fireman."

Why was Natalie such a spoilsport? Why was she acting so bitchy? Carla thought. No wonder Russell left her. Russell was twenty years older than his wife. When they got married, Russell was crazy about Natalie and thrilled to have a young, beautiful wife.

Natalie was as good looking as her older sister, but in a softer kind of way. She possessed a light brown complexion, very dark eyes, and long eyelashes. A true beauty in her own right. While her looks weren't as exotic as Carla's, she had a nice body, too, though not as curvy as her older sister's. But Natalie did have a full head of hair which she permed and often wore in a ponytail because that was easiest for her.

Natalie had to raise three girls by herself. Russell had left her a year ago for an older woman, closer to his own age. Natalie had been heartbroken. She couldn't believe Russell would leave her for an older woman. He said he wanted a more laid-back lifestyle. He said Natalie and the girls were too much drama for him. So he packed up and moved into the house of a woman he had known for years. She and Russell acted like kids, as if they didn't have a care in the world. They went to the movies, the theater, basketball games. Russell loved the Clippers basketball team, which was fine with his girlfriend.

They hung out all the time. Her kids were grown, but Russell forgot that he still had three growing daughters. He didn't spend half as much time with them as he should have, but he did give them money.

Natalie couldn't complain about that. He made sure his girls were provided for. Natalie still had to work, but she drove a beautiful Mercedes Benz, compliments of Russell's guilt. He still had to work, too, in order to afford his guilt. But he played hard, too—with his new girlfriend.

Natalie, the young wife, was forced to be the responsible one while Russell and his girlfriend partied non-stop. Maybe, that's why Natalie was such a sourpuss. She didn't have time for fun, and Carla knew Natalie wasn't dating yet, at least, not anyone steady.

Carla sighed. Sometimes, she wanted to slap the smugness off Natalie's face, but she understood what motivated her sister. She wished Natalie could return the empathy.

"Well, girls, as soon as I see that handsome fireman again, I'm going to bring him by," Carla said, refusing to dim the excitement of her nieces.

"Grow up, Carla," Natalie said.

"Get a life," Carla responded.

The girls went back to their cell phones and games. Only Brittany, the pistol, was looking out the window with the hint of a smile on her face.

CHAPTER 4

Carla's stomach churned. The TiTi Bar had reopened in a new space. Tonight was their grand opening. Wendell refused to be knocked down. Within a few months, he had found a new spot in West Los Angeles, near the airport.

She and Wendell vividly remembered standing in the burnt out remains of the old TiTi Bar. It was depressing, nothing but dirt, soot, and charred debris everywhere. Carla had shuddered when she thought about how close she came to possibly dying. Wendell had sensed her discomfort and put an arm around her shoulder. "You'll be okay," he said. "We're a team. I'm not going to let anything happen to you."

Carla had relaxed against Wendell's arm, but she still felt uneasy. Gutter Joe still roamed free. Nobody could prove that he started the fire. Was it time to get away from the stripping life and put it all behind her? Carla had wondered. Was the fire an omen she chose to ignore simply because she knew no other way of life?

Carla pulled her dress down a little. It was scandalous. She knew she looked hot tonight. That was her intent. She and Wendell were trying to get their customers back after the fire. They were also trying to increase business since this new TiTi Bar was bigger than the former and in a better neighborhood. It wasn't that far from the old club, but it was a more expensive place with more class.

The club had shiny dance floors, plush chairs, and booths. Some of the tables encircled poles so that dancers could perform more private shows for small groups. The main dance floor was raised to give the clientele a better view of the dancers. Railings along the sides rendered just enough distance between the patrons and the dancers. The railings also provided something to grip besides the poles whenever the dancers bent over for customers. There were strategically placed mirrors throughout the club. Like most clubs, the new TiTi had a dark, smoky look. The bar was huge and provided a great view of the exotic dance floor.

Giving herself one last glance in the mirror in her dressing room, Carla wondered if she appeared as jittery as she felt. She was glad Wendell had set aside a small dressing room and office combination for her, away from the other dancers. The private space gave Carla a chance to think and work things out. The memory of the fire still haunted her although it was always relieved by the memory of the strong, handsome fireman who carried her to safety. But life moved on. She had to make a living, and she made decent money managing the club. What other work could she do? Still, she was beginning to wonder if she needed to get away from it all.

Maybe, her sister, Natalie, had a point when she challenged Carla to do something else with her life. What kind of example did she set for her nieces? Six-year-old Brittany was already trying to emulate her, but Carla didn't want any of her nieces involved in the seedy life of stripping.

Carla slipped on her shoes. They were strappy red slingbacks that were almost comfortable, at least as comfortable as a high heel could be. The red satin of the shoes looked good against Carla's skin. Her black lace dress boasted an oval opening in the front that revealed enough cleavage to draw the attention of any man. The dress melted over every nook, cranny, and curve of her body. She had oiled her body so that it shone, slightly iridescent. Her makeup was flawless, heavy as usual, with red lipstick. Her butt was high and round in the dress. She looked stunning and flashy.

When Carla stepped outside of her dressing room, Wendell did a double take. He reached out and touched her ass.

Carla stepped away. "Watch it."

Wendell grinned. "Oh, I am watching it."

"You know what I mean," Carla said smiling, but firm. "Those days are over."

"I know, but you look so delectable."

Carla smiled. "Delectable?" She noticed Wendell was upping his vocabulary since he moved the TiTi to a new place. "Well, you want me to rope 'em in, right?" she asked.

"How about a little test drive?" Wendell prodded.

Carla couldn't believe him. What had gotten into Wendell? He must have watched some incredible porn to approach her like this when they had so many things to take care of before the opening. Where were all the young dancers he usually hung around?

Carla was relieved when right on cue, a couple of sexy young dancers stepped up to Wendell possessively. They wanted to make sure that Carla didn't usurp their money train. With the arrogance of youth, they believed their charms far outweighed Carla's, but just in case, they came to extract Wendell from Carla's clutches. She was grateful for the interruption. These were some new, young dancers that Wendell hired. He hadn't gotten a chance to explore all kinds of sex with them yet because of the chaos after the fire. All of his young dancers were at least twenty-one. Wendell played it safe. He wanted no liability for hiring underage girls who drank and fucked in his club.

Wendell surveyed the young dancers in their sequined bikini tops and sparkly little shorts that left most of their butts hanging out. He obviously had only the girls on his mind now. He turned to Carla. "You're saved by the belles." Wendell almost looked young again. He was still tall, dark, and handsome even though he was gaining weight.

Carla tried to get him to focus on business. "We got a lot to do, Wendell, before this place opens up."

"I won't be long. I'll be right out." He pushed the two young dancers towards an empty dressing room. They giggled like schoolgirls.

Carla shook her head. She figured Wendell was fighting a bad case of nerves because of the grand opening and needed some relief. *Whatever,* Carla thought. As long as he made it quick with the girls, but she knew he would. Wendell was first and foremost a shrewd businessman. He'd take care of business with the girls, then come right out and take care of business with the club.

Carla watched as he ushered the girls into the dressing room. All three were groping and feeling even before they got behind closed doors. Wendell slid his hand right in the crotch of one of the girl's shorts. The other girl rubbed her fanny all over Wendell's dick. Finally, the door closed, Carla could only imagine what Wendell and his girls were doing. Her own crotch felt steamy thinking about it.

Carla gathered her wits and headed towards the bar. The head bartender gave Carla a thorough onceover. Carla ignored it and got straight down to business.

"What's up? How we doing for tonight?" Carla asked.

The bartender forced his eyes away from her cleavage. "I looked high and low, Rae, and I still can't find that gin order. I would have told you sooner, but I figured it was around here somewhere."

"You're kidding, right?"

He shook his head. "Wish I was."

Carla was annoyed. "We're almost ready to open. How come nobody said anything sooner?"

"We can't find the gin, Rae."

Carla spoke to the liquor store manager. "Next time, you gotta do the order right. We open up tonight. How are we supposed to bartend without gin?" She tried to make light of it and smile, but she didn't feel like smiling. She should have been back at the club, doing final prep. *But this was part of the prep,* she reminded herself. Sometimes, she had to take care of things on her own.

"Fifty percent discount, right? Carla asked.

The manager laughed sarcastically. "Yeah, right."

Carla didn't budge. "Opening night, you cut our order, and I have to come down here in person to straighten things out. Twenty-five percent discount is not enough. If you insist on twenty-five percent, I won't argue with you. But I'll know what to do next time."

Carla didn't flirt the way she did with the guys in the club. She was strictly wearing her business hat now. Besides, she had to force the manager and some of the guys in the liquor store to take her seriously. They were so busy looking at her legs and butt in the tight dress. She had taken off the heels and now had on glittery red flats. She still looked stunning, but her demeanor was all business. She was irritated with Wendell for picking a new liquor store, but this store had promised Wendell that they could beat any prices his previous suppliers had given him.

Carla had argued for the old supplier because she believed in loyalty. Their old liquor store would never have cut them short, be it accidentally or intentionally.

The store manager sighed heavily and ran his hands through his stringy blond hair. He could see that Carla wasn't budging. "Fifty percent this time only," he said. He licked his lips and glued his eyes to her cleavage. "You drive a hard bargain." He lowered his voice. "I'll make it seventy-five percent if I can stop by the club when I get off and get a lap dance from you."

"Fifty percent is fine." Carla dismissed his offer. She made sure he entered the discount into his computer and made a notation on her invoice. Then she turned and left, feeling the manager's eyes locking on every curve of her body. She switched her butt from side to side just to fuck with him.

Outside, Carla put a couple of the TiTi's bartending crew to work, stocking Wendell's SUV, a Cadillac Escalade. Wendell used it for work and play. After loading, the guys got into the vehicle with her. Carla drove. She was in one of those moods where nobody could do anything better than she could.

CHAPTER 5

The TiTi Bar was in full swing. Carla had slipped her red satin heels back on. She circulated around the club in impeccable hostess mode. Wendell was back in action too. He had finished his fun with the girls and was all business now.

The club was crowded, and the bar was flowing. Several exotic dancers performed on the main dance floor. Other dancers performed on tables directly in front of patrons. All of the dancers were scantily clad in G-strings, pasties, and sky-high heels so they could tease and tantalize the customers. The TiTi's waitresses were clad almost as scantily as the dancers. The crowd was generous. Bills of all denominations littered the floors in front of the dancers. A few of the dancers performed in a very private area of the club, cordoned off for lap dances and "special requests."

Carla caught a glimpse of herself in one of the club mirrors and smoothed her dress down. She stood up taller and resumed circulating among the customers. Her eyes panned the diverse crowd of all ages and races. A young hip-hop guy with drooping pants planted himself right in front of her. Carla sidestepped him and kept enough distance between them so she could continue moving around the club.

"Why don't you get up there?" young hip-hop said, pointing to the dance floor.

"Not tonight. But I'll let you know when I'm performing," Carla said.

"How about a private lap dance now?"

Carla knew the young man was aroused by the action in one of the side rooms. She could see it, too, from the angle where she stood. A patron with a baseball cap, probably to conceal his identity, was sitting in a chair with a dancer spread-eagled all over him. The dancer's up-and-down motions either simulated penetration or was actually the real deal. The dancer seemed to delight in giving the client extra special treatment.

Carla decided she and Wendell were going to have to rearrange some of the mirrors to protect themselves from liability. While the sight was indeed a cause for arousal, Carla knew she had to get young hip-hop under control.

His eyes penetrated through her dress. "We can go over to one of them side rooms."

Carla kept her distance. "You can go over, or you can watch the show. We got the best dancers in town."

"I wanna watch you dance in one of those rooms," young hip-hop said, undeterred.

Carla pointed to a scantily clad dancer, entwined around the pole on the table nearest them. "Enjoy the show," she coaxed. "You want a drink, young man? I'll send the waitress over." At first, she hated the thought that she was reaching her fiftieth birthday. But at times like this, her age came in handy and gave her the advantage over young patrons. She could adopt a matronly stance with them. But this guy was nothing but trouble. He kept fingering his crotch and licking his lips. He didn't care how old she was. Carla decided to move on.

Wendell came over. "You okay, Rae?"

Carla stared hard at young hip-hop. She nodded. "I'm fine. I was just telling this young man, we got the greatest dancers in town."

Wendell agreed. "Yes, we do. Some of the best girls around, right here." Then Wendell's eyes hardened. "You might want to check them out. Now if you a high roller and want a private dance—not with my manager here—we can accommodate that too."

Wendell's demeanor seemed to intimidate young hip-hop. He sat down at the nearest table and turned his attention to the dancer. The young dancer came over to him and shook her fanny right in his face. He threw some bills in front of her.

Carla nodded a brief thanks to Wendell and began

recirculating. At the bar, she stepped over to a tall, fair-skinned guy in his forties. He was rugged and good-looking.

"Drink up, handsome. Enjoying the show?" Carla asked.

"I certainly am," he said, his eyes roaming all over Carla's body.

Carla extended her hand. "I'm Rae Hepburn. I'm the manager here. Welcome to our grand opening. Don't think I've ever seen you before."

"Don't think I've ever seen you before either." His eyes still feasted on her body.

Then his friend turned around. Carla's breath caught in her throat. Her heart thudded in her chest. The floor seemed to cave in under her. *The fireman!* She'd recognize those beautiful amber eyes anywhere. Without his fire helmet, he possessed a head of thick black, curly hair that matched his rich black mustache. He wore a casual pair of slacks and a russet-colored pullover that fit snugly over his chest and arms. The shirt emphasized the warm brown of his skin. It opened at the neck and exposed some of his chest hair. His arms—those were the arms that carried her, Carla recalled. She wanted to reach out and touch them now. His eyes locked with hers.

"I remember you," he said.

Carla was still flabbergasted and speechless.

"I'll never forget you," she said when she finally recovered her voice. "Captain Rose."

He smiled, then his eyes engulfed her body.

Oh no, Carla thought. *Not you too.* She quickly thrust her hand out to him. She hoped it wasn't shaking. "I'm Rae—"

"I know. Rae Hepburn," he said.

Carla looked surprised.

He smiled again. "You just told my buddy here. Plus, you sent us the nice card and the chocolates. Thanks a lot."

Carla still felt flustered and a little awkward. "That's the least I could do."

He extended his hand. "Let me introduce myself properly. I'm Baxter Rose."

"My knight in shining armor," Carla said. She was thrilled that he wore no wedding band.

"I don't know about all that. I was doing my job."

"Oh, this is the hot stripper you rescued," his buddy said.

"Shut up, man," Baxter said. He turned to Carla. "We work together. Percy was just leaving. He's going over to a table."

"No, I'm not," Percy said. "I'm staying right here. Wouldn't miss this for the world."

Baxter ignored him and stepped between Carla and Percy. "Our fire station is down the street. We stopped by to have a drink and enjoy your grand opening."

His eyes devoured Carla. He didn't hide it.

Carla tugged a little at the front opening of her dress. How could she get this handsome fireman to take her seriously? While he was somewhat more respectful than the usual clientele, his eyes still tried to consume her.

Carla tried to steer him in a different direction. "I'm Carla Rae Hepburn. My professional name is Rae, but I want you to call me Carla."

Baxter's eyebrows rose in surprise.

Good, Carla thought. He was taking her more seriously. "Don't let the dress fool you," she said. "I'm just doing my job. Like you were doing your job when you rescued me."

"Touché," Baxter said, then hesitated. He wondered if she knew what the word meant.

As if she read his mind, Carla snapped. "I know what it means."

Perhaps an educated stripper, Baxter thought. Now he was even more curious about her.

Carla smiled and felt less uptight. Her plan was working. He was treating her with more respect.

Baxter tried to refrain from ogling her. But his eyes still skimmed over her butt and her breasts plumping out of the oval in her black lace dress. His eyes lingered on her legs, anchored in the red satiny heels. What was he supposed to do?

He noticed her hair. He remembered it was thin and almost bald in spots. He realized the long, free-flowing hair on her head was a wig. It was both coarse and curly and looked real. The hair made her look sexy, wild, and young. He thought she wore a little too much makeup, but then he remembered, this was her job. Baxter felt sort of confused.

He had tried to erase her from his mind. But he kept remembering how she clung to him when he carried her from the fire. How she totally trusted him. How she tried to feel all over his arms and chest. He couldn't resist a smile. He was glad staying in shape was a part of his job.

Carla loosened up when he smiled. She wanted to ride off into the sunset with him, but that only happened in the movies. Besides, Wendell approached. He probably wondered why she was spending so much time with one client. Wendell wanted her to move around and stay on top of things.

"Everything okay? Y'all enjoying yourself?" Wendell asked.

Carla felt tongue-tied.

Percy stepped forward. "She's okay. You her bodyguard?"

Wendell stiffened. "Yep. And the owner."

Baxter held out his hand to lighten things up a bit. "Baxter Rose, and this is my buddy, Percy. We work down the street at the fire station."

Percy smirked. "Baxter was the one who rescued your stripper."

Baxter felt ready to slug Percy every time he called her a stripper.

"Why the fuck didn't you say so?" Wendell asked and relaxed his demeanor. He hugged Baxter and Percy with no regard for whether or not they were comfortable with the gesture. "You guys saved the day. You can come here anytime you want. Libations on me—not the girls, but the liquor. You saved my Rae here." Wendell wrapped his arm around Carla's waist and pulled her closer to him.

Baxter's eyes narrowed, and Carla stiffened. Wendell noted the spark between them. He tightened his arm around Carla's waist. She pulled away from him.

Percy felt like instigating. He pointed to Baxter. "That's her knight in fire truck armor. He carried her out. You can't stop that attraction," Percy said to Wendell.

"Man, won't you just be quiet," Baxter said. He addressed Wendell, "I did carry her out. Always glad I can help. Now if you'll do me the honor," Baxter said and held his arm out to Carla.

Since she wanted to feel his biceps, Baxter thought, now he could oblige. Carla laughed and took his arm. Baxter grinned at Percy and Wendell. "Carry on, gentlemen," he said and ushered Carla away to a more private spot nearby.

Wendell started to protest, but stopped himself.

Percy shrugged. "You can't fight that fire."

"Drinks still on me," Wendell said and walked away.

Carla was enamored with her handsome firefighter, and he was enamored with her body. She sighed and shook her head. She grabbed a red cocktail napkin from the tray a passing waitress carried. Then she found herself leading Baxter over to an empty, private room that titillated the imagination. Inside the room, soft red curtains hung on the walls, and red carpeting padded the floors. A plump sectional chair with no arms provided a cushy foundation for both the client and the dancer. A polished dancing table with a pole in the middle provided the perfect metaphor for an accommodating dancer encircling the genitals of a lascivious client.

Baxter's jaw dropped open in surprise when they entered the room. His eyes seared through Carla's dress. "Special treatment?"

Carla smiled coyly. "Yes. Conversation." She opened up the cocktail napkin and stuck the top corners into the collar of her dress. She allowed the napkin to hang like a bib over her cleavage. Baxter got the message loud and clear.

"It's a great dress," he laughed.

"I pulled you in here so we could talk, away from all the distractions."

"Talk? In here?"

Carla nodded.

Baxter forced his mind off her curves. "How are you?" he finally asked.

"I'm doing alright."

"No, honestly. How are you? You could have been seriously hurt. That fire was a possible arson. We're investigating. You could have died."

"I try not to dwell on it."

"That's good, but you might need some counseling. That was some serious shit." Baxter didn't mean to scare her, but he was trying to make his point.

"I'm fine," Carla said defensively.

"You certainly are fine," Baxter said, trying to ease the tension between them. Her smile was back, but she still wore the napkin as a bib. He stared at her smooth, chocolate skin and big dark eyes. The cleft in her chin captivated him. If only she lived a different lifestyle. "I've been thinking about you," he said. "I'm glad I saw you tonight. You've got to get away from all this." He held up his hands in a wide gesture that indicated their surroundings.

Carla matched his gesture. "This is my life for now. But I'm a manager, not an ecdysiast anymore." She smiled inwardly at borrowing one of Wendell's new vocabulary words. She waited for Baxter's reaction.

"I know the word," he smiled wryly.

"Good," Carla said. "Then you know I don't dance anymore. Nothing wrong with it. It paid my bills. Anyway, I'm managing now. There's a difference."

"Not in that dress," Baxter said.

Carla bristled. "You dress a certain way for work. So do I."

"Yeah, but in that dress, every man in here wants to jump your bones."

"That's my intent." Carla decided to go toe-to-toe with him. "We're a business. We want our clients to spend money. When I leave work, I'm a different person."

"You're still a stripper," Baxter said and stripped the napkin from her dress to make his point.

His fingers touched her skin. He felt it, and she felt it, an electric current. They were both surprised by the sudden passion that flared up from his touch. Carla attributed it to the sultry aura of the room as well. She felt a quivering in her loins.

Baxter wanted to release her from the confines of the lace dress, but first, he wanted to stick his fingers through the opening in her dress and pull out one of her breasts and kiss it. He forced himself to get a grip on his feelings.

Before he got carried away by their surroundings, he took out a business card from his pants pocket. He held it out to Carla. "Call me if you want to talk to someone about the fire. I can find you a counselor."

"I don't need counseling," Carla retorted.

"Yeah, you do," Baxter said. "You're still here."

Carla took the card. Even though she knew his rank, seeing the word "Captain" on the card made him even more of a hero in her eyes, but he had rankled her. She tore his card up into little pieces and let them fall to the floor. Then she waltzed out of the room.

As soon as Baxter returned to the main floor, Percy joined him. "Doesn't look like you scored, brother. You need a coach?"

Baxter stood unyielding as he watched her walk away. He still wanted to free her from the lace dress, though she could keep the red heels on. He tried to force his thoughts off her slightly bouncing ass. He felt his pants tighten in the crotch. He had been fighting raw emotions all night.

Damn! he thought. She had been on his mind for quite some time now. And he blew it. Who cared if she was a stripper? He simply wanted to hold and mold that body against his.

Percy laughed at him. "Damn, man. You got it bad."

Carla's emotions were jumbled too. She decided to get back to work and mingle with the patrons. She knew Wendell would be relieved. She knew he regarded Baxter with wariness. Baxter got under her skin, and Wendell wanted to be the only one under her skin. Well, Wendell could forget it and so could Baxter. She'd offer free drinks to everyone from Baxter's fire station anytime they visited. They had saved her life. But she hoped Baxter wouldn't return. He unsettled her.

"Come on, let's get out of here," Percy said as he and Baxter headed for the exit.

"I could never take a woman like that to meet my mom," Baxter said.

Percy stopped in his tracks. "No, you couldn't. You just want to fuck her. If you want to fuck her, do it. Get it over with. But don't go talking that shit about meeting your mother."

Baxter remained silent.

Percy's eyes widened. "Are you serious, man?"

"Of course not," Baxter said.

Carla caught a glimpse of them walking out. She sighed in relief. She could finally do her job in peace, without the presence of the handsome fireman and his disapproval. She was silly to think he would ever take her seriously. She had to let fantasy go. Her knight probably wanted to screw her and move on. She saw the way his eyes had devoured her body. Well, she wanted him too, but in a more substantial way.

She had been caught off guard when he inquired about her emotional state after the fire. She didn't know whether to hate him or hug him for that. Nobody else, not even her sister, had asked about her emotions after the fire. Natalie had only offered that now was a perfect time for Carla to find a new line of work. Well, it was her life and her bills. Until someone offered to pay her bills, managing the new TiTi Bar was as good a job as any.

Carla slipped back to the private room where she had taken Baxter. She swore she could still feel the heat from his body. She wondered if she had left the same impression on him. She had meant to thank him profusely for saving her life, but nothing turned out the way she wanted. Staring down at the floor, she saw pieces of his business card. She wished she hadn't torn it up so thoroughly. She remembered that he had written his personal number on the card. She bent down and tried to gather up all the pieces, but she knew she wasted her time.

"Give it up, babe," Wendell said and watched her curiously. Then he held out his hand to her and tenderly lifted her to her feet. "You don't need him. He's not your type."

Carla was embarrassed. She steadied herself and dusted off her hands. *Damn! Busted,* she thought. "Just cleaning up a little. The room's got to be ready for the next party, right?" she asked with a smile.

Wendell was back to business. "Yep. There's a party on their way now. I need you to move around and do what you do best."

Carla sighed. "Okay. I can do that."

Carla was doing a good job of forgetting Baxter. She laughed and socialized with the patrons as the drinks flowed freely at the bar. The floor in front of the dancers was littered with piles of bills. More bills dangled from the dancers' G-strings. The TiTi Bar's grand opening was a huge success. Carla hoped she and Wendell could sustain the momentum. The new TiTi had more expenses than the old one. As manager, she wanted to make sure they turned a profit. She'd have to ignore her sister and Baxter. This was the only line of work she knew, and this was her only source of income.

Carla's eyes lit up in surprise as Baxter's friend, Percy, strolled towards her. Percy was a nice-looking guy, but he wasn't her fireman. Still, Carla's spirits lifted. Percy was at least a link to her fireman.

"Back so soon," she said. "You forget something?"

"Yep. You."

Carla laughed. "Don't you have a better line than that?"

Percy dismissed her critique. Desire clouded his eyes. "What time do you get off? I know a nice little place where we could relax and have a drink."

Carla couldn't believe him. He was just here with Baxter, and now he was hitting on her as though Baxter didn't exist. She never understood how men could do that. Percy had no qualms whatsoever in pursuing her.

Percy must have read her mind. "Baxter's always going to be my buddy. He knows how I am. Anyway, he's got a girlfriend. Plenty of women are after him. Don't even waste your time. Besides . . . ."

"Besides what?" Carla asked.

"You are a stripper, not exactly his type. Now me, I think you're fine. We can hang out and have a drink, get to know each other better."

"And do what?"

"Let's not play games," Percy said. "I want you, and I can show you a good time."

"I'm not interested," Carla said. She still yearned for Baxter. In no way did she want him to think she desired Percy. Although, who was she kidding? Baxter desired her, but not the way she wanted. She wanted him to take her out on a date. She hadn't dated a man who treated her with respect in a long time. Anyway, Percy didn't appeal to her. She hoped he got the message quickly.

Percy touched her arm. Surprisingly, his touch wasn't as repulsive as she imagined. What a shame. Why hadn't Baxter come back instead of Percy? She would have found a way to win Baxter over.

"I'll treat you right, Rae. We can have some fun," Percy said.

"No," Carla said firmly. She caught a glimpse of Percy's ring finger. She saw the fading line of a wedding band. She figured he was probably divorced.

"You really think Baxter would deal with a woman like you?" Percy asked.

"Well, you would. You know what they say, 'birds of a feather . . . .'"

Percy's eyes flashed with impatience. "Don't even kid yourself. He doesn't want you. I do."

"It's not about what you want," Carla said and backed away from him. "Drinks always on the house for our firefighters." She waved her arms in the air. "Enjoy the dancers. Have a good time. It's our grand opening."

She turned and stepped away, but Percy grabbed her arm. Carla shook his hand off. "You don't want to do that." She could see one of Wendell's henchmen making his way towards them. Carla held her hand up, indicating she had everything under control. Percy backed off.

"No trouble," Percy said. "But we could've had a good time."

"Drinks on us," Carla repeated. "Enjoy."

Percy watched her walk away. He watched her like he did the dancers. He didn't bother to hide his lust.

* * *

As Carla passed one of the stages, long golden legs stepped down beside her. Carla looked up and saw Mimi, the young blond stripper. A beauty in her late twenties, Mimi was one of the exotic dancers who still earned a lot of money in tips, even though she was aging for a dancer. Her G-string was filled with bills, and she carried a duffel bag filled with even more bills.

Mimi's real name was Hermione Rodriguez. She was half-Mexican and half-German. Her mother was German, and her father, Mexican. Mimi had the beautiful golden skin of a Latina, yet delicate blond hair and features reflecting her German roots. She had a tall, slim willowy figure, but still curvy. She probably would have plumped up more, but Mimi liked to do coke, among other drugs. Sometimes, she seemed to have everything under control, but other times, she went on binges. Still, she was like a little sister to Carla. In fact, Carla felt a closeness to Mimi that she didn't feel with Natalie. Mimi didn't judge her the way Natalie did. Mimi couldn't afford to. They worked the same kind of life.

"You don't want that one who just left. You want his friend, right?" Mimi asked.

Carla looked surprised.

"I saw you earlier with his friend," Mimi said.

"Captain Rose. That's the fire captain."

Mimi whistled. "Shit. That's the captain? I was so high that night. Damn, chica. You gotta give him some—for all of us. He deserves it."

"Then I should give you some too. You made him find me."

"You know I don't swing that way. Neither do you. But I'll tell you what. I'll give him some for you," Mimi laughed.

Carla's mood lightened. She grinned. "No thanks. I can handle it."

"He's a good-looking man. I'll sacrifice myself for you."

Carla laughed warningly. "You better not. I owe you, but not that much." Carla's face turned serious. "I'll always owe you, Mimi."

"Stop it, chica. I was just messing with you. You don't owe me anything. We sistahs, right?"

"Always."

Mimi studied Carla's features and issued a warning. "Don't go gettin' your feelings hurt just because he rescued you. He's only interested in your booty. But what's wrong with that? That's what we want, right? But don't go gettin' all gooey-eyed over him."

"I know, I know. Don't take no wooden nickels."

Though Carla was tall and long-legged, Mimi was a couple of inches taller. She draped her arm around Carla's shoulder. "Let me give you some advice. They're nothing more than johns, okay? On a rare occasion, like winning the lottery—actually, the odds are probably worse—you'll find a good man who comes in here, and you can live happily ever after, well almost happily ever after."

Carla sighed. "Okay. I hear you."

"You always buttin' in my business. Thought I'd return the favor."

Carla kept silent. The weight of the whole night came crashing down on her. She felt weary.

"Come on. Let me put my stuff up and let's hit the bar," Mimi coaxed. "I know you don't drink during work hours, but I've got another set tonight. I need some coke."

Carla's eyebrows rose in alarm.

Mimi laughed. "A rum and coke, Rae."

Carla laughed too, relieved.

Percy stood outside Baxter's front door. It was late—after midnight. The street was dark and quiet in an upscale neighborhood in the Baldwin Hills area on the west side of Los Angeles. Stars peppered and illuminated the velvety sky overhead. Baxter's rancher was high up in the hills with a glittering view of city lights.

Baxter opened the door in a T-shirt and his pajama bottoms. They hung low around his hips and accentuated his physique. Percy's face unmasked a pang of jealousy as Baxter led the way.

Inside the house, a décor of rich browns, tans, and plenty of wood predominated. It was a man's house. While not the most stylish décor, the house was decorated handsomely enough, with a big, sturdy couch, chairs, and rugs. African masks and other artwork hung on stucco walls.

Baxter frowned as Percy entered. "What you want, man? You know I'm on duty tomorrow. I have to get up early."

"I need a drink," Percy said.

"I think you had enough already."

"I'll fix it." Percy headed over to a liquor table in the dining area and poured himself some bourbon. He pressed the lever on Baxter's refrigerator and dumped some ice in the bourbon. He took a sip. Baxter waited.

"That woman, Rae. She's not your type."

Baxter started laughing. "You came all the way over here and woke me up to tell me that? You don't need any more liquor tonight."

"I'm saying, she's not your type. I went back there after we left." Percy paused. He knew he had Baxter's full attention now. "She was rolling her ass all over the place. You don't want a woman like that."

Baxter almost felt like smashing Percy in the face. Percy was always after his women. Sometimes, he didn't know why he hung around Percy. But Percy was an engineer, his lieutenant. When it came to firefighting, Percy would go that extra mile for any man or woman in the company, but he was especially loyal to Baxter. He would risk his life for Baxter and had proven it on a number of occasions. Yet he wasn't loyal when it came to Baxter's women.

Amusement crept over Baxter's face. "You're more fucked up over her than I am. Look at you."

"Nah, man. You the one talking all that crazy shit about introducing her to your mother. But I'm telling you, Bax. She was grinding her ass all over every man in that club, including me."

"Whoa, I never said I was going to introduce her to my mother. I said she wasn't the kind of woman . . . ." Baxter's voice trailed off. He didn't owe Percy an explanation. Why was he engaging in such a stupid conversation with Percy?

Baxter seethed. Was Percy lying? Or was she truly a slut? Yeah, he saw her sashaying her ass all around, but that was her job. Would she really mess around with Percy even though Baxter felt some sparks flying from her?

"I came over here to tell you, just in case," Percy said. "So you know what kind of woman you're dealing with."

"Whoa!" Baxter held up his hand. "I'm not dealing with her." He shut up and refused to let Percy goad him any further. He didn't know why he was even holding this senseless conversation with Percy when he had to be up early the next morning.

Percy downed his drink and got up. "I'm leaving. Just thought you'd want to know about Rae."

Baxter had to laugh. "Thanks for the concern. But I got it. I can take care of myself."

"You know I always got your back."

Baxter became more serious. "I know. I always got your back too. Now get out of my house so I can get some sleep."

"Aye, aye, Captain," Percy said.

As he watched Percy leave, Baxter didn't know how to handle this woman, "Rae," "Carla," whatever her name was. But he knew one thing. He wasn't going to let Percy, nor anybody in his unit, touch her.

CHAPTER 6

Carla grabbed her keys and purse and headed out the door of her condo. She glanced around to make sure everything was in order. She loved her place. Her décor was a palette of neutrals with bright splashes of color added from art and pillows. She had gone to great lengths to make her home chic, cozy, and inviting.

Once outside, Carla sailed through the courtyard of her condo building onto the street. Her building was fairly modern with a brick and stucco exterior and Spanish accents. Manicured hedges and azalea bushes added a colorful landscape while trees shaded the courtyard. There was a circular driveway in front. Though it didn't happen often enough for her, Carla always enjoyed having people drive into the circle to pick her up. Then she'd stroll to their cars, feeling like an urban sophisticate. The parking lot for residents and guests was accessed from the side of the building. It was a hip, trendy property that stood at the beginning of West Hollywood near La Brea Avenue.

After the successful opening of the new TiTi Bar, Carla was in great spirits. She and Wendell were still packing in customers each night.

She wore one of her favorite fitness outfits, a royal blue halter top and jacket, black leggings, and sleek athletic walking shoes. She sported one of her more casual wigs that was a curly afro and looked like her real hair. She felt good. She had planned her whole day. Her first destination was a quick walk to the grocery store. She figured she'd pick up a few items plus get some exercise. The sun was shining, and it was a gorgeous day. Carla couldn't have asked for anything more.

Suddenly, she halted in midstride. She blinked her eyes to clear them. Her breath caught in her throat, and her heart picked up speed. Butterflies fluttered in her stomach. On the pavement in front of her building was her handsome fireman. Baxter was standing outside his car, watching her come out of the building. He smiled broadly at her. Carla looked around to make sure he wasn't smiling at somebody else. He wasn't. His smile was for her. She was so glad that she had put her return address on the card and candy she sent him.

He wore a pair of low-slung, narrow jeans and a white open-necked polo shirt with a collar. He had on casual athletic shoes. Though simply dressed, he looked so good to Carla. The jeans and the shirt molded to his body. He grinned as he stood lazily against the passenger side of his car. It was a black Honda Accord, a hybrid. It looked bigger and more modern than the standard. Though certainly not a Cadillac or some other fancy car, it suited him. She liked his car.

Her heart was still racing. What was he doing here? When she finally stood before him, he opened up the passenger door for her, like a perfect gentleman.

"Nice place you have."

"I lucked up and bought it years ago. I could never afford it now," she said absently. She had more pressing matters on her mind, like how to get her emotions under control.

"Have you eaten? Want some brunch?" he asked.

Carla was stunned and unprepared for this assault on her senses. "Uhh . . .," she stammered.

He laughed. "Tell me what you want. Did you eat already? What's on your agenda?"

You. You're my whole agenda, Carla thought, as the canal between her legs moistened. "No, I haven't eaten yet. I was going to buy some cereal and some yogurt," she said huskily, hoping her voice didn't give away her thoughts. She remembered Mimi's words. "Give him some good stuff." Carla smiled involuntarily and shook her head to clear it.

"You do or you don't want brunch?" Baxter asked.

"Brunch would be great. I'm not an early riser."

"I figured, since you work so late. I know a great place we can go."

Carla slid into the car. She pinched herself to make sure she wasn't dreaming.

Baxter laughed. "You okay? You're not one of these people who hurt themselves?"

Carla finally eased up a bit and smiled. "Of course not."

"Good," Baxter said.

"I'm just trying to take this all in. I'm so glad to see you. I didn't know if I'd ever see you again."

"You knew it was in the stars, girl."

Carla beamed. "Girl" sounded good coming off his lips. She found another thing to like about him. Was she setting herself up for instant heartbreak? No matter, she decided. She would enjoy the day. She settled herself more comfortably in the seat and buckled up. The plush tan upholstery conformed to her body and made her relax.

"Nice car," she smiled.

"Yeah, I like it too. Conserves a lot of gas."

The moment they took off, Carla realized Baxter drove too fast. She found herself pressing the floor with her right foot, searching for a brake pedal on the passenger side. He drove on top of cars, weaved in and out of traffic, and exceeded the speed limit. Carla held her breath. She didn't know if the headiness she felt was the result of his driving or the fire in her loins. She liked so many things about him, but she did not like his driving. She sat in silence wondering how to tell him.

Baxter, too, kept silent, navigating LA's eternally heavy traffic like a bat out of hell.

Finally, they reached a little beachside café in Venice and pulled into the parking lot behind the café.

Baxter jumped out of the car and held the door open for Carla. Her right leg felt almost numb from pressing the imaginary brake pedal on her side of the car. She had definitely exercised her right calf muscles if nothing else. She almost swooned into him when he opened the door. She didn't know whether it was his closeness, his driving, or a combination of the two that gave her jelly legs. He had on a very light cologne—good stuff, nothing overpowering, just a whiff to tantalize her senses.

He strode into the restaurant with an air of confidence, as if he had been there before. The manager smiled at them and immediately signaled a hostess to escort them to a table on the patio. Baxter's hand lightly brushed Carla's. She enjoyed the sensation. There was so much pent-up emotion between them. Even the hostess observed them with an air of expectation.

Carla was in her world. She enjoyed the company of a very handsome man who commanded respect and who treated her with respect. They were out on a date, impromptu maybe, but still a date. She didn't know what to do with herself. A long time had passed since she had ever felt so giddy. The hostess seated them at a cozy corner table and observed the sparks flying between them.

Carla inhaled the excitement of the moment, but realized that she had to address something first. "If we're going to have any kind of relationship, you cannot drive like that," she said.

"Wow," Baxter said with a grin.

Carla was determined to make her point. "I'm sure I'm not the first person who's talked about your driving. We're not on our way to a fire."

Baxter raised his brow and smiled wryly. "We're not?"

Carla refused the bait.

Baxter laughed now. "That's me, babe. That's the way I drive."

"Not with me. You cannot drive like that with me in the car. If we're going to go any further, either I drive, or you slow down."

Baxter shrugged. "Okay."

Carla wasn't exactly sure what he conceded. "I'll drive? Or you'll slow down?" she asked.

Wow, this woman wasn't playing, Baxter thought. Since he wanted the booty now more than ever, he reached out and touched her hand. "I'll slow down," he said, well aware of his double entendre.

His touch sparked the electric current running through

them. Carla decided that she no longer cared how he drove. She just wanted to eat and spend some time with him. Her head spun with an intoxicating headiness.

Baxter sensed her acquiescence. It was exactly what he wanted. He knew that his driving and the thrill of the moment created a pulsing connection that neither of them could ignore.

They sat on the outside patio along the boardwalk. The beach stretched lazily for miles in both directions. The water, though murky, still glittered from the sun as frothy waves crested along the shoreline. Carla looked up at the sky. It was almost the color of her top, a cerulean blue. She inhaled and smiled. *What a day.*

Baxter thought the same thing too. He didn't know how the day would pan out, but so far, he was having a good time contemplating the endless possibilities.

"So I caught you just in time for breakfast?" Baxter asked.

"Yes, you did," Carla said. She knew they were playing a bit of cat and mouse. She could slice the sexual tension between them with a knife. She tried to slow down her breathing. "Isn't this a little late for you to eat breakfast?" Carla asked.

"It's brunch. But I can eat breakfast any time. It's my favorite meal."

Carla liked breakfast too. Another plus on his scorecard, she decided. But his driving was still a problem. "Are you a good cook?" she asked.

"Not especially, but I can cook the hell out of breakfast—eggs, grits, sausages, pancakes. You cook?"

"Nope, I'm not a good cook at all. But I still eat healthy—cereal, salads. I can order a mean, healthy vegetable lasagna from this great restaurant I found."

"You on a health kick?"

"For the most part. I gotta maintain."

Baxter's eyes raked over her. "Nice job."

The air was starting to heat up. Carla removed her jacket both to cool off and to entice. She heard his sharp intake of breath.

Good, Carla thought. She was so glad that she had followed the advice of her mother who always insisted that her girls look good even on the most casual of occasions. Carla sometimes felt her mother's standards were too high and unrealistic, but not today. She was glad Baxter liked her outfit.

"That blue looks great on you," he said.

"You look good too." Carla squirmed a little between her legs. How she desired him, but she wanted to get to know him too. "So what's it like to be a captain?" she asked.

Baxter raised his brow in surprise. "I didn't think you cared. You tore up my card. You were pissed when I suggested you might need some counseling after the fire."

"I was pissed that you kept telling me to find another line of work."

Baxter refrained from commenting, but Carla could see from the firm set of his jawline that he still felt the same. She refused to belabor the issue. Instead, she leaned over so that the swell of her breasts pushed against her neckline. She watched his eyes illumine. "You still want to counsel me about the fire?" she asked.

"No. I want to create one." He reached out and touched her arm lightly. Carla was ready to give him a lap dance right on the spot. But the waitress arrived and took their orders. The moment she left, Baxter reached out and touched Carla's arm again. "You free for the rest of the day?" he asked.

Carla hesitated. "I want you, Baxter, but I want more than sex."

Baxter sighed. So he was hanging out with a demure stripper. Well, she could play whatever act she wanted. He was perfectly willing to go along with it for the day.

"I'd like to get to know you, too," Baxter said. Before he could stop himself, he added, "Why can't we just have some fun? I mean, you are a stripper."

Carla stiffened.

"I'm sorry," Baxter said contritely. He didn't want to keep needling her, but there was some undeniable magnetism between them that he was trying to resist. Maybe, her rescue had something to do with it. They were both bound by that one fateful night, yet he didn't want to get things twisted. "What made you become a dancer?" he asked finally. He could see that she was still on guard.

"I'm a manager now," Carla said boldly.

"I know, but what got you started?" he asked, trying to avoid judgment.

"No lectures?" Carla asked.

"No lectures."

"I always wanted to get married and have kids and be the perfect homemaker like my mother. She died years ago. My father . . . ." Carla's voice trailed off. "My mother made it appear so easy and so much fun. That's all I ever wanted was to get married and have kids and take care of home."

Carla tried to gauge Baxter's reaction. He watched her intently. "Anyway, I was always a good dancer," she continued. "I joined a dance company in my late teens. I wore wigs even then. I used some new relaxer in high school, and my hair started falling out. But that's a whole 'nother story. Anyway, I danced this show, and my wig fell off, and some catty girls started laughing hysterically."

"They were probably jealous," Baxter said.

Carla was surprised, yet pleased with Baxter's defense of her. He waited for her to continue.

"Well, I always had a nice body," Carla said.

Baxter nodded appreciatively.

"I had no skills. I was smart, but I didn't apply myself in school. So I started dancing in this strip place. My wig fell off there too, but nobody laughed. I put my wig back on and kept on dancing. They gave me a standing ovation. One guy whooped and hollered and told me I didn't need any hair," Carla recounted defiantly.

Baxter's eyes narrowed, but he suppressed a response.

What the guy also told Carla was that wig or no wig, he could still shoot sperm all over her bald head. Carla avoided recounting that part of the story. She knew that would be too much information.

"I watched this stripper one night and realized I could do it," Carla continued. "I stripped for years and made a lot of money. I made it an art form. My mother and father were so disappointed—and my sister. But by that time, I was living the fast life—parties and drugs."

Baxter didn't know what to make of her. He realized he was treading dangerous waters.

Carla sensed his apprehension, but continued with brutal honesty. "I know it's a rough life. But I'm older now, too old for stripping. That's why I became a manager. And I'm good at it. Do I need to change careers? Maybe. But this is all I know."

Baxter felt mixed emotions. He knew he should probably hightail it from the restaurant and drive her back home, probably faster than he ever drove a fire truck. She was a wildfire indeed. But his thrill-seeking side made him sit tight. He still wanted to feel every part of her body. His pants bulged in anticipation. And while he almost winced at some of her candor, he admired her straightforward honesty. He was never one for bullshit, which he found a constant, living in Los Angeles.

Carla hoped she hadn't scared Baxter off. Was she too upfront about her past? Damn! She could smack herself. What was she thinking? As if that weren't bad enough, she had told him that all she ever wanted to do was get married and have kids. Now if that didn't scare a man off, she didn't know what would. Was she sabotaging herself? Carla breathed a sigh of relief when the waitress came back to check on them and the server delivered their meals.

They had both ordered baked veggie omelets with tomato, spinach, feta cheese, and mushrooms. They ordered potatoes, too, but Baxter added spicy chicken sausage to his meal. Carla found herself giggling like a schoolgirl when they held up their mimosa glasses in toast. She recalled the New Year's Eve toast when he lifted her up.

"Do you remember?" she asked.

"Of course," he said and looked deeply into her eyes. Then he reminded himself that he was trying to keep a level head with her.

Carla felt it best to do the same. "To new horizons," she said and clinked glasses with him.

Right on the money, Baxter thought and smiled. "To new horizons."

They ate in silence for a while. Carla was truly enjoying herself now that Baxter hadn't run for cover from her. It was a special day, and she reveled in the moment. Everything seemed perfect. Here she was sitting across from her handsome fireman. He was even more handsome in the sunlight. The few strands of silver speckled throughout his hair gave him more character. His skin was golden brown, and his mustache was jet black above his lips. Carla couldn't wait to kiss those full, sensuous lips and run her hands across his chest. Her gaze feasted on the biceps that carried her away from the fire. A warm tingling spread between her legs. She forced her mind away from the sensation.

"Let me see your driver's license," Carla said suddenly.

She figured Baxter was younger than she was, but she wanted to know by how much. The way she felt about him now, she doubted that his age would make a difference, but she still wanted no major surprises.

Baxter burst out laughing. "Why do you want to see my driver's license?" But he knew why.

"Before we go any further, I need to know how old you are."

"You'll have to trust me."

"I do. I still want to see your driver's license."

Baxter decided to tease her a little more. "I'm a man, you're a woman. That's the only thing that matters."

Carla put her fork down and extended her hand.

Baxter pulled out his driver's license. He still refused to hand it over, continuing to tease her. "I don't know why I should have to go through this." Finally, he handed her the license.

Carla examined it. Wow! She was impressed. He was forty-five. He looked great. He was still younger than she was, but only by a few years—just young enough to make things more interesting. Carla returned his license.

"Satisfied?" Baxter asked. His voice was tinged with desire.

Not hardly, Carla thought. Between her legs still throbbed.

Baxter smiled knowingly. Carla didn't say anything. She

tried to calm her breathing. Baxter reached out and stroked her arm lightly. He seemed to enjoy toying with her. He was starting to realize the effect he had on her.

Baxter pulled his hand away. "Let's see your driver's license."

Carla was glad for the interruption from her wanton thoughts. She didn't want to pull his hand down inside her crotch and come all over his fingers under the table. What kind of impression would that make?

"You want to see my driver's license?" she asked.

"Yep."

Carla could see that Baxter was as eager for the interruption as she was. They wanted the day to last.

"My age shouldn't matter," Carla said coyly.

"It shouldn't, but hand over that license, girl."

Carla still liked the way he said, "girl." "I don't think so," she said. "It shouldn't matter if I'm in my thirties or my sixties."

"I know you're not in your sixties," Baxter said.

"Close to it."

He looked her over carefully. She was fucking with him. No way was she close to sixty. But he remembered a sixty-year-old he had met recently in a club. The woman was hot—nice body, nice face, lots of energy. But he still wanted somebody closer to his age. Carla had to be joking, he decided.

Baxter extended his hand. "Let's see, young lady."

Carla touched his arm. "I'm fifty-nine," she said with a straight face.

"You're kidding."

"I'll be sixty on my next birthday." Carla watched the play of emotions on his face.

Baxter didn't know what to think. He wanted her. He didn't care how old she was. But sixty would make her almost as old as his mother. She had to be messing with him. Besides, most of the women he knew lowered their age, not raised it.

Baxter was more insistent now. "Hand over that license."

"You sound like a cop."

"We work with cops."

"Okay," Carla said with a sigh. She started digging for her license. "But I already told you how old I am."

Baxter now wondered if he truly wanted to see her license. Perhaps, a little mystery wouldn't hurt.

Carla gave him the license, then burst out laughing. Baxter's eyes narrowed in mock anger. *Whew!* he thought in relief. Forty-nine. She was a little older than he was, but this could liven up the fun.

Carla was still laughing at him. "Scared you, didn't I?"

"No," he shook his head and half-smiled.

"Yes, I did."

He refused to be put on the spot. "So you'll be turning fifty next month in April—an Aries."

"Nope. No more birthdays. Forty-nine was my last one."

"Well, I'm sure you know you look great."

Carla smiled. "Thanks. When's your birthday?"

"August."

"A Leo. That means we should get along."

"We'll see," Baxter smiled. He didn't care if they were compatible. He was only out to have a good time.

She stared at the ring finger on his left hand.

He held his hand up. "I'm not married," he said.

Carla smiled pleasantly. They were both enjoying the moment and each other's company. She sincerely liked him and hoped he liked her. Was she expecting too much?

When the waitress brought their check, Carla was almost sad that the meal was over. "My treat," she offered. "I owe you—big time."

"Nope, I got it," Baxter said. "I keep trying to tell you. I was doing my job."

"I've got to thank you somehow," Carla insisted.

Baxter smiled to himself. He could think of a number of ways she could thank him, but they didn't involve paying for his meal. His eyes fastened on her breasts straining against her top.

Carla slapped his hand playfully as if she could read his mind, but she still pulled out her debit card. After she paid the check, Carla wondered how they would spend the rest of the day. She could easily invite him back to her place and give him a lap dance he would never forget—naked! But she didn't want to move too soon and spoil anything.

Like a perfect gentleman, Baxter walked around to her side of the table and helped her out of the chair. Carla smiled in appreciation.

"Anything for an old lady," Baxter said.

Carla laughed. "Yeah, right."

"So where to?" Baxter asked.

Carla became tongue-tied.

"I know," Baxter said. "How about a tour?"

"A tour?"

"Yep."

"Wherever we go, please drive responsibly," Carla said.

Baxter was on the defensive. "I always drive responsibly. I'll make an effort to slow down if that's what you mean," he conceded. He wasn't too pleased that she was making demands of him already. Although in truth, this wasn't the first time he had heard about his driving. Baxter placed his hand on the small of her back. "For you, I'll do my best."

Carla almost gasped when he touched her. She wanted him to drop his hand lower to her butt, until she remembered that she was playing for higher stakes. He liked her. She could sense it. She didn't know how long this would last, but she would enjoy it as long as she could.

"What tour?" Carla asked, still tempted to nudge his hand downward to her butt.

"You'll see." He gazed at her and smiled. Their eyes locked, and Carla held her breath. Who was she kidding? She just wanted to lie in his arms.

CHAPTER 7

Carla's legs felt less like jelly this time when she got out of the car with Baxter. He had slowed down for her. She found herself giggling again as they stood in the parking lot behind his fire station. It was a low-rise, red brick building that was innocuous, but well-maintained. "You're giving me a tour of your firehouse?"

"Yep," Baxter smiled. He was hoping she would get a kick out of it, but he wasn't sure.

Carla didn't care where they toured so long as she could stay in his company. She guessed she wasn't the first woman he had gifted with a tour, but at least, he was making his interest in her public. Maybe, their relationship could last. *One step at a time,* she told herself.

Baxter couldn't believe that he brought Carla to the fire station. He barely knew her. The "tour" was only reserved for special people. But Baxter knew why he brought her to the station. It was only blocks away from the TiTi Bar. He wanted to institute a "hands-off" policy when it came to Carla. He intended to spread the word that Carla was his for now, until he decided how to deal with her. He would have any man's head who worked under him, or didn't work under him for that matter. Carla was his exclusively until he removed the "off-limits" policy.

Baxter's crew were surprised to see him enter the kitchen with Carla. The captain hadn't brought any special females to the fire station in a while. A few of the men looked Carla over, trying to figure out where they knew her. She smiled at them after the introductions and refused to concern herself with whether or not they recognized her.

At least, Baxter made it clear that she was his date. All she had to do was maintain her composure and not worry about what anyone thought of her as manager of a strip club a few blocks away. She saw a few of the men whispering and nodding in her direction. Carla ignored them. Baxter stared hard at them. They ended their huddle. The few female firefighters in the station seemed friendly enough towards her. Carla guessed they had their own issues being surrounded by a firehouse full of men.

A young rookie walked up to Baxter and smiled. Earl White was tall, dark, and handsome, but rough around the edges. He had a chiseled physique under his uniform of a dark blue shirt and pants. Carla guessed he wore longer sleeves to cover some of his tattoos while on duty. His slacks hung low, but not so low as to run afoul of the station dress code. Though he carried himself like a professional, he was definitely a product of the hip-hop culture. Carla thought he looked familiar, but she couldn't remember where she had seen him.

Baxter pulled him outside the kitchen and introduced him. "This is Earl White, the Earl of Compton. My homie."

Earl laughed as he spoke to Carla. "This is like my dad here."

"Yeah, I got your dad," Baxter said. "Do I look like I'm old enough to be your dad?"

Earl was still laughing. "Yeah, man, you old enough."

Baxter shook his head in mock denial. "This is Carla," he said.

Earl looked her up and down. "Yeah, I know who she is— Rae Hepburn, down the street. I met you on New Year's Eve."

"Ah," Carla said and extended her hand. "You were with Baxter that night."

"I was, but you had eyes only for the captain," Earl stated bluntly.

Carla decided to take the high road and ignore his comment. "Thanks for the rescue. I'm forever grateful."

Earl nodded modestly. "That candy was great."

"Glad you liked it."

An awkward moment of silence fell between them as she and Earl continued to size each other up.

Baxter broke the silence. "Get back to work. I want to show Carla around."

Earl's gaze was direct. "I'll let the captain finish your tour. Don't go breaking his heart."

Carla didn't know what to make of Earl. She wasn't sure if he was an insolent thug, or someone as brutally candid as she was. "I'm sure your captain can take care of himself," Carla said. Though her manner was cordial, she put Earl on the alert that she wasn't taking any nonsense from a man young enough to be her son.

Earl held up his hands in surrender, taking a few steps back. "Everything's cool, miss."

Out of eyesight from the rest of the crew, Baxter grabbed Earl in a bear hug and playfully roughed him up. "I'm a fuck you up, man," Baxter said.

Carla laughed at their horseplay and found herself warming up to Earl. At least, he didn't call her "ma'am." Maybe, he wasn't an insolent thug after all.

Earl laughed and tried to extricate himself from Baxter's bear hug. "You definitely not acting like a dad," Earl said. "You acting like a kid. Go home, man. Ain't this your day off?"

Baxter finally released him, laughing. "I'm taking Carla on a tour."

"Then give her the tour," Earl said.

Baxter held out his hand to Carla. "This way, miss."

Earl pulled Baxter aside for a moment. He couldn't resist ribbing the captain. "I know what you trying to do. We got the message—loud and clear. But Percy is not here today."

Baxter laughed in good humor. "Get back to work. You got a drill this afternoon, right?"

"Yes, sir." Earl playfully saluted Baxter.

"Make him show you his calendar," Earl called out to Carla.

"What calendar?" she asked.

Baxter shrugged. "Nothing."

"You roughhouse all your men like that?" Carla asked, amused.

A wicked grin crossed Baxter's face. "Department rules—no horsing around. But yeah, I mess with Earl mainly. He was a high school hoodlum when I met him, but he was fascinated by our fire station. We adopted him and made him pull up his grades. He's one of our best rookies. I know he looks like a tough guy, but he's a good kid at heart. Straight up honest. Like you," Baxter added.

Carla smiled. She was glad he appreciated her honesty.

First stop, Baxter showed her the garage with its two bright red fire trucks and a rescue ambulance. Carla could picture him driving the ladder truck like a mad man with complete license to do so. She was enjoying the tour, but she could have done without some of the specifics about the triple combination engine. She wanted to enjoy his company more than hear about fire trucks. But he was so animated about his trucks that she had to laugh and poke fun at him. He seemed clueless.

Carla merely shook her head and followed him over to the pole, the infamous firefighter's pole that she could picture everyone sliding down when a call came in. Her eyes brightened with interest.

"It's only for show," Baxter said. "Sliding down that thing can be dangerous. We practice on it sometimes for strength training. That's why you see the mats at the bottom in case anybody falls. But it's strictly for show. Nostalgia."

Carla tried to suppress thoughts of sliding down the pole naked, then pressing against him and dancing in his lap. Yes, she knew all about poles, human and metal. She wondered if Baxter read her thoughts. He breathed a little heavier. She stole a glance at the growing bulge in his jeans. Perhaps, he wanted to see her slide naked down the pole too. Their eyes met for a moment. Carla stifled the ache in her loins and moved on with him to the next part of the tour. She wanted to reach out and touch his butt and let him play with hers.

Baxter took her back to the kitchen again. This time, he called attention to the big stainless steel range and triple refrigerators. Near the kitchen, he showed her the lounge area which had a wide flat screen television. They continued to the living room which had big couches, chairs, and another television.

Baxter showed her the dorm rooms for sleeping and the shower rooms. He presented the exercise room with fanfare and explained how it kept all the firefighters in shape. He showed her a big universal office that also served as a classroom and a study area. Earl and some of the crew sat in the classroom area, ready for a class to begin. Another captain walked in to instruct them. He greeted Baxter warmly and gave Carla a curious smile.

Next, she and Baxter toured the locker room and the storage room. They passed an industrial laundry room the crew used for cleaning their firefighting gear. He even showed her the cleaning supplies. Carla nearly doubled over with laughter as he named and explained all the supplies from regular household products to more specialized station products. Again, he seemed clueless that she could do without this part of the tour.

He took her upstairs to the patio on the roof where he and his crew could relax and enjoy downtime. There was patio furniture and a couple of big umbrellas in the space. Carla thought about straddling him in one of the chairs.

Finally, he took her back downstairs to the captains' dorm which was more spacious than the standard firefighter dorms. The captains' dorm had several rooms with beds that looked more comfortable than the bunk beds in the other dorms. Baxter explained that he shared the captains' quarters with the captain they saw in the classroom and another captain.

"You remember Percy, the guy who came with me to the club?" Baxter's eyes twinkled a bit when he thought about how Percy had the "hots" for Carla too. "The one you made such an impression on. He's one of our engineers, but he's off today."

"Engineer? Is that sort of like a lieutenant?"

"Yeah, you could say that."

Baxter didn't want to give him too much rank in Carla's eyes. And he wasn't worried about Percy missing the "hands-off-Carla" tour. The word would spread, and even if it didn't, he'd personally remind Percy that Carla was "off limits" for now. Baxter shook his head resignedly. Percy might still pursue Carla anyway.

He couldn't blame Percy. Carla was a gorgeous woman, hair or no hair. She had on less makeup today. He liked her fresh-faced look. He wanted to kiss her lips and put his tongue down her throat and in that cleft in her chin. He shook his head to get his thoughts under control.

"Last stop, my office," Baxter said and ushered her inside. He closed the door behind them.

Carla was impressed. His office was surprisingly spacious and well-decorated with dark wood furniture and a plump couch. The walls were white cement with a red brick wall adding contrast. Plants dotted the office and accentuated the décor. A window along the outer wall gave the room a light airiness. Honorary plaques covered the walls, along with pictures of Baxter in dress uniform being congratulated by various government and community officials, including the mayor.

On a wall by itself hung a spellbinding photograph of a building engulfed in flames, leaving nothing but its frame. A curious bicyclist was captured gliding past the hypnotic ruins. Carla shuddered for a moment at the picture. Baxter drew her attention away.

"This is my collection," he said. He indicated a glass showcase of miniature fire trucks. Carla turned her attention to the showcase. It was every little boy's dream, no, every kid's dream. Her nieces would get a kick out of the collection. The trucks were all die-cast metal with rubber tires.

"Wow!" Carla exclaimed. "These are great. My father had a nice collection of miniature cars. He still has a few."

Baxter smiled and opened the case for her. He had organized the cars by year, starting with a replica of a 1925 Ford Model T. It was a Touring Fire Chief car that was red with a black top. Carla marveled at a 1944 Mercedes Fire Engine that was red with black trim and a silver ladder across the top. Baxter handed her a 1960 Mack C Rescue truck in yellow. She could tell it was one of his favorites. He also pointed out a 1988 Fire Department Jeep Vehicle with an open top and sides. A silver ladder stretched across the top of its frame.

Carla examined one miniature after another, thoroughly

enjoying herself. Baxter was pleased with her interest. She rolled one of the trucks over the top of the glass case. She made the "whirring" sounds that fire trucks make.

Baxter laughed heartily. "My mom used to walk me past a fire station when I was about three or four. When the fire trucks pulled in, the guys would honk and wave at me. I've been hooked ever since. My mom wanted me to go to college and study business, but I wanted to be a firefighter and work my way up through the ranks. I still ended up taking a number of courses."

"Must be nice to do what you always wanted," Carla commented.

Baxter nodded. "Yeah, I guess so."

Satisfied that she had touched every single fire truck in his collection, Carla allowed Baxter to close the case. She was crazier than ever about him. Their eyes met. The hunger still flowed between them. Neither wanted to part company.

"So now you've seen everything," Baxter said.

Not everything, Carla thought. Then she noticed a calendar page in a glass frame on a corner wall. She remembered the calendar that Earl, the young rookie, had mentioned. A photograph of Baxter presided front and center on the page. He represented the month of January in the firefighter's calendar.

Baxter looked resigned, but proud when he noticed Carla staring at the picture. "I was a bit younger then," he said sheepishly.

Carla stepped closer to the picture. Her breath caught in her throat. "How old were you when you took this?"

"Not too long ago. They wanted to show some older firefighters who were in good shape."

Carla's eyes locked on the picture. Baxter wore low-slung, light blue jeans. A hint of his white boxer shorts peeped out from underneath. The blue jeans and the white underwear contrasted nicely with the glow of his warm brown skin. His chest was bare, clean-shaven, and muscled. His face and chest were perfectly smudged with well-placed soot. A few smudges emphasized his flexed, bulging arms.

In one arm, he carried a fluffy white Hemingway cat, with the huge paws and extra toes. The end of the cat's fluffy tail was streaked in a burnt orange color. In the other hand, Baxter wielded a long-handled fireman's axe that made him project a strong sense of power. Carla's breath caught in her throat again as her eyes continued to feast on the calendar.

In the picture, Baxter's face glistened a golden brown. His lips were full and sensuous, topped by a thick black mustache. His eyes had been captured so that all kinds of golden flecks sparkled in them. A hint of a smile played on his lips. He wore an orange fire helmet that added a dimension of strength to his sex appeal. His chest muscles bulged and glistened with sweat. His jeans and boxers hung low enough to accentuate the v-section of his groin. The front bulge in his jeans was copious and strong. The camera seemed to have a love affair with all of Baxter. Personifying the month of January, he embodied a fine hunk of a man.

Carla couldn't believe her good fortune. She felt herself openly lusting for him. Baxter felt flattered by Carla's obvious captivation with the picture, but he squirmed uncomfortably as well.

"Wasn't my idea to hang the picture," Baxter explained. "But some of the haters made a bet with me. I lost. They hung the picture."

"In all its glory," Carla couldn't resist saying.

Baxter felt like a sex object himself whenever women looked at the picture. He had to admit he looked good, but he wondered how Carla could do a strip show and not let it bother her.

He couldn't resist asking, "How do you handle it when somebody ogles you with all kinds of stuff in their heads?"

Another time, Carla might have blasted him. But for now, she was so entranced by the picture and the real-life hunk in front of her that she didn't want to argue with him. "You learn to steel yourself."

Baxter's eyes searched her face for a more satisfactory answer.

Carla teased him. "You shouldn't have taken the picture."

Baxter shrugged and threw his hands up. "Hey, at the time . . . ."

Carla moved in closer to him, a hairbreadth away. His resistance to being perceived as a sex object vanished rapidly. He narrowed the blinds, and then returned to her. The heat from the sexual tension between them drew their bodies closer, but not touching.

"I'm glad you took the picture," Carla said. To her, Baxter pretty much looked the same. She noticed that the love handles were a little more pronounced around his mid-section, and his tummy was not as taut as in the picture, but she could definitely live with that. He was a gorgeous man who aimed to serve. *What a man,* she thought. And he was standing right in front of her.

"It's a nice picture, Baxter," Carla said, stepping in closer to him. She could feel the heat from his breath.

"I have to warn you." His voice was husky with desire. "We're in the station. Any moment . . . ."

"I know." Carla pressed into his body. "I want to feel you for a minute." She reached up and caressed his biceps, something she had been longing to do from the moment he rescued her. She felt free to touch and probe as much as she wanted. She ran her hands across his chest and down to his abdomen. She kissed his lips, the lips she marveled at in the picture. His kiss felt even better than expected. Their tongues lashed out against each other.

Baxter gasped. "Let's go," he said hoarsely.

Carla wanted to go, but she couldn't move. She pressed the softness between her legs against the protrusion in his trousers. She heard his sharp inhalation of breath, but he couldn't move either. He pressed deeper into her flesh. Moving in unison, they backed up against the desk for support.

Their bodies were like pulsating magnets that couldn't unlock. Carla knew they needed to stop, and she would in a moment, but for now, she couldn't tear herself away from his hardness. Her body craved the contact that not even the threat of a sudden fire alarm could halt. She and Baxter created their own fire.

Baxter wanted to pull away, but he was trapped by the throbbing in his pants as he pushed harder against her. If anybody suddenly burst in on them, he didn't know what he would do, but he knew he couldn't stop right now.

He rubbed his hands over her breasts through the tight fabric of her top. He felt her nipples harden against his hands, then his fingers. He knew he was lost, but he kept telling himself that he would stop soon, that he had everything under control. He reached down inside her top and fingered her breasts, gently stroking and teasing. Carla's heavy breathing inflamed his.

He continued to play with her breasts with one hand, but he moved the other hand down to her ass, that beautiful round, fat ass that he had been dying to touch. He spent the next moments exploring her butt, rubbing his hand over every curve of it and reveling in the feel. He cupped both hands over her butt and shifted her even more on point between his legs. His thickness pushed against the pliant mound between her legs.

Carla gasped and spread her legs wider. Her legs trembled as her body slid from side to side against the thick fullness in his pants. She reached down and touched the hard outline of his penis. She fingered gently at first, then with a firmer grasp. She knew his stiffness begged to be free. She could feel the warmth of her canal thicken with moisture in anticipation of his entry. Even through their clothes, she could feel him, greedy and throbbing against her. She savored the feel as Baxter slid her hips from side to side.

Then he pushed her pants down and very lightly slid his fingers back and forth over her clitoris. Carla opened her legs wider to him. He slid his finger into her hot canal, exploring and savoring the feel of her as moistness coated his finger.

Carla writhed in surrender to a flood of pleasure. She unzipped his jeans, slid them down, and unleashed the hot pulsing thickness that begged to plunge inside her. Insistently, she stroked his hardness back and forth in her hands. Without missing a beat, he slipped on a condom from the wallet in his jeans pocket. This made Carla even more excited.

His dick was now free to work its magic. She gasped as he slid his fullness inside her. In ecstasy, she felt him gliding in and out of her creamy tunnel. He lifted her up and down on his hardness, and the feeling was exquisite for both of them. Baxter leaned harder against the desk for support and pulled her with him. Her hot slick tunnel engulfed his every move. They were both consumed with such passion that neither could let go of the other. Baxter immersed himself deep inside her, and Carla savored every gliding moment. He was firm, but not rough.

He raised her top up and exposed her breasts. She moaned against his lips as his hands stroked all over her breasts and butt. He pushed deeper, and she opened wider as their greedy bodies locked and slapped against each other. Finally, the exquisite pleasure coupled with the forbidden fruit of fornicating in his office pushed them over the edge. Baxter spurted forth inside her, and Carla moaned in ecstasy and release. She reveled in the warmth of his flow through the condom as her insides contracted with pleasure. Baxter moaned and pulled her against him with one last thrust. Their hoarse breathing subsided.

Baxter finally came to his senses. Carla still relished his softening thickness inside her. He gripped the condom and slid out of her. "Come on, let's get going," he said. He pointed to a side door leading to a bathroom. "You can fix up in there." He looked guilty and avoided her eyes.

Carla didn't know what to think, but she knew she had to freshen up. Maybe, they should have gone back to her place.

Carla felt embarrassed as they left the fire station. Fortunately, most of the men were scattered about the station. Some were still in class or doing paperwork. Some were working out in the weight room, and others were wiping down the truck. As she and Baxter left, Carla held her breath and avoided everyone's eyes. Baxter seemed a bit subdued too, but he also appeared so impersonal. Yet moments ago, nothing could have pulled them apart.

Baxter held the door open for her as she got into his car. *A good sign,* Carla thought, but he exuded an aura that was much different from when they first rode in his car. There had been an air of anticipation then. Now . . . .

"Why so quiet?" Carla asked.

"Nothing," he said and patted her hand absently.

Damn, Carla thought. How could she have let herself get so carried away in the fire station? What was she thinking? Staring at his handsome profile, she realized that she blew it. She might have lost him for good because she gave it up too fast. This was their first date, and she had given it up just like that. No preamble, no nothing. It all started with a picture. She could kick herself. She didn't know what his feelings were for her, but she still wanted to see him again. She finally found someone she liked who seemed to like her, and she blew it because she got all hot and bothered by a picture and the man himself, of course.

Baxter wanted to take Carla home as quickly as possible. He did his best to slow down for her sake. Though he took a longer route, he used back streets that moved fast. He needed to think without her in the car. He didn't want to appear rude, but he had to sort some things out. Was he done with her already? He definitely felt sated. But for how long? Yet he simply did not want to become involved with a stripper. He didn't care how well she spoke.

Carla had just given him all the insight he needed into her character. Was this how she acted with other guys? Did she give it away the first time she hung out with them? He couldn't believe he had screwed her back at the station. He had never done that before. Sure, he had given other women the tour, but only the tour. Everything else happened at his place or theirs or some other wild locale like a boat, plane, or train, but not his office. He was glad they had used the condom in his wallet and not allowed passion to overrule good judgment. Yeah, he knew they both wanted each other. The desire between them was so thick you could almost slice it. But couldn't she have held off just a little?

"So you're done with me, now that you got the goodies?" Carla said, echoing his thoughts.

"Of course not," Baxter said. But he knew he didn't mean it. Yes, he was done with her. Carla wasn't his type of woman. She was bad news. While he would certainly love to screw her again, he couldn't afford the risk of getting involved with her. She was beautiful, honest, and a lot like some of the professional women he dated. Perhaps, she wore a little too much makeup, but he could live with that. But he couldn't deal with a stripper, one who almost lost her life in that seedy environment. Somebody set that fire. He didn't know if they meant to kill her, but they meant to burn down that club. And what would his mother say if she knew he was dating a stripper or even a manager of a strip club? It was best to cut his losses and take Carla home before he became too infatuated with her.

Carla wanted to slap Baxter silly. How could he treat her so coldly? True, she gave up the goodies a little faster than she expected. But she definitely hadn't forced herself on him. He was quite willing and able. She felt betrayed. He had gotten what he wanted, and now he had no use for her. She had wanted something more lasting with him. *Get over it,* she told herself. If he was that immature, she didn't need him. But she had to face it. She still wanted him. She wanted more sex and the pleasure of his company. Maybe, she was kidding herself that she could have some kind of relationship with him. She remembered Mimi's warning. "Don't go gettin' all gooey-eyed over him."

Baxter continued the drive in silence. He took a picturesque route in West LA, driving down palm tree-lined streets, past Spanish style houses, but he drove so fast that everything went by in a blur. Carla should have stopped him from driving so fast, but she didn't care anymore. Was she doomed to a loveless life?

Finally, they pulled up onto the street in front of her building. This time, Baxter made no effort to get out of the car and open the door for her. Instead, he leaned over and kissed her absently on the forehead.

"I had a good time," he said.

Carla simply got out of the car and didn't say anything. She kept hoping he would call her back, but he didn't. He did wait until she entered the courtyard of her building, but she suddenly turned around and walked back to the street. Baxter looked puzzled.

"I need to take a walk," Carla said and widened the expanse between them.

She saw him shrug and drive off. *Why was he acting like such a jerk?* she wondered. She suddenly realized how lonely she was and how silly she was to think that she had found a decent man who cared. He was like all the others who tried to disrespect her. Yes, she could give up the strip club life. She had thought about it many times, especially after the fire. But she would make the decision herself. No one would force it on her.

CHAPTER 8

Carla's heartbeat raced. She took a deep breath to still it. She couldn't believe that she was actually sitting in front of the fire station where Baxter worked. She couldn't believe that he had dumped her. She had to see him again to ask him why.

Carla stepped out of her car, opened the trunk, and pulled out a tray of cupcakes. She was quite pleased with the gourmet collection of chocolate ganache, key lime, and red velvet cupcakes. She planned to give them to all the firefighters in the station. After all, they had put out the fire at the old TiTi Bar. She knew her heart was in the right place. She wanted to give thanks to the wonderful firefighters who saved her, but she also wanted to see Baxter again.

She looked down at the cupcakes and smiled. She wished she had baked them, but she neither baked nor cooked, much to her late mother's chagrin. Her mother knew how to bake, cook, sew, and run a PTA meeting. And she taught her daughters, Carla and Natalie, how to do the same, but once Carla started hitting the fast lane as a stripper, she abandoned all her culinary skills and never looked back. She realized that her dream of being the perfect homemaker like her mother was nothing but a dream. The men she met as a stripper didn't care about her cooking skills. They wanted something hot from her, but it wasn't food. But with Baxter, she thought she had finally found a man who could appreciate her.

Well, hopefully, Baxter and his crew would appreciate the tray of goodies she bought for them. She caught a glimpse of her reflection in the car window. She had taken great pains to figure out what to wear. She wanted to look good without calling too much attention to her physique. She wore a pair of jeans, a soft white blouse, and black gladiator sandals with a moderately high heel. Her nails gleamed with a brand-new manicure and pedicure. She wanted Baxter to see what he was missing. She knew she was a bit heavy-handed with the makeup, but she loved makeup. Maybe one day, she would tone it down, but not today.

Carrying the cupcake tray in both hands, Carla took another deep breath and headed for the station. Earl White, the young rookie, was the first to greet her. He took her to the dining room and placed the tray on the table. The rest of the crew greeted her and swarmed over to the table in obvious delight. They stopped their paperwork, drill work, or whatever else they were doing. Carla laughed. She didn't realize it was going to be so easy.

"For all that you do," Carla said. "Thanks."

A number of the firefighters, male and female, were already feasting on the treats. They thanked Carla with wide grins of appreciation. Earl was munching away and grabbing another cupcake. Carla envied him for a moment. He was young and lean with no worries about his weight.

"Thank you, ma'am," one of the men said. Carla could have done without the "ma'am." Sometimes, "ma'am" came in handy, but not now. She wanted to see Baxter.

"The cupcakes are great, but how about a lap dance?" someone muttered.

Carla swung around. She couldn't determine who said it. "You want a lap dance, you come to the club I manage. We'll be happy to arrange one for you." Strangely, Carla felt a sense of calm as she put the offender in his place.

She began to realize that Baxter was nowhere to be seen. She started to shift awkwardly from one foot to the other until Earl came over and rescued her.

He avoided her eyes. "Not sure where the captain is. He might have gone off somewhere."

"Yeah, not sure when he'll be back," another fireman said. Carla remembered him from the tour Baxter gave her. His name was Frank. He was a sturdy, muscular White guy—blond and handsome, around thirty. He had kind eyes, but even he was avoiding Carla's eyes.

She looked in the direction of Baxter's office. She wanted to barge right in and yell at him, tell him that he was acting like a jerk. She figured he was probably in there, avoiding her. An awkward silence began to form. Somebody coughed. Carla needed no further cue. She stood up taller.

"Well, I just wanted to say thanks for all you do. Hope you enjoy," Carla said and turned to leave.

Then she heard the same smart ass from earlier. "Next time, bring your girls with you and give us some real cupcakes."

Carla whirled around. She saw a young female firefighter try to ignore the comment. Carla couldn't blame her. She figured this young woman probably heard much worse.

Carla still couldn't determine who was making the crude comments, but she did see one of the men snicker. For a moment, she felt the urge to knock the table over and toss the cupcakes on the floor. She'd topple a few chairs as well. If they wanted her to act "street," she'd be happy to oblige them, especially the punk who kept making all the smart-ass comments. But instead of surrendering to her baser instincts, Carla walked away.

Earl escorted her out of the fire house. He shrugged apologetically. "Not sure what happened with the captain." He still refused to meet her eyes.

Carla sighed. The worse was over. She couldn't be more embarrassed than she already was. "Thanks, Earl," she said.

Earl finally looked her in the eye and said, "I think you're cool." Frank stood in the background and nodded.

Carla headed to her car, a late model gold Infiniti that Wendell had given her during a string of good luck. She wondered if she should simply stick with Wendell and ignore his indiscretions, but no, she didn't want that either. Inside her car, Carla welcomed its enveloping sanctuary. She sank deeper into the plush fabric of the seat. She fought back tears of embarrassment and frustration. She couldn't believe that Baxter could be so heartless, that he would use her and seemingly discard her. She knew he was probably there at the fire station, ducking her. Well, she refused to cry over him. She would put him out of her mind forever.

Carla moved about confidently in the new TiTi Bar. She was back in her own arena now. Never again would she subject herself to humiliation caused by Baxter or any man for that matter. Certainly, men would continue to make vulgar, disrespectful comments to her at the TiTi, and she would handle it. But never again would she wear her heart on her sleeve for any man. She had to be more careful. Maybe one day, she would find somebody to love her.

In defiance of Baxter's mistreatment, Carla wore a black halter dress with a slightly flared skirt, but it was her shortest dress ever. It grazed the top of her thigh, just below her ass. She wore high-heeled black sandals and bright red toenail polish. Though short, the dress flared demurely across her butt, yet never hiding the curves underneath. The halter neckline plunged to her waist and revealed more than enough cleavage. Carla delighted in sashaying around the club, titillating the patrons. She felt a ruthless, angry power as she moved about. She'd show all these men that they were just "johns."

Wendell came over to her as she was leaving a patron. "You okay?" he asked. "You seem a little different tonight."

Carla snapped. "I'm fine."

"Whoa. I'm still the boss."

Carla tried to reign in her emotions. She gave a tight-lipped smile. "Everything's fine, dear."

"Then act like it, babe. Be nice to the customers. I detect some latent hostility."

Carla burst out laughing. She found it amusing the way Wendell mixed his new vocabulary with his street talk.

"That's it. Smile a little," Wendell said. He reached out and touched her cleavage lightly.

Carla pulled away from him. "Not tonight, Wendell."

"Does that mean some other night?"

"No, it doesn't. Why this sudden interest?"

"I've always been interested, Rae. You know that."

"No, you been interested in those young girls."

Wendell laughed. "Yep, them too."

"At least, you're upfront," Carla said. She knew Wendell would always have his hands in some young dancer's crotch or all over her ass.

"You know, you haven't been right ever since that fireman showed up. He's not your type, Rae."

"Don't want to talk about it. I'm not feeling him anymore."

"The lady doth protest."

This time, Carla doubled over with laughter. "Shakespeare, Wendell? You're full of shit." She could never remain angry with Wendell for long.

"Laugh at me all you want, but that fireman is not for you. Let it go."

Carla decided to let Wendell have the last word. Maybe, he was right. Then she noticed Wendell tense. His eyes hardened. "Here comes one of your firefighters now."

Carla took a deep breath and turned around, thrilled. She knew Baxter couldn't stay away. She did mean more to him than a cheap lay. Wendell frowned at her reaction. Carla's elation turned to sheer disappointment. Baxter wasn't walking towards her. Percy was. He strode over to her with a confident sense of purpose. Carla tried to look over his shoulder to see if Baxter was anywhere in sight. He wasn't. Her spirits plunged.

Percy's eyes devoured Carla. "You look hot." He totally dismissed Wendell.

"Actually, this dress is a little chilly when I don't move around."

"I'll warm you up," Percy said.

"No. I need to start circulating."

Wendell looked Percy up and down. Carla knew that Wendell was two seconds away from kicking Percy's ass. She imagined Percy would put up a good fight, but she still didn't think he was as strong as Wendell.

Realizing the stickiness of the situation, Carla assumed her role as the ultimate hostess. "Walk with me," she said to Percy. She turned to Wendell. "I'm gonna take Percy around and show him some of our best dancers. Maybe get him a lap dance so he'll spread the word. Good for business."

Carla successfully lowered Wendell's boiling point. She could see the cash registers ringing in his eyes. He was still a businessman.

"Call me if you need me, Rae," Wendell said and strolled away.

"The only lap dancer I want is you," Percy said.

"I know. But that's not going to happen. I'm the manager. I don't do lap dances, but I can arrange one for you with some of our finest dancers."

"Heard you stopped by the station today. Thanks for the cupcakes," he smirked. He licked his lips and fastened his eyes on Carla's cleavage.

"Wanted to show my appreciation for all you guys do."

"No, you came by to see Baxter. I heard he gave you the shaft. No pun intended," Percy taunted.

Carla played it cool. "Did you come here to have a good time or to talk about me and Baxter?"

"Both."

Carla had to acknowledge his persistence. Percy knew no shame. He was relentless. But she'd had enough.

"My business with Baxter is not your business. Now if you want me to escort you around the club for a few minutes, show you how you can have a good time, I'd be happy to. Otherwise, you can escort yourself around, or you can go home. Your choice. It's up to you." Carla turned her back on him and walked ahead. "Come on, I'll take you over to the best dancer in the house."

Carla could feel his eyes raking all over her butt. She could hear his breathing. Normally, she would have swayed her ass even more under the dress just to fuck with him, but now all she wanted to do was get rid of him.

Percy reached out and grabbed her. Carla flung his arm off. He backed down, not wanting a confrontation.

"I want you," he said. "Yeah, I want to fuck you. What's wrong with that? You're hot. You got a nice body."

"I don't want you," Carla said.

"You want Baxter? He doesn't feel the same. You keep harboring some pipe dream about him. He's got plenty of other women."

"I don't care what he has. I don't want you. I can't seem to get that across."

Percy sighed, and his eyes softened. "I'll treat you right. I'd be proud to have you on my arm. I'll take you places. I like you. We could make a dream team." He reached out and lightly touched her arm. Carla was surprised at the pleasantness of his touch. It caught her off guard. Percy noticed her confusion. He pounced. "I can show you a good time. We can have fun. I want to get to know you in every way."

With a feathery touch, Percy caressed the top of her breast. Carla hated to admit it, but his touch felt good. She steeled herself and stepped away. He tilted her chin up and looked her straight in the eye. "I just want to spend some time with you. Enjoy. Go places. Do things together."

Why couldn't Baxter pursue her like this? Carla wondered. *Why couldn't he open up like this?*

For a fleeting moment, she felt like succumbing to Percy's charms. It would serve Baxter right. She knew Percy probably didn't want anything serious, but it would be so nice to hang out with a decent man and enjoy plenty of hot, steamy sex. She would love to let go for a change and simply have fun, date a strong man and go nice places with him. Percy was handsome too—fair-skinned, tall, and rugged.

Carla felt a heat stirring between her legs as she thought of the contrast of Percy's skin molded against hers. But she immediately squashed the thought. Percy was a straight-up wolf in sheep's clothing. He still didn't compare to Baxter in her eyes, no matter how much Baxter vexed her.

"It's not gonna happen, Percy," Carla said firmly.

Percy's face fell in disappointment. Again, Carla felt torn. She looked into his eyes and wanted to let go, but couldn't.

"You and Baxter ain't gonna happen either," Percy said. "But me and you," he said and caressed her arm lightly again. "We can get it on. You think about it. You don't have to give me an answer right now, but think about it." Then he walked out of the club before Carla could answer.

Carla sighed. Mimi, the young stripper, approached. As usual, bills of varying denominations were strung all over Mimi's scantily clad body. Bills dangled from her skinny-strapped bikini top and G-string. Mimi was having a good night, but Carla realized she must have been high as a kite to walk around with all that money dangling off her. Mimi often frustrated Wendell's bouncers as they tried to protect her.

"Now that's the one you should be doing," Mimi said as she watched Percy exit the club. "He's the one who wants you, chica. Give him some. Forget about the other one."

"Don't worry about it. You need to take your ass home, girl. You ain't feeling no pain." Carla gathered up all of Mimi's bills for her, except the ones under the V-cover. "I'm sending you home. Go get some rest and stop gettin' so fucked up."

Carla shuddered when she thought of what Mimi might have taken. She knew coke was involved and probably some downer. Mimi was woozy. Anybody could take advantage of her. Carla figured some of the guys in the club were just waiting for the chance to make a move on her.

Carla nudged Mimi towards a dressing room. She signaled to Wendell. He came over immediately. "Mimi's done for the night," Carla said. "I'll drive her home."

Wendell nodded in agreement and pulled Carla aside. "Talk to her. I don't care how many customers she brings in or how much money they spend, she better get her act together. If she keeps gettin' fucked up, it won't be financially feasible for me to keep her on."

"Financially feasible, Wendell?"

"Yeah, financially feasible. Talk to her."

Carla simply sighed. "I will."

"You come back though. I like that dress. The clients do too."

"Okay, I'll be back," Carla said, but she wasn't so sure. She suddenly felt tired. She couldn't get Baxter out of her system, and she couldn't stop Percy from hounding her. Now she had to deal with Mimi flying high.

* * *

Carla entered the small office beside her dressing room and gathered up her keys and purse. When she returned to the main floor of the club, one of Wendell's trusted henchmen guarded Mimi at a secluded table. Outside the club, the guard escorted Mimi to Carla's car. He waited until Carla started the engine before he left.

Carla shook her head sadly as she drove away. Mimi was barely coherent, but at least, she had managed to stagger out to the car.

In her younger days, Carla herself had gotten more than tipsy, but not like Mimi. Once Mimi sobered up, Carla was going to have a serious talk with her. Mimi was living too dangerously now, and she was becoming so thin.

As Carla reflected on her day, she wondered what would become of her and Mimi. They both had good heads on their shoulders, yet they supported themselves the only way they knew how. Carla fancied herself a dancer, and Mimi fancied herself a singer. Yet they both worked in a strip club. *Well, one day, they'd figure it out,* Carla decided. For now, she had to take Mimi home and get back to work.

She glanced over at Mimi who snuggled half-asleep in the passenger seat. "What am I going to do with you, Mimi?"

Mimi stirred and answered, "I like to get high, chica. I like to get high."

"You're gonna mess up your life, girl."

"I'll stop one day," Mimi said dreamily as she sank deeper into Carla's seat.

Carla certainly hoped so as she drove Mimi home.

A short while later, Carla tucked Mimi in safe and sound, then headed back to work. On the way back to the club, she wondered if Mimi would ever reach her forties. Carla herself had walked a tightrope when she was younger, but fortunately, she survived and never got hooked on drugs and alcohol. She had exercised more discipline than Mimi and avoided losing control. Mimi scared her until she remembered the stories of how Mimi almost single-handedly forced Baxter and his crew to look for Carla. No, she would never give up on Mimi. She had to help her.

CHAPTER 9

Carla walked up the driveway and the steps to Natalie's house. Natalie lived on a picturesque, tree-lined street of single-family homes in the Ladera Heights section of Los Angeles. It was a nice, quiet neighborhood, too family-oriented for Carla, with its manicured lawns and sculptured hedges. But Natalie wanted a safe neighborhood for her girls, and Carla certainly understood. As she rang the bell, Carla saw all kinds of bikes and toys all over the neighborhood, a kid's haven.

Carla remembered the blur of streets like Natalie's when Baxter drove her home from the fire station. She still struggled to block that day from her mind.

Natalie's eyes widened in surprise when she answered the door and found Carla standing there. "Wow. What brings you here?"

Carla shrugged. "I wanted to stop by to see you and the girls."

"Really?"

"I know I never stop by, but I'm seldom invited."

Natalie shrugged.

As Carla entered the house, her nieces, Stephanie and Tiffany, rushed out of their rooms. Even lounging around, Stephanie, the eleven-year-old fashion plate, resembled a model with no effort at all. Tiffany, the five-year-old princess, simply needed a tiara to go with her slick jeans and pink T-shirt.

The girls ran over to Carla and hugged her. Carla laughed and hugged them back. Every time she saw them, she wondered why she didn't visit more, and then she remembered Natalie's constant disapproval of her lifestyle.

"Hi, girls," Carla said. She picked Tiffany up. "Damn, you're a big girl now. Where's that little tiny one, I used to lift up like a feather?" She put Tiffany down.

"I'm growing up, Auntie," Tiffany said in her proper royal voice. Carla wondered how the kids in Tiffany's class accepted the princess air. But then she recalled how her nieces stuck together. They'd punch the lights out of anybody who tried to harass them. And if that didn't work, Russell, their father, would take on anybody in LA who tried to harm his girls. Russell didn't play. He boxed for sport and taught his girls how to box too.

Tiffany jumped up and down with excitement. "Stay for dinner, Aunt Carla."

"Yes!" Stephanie, the pre-teen, exclaimed. She was a bit more reserved, but she smiled with excitement as well.

"I'd love to," Carla said. "You got enough?" she asked Natalie.

"Love to have you. I'm almost done," Natalie said.

"Where's Brittany?" Carla asked.

Brittany finally emerged from her bedroom. Carla's six-year-old niece wore a scandalously short, tight skirt that she must have kept from her toddler days. Her butt peeped out under the skirt. She had hiked her panties up so that it appeared as though she wore a thong. She wore lipstick, eye shadow, and blusher. The tight blouse she wore looked like a bib from her infant days. The blouse exposed her fat, girlish midriff.

Carla stifled a gasp and exchanged hugs with her niece.

"Hi, Aunt Carla," Brittany said, appearing totally unfazed by her outfit.

Carla's eyes met Natalie's, but Natalie refused to discipline Brittany. Instead, Natalie seemed to delight in Carla's discomfort.

"Brittany, uh . . . ." Carla didn't know what to say.

"You talk to her," Natalie said.

"You can't dress like that, Brittany," Carla finally spoke.

"You do," Brittany said.

"But it's my job, an adult job, and I don't dress quite like that."

Natalie raised an eyebrow in disagreement.

Carla immediately defended herself. "Don't you dare," she said to Natalie. "I'm a grown woman who has to dress a certain way for work."

Natalie stared at Carla, unimpressed. Carla's nieces watched and waited, Brittany in particular. Carla felt they were ganging up on her, but she knew she could hold her own.

"There is no comparison between me and a six-year-old. You need to take that stuff off," she said to Brittany.

Brittany refused to budge.

"Go put something else on," Natalie finally directed.

"No," Brittany said.

"Take that shit off now!" Carla insisted. She didn't care what Natalie's reaction was.

Brittany ran crying from the room. Stephanie and Tiffany looked at their mom for guidance. "Let your aunt handle it," Natalie said. She was still hell-bent on proving a point.

Carla ran after Brittany. Natalie kept her other two daughters at her side.

Brittany wailed away on her bed. Her room was fairly neat for a first grader. Posters of the latest singers graced her walls, and a pink ruffled bedspread covered her bed.

"Didn't mean to hurt your feelings, Brittany." Carla hated to see her niece cry. She bent over Brittany. "You're going to mess up your makeup." Amazingly, that seemed to halt the waterworks.

Brittany stood up and stared at her reflection in the mirror on her dresser. She noticed the smudges to her eye shadow and the tear streaks on her blusher. Her lipstick was almost gone.

Carla found some cotton balls and the makeup Brittany used earlier. She started repairing her niece's makeup. Brittany pulled away at first. Carla laughed. "Don't worry. I'm not going to take it all off. Just fix it up so you can show your real beauty. Watch."

Brittany relaxed and let her aunt repair the makeup. When Carla finished, Brittany smiled in the mirror. "You still don't need makeup," Carla admonished.

Brittany was too busy staring at her new reflection to heed the advice. Carla smiled. "Now let's find some clothes. What's in your closet?"

Carla pulled out a nice pair of skinny-legged jeans and a colorful V-neck top and helped Brittany dress. She turned the top backwards so that the V-neck hung in the back. Then Carla found a pair of baby doll shoes that glittered. Since Brittany's hair was already in braids, Carla added sparkly hair ornaments that she found in one of the dresser drawers.

When Carla was done, she stepped back and surveyed her handiwork. Brittany was grinning from ear to ear in the mirror. Carla stood behind her and marveled at how much they looked alike. Though the cleft in Brittany's chin was less pronounced, they both had the same chocolate brown skin and big dark eyes.

All of Brittany's tears had vanished. She hugged Carla warmly, then raced off to show her sisters her new look. Carla shook her head in amusement and followed Brittany out of the bedroom.

Natalie and the girls were in the dining room, waiting. The tableware was arranged, and food sat on the table. Natalie had fried chicken and set out candied yams, greens, baked macaroni, and dinner rolls.

Carla's eyes lit up. "For me?"

Natalie grinned. "Leftovers. I did fry the chicken and popped the rolls in the oven. I know you don't eat fried foods much, but neither do we. So let's dig in and enjoy."

"Aunt Carla, can you do our makeup too?" Stephanie, the pre-teen, asked.

"Me too," Princess Tiffany said.

Carla laughed. "After I finish eating, girls. Okay?"

They nodded. But Stephanie was ready for her makeover now. She merely picked at her food.

"See what you started," Natalie said in fun, but the words still held a double entendre for Carla.

"Okay, Natalie," Carla warned.

Natalie sighed and changed the subject. "Hey, where's the uncle you promised us? You ever see that handsome fireman again?"

Carla snapped. She hopped up from the table and grabbed her purse. "I'm not quitting my job! I don't care what anybody thinks!" She stormed out of the house, leaving everybody staring at her with open mouths.

CHAPTER 10

Baxter and Percy played a game of one-on-one basketball on the court erected behind their fire house. The sun was setting, creating blood orange streaks in the sky. With the advantage of extra height, Percy was winning hands down.

"I'm a wipe this court up with your ass. We won't need to sweep out here for a long time?" Percy taunted in fun.

"One of these days, I'm a fuck you up, man," Baxter said.

"Not today." Percy was still selling wolf tickets. He faked to his right, but swung around to his left, then delivered a hook shot over Baxter's head. Then Percy immediately regained possession of the ball from Baxter and made another shot that swooshed right into the basket. Both men were sweating profusely, but Baxter's shorts and T-shirt were soaked. "Game over," Percy said.

"We still got one more," Baxter said.

"Shit, man, you ain't had enough? I already whupped your ass twice. You might as well quit now. Best two out of three. It's over."

They both stopped and took a break.

"No, I want to play. I'm going to kick your ass at least once today," Baxter insisted.

"It's not happening, man. Look at you. I've never seen you sweat like this. You still fucked up over Rae?"

Baxter bristled. "I'm not fucked up over anybody. That's all history. It'll never happen."

"That's what I told her." Percy waited for his words to take effect.

Baxter's face was unreadable.

"Man, if you don't want her, I do," Percy said. "I told her so, and I saw this look on her face. She wants me. I know it. But she's got this thing for you because you saved her."

"Why you always chasing after my women? Why you always do that shit."

"What you mean—your women? I thought you didn't want her."

"Stop worrying about who I'm hooking up with," Baxter said.

"I'm telling you, don't be surprised if I start hanging out with Rae."

Baxter's blood boiled. He was ready to play ball again. Percy had the ball, confident that he could make his shot. Like lightning, Baxter knocked the ball out of Percy's hand, then shot over his head and scored. Then he took a play from Percy, snatched the ball back, and scored a second time. He played with a ferocity that stunned. Percy couldn't do anything with him. Percy tried to regain his footing, but Baxter was playing like a powerhouse and throwing hook shots.

When Baxter finished wiping up the court with Percy, he told him, "Carla is still off limits until I decide what to do."

"Carla? Well, she was Rae back there the other night, and I know she's got the hots for me. You just fuckin' over her. You don't want her."

"Like you got honorable intentions."

"No need to let all that ass go to waste because you can't make up your mind."

"When I make up my mind, I'll let you know. Until then, back the fuck off."

"You trying to pull rank, man," Percy complained.

"No. I am pulling rank." Baxter strode away with Percy staring after him.

Baxter, Earl, and Frank, roamed around the TiTi Bar. It was crowded, with plenty of women dancing the tables to please the crowd. Some of the women were young and beautiful with breasts and butts toned from dancing. They wore sequined G-strings and pasties. Their faces still held a trace of innocence which proved that they hadn't been totally corrupted by the lifestyle. Other young dancers, while their bodies were shapely, possessed faces that were hardened and puffy from alcohol and drug use.

Clad also in tiny G-strings, the TiTi Bar's older dancers carried fuller, more voluptuous figures. With the confidence borne of experience, they bent over and lifted their butts right in the customers' faces. Because of their fading youth, they knew they had to work harder to please.

Baxter felt his pants constrict as he passed some of the dancers. But he was on a mission. He was looking for Carla. He planned to confront her about Percy. Was she really planning to hook up with Percy? He didn't know what he was going to say when he saw her, but he was going to stop her from seeing Percy.

"How many times we gonna walk around this place, Captain?" Earl, the young rookie, said, frustrated. "I can't stand in front of a table long enough to get hard because you so pussy-whipped."

Baxter's eyebrows rose in surprise.

"Yeah, I know y'all was humpin' in your office. What you think, we stupid? Tell him, Frank."

Frank grinned. "I thought the captain was showing her his truck collection."

"Yeah, he was showing her his collection alright," Earl said. "She's not here, Captain. Get over it."

Wendell walked up and surveyed the small group of firefighters. "Drinks on the house, guys. Not the girls though. You want to go back to the VIP lounge? You'll get the best lap dances in the world." He eyed Baxter competitively. "You looking for Rae? She's off tonight." Satisfied with the annoyance on Baxter's face, Wendell turned to depart. "Drink up, guys. Let me know if you're interested in a lap dance."

"You satisfied?" Earl said to Baxter. "I told you she's not here."

Baxter and his crew stood in front of Mimi's table. Mimi was relatively sober for a change. She was really dancing and steady on her feet, not the least bit woozy from any substances.

She had plumped up a bit, making her curves more pronounced. She wore gold pasties and a G-string. Bills of various denominations hung all over the G-string.

She stopped dancing and walked over to Baxter. "Rae don't work here anymore. She quit. Don't know the details. Haven't had a chance to catch up with her."

Baxter pulled out a twenty for her G-string.

Mimi waved it away. "It's on the house, Captain. You better treat her right or let her alone."

On the one hand, Baxter felt pleased about Mimi's forwardness. It meant that Carla must have talked about him. On the other hand, Baxter was tired of people sticking their noses in his business. He simply wanted to find out how Carla felt about Percy.

Mimi turned her attention to Frank. Her eyes beamed with mischief as she surveyed the husky, blond fireman. She was a little taller than Frank. "What about you, big boy, you know how to act right?" She danced provocatively in front of Frank, bumping and grinding and shaking her ass. She turned around and bent over. Frank was lost.

Earl rolled his eyes. "Aw shit, Frank done fell in love."

Frank ignored him, pulled out a bill, and stuck it in Mimi's G-string. She accepted Frank's money. She moved closer to Frank and bent over again with her ass right in his face.

Baxter laughed awkwardly. He knew Mimi spelled trouble for Frank.

"Let's get out of here," Earl said. He turned to Baxter. "You pussy-whipped. And you fallin' in love with a stripper," he said to Frank. "And I can't even stop at a table long enough to get a hard-on, watching over you two. Get me out of this place. I got plenty of women. I don't need to come here."

Baxter was okay with leaving. He wondered what to do next. Should he ride past Carla's house?

Frank wanted to stay.

Earl was still mouthing off. "You always falling in love with the wrong women, Frank. This one is bad news. You should have seen her on New Year's Eve. She's fine, but she's troubled as hell—just your type. She'll hurt you. Come on, man. Let's go."

Reluctantly, Frank turned to leave with them. "You a pain in the ass, man. Naw, you a pussy," Frank said. "How you gonna walk away from all this."

"Watch me," Earl said and walked ahead of them. Baxter and Frank ran up behind him and started roughhousing him.

Earl laughed, trying to untangle himself. "I'm not coming back here with y'all no more. Frank's fallin' in love as usual, and you, Captain, you ready to search the whole city for somebody you tried to duck a few weeks ago. Next time I come back here, I'm coming by myself. Right now, I feel like I got two kids—one old enough to be my father, and the other old enough to know better."

Baxter and Frank roughhoused Earl even more. Wendell's security watched cautiously. "It's all good," Baxter laughed on their way out the door. "We're teaching him how to respect his elders."

Baxter parked on the street in front of Carla's building and exited his car. He came straight from the TiTi Bar after leaving Earl and Frank. It was late, and the street was quiet. He walked through the courtyard and reviewed the building directory. He didn't know what to expect when he saw Carla, but he had to talk to her. His heart was pounding faster than usual as he searched the directory. He buzzed her apartment. No answer. He buzzed again and still no answer. He pressed the button a third time.

He looked around the landscaped courtyard. He liked her building with its Spanish flair. He wondered if he should wait a few minutes to see if she showed up. What if she had gone out of town? He almost felt like buzzing another apartment to inquire about her, but he didn't want to call attention to himself. He didn't want any problems at work with someone spreading the word that a city fire captain was harassing residents listed in the directory.

He peered through the glass door into the building lobby with its tiled floor and plump, contemporary furniture. He hoped to see someone who might direct him to Carla's apartment so he could at least leave her a note. He should have gotten her phone number. Of course, he could find out her number if he wanted to, but since he was right at her doorstep, a note would show urgency.

Baxter went back to his car. He stared up and down the street, but saw no one. He still wondered if he should wait until she showed up. He wanted to ask her so many things, about Percy, about her job. Did she really quit? Did she think he was a jerk for avoiding her the last time she came to the fire station? Maybe, someone would come along and let him in so he could leave that note. Then he realized that wouldn't look good either. He didn't want to appear like a stalker.

Baxter sighed. He started his car and drove slowly away from Carla's building. He kept hoping that she might appear at any moment. He had envisioned that she would let him in the building and invite him up to her apartment. That all would be forgiven and forgotten, except for Percy. He had to ask her about Percy. He wished he had more time, but he had to catch a plane in the morning. He willed the taut rise in his trousers to soften since he saw no opportunity for relief, but thoughts of Carla and that afternoon at the fire station kept returning.

CHAPTER 11

Carla felt both nervous and excited. She had gotten a job in the medical building where Natalie worked. Located in West Los Angeles, the building housed a number of doctors' offices as well as the executive offices of a nearby hospital. Natalie was an administrative assistant who carried a lot of clout. She had highly recommended Carla for the job.

Carla had mixed feelings about giving up her job at the TiTi. Since her late teens, she had worked in exotic dance clubs. Yet she knew, even as a manager, that the stripping life was not a healthy one for her. Still, she needed to reach that conclusion herself. She didn't want Natalie or Baxter badgering her into making any choices. In the end, it was little Brittany, her six-year-old niece, with her makeshift stripper outfit, who made a lasting impression on Carla. She didn't want Brittany to ever glamorize the life of a stripper. Carla herself was lucky. She hadn't succumbed to drugs or too much kinky sex. But her niece might not be so lucky if she followed in Carla's footsteps.

As manager of the TiTi Bar, Carla liked socializing and mingling with people, ensuring that customers were happy. She had the flexibility she craved when working. Now her movements were going to be more restricted, but she refused to let that dampen her excitement about working in a more respectable environment. In this new world, she didn't have to worry about men trying to stick their hands up her dress or brazenly rubbing against her.

Carla looked around at the medical office's white walls and neutral carpet. The cubicle desks were light-colored laminate.

Fortunately, plants and colorful abstract prints provided relief from what could have been a very monotonous color palette.

It was Carla's first day on the job. She would be working on a temporary basis for now, entering data into spreadsheets. The work certainly didn't thrill her, but she viewed it as her stepping stone out of the strip world. Instead of the very tight, short dresses she wore at the club, Carla wore a slim black skirt and an off-white silk blouse. Both pieces fit well, but they left a lot more wiggle room than her usual work attire. Her curves were all there, just not as visible.

Instead of strappy sandals, she wore low-heeled leopard pumps, and she carried a tan leather purse. She was pleased and excited with her outfit. Her niece, Stephanie, the fashionista, had approved Carla's first-day-at-work attire. Now all Carla needed was one of Princess Tiffany's tiaras.

Carla had always wondered about the experience of working in an office, wearing conservative clothing. Actually, the best thing she liked about the morning so far was walking across the building lobby with her heels clicking. She remembered entering an office building years ago, watching in awe the parade of female workers in high heels clicking across the lobby. At that moment, she wanted to join them. Now, she had actually joined their ranks. If Baxter could see her now, he might not recognize her. She had toned down her makeup, though not too much. She couldn't live without her makeup. She sighed and told herself to forget about Baxter. He didn't deserve her. Yet she couldn't forget him.

Carla thought she had seen him drive away from her building the night before. She had come home late after hanging out with her sister and nieces. She and Natalie had kept the girls up past their bedtime, which suited them fine, especially Brittany.

Carla forced herself to get a grip. After the way Baxter treated her, she doubted that car was his. There were a million black Hondas on the road. Still, she could always hope. No, she should forget him. That was best.

Maria, the office manager, approached. She was a plump, voluptuous Latina in a snug-fitting dress. Watching her, Carla suddenly felt a pang of nostalgia for her own little short, tight dresses. But she realized that her current outfit would keep her out of trouble.

The office manager smiled warmly. "Good to see you again, Carla. You ready for work?"

"Yes, I am," Carla smiled.

Natalie walked past. "See you for lunch," she said and kept walking so as not to interfere with Carla's first day.

Carla nodded, amused. She knew that Natalie was going out of her way to make sure Carla succeeded outside the TiTi Bar.

"Your sister's really looking out for you," Maria said.

"I know," Carla said with a tolerant smile.

A tall White male swaggered towards them. He was handsome and built okay, but he had a slight gut. Carla guessed he and Maria were about the same age, somewhere in their late thirties or early forties. Maria suddenly became giggly like a schoolgirl. She straightened up when she saw Carla observing.

Maria was all business now. "This is our medical offices director, John Rawlins. John, this is Carla Hepburn, Natalie's sister. Carla's going to work on that data entry project. She'll be working on a temp basis, and we'll go from there."

John extended his hand. He gave Carla a firm handshake— too firm. He definitely wanted to capture her attention. "I know I've seen you before, but I can't remember." His eyes bore into hers.

Carla matched his stare, but she didn't recall seeing him at the TiTi. She hoped he wasn't a patron. She realized Maria was beginning to scrutinize her like a rival. Carla bristled at first, but then she decided to employ the same smooth-talking skills she used at the club. "Well, I do favor my sister. That's probably what you remember," Carla said. "I'm looking forward to working with you both." She gazed non-threateningly at Maria who seemed satisfied for the moment.

"Let's get you set up," Maria said. "You need anything before I take Carla to her work station?" she asked John.

"No, I just wanted to meet the new hire."

"Temp, John. She's temping for now."

Carla's spirits sank for a moment. More bullshit, she thought. Then she remembered all of Natalie's efforts to get her the job. She smiled. "You're right. I'm temping for now, but I plan to do such a good job . . . ."

Maria eased up. "Come on, let me show you around. See you later, John."

Carla could feel his eyes penetrating through every pore on her butt. She hoped she wouldn't have many dealings with him. She would do her best to stay out of his way.

Carla and Natalie sat outside and ate lunch at a sidewalk cafe. It was a beautiful Los Angeles day, with not a cloud in sight. Carla lifted her face to the sunlight and smiled. She felt like a regular office worker.

"Everything okay?" Natalie asked anxiously.

Carla laughed. "Relax, Natalie. No, it's not my ideal job. But it's okay. It's a start. I really appreciate all you're doing for me."

"What do you think of John?"

Carla hesitated. "Uh. I think—"

"You think he and Maria got something going? They're both single. Well, Maria's separated."

Carla heaved a sigh of relief. She couldn't tell Natalie that John was hitting on her already. "They might be balling," Carla said. "I wouldn't put it past him."

Natalie frowned.

Carla laughed. "Oops. Sorry. I meant screwing."

Natalie shook her head and laughed. Carla was glad her sister had loosened up a bit. Natalie was lovely when she wasn't frowning in disapproval. Carla gazed warmly at her sister's quieter beauty. Natalie wore slim slacks and a knit blouse both in a berry color. She wore an African necklace of colorful stones. In some ways, her outfit was more conservative than Carla's, but just as hip. Carla was sure her fashion-plate niece had something to do with Natalie's clothing.

"Nice to see you relax, Natalie. I've got everything under control. I'm going to make this job work. Watch." Carla reached over and grabbed some of Natalie's French fries. They both ate tuna sandwiches, but Carla had ordered a salad with hers, while Natalie had ordered fries.

"I thought you don't eat fries," Natalie said.

"I do sometimes. Yours look good. Want some of my salad?"

Natalie wrinkled her nose in distaste.

"How do you stay so slim?" Carla asked in amazement. "Eat your vegetables, girl," Carla admonished.

Natalie rolled her eyes.

Carla grinned. "Fine. I'll stop lecturing if you will."

"Deal," Natalie said, but couldn't resist. "For now."

They both smiled and basked in their sisterhood and the afternoon sunshine.

After lunch, Carla focused on cranking out as much work as she could. She wasn't the fastest typist, but after working as manager of the TiTi, she had improved her typing skills and comfort level on the keyboard. She was on a mission to type as much data as she could into the spreadsheet on her screen. Keyboarding kept her from succumbing to the boredom she truly felt. It also helped her suppress thoughts of Baxter. If only he could see her now.

Carla suddenly felt breathing on her neck. She swung around and faced John Rawlins, the medical director. Her reaction caught him off guard, but he quickly regrouped. "Didn't mean to scare you," he said.

"You didn't," Carla said. She made a mental note to watch him from now on. After working at the club, her instincts were well-honed. She could always sense if some horny bastard was trying to slide up behind her for a quick feel or a grind on her ass. But she hadn't sensed John Rawlins coming up behind her. She had to be more vigilant and keep him at bay.

John drew himself up to full height and stepped in front of her desk. Carla saw his dick harden and forced her eyes away. Even though she was seated, she knew she towered above him because he was acting like such a sleaze ball. She sighed in exasperation. "I'm trying to get this work finished before I leave. Do you have some more items for me to add?"

"No, just wanted to make sure everything's going okay and that everyone's treating you right."

Everyone but you, Carla thought. *You slimy asshole.* But instead she said, "I'm getting a lot done, and everybody's been very helpful."

"Good," he said and turned to leave. Carla could see the profile of his dick jutting out further. She looked away and wondered how she was going to handle him. She couldn't believe she was having problems on the job already. This was her first day. There was no way she could cry harassment yet—not against a White male who was director of the medical center. Well, she wasn't going to let him run her away. She was determined to keep him from interfering with her work. She laughed to herself. No way did she want to hear Natalie's mouth if the job didn't pan out.

Carla felt proud of herself. She had survived a week on the job, partially because John Rawlins had been out of town for the past few days. Coincidentally, Maria was out the exact same days. Carla didn't care so long as she didn't have to deal with John. Carla welcomed whatever diversion Maria provided him.

The following Monday, both John and Maria were back. While they were gone, Carla had entered large amounts of data involving medical statistics for a report. Though she was bored out of her mind, she had forced herself to create mini goals to overcome her boredom. Surprisingly, the goals worked. Her spreadsheets had increased daily. She actually felt a major sense of accomplishment that she had survived her first week and resisted the urge to head back to the TiTi.

Carla was finishing up the day's work when the phone rang on her desk. She picked up and heard John's voice on the other end. "Could you stop by my office for a minute?" he asked. "I have some more figures for your spreadsheets, some patient statistics."

"Sure. But I'm almost done for the day. I'll have to enter that data tomorrow."

"Fine. That's when I need it."

"I'll be right there," Carla said in her most professional tone.

She knew he was up to something, asking her to come to his office so late. She sighed and wondered what avoidance tactics she could use to ward him off.

When Carla reached John's office, his door was closed. She knocked.

"Come in," he said.

Carla entered, but left the door wide open.

John seemed amused. He handed her a stack of pages to input. "I know your day is almost over, and you want to get out of here. Somebody just gave me these figures. I need you to input them first thing tomorrow morning."

Carla nodded. "As soon as I come in."

"Good." He rose from his desk. "Everything going okay? You being treated right?"

Carla nodded warily. She wondered what he was scheming. She couldn't resist stealing a glance at his dick. He seemed to have his libido under control for the moment. He walked over in her direction. Carla stiffened. But John bypassed her and walked over to his briefcase on the chair beside the door.

Carla relaxed. She looked around his office. It was standard fare for an administrator. The furniture was good quality. It included a table and chairs so that he could hold an impromptu meeting if needed. He kept his office neat and orderly. But like Carla, he must have felt that the medical offices were too sterile because he had hung an incredible collection of photographs on his walls. His collection showcased stunning photos of Berber women with blue eyes and bejeweled headdresses. He had hung a captivating photo of a Berber chief leading a camel through a stretch of sand dunes, turned orange by the setting sun.

Carla found herself mesmerized by the photos. "Wow!" she said in awe.

John nodded and stuffed some papers in his briefcase. "Yeah, they're great. I'll be leaving now," he announced. "I wanted to make sure you got those figures."

Carla was shocked. John made no harassing gestures whatsoever. He seemed all business. Carla felt somewhat guilty for thinking the worst of him when she first entered his office. After all, he must have done something worthwhile to earn the title of medical director.

"Have a good evening," Carla said and left his office. She was pleasantly surprised that things turned out much better with John than she thought they would. She might actually start liking the job, despite the boredom.

By the middle of the second week, Carla was cranking out plenty of work. She had gotten into a rhythm. While she longed for a more flexible work atmosphere, the keyboarding had become therapeutic for her. It dulled the ache for Baxter.

Carla had spent almost two weeks on the job. She was fitting in nicely and even dressing the part—hip business casual, yet conservative enough to tone down her physical attributes. She smoothed her sweater before she entered the conference room. She wore nice slacks and heels that matched her sweater. She had copied her sister's style, except her pants clung tighter and she wore more makeup. She knew Natalie was thrilled that things were working out.

The office was having its monthly birthday celebration, honoring all celebrants born in April. Carla didn't necessarily want to go, but she knew it was good PR to attend at least some office functions.

April was Carla's birthday month, but she had sworn Natalie to secrecy. Carla's birthday had come and gone with no Baxter. But Natalie and Mimi had helped her celebrate whether she wanted to or not. Natalie and her girls had taken Carla to an amusement park where they rode roller coasters and other rides all day. It was a great release for Carla. She couldn't remember the last time she had so much fun, and she loved the company of her nieces. Mimi, on the other hand, had found this swank restaurant in Beverly Hills. She and Mimi dressed up, toned down the flash, and strutted into the restaurant as though they owned the place. Mimi kept her drinks to a minimum as they ate, laughed, and partied, ignoring the men who tried to pick them up. Carla had a ball.

As she stepped into the conference room, Carla was relieved to find Natalie waiting for her beside the door. This new office life was all foreign to her, and the work hours taxed her nerves. She was used to staying up late and getting up late as well.

Natalie squeezed Carla's arm. "Glad you got away from your desk."

Carla smiled. "Told you I'd be here."

Her supervisor, Maria, was on the other side of the room engrossed in conversation with other workers. Carla and Natalie headed over to the conference room table to admire the huge tres leches cake purchased for the occasion. John walked in and decided to join them. Carla still didn't trust him, but so far, he hadn't bothered her. Maybe, she misjudged him.

"Here, we have two sharp, lovely workers and both from the same family," John said.

Natalie smiled tolerantly. Carla figured that Natalie didn't trust John either. Apparently, neither did Maria. She rushed over to them to protect her interests. Carla wanted to shout that Maria could have him. She had no desire whatsoever for John.

Everybody moved up closer and crowded around the big decorated cake. The birthday people were encouraged to come forward. Their names hung on a colorful list on the wall. Carla suspected that she wasn't the only who hadn't come forward. Still, she found herself getting caught up in the celebration as everybody sang happy birthday amid big grins from the birthday folks. Carla hugged her sister, grateful for the chance to feel like part of the work crowd.

Though it was the birthday celebrants' spotlight, people were starting to notice Natalie's stunning sister. Curiosity about Carla began to overshadow the birthday fete. Carla was glad that she hadn't revealed her birthday even though she was tempted to. This was a major birthday for her. She turned fifty. She didn't necessarily want the whole world to know.

Carla smiled and graciously answered questions as the birthday cake was being sliced and passed around. She tried to downplay that she was Natalie's sister. She didn't want anyone accusing Natalie of nepotism. Already, among the crowd, she could spot the gossipmongers exposing their talons.

"When's your birthday?" somebody asked. Many eyes turned to Carla.

"I'll never tell. That's—" Carla halted in mid-sentence. Somebody had grabbed a firm handful of her butt. It rivaled some of the feels she'd fended off at the club. She swung around. John Rawlins and another male worker stood behind her. Both men appeared to be innocently enjoying the birthday party. Carla waited for some sign from either of them, but she saw nothing.

"You okay?" somebody asked.

Carla nodded, but she was disgusted. *Scuzzy bastard,* she thought. She knew it was John Rawlins, but she couldn't prove it. He had struck when everyone was crowded around the table, and all eyes were away from him. Carla had to admit that he was an A-1 scuzzball.

Natalie was back at her side. "You alright?"

"That bastard just felt me. He gave me a good one."

"Who?" Natalie asked.

"Who do you think?"

Natalie sighed and turned around. John looked as though butter wouldn't melt in his mouth. "How do you want to handle it?" Natalie asked.

Carla shrugged. "What can I do? I can't prove it. Could have been that other guy standing next to him, but I doubt it."

"I really wanted this to work out for you. You seemed to be on a roll."

"I know you want this to work, but I'm not going to let people feel me whenever they want," Carla hissed.

"I know. I know. You're right," Natalie acknowledged.

"Relax. I still want the job, but I'll have to avoid that bastard, John."

Concern etched Natalie's features.

Carla picked up two big slices of cake. She handed one to Natalie. "Let's eat, drink, and be merry," Carla said. "I'll figure it out."

For the moment, Natalie seemed relieved. Carla glanced over at John again, but he seemed innocent.

"Eat your cake, Natalie. Believe me. I've handled worse."

"You have?"

Carla laughed. Natalie was downright prissy at times. "Come on, I worked at a strip club." Carla kept her voice low. "But it's okay. I can handle it." She took a bite of cake. "Umm. This is good."

Natalie's mood lightened. She took a bite of cake also. Carla smiled, refusing to let thoughts of John dampen her spirits.

Carla was feeling great. It was Friday. She had managed to last a month on the job. She was starting to feel like a full-fledged office worker. She hadn't seen John the past few days, and that helped too. She tried to tell herself that maybe he hadn't felt her ass so blatantly that day in the conference room. But she knew better. She had to figure out a way to hold onto her new job, but keep John Rawlins in his place. While the job was mighty boring at times, she was determined not to go back to the club.

Evening approached. Carla was keyboarding her last bit of data for the day. Maria had asked her to stay late to finish. From her cubicle, Carla peered through one of the office windows. The evening was gorgeous with burnt orange highlights sweeping across the sky. Carla had nowhere to go that night, no man to date, no Baxter, but she planned to make the best of her Friday evening. She smiled—until she saw an email notification flash on her screen. Scuzzy John had sent her an email requesting that she stop by his office and pick up more data that he wanted her to input on Monday. He indicated that he was out of the office, but she could pick up the reports on his chair. Carla breathed a sigh of relief. At least, she didn't have to face him. She always felt two seconds away from cursing him out.

Carla stood outside John's office. The door was closed, and almost everybody had gone home. She moved closer to the door and listened, but heard no sound. She opened the door and peeped in, but John wasn't there. Carla heaved another sigh of relief. Perhaps that feel at the birthday party was the end of his harassment. She found herself hypnotized again by the phenomenal photographs on his walls. This time, she noticed additional photographs of spellbinding landscapes and ocean vistas. The pictures made her dream of freedom. No more office confines or dimly lit dance clubs.

She pulled herself out of her reverie and bent over John's chair to pick up the reports. Suddenly, she felt an arm grip her waist and swollen maleness press against her butt. Carla gasped and turned around. It was John. She wondered how he managed to sneak up on her like that. She immediately tried to jerk free, but he was stronger than she thought, and his dick was getting harder. He seemed to delight in her struggle. Finally, Carla did what she dreamed of doing all along. She brought her heel down hard on his instep, then she brought her elbow up into his chin. By that time, it was easy to knock him over with a knee to the groin. John's eyes burned furiously at her, but he was in too much pain to subdue her.

"You bitch," he snarled. "You know you wanted it."

"Yeah, right. That's why your ass is lying on the floor, all fucked up." Carla stood over him ready to give him a kick in the groin if he made even the slightest move towards her.

"You're nothing but a no-good hooker, trying to pretend you fit in. Yeah, I've seen you at that club, that Titty Bar."

"It's the TiTi Bar," Carla corrected him. She raised a pointy-toed pump in the direction of his crotch. She was ecstatic that she had worn her "roach killers."

John winced.

"Don't ever touch me again. Do I make my point? Pun intended," Carla smirked. Reassured that he was still incapacitated, she ventured towards the door.

"You can forget about coming back to work on Monday and so can your sister," John sneered.

At the thought of Natalie losing her job, Carla faltered for a moment. Then she stopped in mid-stride. "Natalie's going to be working here as long as she wants. You know me and the kind of work I do. I'll have somebody from the TiTi fuck you up so bad you'll make Natalie director."

"You threatening me?" John had the nerve to appear outraged.

"No, it's a promise. My sister better have her job on Monday.

You don't have to worry about me though. I have no intention of coming back and working with a slime bucket like you." Carla grabbed up the report pages, unclipped them, and threw every page on top of him. "You keyboard that shit, asshole." She stormed out of his office without looking back. She dared him to sneak up on her. She'd castrate him with her pumps if he did.

CHAPTER 12

Carla got out of her car and marched straight into the TiTi Bar. She froze in her tracks. Gutter Joe stood in Wendell's office. *Another slime bucket,* Carla thought. Only this one was much more dangerous. What was Joe doing here? Carla couldn't believe she blew her job at Natalie's medical center only to find Gutter Joe in Wendell's office.

Her eyes widened in shock. "Why is he here?"

Joe's pale skin flushed beneath Carla's wrath, but his hazel eyes still burned with a coldness that would have chilled most people.

A few characters who visited the club on occasion made Carla shudder, but not Joe. She found him so repulsive that she lost all fear of him. She would fight him to the death if she ever had to, and she might lose, but he would know he was in a fight.

Joe's eyes smoldered because of his lack of control over Carla. He turned towards the door. "I'll let you handle things," he said to Wendell and left.

Carla stared at Wendell in disbelief. "What's he doing here? You know he set that fire. Why would you let him in?"

Wendell was busy appraising her transformation. She looked like one of those slick office women with her slim pants, silk blouse, and heels. Her makeup was toned down.

"The prodigal daughter returns," Wendell said.

"I guess." Carla shook her head sadly. The weight of what she had done to John Rawlins came crashing down on her. She knew Natalie would be so disappointed. While it was a boring job, Carla liked the idea that she was finally working in an office. She had always wondered how it would feel. Now her office job was over, and here she was back at the TiTi Bar with Wendell. She felt shaken.

Wendell looked her up and down with approval. "You went and got all businesslike on me—in just that short a time. I missed you, Rae."

"I missed you too. But not the club."

Carla surveyed Wendell's office. Although the new TiTi Bar was more high class than the old one, this didn't apply to Wendell's office. He used mismatched furniture that had little style. A big oak desk was stacked with papers already. Wendell did have a nice modern swivel chair, but it clashed with the heavy oak desk. He had hung some beautiful collages of boxers that included Muhammad Ali and Sugar Ray Leonard. Carla had talked Wendell into buying the pieces. Crafted by an artist in Leimert Park, the pictures gave Wendell's office a sense of style that otherwise would have been missing.

Though the TiTi had been her second home, Carla kind of missed Natalie's office with its more antiseptic feel. It provided a safer haven for her from the men, the drugs, and the seediness. After the fire, Carla realized that the TiTi Bar didn't feel quite the same for her. Or was it Baxter who had influenced her thinking? Whatever. She would miss going to her office job on Monday, but she had to let it go. That was all behind her now. She had other plans.

But first, she had to find out what Joe was doing at the TiTi. "You doing business with Joe now?" Carla asked.

Wendell hesitated, then looked away. "Yes."

Carla waited.

Wendell heaved a sigh. "He owns the place."

Carla's blood ran cold. "He owns the place!"

Wendell nodded. "He's part owner until I pay the loan back. After the old TiTi burned down, I couldn't get all the money I needed to buy this place so I looked around for some unconventional money and found it. I didn't realize that Joe was behind the financing until he started showing up here. I tried to stop him from coming in, but then I learned that the money I borrowed is partly his."

"Damn, Wendell, we both know he probably set that fire because you wouldn't let him do his drug deals. Now he can come in here anytime he wants."

Wendell shrugged. "I know."

Carla sank down on the chair across from Wendell. "We're both up shit's creek. I just lost my job, and you borrowed money from Gutter Joe."

Wendell raised an eyebrow. "You lost your job?"

Carla nodded. "The director of Natalie's office used to visit the club. I don't remember seeing him, but he remembered me. He's been trying to feel me up ever since I started. I had to practice some self-defense on him. I know I can't go back there on Monday."

Wendell chuckled. "That's my girl. What about your sister? She okay?"

"I told him somebody from the club would fuck him up if Natalie lost her job. I'm pretty sure he believed me."

Wendell's eyes brightened. "So what you gon' do, Rae? You coming back?"

"Here's the deal. I want to come back and do a show."

"A show?"

"Yep. A show."

Wendell looked her up and down with a grin. He reached out to touch her breast through the silk blouse.

Carla could see a bulge rising in his pants. She moved herself out of reach. "Not you, too, Wendell. I've had a rough day."

Wendell was somewhat offended. "You look good, Rae. A model of feminine pulchritude. But you ain't no spring chicken to do a show. Come back and host for us. We miss you. I need a good manager."

Carla felt the sting of Wendell's words, but she knew she had to push forward anyway. While she certainly wasn't in her twenties, she still had some youth left. And if she ever wanted to strip again, she'd better do it now, while she still had the body. She pressed forward. "I want to do a show. We can print out posters and flyers. Since Mimi is such a whiz, she can spread the word for us on social media."

"If she's not strung out," Wendell remarked.

"She'll be okay," Carla assured him. "I'll be the headliner, and Mimi can open up for me. She's always wanted to sing. I'll put a show together like you've never seen."

"Clients don't want to hear Mimi sing," Wendell said flatly, "unless they're lying on top of her."

Carla refused to be dissuaded. "I need this, Wendell. My last big hurrah. I need the money. I can't make any money in these office jobs. Even if I found another one, I still might have to hassle with some other slime bucket who knows me from the TiTi."

Wendell looked at her butt and shrugged.

Carla ignored him and laid all her cards out on the table. "After this show, I'm getting out of this business. I've got to, especially now that Joe is part owner."

"It's still my bar."

"But you've acquired some nasty baggage with it."

Wendell watched her intently. "You want me to help you do a show so you can jump ship and start a new life? You're the best manager I ever had, Rae. I'll give you your old job back, but I'm not bankrolling a show so you can leave me. That's some crazy shit. You ain't twenty no more or even thirty. Didn't you just have a big birthday?"

Carla was still determined. "You need to get out of this business, too, or at least away from the TiTi. We can put on a big show and run with the money."

"I need a lot more money than that."

"But it's a start."

"You really think you can pull it off?" Wendell asked.

Carla stood up tall and gyrated a little. She undid a couple buttons on her blouse. Wendell got the picture. He licked his lips. Carla stopped in mid-tease. She was pleased with the effect on Wendell, and she hadn't even gotten started.

"I know I can still do a show, Wendell. A big show. We can put up a gauzy screen or curtain, add an air of mystery, make me look younger."

"You gonna perform behind a curtain the whole night?"

"Oh, I'll come out, but we can arouse some curiosity before

I do," Carla said, excited. "We'll up the cover charge and the drinks." Carla could almost see the wheels spinning in Wendell's head. "We can do two shows in one night. The first one we'll call the matinee, and the second one will be the blockbuster. We'll charge higher for the second show."

"What about your fire boys?" Wendell asked sarcastically. "You want them to see you do a show?"

"If they want to," Carla said. "But they get in free."

"Free?" Wendell balked.

"You don't think they deserve a free show after saving me?" Carla lashed out.

"Sure, they do." He dropped his opposition immediately.

Secretly, Carla hoped they wouldn't attend and certainly not Baxter. If he did show up, oh well. This was strictly business, her business and not his. He had dropped her like a hot potato. She could do the same.

Wendell was checking Carla out, assessing whether or not she could pull it off.

Carla read his mind. "I'll work out even harder, get my body really firm. We can call it 'The Greatest Strip Show on Earth,' or something like that, some kind of burlesque-stripper show. We'll play up my maturity and experience—not too much though," Carla said with a laugh.

Wendell was almost convinced.

Carla kept pushing. "Our promo can say, 'Come spend an evening with the hottest stripper of all time, the infamous Rae Hepburn.'" She paused, noting that she had Wendell's full attention. "Think of the money you'll make from tips that night from all the girls, plus me and Mimi. We'll pack the house. I'll work the clients up for you, Wendell. Think about your cut from the lap dances and those tips." Then Carla delivered the final attention grabber. "We split 50/50—the door, the bar, my tips. And Mimi gets more than her usual."

Wendell's eyes grew big. "Whoa! No way. No 50/50."

"I'm bringing in the crowd. Without me, you won't be able to do that kind of show."

"You hope you can bring in the crowd."

"I know I can."

She knew Wendell admired her bravado, but he was still hesitant. "I don't know, Rae."

"I figured everything out, Wendell, while I'm sitting here talking to you. If you're not interested, I'll find somebody who is, or I'll promote the show myself."

Wendell's stance hardened. "Sure. Go do that. Who's going to hire a fifty-year-old stripper?"

"You hire older dancers. Look how long you kept me on before I started managing. I'm in good shape, and I can pass for younger. Somebody'll take me up on my proposal."

"I kept you on because I tried to protect you as much as I could. Stripping can be a hard life."

Carla spoke earnestly. "I know, and I appreciate your protection. Always have."

Wendell was still mulling things over.

"What have you got to lose? I'm presenting you with a win-win proposition." Carla paused. "You think about it. Not too long though, or I'll ask somebody else."

"I got a major problem with that 50/50 split on the door and the bar."

Carla was undeterred. "Think about it."

She turned to leave, exhausted. She had lost one job. Now here she was going after another, one that she was trying to quit. She was seriously putting her ass on the line in the hopes of capturing the audiences of her younger years. All because she needed to pay her bills while she figured out what to do with her life. What if nobody came to her show? Carla dismissed the thought. Men would always show up at the thought of uniquely presented pussy. She knew that much. She would make sure her nieces never found out about the show, and certainly not Natalie. As for Baxter, she couldn't afford to worry about him. She had to earn a living so she could find another way of life.

"You're really serious about this," Wendell said.

"Yes, I am," Carla responded.

Wendell's stance softened. He tried to pull her close. Carla could tell he liked the satiny feel of her blouse. He tried to put his hand inside.

Carla eluded him. "Stop. This is a business proposition only."

"Don't I get to sample the goods before I consider my investment?"

Carla smiled. "You've already sampled the goods. Plenty of times."

"Not recently."

"That's because you've been sampling younger goods." Carla was glad she had an excuse. No more sex with Wendell. They were beyond that stage now.

Wendell wouldn't take "no" for an answer. He reached out and caressed her breast anyway. Against her will, Carla felt a sudden stirring. Wendell felt it too. Carla realized that if she didn't move out of Wendell's reach, she might end up in bed with him. Then he would end up watching porn to keep his dick hard, or go find some of his young dancers and enact some of his fantasies. No, she didn't want to fall back into that routine with Wendell. She still wanted Baxter. Why couldn't she get him out of her system?

Carla shifted her attention back to Wendell and pulled away from him. "Strictly business, Wendell. Take it or leave it. I'll call you tomorrow."

"Aw, come on, Rae."

"You'll have to come with somebody else," Carla laughed as she made her exit.

After she left Wendell's office, Carla almost collided with Mimi. They hugged.

"Buenas tardes, chica. Heard you were here," Mimi said.

When she spoke Spanish, Mimi had a lovely Mexican accent that she inherited from her father. Carla tried to learn Spanish from Mimi, but their lives didn't allow much time for tutoring. Mimi also spoke German, though not as fluently. Mimi lived in the fast lane and didn't have much time to practice German. She mainly spoke the language with patrons or tourists who came to the TiTi on occasion.

Mimi's father was a leftist political leader in Mexico at one time. His politics pit him against the ruling party, so he was kidnapped along with Mimi's mother and never heard from again. Mimi, who was around ten at the time, fled with other relatives across the U.S. border, but she was immediately captured by a ruthless band of human traffickers. Mimi had endured many lives before she reached Los Angeles, yet she was only in her teens when she arrived.

"You're here early," Carla observed.

"Gonna do a couple shows. Then I got a hot date tonight." Mimi glowed.

Carla was happy for her. "Who?"

"I found me a handsome fireman."

"Who?" Carla demanded.

"Not your guy, chica. But somebody who works with him. They came in here one night after you quit—"

"Baxter came here." Carla's heart skipped a beat.

"He was looking for you, but I told him you quit. So they left."

"Why didn't you tell me?"

Mimi shrugged and looked away. Carla realized that Mimi had probably been absorbed in one of her binges and didn't remember much about Baxter visiting the club.

"You got to let those drugs alone," Carla warned.

Mimi bristled. "No lectures. You're so into yourself, Rae. You don't even care about me and my fireman."

Carla tried to feign interest, but all she wanted to hear about was Baxter. "Sorry. Tell me about your guy." She finally succumbed to Mimi's beaming smile and laughed. "Let me guess. It's the guy named Frank, right?"

"How'd you know?"

"A good hunch. I met him at the firehouse when Baxter gave me the tour."

Mimi looked away.

Carla sighed. "It's okay. I've gotten over that day. Well, Frank seems like a nice guy." Carla appeared to be holding something back.

"What?" Mimi asked.

"Nothing."

"What?" Mimi persisted.

"He seems like a really nice person."

Mimi bristled. "And I'm not?"

"I love you like a little sister, Mimi, but you're a wild child."

"Frank likes me, and I like him."

Carla backed off. "Great. I'm happy you met somebody. He's okay with your work?"

"You know me. This is what I do. A girl's got to support herself. He can accept it or reject it." Mimi paused. "Why are you back? I thought you had escaped."

Carla realized that Mimi was secretly rooting for her to break away from the club. Carla hated to disappoint her. "I am getting away from the club, but I've got to do one more show, a big one, my last big thriller. I need some money to tide me over until I figure out what I'm going to do. I just lost my job because some guy kept harassing me. He remembered me from the old TiTi."

"Asshole," Mimi said.

"Yeah. Anyway, I got to do this one last show, and I need you to do it with me."

Mimi perked up.

"You'll open for me," Carla said. "You can even sing a little."

Mimi's eyes widened. "You're going to do a strip show?" She surveyed Carla up and down, trying to determine if Carla could pull it off. "You look good, chica, but let's face it, you're not even forty no more. Plus, you been working as a manager."

"You sound like Wendell," Carla snapped. "I'm doing this show. Now you can open up for me and sing, or I'll get somebody else to open."

Mimi shrugged. "Fine. I'll open. You still look hot." She laughed slyly. "I'm sure they'll come."

Carla narrowed her eyes playfully in response.

"I definitely get to sing?" Mimi asked.

"More dancing than singing."

Mimi nodded. "I know. They're not coming to hear me sing, but I can sneak a song in."

"Yes, you can. But you gotta dance your ass off. No drugs, Mimi. And we need you to do your social media thing to spread the word."

"I've been pretty clean since I've been seeing Frank. But I

don't want him to hear me sing, and I don't want him to see me do my raunchiest dancing. You don't have to worry about Baxter though. Frank says he's been doing a lot of traveling lately—speaking engagements and conferences." She hesitated. "He might be dating somebody out of town."

Carla took a deep breath and steeled herself. This was not something she wanted to hear, but Baxter was a good-looking guy. He had a life before they met. In a way, she hoped he did have someone so she could stop thinking about him and get him out of her system. She hoped he'd be out of town for her performance. She didn't want to worry about him showing up at the TiTi for her final hurrah.

"It's okay, Mimi. I'm over Baxter."

"No, you're not."

Carla shook her head and laughed.

CHAPTER 13

Baxter inhaled deeply. He was glad to be back in Los Angeles. He had learned a lot from the firefighter conferences he attended and shared his own knowledge as well. But he welcomed the break from traveling. As he entered the local sports bar where he and his crew hung out, he almost collided with Percy, Frank, and Earl as they were leaving. They were all spruced up in their civilian clothes. Baxter caught a whiff of somebody's cologne. They looked away when he saw them.

Baxter blocked their path. "What's up? I've been texting, and nobody gets back to me."

All three appeared tongue-tied. Percy finally spoke up. "Hey, we missed you, man, but we're on our way out."

"Where you going?"

"We're going to have a drink someplace else."

"Thanks for the invitation."

"It's not like that, Captain. We thought you were still on the road."

"Well, I'm back. I'll join you."

Earl cleared his throat. "I don't think you want to do that."

"Why not?" Baxter knew what was up. It was all over the Internet. He stared at Frank.

Frank sighed. "Okay, if you want to join us, but I don't think . . . ."

Earl pulled out a flyer and shoved it into Baxter's hand. Baxter had seen the flyer online. It read, "The Greatest Strip Show on Earth: An Evening with the Last Stripper." Baxter's eyes squinted in anger as he focused on the headline.

"I'll go with you. That's why I came back early," he said. His demeanor dared them to refuse.

"Aw, shit," Earl said. "Man, you gonna spoil our fun. You sure you can handle Rae on stage half-naked with us watching, too?"

Baxter nodded, tight-lipped. "I can handle it."

As he headed to his car, Baxter's crew regretted that they had run into him. "I told y'all we should catch the first show instead of waiting around," Percy said.

"Nah, man. I want to see the second show. This is the big one," Earl responded.

"How about you, Frank?" Percy asked.

"Frank don't care what show he sees as long as Mimi's onstage," Earl said. "Frank loves those wild women."

Frank shook his head in denial. "Shut up, man."

Baxter led the way as they all drove to the TiTi Bar in procession. Baxter drove as though he was on a mission.

Carla took a swig of water and smiled, elated. She had just finished the first show. It sold out. The house was packed— standing room only. Mimi and Wendell had embarked on a marketing campaign that relied heavily on word of mouth and social media. Carla handled more of the traditional marketing like the flyers and posters. The goal was to create a major sensation and rake in the dollars.

Mimi had created a Facebook page and tweeted her ass off. She had garnered a sizeable following in the month it took to pull the show together. To tease and tantalize followers, Mimi exploited the hell out of other social media too, sending pictures of her and Carla, dressed provocatively in their street clothes.

Carla wanted to rest between both shows, but she was too hyped. She felt that some of her dance moves could have been smoother in the first show, but she would make sure they were flawless in the second. Because her bra didn't unhook as easily as it should have in the first show, Carla had the wardrobe assistant she hired for the night re-check every snap, zipper, and string on her costume for the second show.

As she prepared, Carla tried to lessen the butterflies in her stomach. She was having fun with her last hurrah, but she still felt guilty. Was she doing the show more for vanity's sake? Or like a junkie trying to get clean, was this her last binge? Whatever the reason, she decided to make this her best show ever and enjoy the moment. She knew the butterflies would vanish once she started performing.

Taking a deep breath, Carla peered through a curtain. The club was filling up again. She noted that the number of women, both straight and lesbian, for this show had increased. A few patrons from the first show had paid to stay for the second show. Wendell didn't care, neither did Carla, since these patrons increased publicity.

Carla stole another glance at the audience. Her throat constricted, and her heartbeat pounded wildly. The floor seemed unsteady beneath her feet. Baxter and his crew sat ringside. Frank was there too. Mimi had tried to downplay the show to Frank, but Carla figured that merely enticed him. Besides, everything was all over social media. Frank didn't want to be left out.

As for seeing Baxter in the crowd, Carla wanted to bolt from the club. How could she go out there and perform in front of him? The plans for her last big fling did not include him. His face looked grim. *Dammit!* Mimi said he was still out of town. Carla swallowed. She knew it was too good to be true that he would be on the road during her performance. That would have been too perfect. Now what was she supposed to do?

Mimi pulled Carla away from the curtain. "They're out there. Did you see them?" Mimi asked, distressed.

Carla sighed deeply. "Yeah, I saw them." She studied Mimi's face. Mimi was high, not plastered yet, but high. Carla wanted to dig a hole somewhere and crawl inside. She took several deep breaths and steadied herself. She decided that she would perform her ass off in front of Baxter. She'd perform for him and her nieces so she wouldn't have to strip anymore. She would make this her best performance ever so that she could haul in the cash and find something else to do with her life and never look back.

The manager side of Carla kicked in. "Are you high?"

Mimi started to deny it, then stopped. "A little," she admitted.

"Can you do the show?"

"I'll sing and dance like you've never seen, chica. I just got a little buzz on. It'll help me perform better. Here." She held out a drink to Carla. "Have some of this. It'll make you feel better too."

Carla made it a point to avoid drinking or drugging on the job. In her younger days, she would get high and strip, but as she got older, she wanted a clear head when she worked. She knew many of the customers were jerks who would try to brazenly fondle a dancer or even force her into a dark corner. Carla never wanted to go onstage high every night. She didn't want to get hooked on anything or rely on any drug as a crutch. She was incredibly blessed. She did not have to get high to perform—except tonight in front of Baxter. She found herself accepting Mimi's offer.

Carla sniffed Mimi's drink.

Mimi grinned. "It's rum and coke, chica. No additives."

But Carla knew that Mimi had imbibed more than rum and coke.

Mimi read her mind. "Don't worry about what I'm feeling. That's rum and coke. I can put a tiny bit of an upper in there if you want it."

Carla was tempted, but she shook her head. "No, only the drink."

"You sure you don't want me to add anything?"

Carla was a bundle of nerves. "Okay, fine. But whatever you add, I need to be able to function."

"Oh, you'll do fine, chica. I wouldn't give you anything to hurt you. Just give you a slight buzz."

Mimi broke a pill in half and slipped a piece into Carla's drink.

Carla took a big gulp. "Why did you say Baxter was out of town?"

Mimi shrugged. "He was."

Though Carla knew it was too soon for the drink to take effect, she felt more relaxed already. She couldn't worry about Baxter any longer. The business side of her was taking over. She needed to reassure herself that Mimi could perform. "You sure you're not going to crash and burn out there?"

Mimi took a deep breath. "I'm in control." But she seemed a bit anxious.

"I know you're not afraid of Frank. He's seen you dance before. I'm sure he's seen more than that," Carla laughed.

"He's seen all up my ass, but he's never seen me sing," Mimi finally blurted out.

"You don't want him to hear you sing?"

"No."

"You let him watch you strip butt naked, but you're nervous about him hearing you sing."

Mimi nodded.

"Well, you sounded fine," Carla reassured her.

"I did okay, but I saved up my best for this show. What if I can't sing in front of Frank?"

Carla started laughing. "Keep throwing your ass in his face. He likes that. He won't care about your singing."

Mimi still wasn't convinced.

"You'll be fine, Mimi. Don't worry about it," Carla insisted.

Mimi brightened.

"Now get ready. The show must go on," Carla urged.

She scanned the audience again. She froze. Gutter Joe sat ringside as well. He always spelled bad news. Carla dismissed thoughts of Joe, knowing that after tonight, she'd never have to see him again. It was a wonderful thought.

Wendell came backstage. "You ready, Mimi?"

She swallowed and nodded.

"You're up after her, Rae," Wendell said.

Carla was forced to smile. How could she forget?

Wendell seemed on edge too. The three of them wanted a night to remember, but they also couldn't wait for it to end.

"The fire boys are out there," Wendell said. "I don't want y'all gettin' all infatuated and fucking up my show."

Carla's jitters were evaporating. "No problem."

Wendell left. Carla peeped out and watched him go over to the DJ booth. The first strains of an instrumental version of Donna Summer's "Love to Love You Baby" started playing.

Mimi sauntered out. The lights were dim onstage. She moved forward, gradually coming into view. Then her voice rang out to the song. *Wow!* Carla thought. Mimi did save her best for last. For the first show, Mimi sang a different song. But this second song worked better. Mimi's voice was haunting and lilting. Her vocal clarity was amazing. The audience sat up straighter. Frank watched her intently.

She was dressed in a scandalous, slinky white gown that contrasted beautifully against her golden skin. The gown boasted a halter top that showed much of her breasts. Whereas Carla had toned and trimmed down for the show, Mimi had plumped up to round out her curves. Mimi's dress was slit up the sides, all the way to her waist. The thread of her silver G-string gleamed through the slits. The dress fell softly over Mimi's hips. Since the midriff and back were cut out, skinny straps crisscrossed her midriff to hold the dress together. She wore silver stilettos.

As Mimi continued singing her version of the song, she started bumping and grinding so that the slits on her dress flapped open, showing her legs and butt. She rubbed her body up and down sensuously. Mirrors throughout the club captured her motions and provided double viewing pleasure for the patrons. Gradually, she stopped singing and gave the audience more of what they wanted. She licked her lips teasingly, then turned around with her back to the audience and bent over. She shook her butt. Then she slid up and down the pole at the front of the stage. She started singing again in a sultrier, more lilting voice. She gyrated around the pole with her sexy white dress on. Carla could hear the men howling and egging Mimi on.

With a flourish, Mimi pulled one of the neck strings on her dress, and the halter top fell down, displaying silver pasties on her nipples. That was the end of her singing. She immersed herself into the pole dancing instead. She danced in front of the pole with the halter top falling down and grazing her hips.

Then she pulled loose another string around her midriff, and the entire dress fell at her feet. Mimi stepped out of the dress and made grinding motions up and down the pole with her legs wide open. She was now the ultimate exotic dancer. She performed all kinds of bumps and grinds. She even performed sexy acrobatics, twirling around the pole, legs spread wide. She cupped her breasts and shook her fanny at the audience. She danced with such abandon that the patrons threw all kinds of tips on the stage.

Mimi hadn't completely forgotten about Frank, however, because when she bent over to solicit tips, she went to the side of the stage opposite from where Baxter and Frank sat. Drooling in awe, Frank couldn't take his eyes off her. Mimi's G-string quickly filled up with bills, and money was still being thrown onstage. Carla peeped out at the audience. Gutter Joe got up and put money in Mimi's G-string. He tried to give her a greedy feel, but Mimi was a pro, even against a slimeball like Joe. She got the tip and quickly eluded Joe's feel.

Frank watched him coldly. Percy and Earl whistled, hollered, and threw money on the stage. They enjoyed the show and seemed oblivious to anybody's discomfort. Frank was more subdued, and Baxter seemed torn between watching Mimi and holding back. Carla sighed. Her turn was coming up soon.

When Mimi's set was over, she grabbed her dress and strutted offstage. More whistles followed her. Behind the stage, Carla gave her a high-five.

"Wow! You were awesome, Mimi. Your singing, your dancing. You blew it away out there. I bet you got every dick in the place hard, except for Baxter's," Carla said, teasing.

"His too," Mimi laughed. "I saw him trying to play cool and collected."

The drink was taking effect on Carla. She felt she could face anything. Next was her turn on stage.

Mimi took in Carla's appearance. "You look hot, chica."

"Thanks."

Mimi headed for the dressing room. "Strip your ass off. I'll be out there watching with Frank."

Carla took one last sip of Mimi's potion and put it down. Wendell was back. "You ready?"

Carla stepped out onto the stage. Since she was the headliner, Wendell had gone to great lengths for her performance. A sheer curtain fell from the ceiling onto the stage to tantalize, yet provide mystery. The gauzy curtain separated her from the audience. Carla strode out fully covered in a black satin trench coat with a hood. The coat was belted and flowed gently over her body. The hood softly covered her head and hid her features. The coat itself showed a hint of cleavage and reached mid-thigh.

Meeting the trench coat were thigh-high leggings of black leather. They zipped on the inseam and sat firmly atop satin gladiator heels, forming a boot. Long fingerless gloves of black lace caressed her arms and revealed freshly manicured red nails. Pedicured red toenails peeped out from the toes of her gladiators. Carla wore plenty of makeup and red lipstick. She looked stunning, even behind the curtain in silhouette. She felt Baxter's eyes upon her and didn't flinch. She'd deal with him later.

The audience was somewhat hushed, until someone hollered, "Take off the coat!" Carla beamed a sultry smile and moved effortlessly to the music. The DJ played a jazzy tribute to traditional burlesque, a funky remix Carla found of the 1962 classic, "The Stripper." It was a fun piece of music that set the audience whistling. Carla turned around with her back to the crowd and stood wide-legged in the coat. She swayed her butt from side to side in her high-heeled faux boots. Patrons watched the stage and the mirrors.

Even though she hadn't removed a stitch of clothing, more and more men were howling in anticipation. Carla was glad. It made her job easier. She was going to enjoy her last stand. She caressed herself in the coat with her back to the audience. Then she turned and faced the audience, still caressing herself. She stood wide-legged and circled her hips. She bent down low and rose effortlessly in a smooth motion. She raised her hands in the air and started grinding under the coat.

"Come on, baby. Take it off!" the men hollered.

Carla dropped the hood and revealed a long black wig that she had styled into a ponytail at the nape of her neck. For the show, she decided on smooth, straight hair. As the hood fell to her shoulders, she heard more whistles.

Unable to fight his urges any longer, Baxter decided to enjoy himself. The waitress had returned with their drink order. Drinks were on the house for him and his crew. Mimi sat with them.

Baxter felt his pants straining as he watched Carla. The scantily clad waitress wasn't helping matters, nor was Mimi. She had changed into a brazen white mini dress with see-through netting and strategically placed bits of fabric that barely covered anything.

Baxter shifted his focus back to Carla onstage. She smiled teasingly and opened the top button of her coat. The mounds of her breasts became more visible. Money was being thrown on the stage now in front of the diaphanous curtain. Wendell's security circulated among the audience to ensure the money stayed there. Carla unbuttoned the coat to the waist, but still didn't open it all the way. A trace of pink showed under the coat. Finally, she opened the bottom button. More cleavage and more pink showed under the coat, but it was still belted. Leisurely, Carla untied the belt, and the coat sprang open to reveal a curve-hugging mini dress that resembled a scuba diving outfit. The strip of pink satin in the front anchored a zipper. The rest of the tight dress was wet-look black satin.

Carla turned away from the audience again and caressed her breasts and gyrated her hips. The men howled in response. "Come out of the curtain!" they shouted. She turned back to face them and continued caressing and gyrating. Then she dropped the coat to the floor and kicked it aside. A stage assistant discreetly removed the coat. Carla now strutted about the stage in fingerless lace gloves, the tight satin mini, and thigh-high boots. Lace top stockings now showed between the hem of her dress and the top of her boots. She heard renewed howling as she raised her arms invitingly and stripped off one black lace glove, then the other. Her strong, taut arms were bare now.

To the sultry beat of a new song, Carla began unzipping the dress. The gauzy curtain parted down the middle as she unzipped the dress down the middle. In full view now, she sashayed forward, still grinding and caressing. She turned around to wiggle her hips for the patrons. She faced them again and slid the zipper of the dress all the way down. The dress parted. Every eye was upon her. Some of the men held their breaths. Beneath the scuba dress, Carla wore a sheer skinny-strapped mini that clung to every curve. Her pasties and bikini panties were displayed under the mini. The straps of a garter belt hung below the dress and fastened to the lace top of her fishnet stockings.

Baxter's dick was hard as a rock now. He kept his eyes locked on Carla. He couldn't believe how good she looked and how lithely she moved. She danced like a much younger woman, and she must have been working out a lot. She was in great shape, better than he remembered. Her body was tight and curvy. She looked so hot, and she had such an alluring stage presence.

Carla opened the scuba dress wider to show more of the sheer mini underneath. She heard all kinds of whooping and hollering from the crowd. As more money poured onto the stage, Carla peeled off the scuba dress and let it fall to the floor. She stood in all her glory in the breathtaking sheer mini dress that showed every contour of her butt and breasts.

The DJ upped the tempo of the music. Carla raised her hands in the air and kept grinding and circling. Her hands lightly grazed her breasts as she continued the gyrations. Then she squatted, legs opening wide as she circled her hips. With one hand over each seam, she unzipped the inseams of the leather leggings in one smooth, coordinated motion. The leather dropped to the floor as she rose to full height and continued dancing to the music. The men cheered loudly. More money flew on the stage.

Carla now stood in a sheer mini, gladiator sandals, fishnets, garter belt, and underwear. She played with the straps of the garter belt and finally unclasped them. They hung loose and sexy. She turned her butt to the audience, allowing the men to feast their eyes on her butt and her legs through the fishnets. The footless stockings meshed right into her gladiator sandals. The stockings had a lace top and glittery back seam. She caressed her legs through the fishnets, all the while bending over with her butt to the audience. She ran her hands up and down the back of her legs and thighs, teasing and tantalizing. She gyrated and opened her legs wider. The audience was amazed at her agility.

Then to the beat of the music, she caressingly ran her fingers down the glittery back seam of each stocking from the lace top to the ankle. The fishnets parted on both legs and fell to the floor. The men whooped and hollered. The noise was almost deafening. Barelegged, she rocked and shimmied, with the garter straps still hanging. Carla turned back to face the crowd and wiggled suggestively. She unsnapped the garter belt and let it fall to the floor.

Mimi screamed. "Do it, chica!"

Carla now faced the audience in her strappy satin gladiators and the sheer mini dress. Her bikini panties and iridescent pasties still showed beneath the dress. The DJ elevated the tempo again. Vanity's "Nasty Girl" poured from the speakers. Carla unclasped the ponytail and allowed her hair to cascade around her shoulders. She started fast dancing. She bumped and twerked like the video mavens. She performed backbends that exposed her crotch seductively.

Baxter was spellbound. Not only did she make his dick hard, but she could dance too. He was stunned.

Carla twerked again and presented a side and back view. Her pasties gleamed underneath her dress. She faced the crowd and massaged her hips and thighs. She wiggled out of the bikini panties. They dropped to the floor around her ankles. She stepped out of one panty leg and allowed the other to dangle. She finally kicked the panties off, and the crowd went wild. Now only an iridescent V-string and pasties appeared under her sheer dress. All kinds of money rained onto the stage. The tempo of the music slowed.

Carla licked her lips and caressed every part of her body. She circled her hips round and round. She made sure her profile showed every curve of her breast and ass through the tight dress. Except for the glittery pasties and V-string, she now stood bare-bodied under the scandalous dress in her gladiator heels.

Baxter was awestruck. His erection had a mind of its own while watching her. He had never seen a show like hers. It was a shamelessly brazen performance. She had captivated and spellbound her audience. Baxter swallowed and held his breath for the grand finale.

Carla kept dancing and caressing herself through the dress. She turned her shapely back to the audience and pulled the skinny straps of the dress down over her shoulders. She shook and shimmied so that the men hollered for her to turn around and take it all off. Carla wasn't ready to comply yet. She caressed her breasts and wiggled her ass at the crowd.

She finally faced front again with the dress around her waist. Then she performed the final coup de grâce and teasingly lowered the dress over her hips and thighs, then over her legs. She stepped out of the dress and now wore only her heels, pasties, and the V-string. The few dimples flecking her thighs only added to her allure. She continued dancing and touching herself. Then the trumpet riffs began of a remix of "This Girl" by Kungs and Cookin' on 3 Burners. To the funkiest parts of the song, Carla twerked, lunged, and gyrated around the pole. She made every man in the place feel that she was dancing only for him. Both men and women rooted and cheered for Carla. The money still poured onto the stage. Her body glistened with scented oil and sweat, enhancing her seductive appeal.

Carla escalated her bumps and grinds as she snaked around the pole. She did a few acrobatics around the pole and flung her legs wide, but for the most part, her dancing was more sensual than gymnastic. She dropped to the floor and did a few acrobatics without the pole. She lifted her legs high overhead and plowed backwards, showcasing her butt for the audience. Then she rose smoothly to her feet and performed a final round of lunges and gyrations. Under the stage lights, the iridescent V-string and pasties sparkled against her skin.

She moved closer to the ringside tables, enough to tease and further entice. Though she avoided lingering in front of Baxter's table, she still sensed the heat of the firemen's eyes all over her body. Carla now accepted tips. She allowed only those patrons with crisp one-hundred-dollar bills to slip the currency into her V-string. If a patron, male or female, raised a bill with the face of Benjamin Franklin on it, she shimmied over to them and made herself available. Gutter Joe raised two hundreds. Carla bypassed him. When her V-string was full, she stepped back and performed one closing round of grinds and twerks to salivate the audience.

Finally, she bent over and grabbed her remaining clothes off the floor. She strolled off the stage almost naked in her heels, pasties, and V-string. She shook her butt one last time and exited the stage in all her bold magnificence. The crowd roared, and the final downpour of money rained onto the stage.

CHAPTER 14

After the show, Mimi ran into the dressing room to greet Carla. "Damn, chica. I didn't know you could still move like that. Where did you get those clothes, that coat? You were awesome."

Carla gave Mimi a fist bump. She didn't want to get Mimi sweaty. "Thanks. Would you believe most of that stuff came from my closet? Otherwise, I'd have to spend all the money I make tonight paying off my clothes."

"I hear you," Mimi said. She paused. "You ready to face the real music?"

Carla nodded, butterflies returning to her stomach. Mimi's drink was starting to wear off. "You think he liked the show?" Carla asked.

"I don't care what Baxter tells you. He loved the show. He couldn't take his eyes off you."

"Really?"

"Who could?"

Mimi had a fresh drink in her hand. She held it out.

Carla managed to resist temptation this time. "I need a clear head when I see him. Don't you need a clear head, too?"

Mimi took a big sip of her concoction. "I've got one." She finally put the drink down in reaction to Carla's disapproval. "Freshen up, killjoy, so we can go hang out with our men," Mimi said.

Wendell flew into the dressing room, hyped. "Damn, baby," he said to Carla. "You rocked the house tonight—with a little help from Mimi here." He made sure he gave Mimi some credit.

Mimi smiled appreciatively.

Carla figured Wendell had pulled in some big money tonight and was giving Mimi her kudos just in case he wanted to do another show. While Carla's spirits soared after her performance, she didn't want to do any more shows. She had to get high to perform this one, and now she had to face Baxter. She couldn't wait to see him, yet she didn't know why after the way he treated her.

"Go see your fire boy," Wendell snorted, realizing that Carla's mind was on Baxter.

For the moment, Carla didn't care what Wendell called him. She simply wanted to sort things out with Baxter.

Carla strolled through a sea of wolf whistles and suggestive comments meant to lure her over to some of the tables. She wore a red mini dress, shredded on the sides into slits that revealed a red push-up bra and bikini panties. The dress showed plenty of skin and all her curves. She wore silver gladiator sandals with the dress. Carla felt obligated to greet customers she hadn't seen in a while. It was part of her deal with Wendell. She and Mimi had agreed to circulate among the customers and do more teasing and tantalizing. Wendell wanted to sell plenty of drinks and lap dances.

Any other time, circulating among the patrons wouldn't have presented a problem for Carla, but she wanted to head over to Baxter's table right away. So she put her best face forward and circulated among the customers as she advanced in Baxter's direction. She stuck her elbows out numerous times to elude slime buckets who wanted to touch her. But some of the men really appreciated the show. They made Carla feel like a celebrity.

As she walked through the crowd, Wendell's security kept an eye on her. Carla liked the attention, but she was still determined that tonight was her last stand. On her way over to Baxter's booth, plenty of men tried to lure her over to theirs. Carla smiled and exchanged good-natured banter with them, but she was on a mission. Finally, she stood in front of Baxter's table. He and his men were still awestruck by her show. Their table now became the hub of excitement. Wendell came over and spoke to Baxter even before Carla could.

"Y'all treat my girls right," Wendell said, but everybody at the table knew his words were meant for Baxter and Frank. "Don't forget they gotta mingle with the clients, part of their contract. Don't monopolize my girls."

Baxter and Frank ignored him. They only had eyes for Carla and Mimi. Baxter couldn't take his eyes off Carla. In the hot red dress, she was as much of a showstopper offstage as onstage. He was torn. He wanted to reach inside the dress and explore every curve of her body, but he also desired just a simple conversation with her. He turned to Mimi whose dress displayed as much as Carla's did. Right then, Baxter decided that he and Frank were screwed from the moment they met these two women.

Wendell gave up and walked away. Carla knew Wendell didn't want his star attractions hanging at one table for the night. That wasn't the deal. But she had to talk to Baxter first, then she could decide how to handle the rest of the night.

Carla dispensed her hellos and sat on the end beside Baxter. Mimi sat on the other end beside Frank. Though Baxter hated to admit it, he was flattered that Carla sat beside him. She seemed like a celebrity. The whole table was riding high with the two showstoppers gracing their booth. Baxter knew he and his crew were the most envied patrons of the night. He tried to ignore some of the lewd comments he overheard.

Earl could no longer contain himself. "Gonna be some fireworks tonight. That was a hot show," he said to Carla. "You still got it."

Percy nodded in amusement as he watched Carla and Baxter.

"Thanks," Carla said weakly.

Baxter's face was unreadable. Percy and Earl shifted everybody around and got up from the booth. They headed towards one of the dancers at another table.

Earl couldn't resist turning back. He grinned. "You okay, Captain? You need any help?"

Everybody started laughing, including Percy. "We'll be right around the bend if you need us," Percy ribbed.

"You know Percy will help you out," Earl teased.

Baxter smirked. "I got this, guys. I know what I'm doing."

"You sure?" Earl feasted his eyes on Carla and Mimi. "Damn, you ladies look good tonight."

"You better take your ass over to that other table," Baxter laughed.

"Before we carry you," Frank added.

Percy and Earl left, but not before Percy turned around and stole another glance at Carla in her tight red dress. Carla ignored him and turned to Baxter. Mimi and Frank had eyes only for each other.

Carla and Baxter spoke at the same time. "I didn't expect to see you—" Carla started.

"I've been on the road, but I did try—" Baxter's words tumbled out.

They both regrouped. "That was an amazing show," Baxter said. He didn't know how else to start since he had so many things to say. "You tired?"

Carla shook her head. "No. I still feel excited, exhilarated."

Baxter was part of her exhilaration. She was finally sitting beside him. He looked so good. He wore a knit sweater and low-slung slacks. The sweater fell softly on his broad shoulders. Carla was torn between hugging and kissing him affectionately and giving him the lap dance of a lifetime.

Baxter's eyes lingered on her dress. "That's an incredible dress," he said.

Carla tensed up. "It's part of my job,"

"I heard you gave up your job."

"I did, but I needed some money," she admitted.

"You want to do this for the rest of your life?"

"You mean managing the club or stripping?"

"Both."

"Before you judge anybody, you need to take a look in the mirror. That was some pretty lame shit you pulled at the fire house."

Baxter looked away guiltily. "I had a lot of work to do that day. I didn't want to be distracted."

"You had so much work that you couldn't even come out and say hi?"

"It wasn't like that." He shrugged. "I don't know. I've been dazed and confused since I met you."

Carla was ecstatic with his admission, but she wasn't going to let him off that easy. "Do you know how much you embarrassed me? In front of everybody at the station?"

"I wasn't ready to see you," he said.

"So you got what you wanted from me, and you were done, right?" Carla's voice was rising. Mimi and Frank looked over, but Carla didn't care. "You still refuse to admit that you did anything wrong. Yet you have the nerve to pass judgment on me. I will never let you embarrass me like that again." Carla got up from the table. She almost toppled some of the drinks.

Baxter reached out and grabbed her arm. "I won't ever do that again," he said.

Gutter Joe suddenly appeared. "Is he bothering you, Rae?

Carla whirled on Gutter Joe. She didn't need that slime bucket to rescue her from anybody. "Mind your business, Joe."

"Wanted to make sure nobody was mistreatin' you." He reached out and caressed her arm. "Not after you made my dick so hard and all the guys in here."

The weight of the whole night came crashing down on Baxter. His nerves were stretched taut by all of his pent-up sexual tension and all of his confusion about seeing Carla dance almost naked in front of everybody. In a flash, he jumped to his feet and with a swift one-two punch knocked Gutter Joe to the floor. Joe's lip bled. His eyes blazed furiously, but Baxter stood over him menacingly, daring Joe to get up.

Carla was stunned by Baxter's ferocity. But she knew Gutter Joe was a vicious snake you couldn't turn your back on. "Come on, Baxter. Let's get out of here," she said, trying to calm him.

Baxter maintained his stance. He stood over Joe and glared at him. "You ever say anything to her again, and I'll knock your fucking teeth down your throat."

By now, Frank was on his feet. He slid Mimi out of the way. She looked worried. Carla understood Mimi's concern. Everybody knew Gutter Joe was bad business. His pale face was flushed with anger, and his hazel eyes were cold and murderous. But Frank obviously had Baxter's back. A few of Joe's men tried to close in on Baxter and Frank, but Percy and Earl returned. They swung immediately to the defense of their crewmates. Percy and Frank suspended their hands over their waistbands. Carla figured they carried guns. Surprisingly, young, hip-hop Earl didn't appear to be armed, but he stood squarely beside Baxter.

Carla was impressed by the loyalty of Baxter's men, but she definitely didn't want to witness a gun battle. Fortunately, Joe's men didn't want to take on Baxter's crew. Percy, Frank, and Earl faced them, unyielding. Carla could only imagine how they backed up one another in a fire. Baxter finally allowed Joe to rise to his feet. Joe's eyes smoldered with fury, but Baxter's fury outmatched his. Joe looked away.

Wendell and his bouncers moved in. "We don't allow no altercations in here," Wendell said.

Baxter was in no mood to comply. "We can take it outside if we have to."

Carla reached for his arm again. "Baxter, please."

His stance remained unbending. He knew the type of snake Joe was. But amazingly, Joe gathered his men and left. He strode out as arrogantly as he strode in.

Baxter watched him coldly as he left. The club returned to normal. Wendell and his bouncers started to circulate again.

Still struggling to control his temper, Baxter turned to Carla. "You satisfied now? That's why I have a problem with you working here. See, I'm not Frank. He can ignore all this shit." He paused. "I bet that motherfucker, Joe, burned down the old bar. What's he doing here?"

Carla didn't say anything.

Baxter's jaws clenched. "Come on, let's go."

Carla hesitated. "Mimi and I are under contract. I can't leave yet. I've got to walk around and mingle. I told you I'm trying to give this up, but I needed one last show to give me some money to figure things out."

"You should have come to me," Baxter said.

"I want my own money. And why would I come to you after the way you treated me?"

Carla felt elated at his offer, but the fact remained that he had dissed her horribly. Besides, she wanted to sashay around in her red dress and mingle at the TiTi Bar, hopefully, for the last time. Was she acting like a junkie, splurging before detox?

Baxter shook his head in annoyance. "You really like this shit."

"This is my job for the night, Baxter."

"No matter how unsafe it is?"

"I'll be okay. Wendell's got security here."

"You want to stay. Fine. Frank can watch out for you. Earl can stay too."

"What about you? I'll walk you to your car."

Baxter's eyes softened in amusement. He stroked her arm lightly. "You going to protect me?"

She nodded with a straight face.

Baxter smiled wryly. "Don't worry about me. I'll kill that bastard if I have to."

That's what Carla feared. She was so sorry Baxter had gotten pulled into this, but she had to finish her contract. And she was still angry with him because he wouldn't apologize for embarrassing her at the fire station.

"You sure you're not ready to leave?" Baxter asked.

"Positive," Carla said. She tried to ignore the current that flowed hot and heavy between them. She could feel his eyes burning through the red dress. He couldn't hide it. She was glad, at least, for this connection between them. She turned to Mimi and Frank. Baxter's eyes continued to rake over every curve under her dress. Carla turned back and caught him in the act. He smiled guiltily, then started talking with Frank.

Mimi tried to stifle a devilish grin. She whispered to Carla. "Did we luck up or what? Our fire boys, they some bad motherfuckers. Did you see the way Baxter flattened Joe out?"

She gave Carla a high-five. Carla tried to stifle her own devilish grin.

Baxter fumed when he saw the high-five. He spoke to Carla. "If you want to stay, Frank's going to watch out for you and Mimi. So is Earl. But I'm out of here." He turned and left with Percy.

When they were out of earshot, Earl glanced at Carla. "You notice he didn't leave you with Percy." Everybody laughed.

Frank spoke up. "Nah, Percy wanted to leave. He'll make sure the captain gets home safely." Frank paused. "Then he'll come back and hit on Carla."

They all laughed again.

CHAPTER 15

Carla walked purposefully over to the front desk. This was her second visit to EveryDay Fitness Center. The first time, she had walked in off the street to apply for a job, any job that would help her break away from the TiTi Bar. A smart-assed young woman behind the counter had told her to apply for a job online since there were no jobs at this particular center.

Carla knew her method of walking in off the street had become outdated, but she figured since the center was new, they probably needed staff. The center was located in the Crenshaw/Leimert Park area, not too far from where she lived in West Hollywood. Carla figured a new fitness center, a new start. This was perfect for her. She just had to get past the smart-assed young woman at the counter.

Armed with the name of the manager, Carla decided to apply in person again to see if her luck would change. Young smart ass was at the counter. Carla took a deep breath and approached her anyway.

"Is Jasmine Sykes, the manager, available?" Carla asked.

"Weren't you already here looking for a job? I thought I told you to apply online."

"I did. But I haven't heard anything."

"It's only been a week."

Carla was becoming impatient with young smart ass. "Listen, I'd like to work here. This could work well for you and me." Carla's words fell on deaf ears. "Is Jasmine available?" Carla pressed.

Before the young woman could dissuade Carla further, another young woman in her early thirties came out from one of the side offices. She was very pretty and possessed a fit, curvy body that was a walking advertisement for EveryDay Fitness.

She extended her hand to Carla. "Hi, I'm Jasmine. You looking for me?"

Carla liked this young woman. She was no-nonsense and secure with herself. She didn't appear to have anything to prove. Still, Carla felt a bit nervous now that she had come face-to-face with the manager.

Carla gave Jasmine a hearty handshake. "I'm Rae, I mean Carla Hepburn. I'm looking for a job."

"Did you apply online?" Jasmine asked absently. Staff members were coming up to her and asking questions. Jasmine began delegating duties to other staff members. Then she became engrossed in a text on her smart phone. Carla's spirits sank. Jasmine was more cordial than the smart ass at the counter, but she was much more preoccupied.

"I did apply online, but I haven't heard anything," Carla said.

Jasmine smiled tolerantly. "Give it a few weeks. I'm sure we'll get back to you."

"I know I'd be a good fit here. I can bring in more clients."

Jasmine perked up. "What's your background? Where else have you worked?" She gave Carla her full attention now.

Carla hesitated.

Jasmine lowered her voice. "You a stripper?"

"Why do you say that?"

Jasmine shrugged. "The makeup. You've got an incredible body."

Carla started to deny her stripping experience, then decided to use it to her advantage. "Like I said, I could bring in more clients. I could work with your mature clients. I've worked as both a manager and a hostess."

But Carla didn't get a chance to explain further. Jasmine was interrupted by her staff and her phone. "Wait a few weeks," Jasmine said in encouragement. "If you applied online, I'm sure you'll hear from us. Nice meeting you." She was pleasant enough, but firm in ending the conversation.

Carla decided not to press any further. "Thanks, Jasmine. I'll stay in touch."

The smart-assed young woman at the counter seemed to gloat. Carla turned and left the fitness center a bit discouraged. While she certainly hadn't done an extensive job search yet, she wondered what she was up against. This was all new to her. She was aware that she had much to offer, but she wasn't sure how to present it. She knew how to manage. She knew how to socialize. How could she get that across? No wonder she had worked in dance clubs for so long.

Carla sat at a little sidewalk cafe and checked her watch. Right on time, Wendell strode over to the table. He bent over and kissed her cheek.

"I know why you picked this place," Wendell said. "So I don't get no feels."

Carla laughed. "I figured we'd try something different. I'm trying new things."

Wendell shrugged and looked around. "Nice day, nice place. Nice company." His eyes devoured Carla in her denim dress and strappy sandals. The dress was cut low, but not too revealing, and it hung well in all the right places.

The waitress came over to check on them. Wendell politely dismissed her so he could review the menu.

Carla smiled. "You look like you lost a little weight."

Wendell beamed at the compliment. "I'm trying. I need a little more energy."

Carla laughed. "To keep up with them young girls."

Wendell couldn't deny it.

"So what's this business deal you're proposing?" Carla asked.

"I need you to come back to the TiTi and do one more show."

"You been leading me on, Wendell. I thought you really came up with something."

"That's all I came up with, Rae. The TiTi made a lot of money that night. I put a little money away for a rainy day, but I need more."

"Nope. No more shows. That was the last one."

"Let's strike while the iron is hot, while you still got the goods. You and Mimi, you're fresh off that show. We can do two more shows. And that's it."

"I thought you said, one."

"One, two, what's the difference?"

"I made some decent money off that show," Carla acknowledged. "But I want to quit while I'm ahead. Besides, I don't like the fact that Gutter Joe automatically gets a piece of my pie."

"I don't either. That's why I want to do these shows so I can get him out."

"You can't make enough money off those shows to buy Gutter Joe out."

"I know, but I can go to Vegas with that money, win big, then buy him out."

"I don't believe you, Wendell. You tell me you got some new proposition, and it's the same ole, same ole."

"Two more shows. We'll pick up those guys who missed the first shows. We can go all out and bring in the crowd. We can escalate the price of the tickets. Maybe, you could do a special lap dance onstage. Come on, Rae," Wendell coaxed. "How's your job search coming along? How long you think your money is gonna last?"

Carla was forced to remember her job search at the fitness center. While she thought the center would be a perfect new start, who was she kidding? She was a mature stripper who didn't know much else. She realized Wendell had struck a nerve. He realized it too. He observed her reaction.

But Carla refused to relent. "I know it's not going to be easy to find a job, but I'm determined. So give it a rest."

"Good as you look, I can't give it a rest." Wendell spooned some ice from his water glass and slid it down Carla's cleavage.

Carla gasped from the cold. She reached inside her dress, grabbed the ice, and flung it on the ground. "You do that one more time, and I'm out of here."

"Okay, okay," Wendell offered with a sly grin. "Couldn't resist all that décolletage."

Carla was irritated with herself for being aroused by his

action. She felt a stirring between her legs. She felt her nipples harden from both the cold and her arousal. Wendell seemed to gloat. He could tell the effect the ice had on her.

"Listen, Rae. One night, two more shows—while you still got the goods," Wendell urged. "This could be your fantasy showcase, where you can really get off onstage. Go all out creatively. I'll even let Mimi sing longer. And if you two would give special lap dances, we could make all kinds of money."

Carla refused to address his proposal. "No more ice, Wendell."

"Aw, you know you liked it."

Carla tried to ignore the growing moisture between her legs. She and Wendell could easily go to his place or hers, or better yet, find a nearby hotel. That would be different. She was tired of holding out for Baxter. For what? They simply didn't get along, and she was never going to get an apology out of him. She might as well screw around with Wendell. She and Wendell would always be friends. A sexy afternoon tryst couldn't hurt.

Wendell sensed her resistance waning. "How about a nice little rendezvous—someplace nearby?"

Carla's breathing was heavier. She squirmed in her seat. But then, a gorgeous young woman in her twenties strode by in a skin-tight mini. Wendell's laser vision kicked in. He couldn't tear his eyes away from the young woman's breasts and ass. His reaction to the young woman was like a shock of icy water in Carla's face. She decided that the desire for a harmless afternoon tryst with Wendell wasn't worth her time. She wasn't going back to the same old bullshit.

Wendell finally caught himself and turned back to Carla with a sheepish grin. She grinned back. "You just blew it."

Wendell sighed. "Hopefully, not the show."

"I'll think about it."

Carla prayed that she wouldn't have to do any more shows, but the reality was that her money wouldn't last much longer, and the job search might never go well, given her background. She decided to stop worrying about it. She smiled and sat back leisurely. "Let's enjoy the afternoon. Lunch is on you, right?"

Wendell still pressed. "And the hotel."

"Nope. No hotel, but I will consider the show."

CHAPTER 16

Baxter smiled at the lovely woman sitting across from him. Simone Winston was hot with beautiful brown skin, a voluptuous body, and long, thick hair. He had forgotten how gorgeous she was. She would never disclose her age, but he guessed she was in her late thirties. They dined on a late supper at one of those trendy new restaurants in downtown LA, near the theater center.

Simone was a model and actress who loved the arts. She had made it big in modeling for a while, but now she was pursuing theater, behind the scenes. She had invited him to see a play that showcased one of her friends. But Simone hadn't invited her friend or any of the other actors to join her and Baxter after the show. She wanted Baxter all to herself since she hadn't seen him in a while. That was fine with Baxter. He didn't feel much like mingling tonight.

Lately, he hadn't done much dating. He'd been traveling a lot, attending firefighting conferences and trade shows. He was still dazed and confused when it came to Carla, but that was all behind him now. He had to get her out of his system if he wanted any peace in his life. Carla and the TiTi Bar caused him too many problems. Frank loved those wild, roller coaster women who bounced his heart around like a yo-yo. But Baxter couldn't afford to have his life turned topsy-turvy by any woman.

He reached out and touched Simone's hand. "You look good."

Simone gave a sexy smile. She wore stilettos and tight pants with a crop top. She looked stunning, and she was well aware of the effect she had on men. Baxter tried to ignore the little voice inside his head that said she wasn't Carla. He decided to have more wine and truly relax in the presence of a beautiful woman. He wanted to reignite the passion he once felt for Simone.

"That was a good play," Baxter said.

"What did you think of my friend?" Simone asked curiously.

"Great performance. She went from plain Jane to vixen in no time. She's a gorgeous woman even without makeup."

An insecure look crossed Simone's face. She shrugged. "I think she overacted a few times, but other than that, I think she did a good job."

"She's a sharp woman, but not as sharp as you," Baxter said in reassurance.

Simone appeared more secure again. Now Baxter remembered why he had stopped seeing her. She sometimes acted too Hollywood. He had to constantly reassure her that she was beautiful. When she forgot about her insecurities, they had a great time together. They ate. They drank. They went to the movies, all kinds of shows and exhibits. And she rocked his world in bed. He sure hoped he got laid tonight. That would be a great way to rekindle their old flame, help him forget about Carla.

"You look good, Baxter," Simone said.

He was dressed in tan slacks and a soft white shirt that opened at the neck. He had removed his jacket. Simone's eyes followed the outline of his chest and shoulders in the shirt.

"You miss me?" she asked playfully. She stroked his thigh.

Baxter decided to loosen up and enjoy the night. He could feel the beginnings of an erection.

Guessing his reaction, Simone smiled. "You seeing anyone?"

For some reason, Baxter found himself stammering. "No . . ., I'm not."

"You sure?" Simone teased.

"A little fling. Didn't work out. It's over now. She doesn't compare to you." Baxter immediately regretted saying the words. Carla more than compared. He simply couldn't deal with her lifestyle.

Simone seemed satisfied. "I missed you, Baxter. We always had fun together."

"I agree." Baxter lifted his wine glass in toast. He was really enjoying himself. He should have gone out with Simone sooner. Of all the women he had dated in the past, she was tops on his list. She was the most satisfying in bed—with the exception of Carla, a little voice nagged at him. He wasn't as restless with Simone as he was with most women. He and Simone had plenty of fun. Maybe, it was time he settled down with someone who could make him forget about Carla.

Simone lightly touched his thigh again. His maleness responded immediately.

"You have to get up early in the morning?" Simone asked huskily.

"No, I don't," Baxter responded, his voice hoarsening with passion.

"Fine. You want to stop by my place after we eat?"

Baxter smiled and nodded. "Best offer I've had all night."

"It better be the only offer you had all night," Simone teased. But Baxter knew she meant it.

"Just the two of us. That's all that matters tonight," Baxter assured her. He hurried up and finished his food.

Simone grinned. "We can do dessert at my place."

"What's on the menu?"

"It's a surprise."

Baxter couldn't wait to reach Simone's place. The hardness in his slacks throbbed, eager to soar like a rocket.

Simone lived in a stunning downtown loft that had two levels and plenty of space. High-end decorating and a skyline view were the hallmarks of her apartment. The place had a New York vibe to it and matched Simone's level of sophistication.

Baxter loved watching the view of city lights when he came to visit Simone. He sometimes wondered if he should move downtown to a similar spot. But his Baldwin Hills home was fine with him. He had a nice view too, a different kind of view, but a striking one nonetheless.

Simone walked over to her wine rack, pulled out a nice

bottle of Port, and poured two glasses. She cued her music, and a sultry jazz tune poured from the speakers. Baxter smiled. The music suited his mood. Simone was good at figuring him out. She was almost perfect. He felt relaxed in her apartment with its sophisticated artwork and sleek furniture. If he became serious with Simone, he could have the best of both worlds—his place and hers.

Simone eased up behind him as he stood at the window admiring the view. She handed him a glass of wine. He sipped and watched the skyline. As she leaned into him, he could feel her breasts against his back. His whole body warmed up, and his fullness strained against his pants.

"Wouldn't you rather be with me than with her?" Simone asked.

Baxter tensed for a moment. "Huh?"

"I saw you watching my friend after the show. You had eyes only for her."

Baxter wasn't sure he liked the way the conversation was going. He turned to face Simone. "She was the star of the show. I told you, she's a fantastic actress, but that's it. I don't want her. I want to be with you. That's why I'm here."

Simone finally seemed reassured. She reached for Baxter's hand and placed it on her breasts as they stood at the window. Baxter felt his insides stirring again. He wanted to lose himself in her breasts and thighs. Then suddenly, his erection fizzled. He didn't want her anymore. He willed himself to harden, but nothing happened. He took Simone's hand and led her over to the sofa, hoping to regain his desire. But he still felt no sexual attraction to her.

"What's wrong?" Simone asked.

"Nothing." Baxter suddenly wanted to get away from her. He didn't know what was wrong with him. "I got a lot on my mind. Maybe, I better leave."

"I didn't mean what I said about my friend."

"That's not it. It's me. I've got some things to work out." Without waiting for her reaction, he grabbed his jacket, kissed her cheek, and left.

* * *

Baxter strode up a short walkway and rang the doorbell. A gorgeous mature woman, bearing a striking resemblance to him, opened the door. His mother, Lillie Rose, smiled in delight at seeing him.

"Surprise, surprise," Lillie said. "What's up? Haven't seen you in a while."

"I've been calling, Mom."

"Yeah, but you haven't stopped by."

Baxter shrugged.

Lillie's eyes bore into his as if trying to read his mind. Then she sighed apologetically. "I've got to run over to the mall. I'm on a mission. I need a dress for a wedding. You want to go with me?"

"Sure."

"You're going with me to the mall?"

"Yep. You're not going to take all day, are you?"

Lillie stared at him, open-mouthed. Finally, she regrouped. "I'll try not to take too long. Let me get my things."

She went back inside the house, but Baxter stayed outside. He felt restless. He wanted to breathe the crisp air. It was a cool spring day. He liked his mom's neighborhood. She lived in Atwater Village in the northeastern part of Los Angeles. She lived in a small Spanish style bungalow on a quiet street of similar homes. It was a trendy neighborhood that worked well for his mom. He knew she was surprised to see him. He seldom dropped by without calling, but he wanted to hang out with her.

Baxter sat outside the fitting room, bored. He hoped his mother wouldn't take long. So far, she had tried on several dresses, and none seemed to work. She came out of the dressing room again, this time in a beautiful blue sheath that contrasted well with the golden brown of her skin. And she still had the curves, plenty of curves, Baxter noted. His mom had a bountiful figure. She was tall and big-boned, definitely not skinny.

"What do you think?" Lillie asked.

"Looks great. It's a little low in the front, isn't it?"

"A little," Lillie teased. "But it should be okay for a wedding."

His mom enjoyed weddings so long as it wasn't her own. She got pregnant with Baxter in her late teens, and his father, who was young and dumb, never stuck around. Lillie did marry in her forties, but that marriage didn't work. Baxter's stepfather worshipped the ground Lillie walked on, but she never felt the same spark for him. Lillie said he was a good man, and she thought she could fall in love with him, but it never happened. Eventually, she wanted her freedom. After her marriage dissolved, she started dating and never looked back. She always kept a boyfriend, but she was a confirmed bachelorette.

She was still a good-looking woman in her mid-sixties. Hardly any lines or wrinkles etched her face. Baxter looked just like her. They both had inherited his grandfather's amber eyes. Lillie got a kick out of hearing people exclaim how much her son favored her. Baxter had seen a few pictures of his dad and wished that just once someone had noticed a resemblance. But as Baxter got older and realized that he might never meet his dad, he was glad that he resembled his mother.

Lillie headed back to the dressing room. "See, that didn't take long, did it?"

Baxter grinned. "Only a couple hours."

"I'll take you to dinner for your time. There's this cute little place I found. They've got some decent soul food."

Baxter brightened. He enjoyed hanging out with his mom.

Baxter and Lillie sat in a quaint little restaurant that had tablecloths and flowers. He and his mom ate chicken meatloaf and gravy, candied yams, greens and mashed potatoes. Baxter was in his world.

"You didn't have to order what I did, Mom."

"If I cooked for you at home, we would have eaten the same thing."

"Okay," he said with a shrug.

"How's the food?" Lillie asked.

"It's good, Mom. Almost as good as yours."

"You're right—almost. I'm glad you like the place."

They ate for a while in silence, savoring their food and companionship.

"Who is she?" Lillie probed.

"Who?"

"Come on, Bax. You visit me unexpectedly, shop with me a couple hours, and don't complain. You got something on your mind?"

"Nothing. Everything's fine."

Baxter looked up from his plate and stole a glance at his mother. He could tell that his mom didn't believe him. She had a smirk on her face, but she wasn't going to press him. They resumed their meal in companionable silence.

Lillie couldn't refrain. "I know you got something on your mind. Say it. You can tell your momma anything. Talk to your momma," she teased, but her eyes were serious.

Baxter still ate in silence.

"How's the job?" Lillie asked. "How's your crew?"

Baxter was full now and toying with his food. "I met this woman," he finally divulged.

Lillie smiled smugly. "I knew it. But what's the problem?"

"I keep thinking about her, and that's not something I want to do."

"Why not?"

Baxter sighed. "She's a stripper."

"Ah, the one you rescued."

"Yeah, that's the one," Baxter admitted.

Lillie cleared her throat. "I should've known when you mentioned her, there was something to it."

"Well, I didn't give you any indication."

"You did. I chose to ignore it. What about Simone?"

"I saw Simone last night. It's not working. I can't get Carla out of my head."

"Sounds to me like you're confusing rescue with love," Lillie said.

"I didn't say anything about love. I just can't get her out of my head."

Lillie's eyes probed Baxter's face. "Whatever it is, you're

serious. I can tell. I love you, Bax, and I want you to be happy. But I don't think a stripper is the kind of person you want to get involved with. You worked hard. You're a captain."

Baxter nodded in agreement. He hoped his face didn't show the confusion he felt on the inside. He didn't dare tell his mother that he'd probably have to watch his back from now on because of Gutter Joe.

"Didn't you say somebody set fire to that club?" Lillie asked.

"We can't prove it yet. The Arson team is investigating."

Lillie's eyes filled with concern. "Sounds like Carla is involved in some shady business. Does she want to be a stripper all her life? How old is she?"

Baxter swallowed. "Fifty. I think she had a birthday recently."

"Fifty? Shit. She still stripping at fifty?

"She manages the club now. Did manage the club. I think she's trying to get out of the business. I don't know for sure," Baxter finally admitted.

"It's your life, Baxter. But girlfriend may be pretty set in her ways. She's almost as old as I am."

"Not quite," Baxter said defensively.

"She's not far from it," Lillie countered.

"That's because you had me in your teens, Mom."

"Late teens." Lillie shook her head and sighed. "You know I wanted you to go to college, but you decided to do your own thing. And I'm proud of you for it. You've excelled in your own way. You helped me buy my house." She paused. "But you don't want to throw everything away over some woman who could wreck your life. It's not always about the heart, Baxter. You need a partner, too, someone who shares your values."

"I hear you, Mom. That's why I'm talking to you. Help me to clear my head."

Lillie started laughing. "I'm trying to help, but you got a thing for this woman, no matter what I say."

They both fell silent.

Lillie made one final attempt to dissuade him. "You've dated some nice women. What about the one you brought to the concert?"

"Not feeling it."

Lillie sighed. "If you want a stripper, I guess it's not the end of the world. It's your life."

CHAPTER 17

Carla wasn't used to rejection. At the TiTi, men swooned over her. Even the ones who wanted the younger dancers tried to gain her favor. But the club life was all she knew. How could she get anyone to take her seriously in a work setting outside the club? She had to find a way. She took a deep breath and braced herself. This was her fifth time at EveryDay Fitness Center, and this would be her last, she vowed, if they didn't hire her.

Young smart ass was at the reception counter again. Carla learned her name was Regina. She tried her best to be diplomatic with Regina, but it never worked. Carla wondered if she was just banging her head against the wall.

"Again?" Regina said, trying to stop Carla in her tracks.

Carla marched forward with a smile and a steely exterior. "I want to speak with Jasmine. Make sure she doesn't pass up a good hire before I move on and offer my services somewhere else."

Regina looked Carla up and down enviously. While Regina was in her twenties and in good shape, she couldn't match Carla's curves.

"Give it up," Regina said. "Jasmine is pretty busy today, and you still have to apply online like everybody else.

"I've already done that and still haven't heard anything."

"You will." Regina dismissed her and started processing clients. Carla overheard Regina say to one of the female patrons, "Damn. Girlfriend can't seem to take a hint. We don't have a job for her."

A young male patron observed Carla's figure. "Y'all need to give her a job. She can be my trainer."

That was the last straw for Regina. "Bye. I'll let Jasmine know you were here. Please don't come in again unless we call you." She turned her back on Carla.

Carla wanted to snatch Regina over the counter and slap her a few times. Instead, she said, "You sure Jasmine is unavailable? I wanted to let her know that I'll be moving on. I could revolutionize this place and bring you more clients."

Jasmine finally came out of her office and smiled. She shook her head. "Gotta hand it to you, Carla. You don't take 'no' for an answer. But we're fully staffed now, and you do have to follow online procedures. I wish you the best of luck in your job search."

"Thanks," Carla said sincerely. She appreciated Jasmine's frankness. "We could have worked well together," Carla added. She stood up straighter and decided that Jasmine's loss was somebody else's gain—hopefully not Wendell's. She was trying to do everything in her power not to return to the TiTi. The fitness center still seemed ideal for her.

As Carla headed for the door, Jasmine noted the attention Carla commanded from the patrons. Jasmine also noted the smirk on Regina's face.

Jasmine ran after Carla. "Alright. Let's see what you can do. Don't disappoint me."

Carla squelched the sting of tears in her eyes. She beamed in appreciation. "I won't."

The sun dazzled overhead in a clear blue sky as Carla pulled into the parking lot of the fitness center. Excitedly, she grabbed her tote bag and rushed inside. While she missed clicking her heels in the office building where she worked with Natalie, she was thrilled to have found a job at the center.

Natalie was thrilled too. Carla had explained what happened during her last encounter with John Rawlins, though she neglected to mention threatening him. Natalie guessed, however. "I don't know what you said to him, but he gives me lots of leeway," Natalie said. "But rest assured, I'll sue the shit out of him if he ever goes after my job."

Carla had raised her eyebrows in surprise. Natalie seldom swore. Carla had hugged her younger sister in amusement. "Between the two of us, I bet he won't fuck with nobody else."

Natalie had simply smiled and shaken her head at Carla's language.

In her new job as a trainee for EveryDay Fitness, Carla handled the front desk, but she was also being trained in sales and marketing so that she could recruit new clients. To excel in her new position, she was also required to enroll in a fitness certification program. Once she received her certificate, the sky was the limit. A whole new world had opened up to her, one that would make good use of her smarts and energy. She hoped she could stick to this new life.

Since Jasmine gave her plenty of freedom, Carla knew that at some point, she could incorporate some of her stripper moves into the dance courses she would teach after she became certified. She was pleased with herself. So far, she hadn't succumbed to the lure of returning to the TiTi. She hadn't told anybody at the club about her new job, except Mimi. She wanted to make sure that she could keep the job first.

As Carla stepped behind the counter beside Regina, the young woman barely spoke. Carla simply ignored her. She was so delighted to have a regular day job that not even Regina's ill temper could dampen her spirits. Carla pulled up the computer information she needed to get her day started. Though it was early in the morning, patrons were lining up at the counter and signing in.

Carla began processing a patron whose membership had expired. With her eyes glued to the computer screen, she hit all the requisite keys to initiate the process. Somebody else was at the counter too, but Carla was busy figuring out how to help her current client. Her computer froze. She looked up and saw Regina staring at her.

"What?" Carla said, flustered. "I'm trying to get this lady reinstated." Regina was staring at her oddly, but Carla still tussled with her computer screen. Regina looked up over Carla's head. Baffled, Carla followed her gaze, and then she saw him. Baxter stood at the counter in gray sweat pants, a blue T-shirt, and a hoodie. He looked handsome and relaxed with his gym bag flung over his shoulder. Carla held her breath and locked eyes with him. Her legs felt like jelly. All of her computer training for the job flew out the window. A line was starting to form, and she still had not reinstated her current client.

"Please take over for me, Regina," was all Carla could say. She apologized to the client and told her that Regina would help her. Still standing behind the counter, Carla steadied herself and walked over to Baxter.

He smiled at her. "You work here?"

Carla nodded. She didn't trust herself to speak.

"Good." He hesitated and swallowed. "I'm sorry about how I treated you that day at the firehouse. I really am."

Carla almost reeled. She stared at him, open-mouthed, and fought off the tears stinging her eyes. "Apology accepted." Her voice was barely audible because she couldn't believe what was happening.

They both exhaled and reveled in the moment.

"I've got to take my class," Baxter said. "I'm checking out that new mixed martial arts class. I'll see if we can use it at the station. Before I go, give me your number so I can call you. We've got a lot to talk about."

"We do." Carla's face lit up as she gave him her number.

"I'll call you later," he said.

Carla nodded. She saw Regina smirk in envy. A steady flow of patrons still streamed to the front desk. Jasmine came out of her office.

"Everything okay?" she asked Carla. Jasmine couldn't resist smiling broadly at Baxter. "Don't forget she's at work," Jasmine informed him.

"Everything's fine," Carla beamed. She tried to stop smiling like a lovesick schoolgirl, but she couldn't.

* * *

Carla and Baxter ate lunch in the mall at a small restaurant across from the fitness club. They sat outside on the patio. Apparently, Baxter couldn't wait to see her. He made lunch plans with her right after his class.

Carla wore her uniform of black leggings and a red T-shirt. The T-shirt was snug and stylish. She liked the uniform. Apparently, Baxter liked it too. His eyes followed her contours under the shirt. She recalled their first lunch and their tryst at the fire station. Her insides warmed, and she felt a tingling between her legs. None of that, she warned herself. She and Baxter still had some things to clear up.

Baxter lifted his juice glass in toast, and Carla lifted hers. "To brand new starts," he said.

"To new starts," Carla agreed.

"This reminds me of our first lunch," he said.

Carla was pleased that he remembered. "It's a little different," she said.

"Yes, now you're working at an honest job. I mean a different job, a safer job."

"For now." Carla couldn't resist taunting. "I may have to return to the TiTi. I hate getting up early. I'm working this job because with my background, this is the only job I could think of. But I'm starting off at the bottom. I don't have the flexibility that I had at the TiTi, and I have to be careful that nobody feels threatened because of my skills."

Baxter touched her hand. "You do have so many skills. That's why you don't need to work at the TiTi."

Carla sighed and tried to feel reassured. She withdrew her hand from Baxter's when she felt a quivering sensation spread between her legs. She wondered if he guessed because he simply smiled.

Carla bit into her veggie burger to take her mind off a different hunger. Baxter was eating healthy too. He bit heartily into his tuna sandwich.

"How'd you get the job?"

"Persistence," Carla laughed. "I kept coming back, and finally, Jasmine—she's the manager—agreed to hire me. It's a good job. It gets a little monotonous at times, but overall, I'm pleased."

"Do you really miss the TiTi?"

"Sometimes. But I don't miss the lechers, the lewd comments, the—"

"The fire."

Carla refused to discuss the fire. She concentrated on her burger instead. After a few bites, she spoke. "I miss the attention and getting dressed up. I miss running things. Taking charge. Now I'm starting from scratch—at fifty."

"It's all going to work out if you let it. You can't work at the TiTi forever."

Carla seemed unconvinced.

"You got plans this afternoon?" Baxter asked.

"Yes, I do. I have to go back to work."

Baxter touched her arm lightly.

She was ready to jump across the table and straddle him. The urge hit her so suddenly. She forced her mind in a different direction. "Take me out on a proper date," Carla said. "Make plans with me. Woo me a little. Not just lunch, and we hop in bed."

Baxter grinned. "What's wrong with that?"

"We moved too fast the first time, Baxter. I moved too fast and so did you. You have no idea how humiliated I was when you shut me out—just like that." Carla snapped her fingers.

Baxter sighed. "I know. I was wrong. But everything happened so fast, and I didn't want to get involved with—" He realized that he was about to put his foot in his mouth again for the umpteenth time. He reached out and held her hand. He tried to ignore the growing tumescence in his pants. "What are you doing this Saturday? How about a movie?"

Carla was surprised that he was asking her out on a date even though she had insisted on it. She hadn't been invited on a proper date in so long. In fact, she had seldom been asked on a proper date while working as a stripper. Wendell had romanced her a little, but that was so long ago.

"I'd love to see a movie," Carla said. "But I'm not giving it up this time. Neither should you."

Baxter laughed. "We'll see."

For the remainder of the meal, they basked in each other's company and the sexual promise that flowed between them. Carla hated the thought of going back to work, but knowing she had a movie date with Baxter would make it easier.

CHAPTER 18

Carla examined the three dresses lying on her bed. Two were black, and one was a siren red. She couldn't make up her mind. She chided herself for acting like a love-struck teenager. Baxter would arrive in less than an hour, and here she was agonizing over which dress to wear. *Just pick one,* she told herself. Baxter was taking her out to dinner then a club affair that one of his buddies had invited him to.

"You want to go dancing next week?" he had asked when he dropped her off after their movie date.

Carla had insisted that he take her home after the movie and that she wasn't going to his house, nor was he invited to hers. She was afraid that she had antagonized him, but she should have known better. He was a man, and he was hot and ready for the challenge. She was hot and ready too, but she was determined to get to know him better and enjoy his company before they jumped into bed again.

Carla finally settled on the red dress. It was the one she wanted to wear all along, but she didn't want to give off any signals that she was ready to end her self-imposed abstinence. The dress was a low-cut mini, but not too excessive. It hugged her assets, but it wasn't as raunchy as the dresses she wore at the TiTi. She knew she looked good in the dress, but she still felt jittery as she waited inside the lobby of her building for Baxter. She wasn't used to dinner and dancing with a handsome, decent man who genuinely seemed to respect her.

She peered through the glass door of the lobby. A shiny red Thunderbird pulled into the circle of Carla's driveway. For a fleeting moment, she wished Baxter drove a fun car like that, but his Honda was cool with her. In fact, anything he drove was cool with her. He could have picked her up on a skateboard, and she would have enjoyed the ride, especially now that she worked at the fitness center.

Carla fidgeted and smoothed out her dress. Baxter was usually prompt, even a little early. She hoped he wasn't going to stand her up. This wouldn't be the first time that she had been stood up by somebody who decided they didn't want to date a stripper after all. Maybe, she had been naïve to think that she and Baxter could really have a relationship. Carla opened her purse and checked her cell phone. He wasn't late yet, a few minutes to go, but she still wondered if he was going to show up.

Then the driver's door of the red Thunderbird opened, and Baxter got out. Carla gasped with pleasure. He looked hot. He wore a black sports coat and open-necked shiny black shirt. His gray trousers kept his outfit from being too formal, yet added pizazz. He smiled broadly and signaled for her to come outside.

Carla ran out and laughed. This was her idea of heaven—being picked up in her driveway in a red Thunderbird. She circled the gleaming car. "Is this yours?"

Baxter's face lit up. He kissed her cheek in greeting. "It is, young lady."

Carla couldn't believe it. The Thunderbird was a dream car, a red convertible. The top and the interior of the car were black. Though it was a warm night, the top was up.

"Wanted to surprise you," he explained. "I can put the top down now."

Carla squealed in delight. "2002?" she asked.

Baxter smiled, pleased that she knew the year.

"I told you my father used to collect miniature toy cars. You got a hard top for it too?" she asked.

Baxter nodded proudly.

"Where's the Honda?"

"Home. This is my dress car."

Carla laughed. "Your dress car?"

"Yep," he answered. He swung around to the passenger side and held the door open. Carla stood still and marveled for a moment. She was a bit overwhelmed by the lovely car and the man who drove it. She didn't know if she deserved such good fortune. She blinked her eyes, elated that nothing disappeared.

"Hop in, girl," he said.

Carla melted into the interior. "It's roomier than I expected."

Baxter sighed. "Trust me. I've had all kinds of work done to make it comfortable. It's best with the top down."

Carla's dress rose higher as she settled herself into the seat. "My dress matches your car. I'm glad I wore it."

Baxter made no effort to hide his admiration of her legs. "I'm glad you wore it too."

He slid into the driver's seat, cranked the engine, and lowered the top. Then he reached over her and popped open the glove compartment to reveal an assortment of women's scarves. Carla raised an eyebrow and wondered who else rode in his car. Baxter offered no explanation. Carla decided not to probe. Instead, she picked a scarf that matched her dress. She certainly didn't want her wig to blow off.

As Baxter shifted into gear, his hand deliberately brushed her leg. "You look lovely," he said as he eased the car out of the circle.

Carla couldn't resist. She touched his leg too. "So do you."

Baxter was in high spirits. "We'll eat, then party. You think you can hang?"

Carla giggled. "I think so. You a good dancer?"

"Uh, not as good as you. But I promise not to embarrass you."

Carla didn't care whatever else happened in life. She would always remember this night.

Baxter reached over and brushed her thigh again.

Carla wanted nothing more than for him to insert his finger inside her and glide it in and out. But she pushed his hand away. "Let's take it slow."

"Oh, I can do it slow."

Carla grinned. "I'm sure you can, but that's not what I meant."

He sighed resignedly. "Beautiful weather we're having. You agree?"

She burst out laughing. "Yes, lovely."

Carla enjoyed a wonderful time for the rest of the night. They had dinner at a new restaurant in Silver Lake on the northeast side of LA. It was a trendy, yuppie area, a bit too yuppie for Carla's taste, but she didn't care as long as she hung out with Baxter. On the tables inside the restaurant, mini Tiffany lamps emitted a soft glow. Baxter liked the lighting. From time to time, he was able to graze Carla's legs under the table without scrutiny. But for the most part, he behaved himself.

On their way to the club, Baxter drove fast, but not as fast as usual. She hoped she was partially responsible. After a while, she forgot about his driving and simply enjoyed the ride in his red Thunderbird.

At the club, Baxter introduced the guys who were hosting the affair. The club was in Hollywood, not far from the restaurant where she and Baxter dined. The guys he introduced were friendly enough, and out of respect for Baxter, they kept their eyes on her face and not on her body. Carla prayed that none of them had frequented the TiTi. She breathed a sigh of relief when she caught no glimmer of recognition in anyone's eyes.

"Where's Percy?" Carla asked.

"No Percy. Not tonight."

Carla felt even more relaxed. She relished Baxter's company. She felt that she had embarked on a fresh new start.

Baxter ushered her over to one of the tables where his friends sat. He introduced her to a few more people, then got up from the table. "I'm going over to the bar to get us drinks," he said, but Carla knew he was eager to greet a few more of his buddies standing at the bar.

Carla nodded and took in everything around her. It was a nice club with a softly lit ambience. Tables and booths surrounded a gleaming hardwood dance floor. The booths were traditional dark red velvet, plush and well-maintained. Very few couples partied on the dance floor. The mixmaster DJ wasn't much of a master in Carla's opinion. Hopefully, he'd play some better music. She really wanted to dance.

At the table, Carla engaged in small talk with some of the wives and girlfriends of Baxter's friends. The women weren't very friendly though. Their eyes flashed distrustfully at the curves under her red dress. Carla was used to this kind of reaction. She ignored them.

One of the women was fair-skinned and gorgeous. She had beautiful eyes and a head full of long, curly hair. She had a nice body too. She and Carla bonded somewhat since they were both being hated on by the other women. Carla welcomed the beautiful woman's conversation.

Carla talked with a few of the men too. There was one she really enjoyed talking to, but his wife glared at her the whole time. Carla looked around for Baxter. She wondered what was taking him so long. Baxter was still at the bar with some of his buddies. He seemed engrossed in conversation with one of them. He was nodding and listening intently. Then they started looking at Carla. She squirmed a bit and wondered what Baxter and his friend talked about. Did his friend recognize her from the TiTi? Was his friend trying to talk Baxter out of dating her? They turned back to the bar, still conversing. Then one of the other guys joined in. They appeared so intense in their conversation.

Carla studied Baxter and the two men. She wondered how he knew them. She'd ask him if she could ever get his ass back to the table. She hoped they weren't saying bad things about her to Baxter. She tried to calm down and relax. Then a thought occurred to her. She was so busy wondering if Baxter and his buddies were discussing her that she hadn't noticed how smooth they were. They dressed sharply and moved with an air of confidence. One of them appeared more street-smart than the others. He and Baxter got along well. A question started to nag at her. Was Baxter some kind of drug dealer? Was he too good to be true?

He dressed well. He had two nice cars, and he was smart, smart enough not to be flashy with any drug earnings he made. How could he afford to live the way he did on a fireman's salary? True, he was a captain. Maybe, he managed his money well. But Carla wasn't convinced. She sighed heavily. It would be just her luck to fall for a drug dealer when she was trying to do everything in her power to get out of the strip club life. She felt a sinking feeling in the pit of her stomach. Maybe, she should get up and leave quietly. She shook the thought off and decided to get up off her butt, walk over to him, and ask him if he was dealing drugs. *Please don't let it be so,* she prayed. Carla got up from the table, stood tall, and headed for the bar.

As she walked over to him, Baxter tried not to stare, but she was so lovely in the red dress. He knew he was the envy of almost every man in the club. He openly feasted his eyes on her. He didn't bother to conceal it anymore. She could think him a lecher if she wanted. Maybe, he was—for her. He liked everything about her. She was beautiful, smart, and fiery. She appeared a little hard around the edges, but that added to her character. He enjoyed her company. More than anything, he hoped she wouldn't go back to that strip club.

Baxter secretly noted the way his buddies tried not to stare at Carla. He was amused. He couldn't fault them if they did steal a glance. Carla strode over to him purposefully. He could tell that she was used to men gaping at her. She took it all in stride.

Baxter reached out for Carla's hand and made a round of introductions. Then he addressed her only. "Sorry. I got waylaid. I'll get our drinks now."

"Uh, before you do, I want to talk to you for a minute."

Baxter tensed. "What's up?"

They stepped away from the bar.

Carla suddenly felt tongue-tied. She didn't know how to question him about her suspicions. She fidgeted uncomfortably. He was so honest. What if she didn't like his answer?

"What's up, Carla?" he asked curiously.

Carla steeled herself. "Are you a drug dealer?"

Baxter burst out laughing. Carla lowered her eyes sheepishly.

"Why do you ask that?" His eyes still gleamed with amusement.

Carla shrugged. "You were huddled over here in secret with your friends. I thought you forgot about me."

"I didn't forget about you. I wouldn't do that. My buddies and me, we got into some heavy conversation."

Carla still wasn't satisfied. "You seem too good to be true. You dress nicely, the cars. You don't seem to worry about money."

"I get concerned about money like everybody else. That's why I was in a huddle with my buddies. We got an investment club going. We give each other tips about trading—"

"Not insider trading," Carla said warily.

Baxter laughed. "No insider trading. My mom would kill me. It's all legit."

Carla was surprised at the reference to his mom.

"You know about insider trading?" he asked with a smile.

"I've heard about it," she smiled back.

Baxter pulled her close. "You think I'm too good to be true?" His lips were a whisper away from hers.

Carla tried not to melt in his arms. "We'll see," she said, spellbound.

Baxter released her when he felt an erection forming. "Let's get our drinks and go boogie on the dance floor."

"With that DJ?"

Baxter laughed. "Look over at the booth. My buddies replaced him. Too many complaints."

"Wonderful!" Carla exclaimed.

Right on time, the new DJ played the party anthem, "This Is How We Do It" by Montell Jordan. The dance floor filled up. Carla was starved for some good dance music. She grabbed Baxter's hand and headed for the dance floor. They forgot about the drinks.

Carla and Baxter rocked hot and heavy to the song. Carla had hoped that he could at least dance a little. But she was in for a big surprise. He could really move. He almost rivaled her on the floor. She loved it. She finally found someone who could keep up with her. She was able to cut loose with him. He took his jacket off and really got down. He was a ham on the dance floor. Carla laughed in delight as they partied.

A few drinks later, Carla was having such a good time with Baxter that she didn't care what he did for a living. She didn't believe he was a drug dealer, but she no longer cared. He had charmed her so much during the evening.

Throughout the night, Carla exercised a modicum of restraint on the dance floor. While she danced provocatively with Baxter, she held back a little until the DJ played "Don't Cha" by The Pussycat Dolls. Then Carla showed some of her racier moves. She held Baxter captive under her charms. She bumped and gyrated all over him. She took advantage of their spot in the middle of the dance floor where they were camouflaged by the throng of dancers surrounding them.

Baxter shook his head and laughed. "Girl, what you doin'?" His breath was hot and steamy. "Okay now," he warned.

He was still trying to act the gentleman, but Carla was all over him. He finally decided to let her do her thing, and he would kick back and enjoy it. He was starting to sweat a little. His satiny shirt was becoming damp in spots. He opened up another shirt button, exposing more of his chest. Carla hollered. She kept grinding her butt all over him. He was lost. He needed rescue. He found it when the DJ played Marvin Gaye's classic, "Let's Get It On."

The song gave Baxter an excuse to pull Carla close. She welcomed the excuse too. They were both slightly damp, which only heightened their arousal. Baxter couldn't hide the swelling in his slacks as he pressed against her. Carla pressed back. She molded every contour of her body against his.

"You got me so hard. How we gonna walk off the dance floor?" His voice was low and husky.

"Oh, I won't have any problem," she teased. Carla felt him shake with laughter.

"That's cold," he said.

As Baxter held her close, they stopped talking and yielded to the moment. Carla felt safe and secure in his arms. She allowed his hungry maleness to probe the softness of her loins.

She melted her breasts against his chest as they locked together on the dance floor.

When the song was over, they headed back to the table. Carla walked slightly ahead of Baxter to give him cover and time to soften. But to mess with him, she stopped suddenly so that his softening organ pressed against her butt. Immediately, he was hard again.

"Wait 'til I get you home," he whispered against her ear.

Carla pulled away from him so that he could compose himself before they reached the table. Once there, they sank down, flushed and exhilarated.

"Somebody's been having a good time," one of Baxter's friends said.

Baxter simply leaned back against Carla as she put her arms around his shoulders and pressed her breasts against his back.

Outside the club, a blast of cool night air helped Carla come to her senses. She wanted Baxter so much, but she still wasn't ready to give up the goodies yet. She knew he was going to have a fit, but she'd risk it. She wanted him for keeps.

They stood in the parking lot, leaning against his car. Baxter pulled her close. "Your place or mine?" he whispered against her lips.

One of Baxter's friends pulled up and laughed. "Y'all better wait 'til you get home," he said and drove away with his date.

Baxter ushered Carla into the car and pulled out of the lot. "We going to my place?" he asked.

"No mine. I'm going to my place."

"What do you mean by that?"

"I'm not ready to give it up yet," she said firmly.

"Am I still being punished?"

"No, you're not being punished. I want to get to know you, and I want you to know me. We moved too fast that first time, and you couldn't handle it."

Baxter brushed his hand against her thigh. "I can handle it now."

Carla moved her thigh out of his reach. "I'm serious. I want to get to know you better."

Baxter was losing patience. "You were all over me on the dance floor, and now suddenly, you want to play innocent. You led me on back there."

"I got carried away in the moment. We were having a good time."

"How long am I on punishment?"

Carla stifled a laugh. "You're not on punishment. We're going to take it slow, that's all."

"I don't want to take it slow. Look, I said I'm sorry. What I did was wrong. How many times do you want me to say it?"

"No more apologies needed, but I still want you to take me home."

"You really want me to drop you off, and then I go home?"

"Yes."

"I don't know if I want to see you anymore."

Carla burst out laughing. "Listen to yourself. You only want to sleep with me?"

"No, that's not true, but we're both adults. And you're no stranger to guys wanting you."

"That's exactly why we need to move slow—so you see me in a different light."

"I do see you in a different light, or I wouldn't hang out with you."

"I want a platonic relationship with you right now. That's the word I wanted."

"Well, I definitely don't want a platonic relationship with you—now or ever. But I'm certainly not going to force myself on you."

"Good."

They rode in silence for a while until Baxter started picking up speed.

"Slow it down," Carla warned.

"I am. You wanted platonic."

"I meant the car," Carla said.

Baxter stifled a grin. "Okay. Okay. No sex. No racing. You're a drag. I should put you out of my car."

"Try it."

"You ought to be glad I like you, girl."

When they pulled into the driveway of Carla's building, Baxter asked, "Do I, at least, get a kiss?"

Carla puckered up and gave him a quick one. She noted the rising tent pole in his slacks. "We're still friends?" she asked.

"Yeah, I guess."

"I'm glad." Carla couldn't resist. She reached down and gave his dick a firm, heartfelt squeeze. Then she hopped out of the car.

He jumped out immediately to catch her, but she moved swiftly out of his reach. "Call me," she said with a laugh and hurried away.

"That's wrong, Rae," he hollered after her.

She swung around before she entered her building. "It's Carla."

"You're wrong, Carla." Baxter was pissed.

CHAPTER 19

Carla's heels clicked in the hall. She liked the sound, but she wished she were in a different building. She wore a simple dress with a fitted bodice and loose skirt. The fabric was a print with vibrant colors that contrasted well with her skin. The dress was a definite departure from the tight-fitting clothing she usually wore.

She took a deep breath and continued through the hallway of the nursing home. Family members, from middle-aged adults to teenagers, rolled their loved ones in wheelchairs through the hallway. They stared at Carla curiously. Despite infirmities and wheelchairs, some of the elderly men watched her with a gleam in their eyes. Carla smiled and shook her head. She should have worn one of her tight dresses and higher heels and did a few bumps and grinds for everybody, including the staff.

The Silver Lining Nursing Home was clean, antiseptic, and modern. Decorative artwork hung from walls painted in muted pastels. Comfortable cloth chairs in warm colors dotted the hallways and provided seating for residents and visitors alike.

Carla bent over a water fountain and drank thirstily. She wiped water from her bottom lip. She hesitated, then breathed deeply and entered a room.

A man in his mid-seventies sat in a wheelchair staring out the window. Though his back hunched slightly, he was big-boned with a sense of power emanating from his physique. He was brown-skinned and handsome. Though his hair was thinning, he still possessed a full head of hair. Carla envied his hair.

"Hi, Dad," she said softly.

Aaron Hepburn turned around and faced her. "Hi Natalie," her father said with a smile.

"I'm not Natalie."

Aaron chuckled. "I know who you are. Thought I'd mess with you since y'all think I'm losing it."

Carla waited for a minute to see if her father really knew who she was.

He sighed and smiled softly. "You're my long, lost Carla."

Carla leaned over and hugged her father. He hugged her back and studied her.

"Who is he?" Aaron asked.

Carla looked puzzled.

"The new man in your life?"

How did her father know she was seeing Baxter? She hadn't told Natalie yet in case things didn't work out. Her father possessed an uncanny intuition at times. Carla decided to evade the question.

Instead, she ran over to her father's toy car collection. He kept his cars locked up in a glass case. He had about ten cars in all, among them a 1962 Corvette convertible, a 1963 Thunderbird, a 1965 Mustang convertible, and a 1967 LeMans. He had a few old model Buicks, too, from the 1940s.

Aaron's car collection had dwindled. Natalie thought some of the staff might have taken his cars. When Natalie told her ex-husband about it, Russell came up to the nursing home and read everyone the riot act. He threatened to come back with his boxing gloves. That seemed to stop Aaron's car collection from dwindling.

Aaron got a kick out of watching Carla's reaction to his cars.

"A friend of mine collects miniature fire trucks," she said.

"The same friend who got you to give up stripping?"

Carla was ready for her father now. "No one influenced me to give up stripping. I quit on my own. How did you know?"

"I can tell," Aaron replied. "But you still had a little help."

"It wasn't a bad way to earn a living, Dad. Besides, these last years I wasn't dancing. I was managing."

"It's still no place for my daughter."

Carla sighed in resignation and plopped down in a chair. "Whatever."

"Don't be a smart ass," Aaron warned.

Carla forced herself not to respond.

"So who is he?" Aaron asked.

Carla was surprised by his clarity and persistence.

"It's a good day," Aaron said as if he read her thoughts. "You're here." He still waited for an answer to his question.

"His name is Baxter Rose. We're sort of dating. He's a fireman. But he's not the reason I quit. I made the decision myself."

"I'm glad you're out of that club. What are you doing now?"

"I work at a fitness center."

"That's good. Suits you fine."

"You shut me out, Dad. That was so unfair."

Aaron's mouth formed a grim line. "I didn't want my daughter working in a strip club, plain and simple. Your mother didn't want it either."

"Yeah, but she didn't shut me out."

"I had to. When your mother died in that car accident, all I kept thinking was I'm going to lose my oldest daughter too. That club life, that's a rough life."

"I was fine. I'm still here. I'm a survivor."

"And I'm not?"

Carla didn't say anything.

Aaron shrugged. "I miss your mom."

"I do, too, but we can't just give up on life. You've never been the same since mom died. You went to pieces over her death."

"I know you want me to get out of this nursing home so you and Natalie and Russell don't have to pay anymore. Don't forget I drove a bus for years, and that's helping to pay for this too."

Carla shook her head in denial. "I don't care about the money, but you look so strong."

Aaron refused to debate. He studied Carla's face. "You're beautiful. You look like me and your mom. You got my eyes and her color," he bragged.

Then he suddenly stopped talking. Carla knew she couldn't

reach him when he clamped down like that. She felt angry and frustrated because her father seemed too strong and sturdy for the nursing home and his wheelchair. Yet he seemed to have no desire to live after her mom died. For almost fifteen years, he had mourned and gradually deteriorated. Carla and Natalie had wondered if he was racked by guilt for some reason, but they could never confirm.

Carla sat watching him for a while, hoping he might come out of his private world. But her father had retreated into that space in his head that pushed everybody else out.

She loved her dad, but she wanted to shake him at times like this. She wanted him to carry on, to fight for life. Carla rose from the chair and hugged him. He was still in his solitary world.

As she turned to leave, her father called out in a distant voice. "A fireman, huh? Bring him around."

"We'll see, Dad." She wasn't sure her words registered until she saw the faint trace of a smile on his lips.

CHAPTER 20

Carla was thrilled. Baxter had invited her to the Fire Engineers Charity Ball, a black-tie community event that included various neighborhood and city officials. Carla felt both giddy and nervous as she and Baxter entered a country club ballroom on the west side of Los Angeles. This year's ball was being held in Marina del Rey. Inside, they could dine and dance. Outside, they could stroll along the promenade and watch the boats and harbor lights.

Baxter was ecstatic that one of the charities benefitting from this year's ball was PowerForward, a watchdog program designed to post bail for young people of color who were wrongly detained or imprisoned. The program also offered sports activities for youth and gave out college scholarships. Baxter had lobbied hard for PowerForward since he was on the committee that planned the ball.

Carla turned to him and smiled. He looked so handsome in a bone-colored tuxedo jacket made of African cloth. A pattern of black antelope images covered the jacket. He wore a white shirt, black slacks and bow tie, and a yellow boutonniere. He bought the jacket after Carla told him that she was wearing a yellow gown that she found at an African boutique. Baxter rocked the jacket. It coordinated well with her gown.

They had found their attire at the Pan African Arts and Film Festival, one of the biggest film festivals in the world. Someone had given her a flyer about the festival, which had been moved to late spring. The timing was perfect for Carla. Now that she was enjoying a whole new way of life, she had invited Baxter to go with her to see some of the films. Besides the films, she attended a wonderful African fashion show and experienced a completely new way of looking at African fashion. The moment she saw the yellow gown on the runway, she knew it was made for her. So she went back to the festival without Baxter and tried the dress on. She negotiated heavily to get the price down. Now she was enjoying the fruits of her bargaining.

The dress was a sleeveless, form-fitting sheath above the knee. Sheer chiffon, flecked with dainty cowry shells, covered her décolletage and shoulders. The rest of the bodice and skirt were made of silk. The bottom of the dress flared from the knees to the ankles and was comprised of a layer of chiffon over silk. Carla had found some African jewelry, a big beaded cuff and dangling gold earrings to go with the dress. She wore a neutral shoe with a moderately high heel and platform. And she wore one of her favorite wigs, a curly Afro-bob that looked stylishly mussed up and natural.

Carla had no regrets about splurging on her outfit. Who knew when she would get the chance to attend another ball? She hoped that she and Baxter were on the road to some kind of promising relationship, but she might wake up one day and have the carpet yanked from under her. She hoped not, but she could never be sure. All she knew was that she was starved for a good, decent man, and she had found one. She prayed that the fun would continue.

Baxter smiled warmly at Carla. He placed his hand on the small of her back possessively as he guided her into the ballroom. Her back was bare to the waist. Yet the front of the dress was more demure even though it displayed ample cleavage through the sheer chiffon covering her shoulders. He realized he had a true beauty on his arm. Maybe, she'd finally give up the booty tonight.

He was tired of the platonic shit. How long was she going to dangle the carrot? Besides, she had already let the horse out of the barn. Correction, he had already let the horse out of the barn into her pastures. So what was the big deal? True, he was getting to know her better, but by now, he knew her well enough. It was time to get down. Regardless, he still planned to have a good time tonight. After all, he was escorting the belle of the ball. But later, he and Carla were going to have a serious talk about ending this platonic business.

Carla liked the feel of Baxter's hand against her back. His touch warmed her insides, but she still wasn't ready to give up the booty yet. She didn't know how she was going to resist later, but she'd cross that bridge when she got to it. As for playfully touching his dick, she wouldn't do that again. He had read her the riot act afterwards. He said, "If I can't touch, you can't touch. Either you want us to abstain or you don't."

Carla was forced to admit that he was right. Still, she had to stifle a laugh at his lecture. Perhaps, the next time she touched him intimately, she'd deliver.

As they made their way to the reception area, Carla's eyes lit up. Mimi and Frank stood at the bar. Carla squealed in delight and hugged Mimi. "Wow, you look awesome," Carla said.

Mimi wore a cream-colored gown and gold sandals. She was a knockout and lucky that her drug binges hadn't taken a noticeable effect on her looks yet. Mimi appeared as animated as Carla was about attending the ball. "Look at you, chica. You look so hot."

Baxter and Frank stepped aside to talk. Carla nodded and smiled at Frank. He was dashing in a black tux with a gold vest.

The reception area was starting to fill up. Various appetizers of caviar, artichoke hearts, and stuffed mushrooms were delicately arranged on buffet tables.

"Can you believe this?" Mimi squealed. "I feel like royalty."

"You look like royalty. How's everything going?"

Mimi shrugged. "You know me. Everyday's a struggle."

"You have to leave that club, Mimi."

"And do what?"

"Are you kidding? You're so great with that social media stuff. You could work in a PR firm or start your own. Set up your own website. Work as a consultant. Maybe even sing?"

"I'm getting too old to sing."

"You're only twenty-eight."

"That's old for singing."

"Only if you buy into that. Or you could teach singing. There are so many things you can do."

"You sound like Frank. First, he was okay with me working at the TiTi. Now he wants me to leave." Mimi hesitated. "Gutter Joe comes in a lot now. I try to steer clear of him, but he gets the best drugs," she confessed.

"I hate that mother fucker," Carla said vehemently. "Don't let him get to you. Don't lose everything you have with Frank. He's crazy about you."

"I know, and I care for him too, but . . . ."

"What?"

"I still got that wanderlust in me."

"I don't know what to say, Mimi. You're treading very dangerous waters. You always have. Get away from the club and that fuckin' Gutter Joe before it's too late."

Earl and his date approached the table. Carla's and Mimi's mouths dropped open. Mr. Hip-Hop looked like the perfect gentleman in a blue and black tuxedo. His date was lovely and in her early twenties, around Earl's age. She seemed mild-mannered and reserved, yet comfortable in her surroundings. Her royal blue gown with its halter neckline fit snugly over her slim frame.

Earl grinned at Carla and Mimi. "Stop staring. Y'all didn't know I could dress up like this, did you?"

Baxter and Frank joined them. "Don't nobody want you, man, except this young lady," Baxter teased. Everybody laughed. Earl's date seemed to enjoy the good-natured banter.

Percy was the last one of Baxter's crew to arrive. Percy's date was tall and full-bodied, somewhere in her forties. She was a confident, brown-skinned beauty with reddish hair. Her ample curves poured into her dress. She wore a green glitter strapless gown that almost came across as tawdry. But her carriage and stature made the gown acceptable. Carla wanted to like this woman. She carried herself strongly the way Carla had done at the TiTi.

Percy himself looked handsome in a black and gray tux. Even though he had a gorgeous date, his eyes immediately pounced on Carla's curves. She ignored Percy and extended her hand to his date, but the big-boned goddess gave Carla a rather cool reception.

Percy introduced her as Theodora.

"Do not call me Dora. Call me Teddy," she said.

Carla smiled. In no way did this woman look like a "Teddy." For that matter, the name, Theodora, didn't suit her either. Carla decided that she could forget about enjoying any kind of friendship with Percy's date. The woman considered Carla too much of a rival, and Percy wasn't helping matters with his roaming eyes.

"Show some respect," Carla hissed at Percy when his date was out of earshot.

Percy appeared clueless. "What?"

"Nothing." Carla decided not to waste her time explaining.

Besides, Baxter was back at her side. The way Baxter greeted Percy's date, Carla knew they had met before. She wondered when and where. She fought off a wave of jealousy. She was sure Baxter and somebody he used to date had hung out with Percy and Teddy before. Teddy gave Carla a smug look, but Carla refused the bait. Baxter certainly had a life before her, she reasoned, and so did she.

After the cocktail reception, an emcee picked up the microphone and urged everyone to take their seats. Carla and Baxter sat at a head table along with Percy and his date. Earl and Frank sat nearby with other guests. At the main table sat the director of Fire Safety and Community Security. This was a new liaison department, Baxter explained to Carla. He hoped the department succeeded because he got along very well with the director, a Black female. He did not interact well, however, with her deputy.

Baxter had pointed out the deputy director to Carla. He also sat at the main table. Carla noted that Baxter and the deputy locked eyes for a moment. But then, Baxter turned his attention back to the emcee. Carla was glad. She was in high spirits and didn't want anything to spoil her mood, even though Mimi had somewhat spoiled it already. Carla wished she could somehow get Mimi out of the TiTi.

Carla appraised her surroundings and smiled. True, she

sometimes missed the TiTi and all the attention she had received. But she didn't miss the disgusting sleazeballs who wanted to grope her and propose all kinds of lewd acts. She hoped that was all behind her. Her new life and this charity ball suited her much better. She leaned in closer to Baxter. He squeezed her hand.

"You okay?" he asked.

"I'm having a ball," she answered.

The food was being served. Carla and Baxter ate a salmon dish with a French cream sauce, baby potatoes, and asparagus. Others at the table dined on filet mignon. The food was delicious, and the wine. She and Baxter drank an oaked California Chardonnay that she had read about when she managed the TiTi.

Baxter offered a toast at the table, and everyone joined in. "To powering forward in our own lives," he said. Everyone clinked glasses. They talked and laughed more freely after the toast. Carla wished the gaiety of the moment could last forever. She watched Mimi at the next table capturing attention like an ethereal goddess as she smiled and gestured to Frank and the tablemates closest to them. Earl was clearly enjoying himself, laughing with his date and their tablemates. Carla noticed Baxter smiling proudly at Earl. She guessed that Earl and his date barely passed the legal drinking age. In a club, they would have been asked for ID.

Now that Percy had stopped gawking at her, Carla noticed that Percy and his date seemed to be enjoying themselves as well. Besides Percy and Teddy, Carla had her choice of interesting tablemates. On her left sat a banking executive and his wife, who was a teacher. On Baxter's right sat a public relations specialist and a male nurse. A young female firefighter was there with her date. And LA's entertainment industry was represented by an actor and a budding filmmaker. Carla was able to talk to all of them.

She had to give credit to the TiTi. The same social skills that she used there served her well anywhere. She felt comfortable in her surroundings. So did Baxter. Every now and then, his hand grazed her thigh, or his arm brushed up against her breast. Apparently, he had forgotten about their moratorium on touching. She refused to believe that all of his touches were innocent or accidental. She didn't mind though. Her loins warmed whenever he touched her. It was a good feeling. She still wasn't sure if she would sleep with him tonight. But for now, she would enjoy their stolen moments of foreplay.

Dinner and the evening program were brief. The program consisted of various speakers who showered accolades on one another. Other speakers praised the merits of each charity that would benefit from the ball. Baxter spoke briefly and introduced the organizers of PowerForward, the social justice program he favored for youth.

After the speakers, a jazz fusion band and two female vocalists provided entertainment. Carla was still learning to appreciate jazz. But when one of the vocalists sang a Gloria Lynne song, "I Wish You Love," Carla sat up straight and listened. The woman sounded almost as good as Lynne. The song reminded Carla of her parents who liked to slow dance to the song. Then both vocalists brought the house down when they did a rocking rendition of "Get Your Kicks on Route 66." The song had never held much appeal to Carla until she heard this band's performance. She learned a whole new appreciation of the song when they finished.

Before anyone had a chance to become restless, the program moved on to dancing, mingling, and strolling along the marina. Carla wanted to do it all. Baxter was introducing her to so many people. Fortunately, she was good at remembering names, another skill she credited to the TiTi. Finally, Baxter ran smack into the deputy director of the new liaison department.

The deputy director was a big Italian guy with dark hair, bushy eyebrows, and olive skin. His eyes narrowed at Baxter. "You know we still get to review your budget. We can't recommend those fancy computers you requested. And definitely not that new turnout gear with cooling tubes in the jackets. That technology is too expensive."

Baxter's eyes flashed. "That technology saves firefighter lives. You should know that. It's a reasonable budget."

The deputy refused to be swayed. "And don't go running to mama behind my back."

Baxter went toe-to-toe with the deputy. "You're the one who runs to mama. Then you try to take credit for my recommendations."

Carla's eyes widened in surprise at their overt hostility.

The deputy noted Carla's concern. He switched gears. "Carla Hepburn, right?"

Diplomatically, Carla extended her hand to tone down the hostility between him and Baxter. "Yes, I am. So we get to meet—up close and personal."

"That's a lovely dress," the deputy remarked. "You've been the talk of the evening."

"Only good things, I hope," Carla said.

"Well, I certainly wouldn't tell anybody how I know you."

Carla frowned. She felt Baxter tense at her side. Carla maintained her cool. "We've met before? I don't remember your face."

"From—gotta make sure I pronounce it right—the TiTi Bar."

Carla racked her brain. She didn't remember seeing him at the TiTi. Damn, the world was small. Would she ever be able to put the TiTi behind her? She was trying so hard. She didn't want to embarrass Baxter either. She could handle disdainful comments because they generally came from hypocrites. She had developed a tough skin, especially considering the vulgar remarks she had endured almost every night at the TiTi. But Baxter was a different story. He was taken aback for a moment by the deputy's comment.

"You sure you don't have me mixed up with somebody else?" Carla asked the deputy.

"Oh, it's you." His eyes raked over her. "You're not someone I'd forget."

Carla suddenly felt like one of those defensive basketball players. She stealthily planted all of her weight against Baxter so that he would have to exert quite a bit of energy to move her. It both halted and amazed him for a moment.

"Whatever you think you know about me, you don't," Carla said with finality.

"Rose," the deputy said, calling Baxter by his surname. "I don't think you want the word spread around that one of our finest fire captains is dealing with a stripper." He emphasized the word 'finest' derisively. "Is that part of your budget?"

This time, Carla couldn't hold him back. Baxter stepped right in the deputy's face.

Carla pushed her hand between them to intervene. Baxter stared at her incredulously. "Step back, Carla."

"No worries," Carla said smoothly. "I'm sure if the deputy here wants to spread the word about how he knows me from the TiTi, he's going to be asked why he spends so much time there. Is the TiTi in your budget, deputy?"

Baxter lightened up and smiled reluctantly at Carla. "Good point. He would have some explaining to do."

The deputy had no choice but to lighten up as well. "Carry on, Rose," he said and walked away.

"You too," Baxter called after him, pleased to have the upper hand.

Carla heaved a sigh of relief. "Whew!"

"Good thinking, baby, but don't ever do that again. You should never step between two people—"

"I know, but I had to do something. Please don't let that nut case get to you. He's not worth it. You've got a lot at stake."

"Can't live by fear."

"Yeah, but you don't want to lose your job because of somebody like him."

"Let me tell you, if I go down, he goes down. He's always meddling in my station, trying to get policies changed and things removed from our budget. I've had to battle him ever since he took that job."

"How well do you get along with the director?"

"Who, mama?" All of a sudden, Baxter smiled warmly. His eyes went to somebody behind Carla. "We get along fine."

Carla turned around to face a beautiful woman in her forties. She looked even better up close than she had seated at her table. She was hip, shapely, and dressed in a ball gown that hugged her shape, but in a classy way. Even though the gown was high-necked, showing no cleavage, the director was still a stunner.

"We do click," the director said and smiled at Baxter.

"This is our Director of Fire Safety and Community Security, the new department I was telling you about," Baxter said, making introductions.

"See, that's why he didn't introduce us earlier," the director laughed. "I'm the new kid on the block, and he had to go schmooze with other officials first."

Baxter laughed and shook his head in denial.

"How are you and my deputy doing?" the director asked.

"Fine," Baxter lied.

"Glad to hear it," the director said. She and Carla talked pleasantly for a few moments, then she excused herself to mingle with other guests.

Carla watched her walk away, feeling a twinge of jealousy. *How well did Baxter and this woman get along?* Carla wondered. She turned to Baxter and raised an eyebrow. "You told her you and the deputy get along fine?"

Baxter shrugged. "What am I going to say? I hate his stupid guts."

"No. I guess not." Carla cleared her throat. "So how well do you communicate with her?" Carla wanted to know if Baxter and this woman had some kind of ongoing affair.

Baxter dispelled her fears. "The director's beautiful, but she's lesbian. Not too many people know about it. She doesn't advertise it. She faces enough battles every day—incredible sexism in a predominately male field. Racism—she's a black female. Now add gay. That's why she and I connect so well. I've had one battle after another being a Black fire captain, and I'm a man. Can you imagine what she faces?"

Carla understood immediately. Still, she was glad the director preferred women over men in the sex department. "How did you find out she was gay?" Carla asked, relieved. The guilty look on Baxter's face was enough answer for Carla. She frowned.

"I didn't know you then," Baxter defended himself.

Carla decided to let him off the hook.

"Come on, let's get out there and dance," Baxter suggested. His hand brushed up against her breast.

Carla figured it wasn't an accident.

"Oops. I forgot," he said.

CHAPTER 21

Carla and Baxter danced to an eclectic mix of music. They were always among the first on the dance floor. Carla's head was spinning just as much as her body from the thrill of it all. The DJ, a wiry young Asian man, looked like a high school kid, but played a diverse mix of sounds. His playlist included pop, R&B, salsa, and hip-hop. He even played some Afro Funké music that got everybody on the dance floor with its pulsating Ghanaian and Ethiopian beats.

Carla enjoyed hanging out with Baxter. He was a good dancer and danced to anything. She laughed in delight when the music seamlessly shifted into Offenbach's "Barcarolle" from *The Tales of Hoffman*. Baxter swirled her around on the dance floor as they performed their own version of a waltz. He had to remind her a few times to let him lead.

At one time, Carla hated opera music, but one day, when she and Mimi had been stoned on some good marijuana, Mimi played a CD, advertised as the greatest opera album ever. Carla found herself enjoying a number of songs on the CD and even went out and bought it. She especially remembered the "Barcarolle" because of its beauty. As she waltzed in Baxter's arms, Carla loved the way her dress flared at the bottom. But had she known in advance that she would glide to the "Barcarolle," she would have found a flowing ball gown from a designer thrift shop.

Still, her yellow gown turned heads. She and Baxter were amused at the reactions of some of the upper-crust attendees who couldn't hide their surprise as she and Baxter whirled around to the music. As if dancing with the stars, she and

Baxter maintained good form and posture. They tried to coax Earl and his date onto the dance floor, but Earl was adamant that opera was not his kind of music. He was having no parts of it. Carla detected that Earl's date might have considered joining in, but she would have had to cajole somebody other than Earl or waltz by herself.

Mimi and Frank were holding their own on the dance floor. They swirled closer to Carla and Baxter.

Mimi laughed. "See, chica. Glad I turned you on to Offenbach?"

She and Mimi exchanged a quick high-five and immediately resumed dancing. Baxter and Frank laughed. Mimi seemed more relaxed than earlier in the evening, and she still appeared sober. Carla hoped Mimi's mood would continue.

Baxter was in a touchy-feely mood on the dance floor. Carla could feel the heat from him as they danced. Or was it her heat bouncing off him? Whatever it was, her body reacted. A warmth spread between her legs. She wondered if Baxter felt it. He must have, or he wouldn't have pressed his body so close. He wouldn't have allowed his thigh to mold against the softness between her legs. Her breath quickened. Then the dance was over, and Baxter pulled away from her totally in control. She hated to let him go. She felt bare without his hard body pressing against hers. He smiled teasingly. Carla forced her breathing back to normal.

Mimi and Frank stood beside them. Upon close inspection, Carla realized that Mimi was under the influence of something, but Carla didn't want to speculate. She pulled Mimi aside. Baxter and Frank headed in different directions across the ballroom.

"You okay, Mimi?"

"Relax. I'm fine. Hey, aren't you glad I turned you on to opera that time we got stoned?"

"You're still stoned."

Mimi's eyes narrowed defiantly.

Carla sighed and conceded. "Yes, Mimi. I'm glad you introduced me to opera."

The deputy director walked past. His eyes were steely as he tried to avoid Carla and Mimi.

"Prick," Mimi said. "Frank says nobody likes him. You remember him from the TiTi, right?"

"No. He tried to scare me, said he knew me. But I don't remember him."

Mimi lowered her voice. "That's because he hangs out in that private room."

"Ah, he's the guy with the baseball cap. Wendell lets him break the dress code."

"Yep. That dancer at the front table does him on a regular basis."

Carla's eyes twinkled with amusement. "Wait until I tell Baxter."

Mimi giggled. "I already told Frank."

"We owe you, Mimi. Thanks. Here, I got something for you." Carla pulled out a card from her clutch bag. "This is one of the women who sat at our table. She's in PR. You should talk to her. Let's go find her."

"I already talked to her. I don't want to talk to her anymore. I know I'm high. I don't want to fuck things up."

Carla was glad that Mimi didn't want to screw anything up. "Well, I've got her card whenever you're ready," Carla said. "I think Percy's date is involved in PR too."

"Right now, I'm ready to let my hair down. I been a good girl all night."

"Yes, you have. But—"

"Don't," Mimi warned. "Let's go find our men."

Baxter conversed with Earl at one of the bars in the ballroom. They stared out the window at the marina outside. Baxter felt relaxed as he observed the beauty of the shoreline. City and harbor lights illuminated the water. Sleek sailboats and yachts added their own sparkle to the marina. Baxter was enjoying himself, content to be with his crew. Frank stood nearby with Percy and Teddy who were ordering drinks. Earl's date was conversing with one of the female firefighters. Carla and Mimi were still schmoozing with other guests as they made their way over to the bar.

Baxter turned back to Earl. "I'm proud of you, man. You handled yourself well tonight."

Earl chuckled. "I told you I know how to act."

"I know you do. You did good, really good."

Earl was basking in the kudos. Then in typical, youthful fashion, he could no longer contain himself. "Now can me and my date get the hell out of this place? We want to hang out and do our thing."

Baxter started laughing. "Go for it. You've earned it."

Before Earl took off, he and Baxter exchanged a fist bump and hug. "Captain, I appreciate everything you've been teaching me," Earl said.

Baxter smiled in acknowledgement. But before Earl could escape, he ran straight into the director. She smiled at Earl and his date. "I know you're not leaving yet."

Earl was busted. "No, ma'am," Earl said. "We were just heading your way."

"Fine," the director said. "I want to introduce you to a few people."

Baxter stifled a laugh as Earl and his date accompanied the director. Mimi had returned. She and Frank tried to relay their farewells too.

"We're outta here," Frank said, holding Mimi's hand.

"No, you're not," Baxter said. He was still struggling not to laugh. "She's waving you over."

Indeed, the director was signaling for Frank and Mimi to join her. Frank dutifully obliged. Earl gloated over the fact that he wasn't the only one forced to stay.

Carla had rejoined Baxter. She could see that Frank and Earl had been waylaid by the director. Carla smiled warily. "I hope Mimi can get out of here soon. Girlfriend is ripped. She needs to go home." Carla sighed. "Mimi's a pistol."

Baxter grinned. "Frank loves pistols, literally and figuratively."

They both laughed.

"I've got some news for you," Carla said.

Baxter was all ears.

"Your deputy director's been getting private lap dances from—you probably don't remember her—that dancer at the front table. He hides under a baseball hat."

Baxter nodded. "Frank's been trying to tell me, but we keep getting sidetracked. I remember that dancer."

"You do?" Carla stared at him curiously.

"Well . . .," Baxter stammered. "Who wouldn't?"

Carla let him squirm. She was surprised that Baxter remembered the dancer. *There was no accounting for taste,* she decided. Men loved that dancer at the front table. She was raunchy as hell and always on top of somebody's lap. She made it hard for the other dancers.

"Anyway, thought you'd want to know what the deputy's been up to," Carla said.

"Thanks. Good to know. But I don't want to use it against him unless I have to. I don't want to stoop to his level."

"Well, he obviously doesn't feel the same."

"Let's enjoy the night," Baxter said and guided her outside to the promenade. They strolled along the waterfront for a while. Then they stopped in front of a railing and looked out over the harbor and its glistening lights. Carla inhaled and smiled dreamily.

"Finally, just the two of us," Baxter said.

Carla relaxed and let go. The crowd had thinned out. Only gregarious hipsters and steadfast partygoers remained. Earl and his date had finally escaped. Percy and his date were flirting heavily with each other at a table inside.

Carla stood close to Baxter, their shoulders touching. "Your place or mine?" Baxter's tone was insistent.

Carla laughed. "Is that an ultimatum?"

Baxter eased up. "Just a question, baby."

"We'll see. Depends on how you treat me?"

"How I treat you? Didn't I show you a good time tonight?"

Carla had to admit that she had a fabulous time at the ball. She smiled at him. "You're a wonderful escort, Baxter."

He beamed. "I tried. So your house or mine?"

"Your pick."

Baxter's eyes lit up. "Really?"

Carla nodded teasingly, then out the corner of her eye, she saw Mimi hop up on one of the tables inside and start dancing. Baxter noticed her too. He swore as they returned to the ballroom.

The DJ was gone so Mimi danced to a pulsating R&B tune from a cell phone. A young man, flushed from alcohol and somewhat disheveled, jumped up on the table with her. Mimi was dancing her butt off and obviously high. Frank was doing damage control by trying to lure her off the table. But Mimi's young suitor would have none of it.

Baxter didn't crack a smile. Carla knew he was seconds away from walking over and demanding that Mimi get down off the table.

Frank beat him to it. With surprising agility, he hopped up between Mimi and her suitor. Carla couldn't hear what Frank said, but the young man jumped down off the table. If only Mimi would do the same, Carla thought. But Mimi was escalating to some of her strip club moves. The gyrations were becoming more pronounced. She seemed oblivious to where she was. Frank was trying not to lose his cool and create a scene. A few guys standing around were egging her on.

Carla crossed the room to where Mimi danced. She knew Baxter was right behind her.

Carla didn't care who was watching. "Get down from there, Mimi," she said in a firm voice.

"Get on up here, chica. I know you want to dance."

Carla remembered many nights at the TiTi when she had to force Mimi off the stage and home so no one would take advantage of her.

"Hand her to me, Frank," Carla said confidently.

Frank appeared relieved. Before Mimi could make more of a spectacle of herself, he grabbed her and lifted her off the table into Carla's arms.

"Get your act together, Mimi," Carla hissed.

Mimi laughed hazily. "I was—before you and Frank snatched me down."

"We need to take you home," Carla said. She turned to Frank. "Give me a second."

Baxter watched, grim-faced. Carla walked over to him. "I've got to take her home."

"Frank can do that," he said, unyielding.

"I need to talk with her."

"Talking won't stop her. She's gotta stop on her own."

"I have to do something, Baxter. I can't let her continue. She's getting worse. I know Gutter Joe is behind this. He's trying to destroy her so he can get to me—and you," Carla finally admitted. "I can't walk away from her. I need to find out what's going on in her head. Girl talk."

Carla knew Frank was listening, but he didn't say anything. He anchored Mimi in place so that she appeared steadier. He seemed grateful for Carla's intervention.

Baxter sighed in resignation. Carla leaned into him and smiled apologetically. She pressed her body against his and gave him a lusty kiss. "I know you're not a happy camper right now."

"You got that right," Baxter agreed. "I'm ready to fire the camp counselor."

Carla smiled, half-teasing. "Don't do that."

"Make sure Carla gets home okay," Baxter addressed Frank.

"I will."

Baxter stared intently at Frank. "We'll talk later."

Frank nodded, but stood firm beside Mimi. Baxter tried to suppress his irritation as he watched them all walk away.

Percy came over and patted his buddy on the back. "This is Frank's MO. Why are you so surprised?"

"I'm not," Baxter answered. "But they messed up my night."

"Come on. Let's have a nightcap."

Baxter decided that he might as well. A drink might be the most fun he'd have for the rest of the night. Over drinks, he and Percy talked and bantered for a while until Percy's date came back to claim him.

"You ready to go?" Teddy said with gift bags in hand for her and Percy. "These are nice," she said to Baxter.

"Thanks," he said. "There's more if you want them."

Teddy shook her head and smiled. "These are enough."

Percy finished his drink. "I am ready to go, madam."

"You want to shoot some hoops in the morning? I'm ready to kick your ass," Baxter said.

Percy grinned. "In your dreams, sucker." Percy grabbed Teddy's hand. She smiled girlishly. "Nah, man, I'm not going to be able to make it in the morning. I got better things to do," he ribbed Baxter.

"Have a good evening. Don't worry about me," Baxter said.

"We won't," Percy laughed and took off with his date.

Baxter was angry with the world. He couldn't believe he was standing alone at the bar with no Carla. Not even the beautiful lights along the marina brightened his mood. He stared at the extra gift bags in front of him that he couldn't seem to give away.

"All alone, Captain?" The deputy director stood at the other end of the bar. "Where's your girlfriend?" he taunted. Then he noticed the extra gift bags in front of Baxter. "You get to keep all of those? I never got one."

Baxter slid a bag down the bar to the deputy. He wanted to hurl it. "Here. This one's especially for you, the VIP bag."

The deputy glared for a moment, then said, "My wife didn't get one either. She's in the restroom."

Baxter slid another bag down the bar more gently. "For your wife. I think some of the bags are different."

"Thanks," the deputy muttered grudgingly. He opened the first bag. In a flash, he confronted Baxter, eyes blazing. "You trying to be funny, Rose?" He held up a unisex baseball cap with a moderate amount of bling.

Baxter frowned. "Don't wear it then. Give it to your wife."

The deputy became even more incensed. "You trying to blackmail me?"

Baxter was totally baffled and ready to slug him. Then Baxter recalled Carla talking about the baseball cap the deputy wore with the dancer. Baxter burst out laughing. "We gave out caps because of our sports program for kids."

The deputy's wife returned. She was a tall, leggy brunette. She looked Baxter up and down scornfully. Baxter knew she was undoubtedly under the negative influence of her husband.

Baxter was still smiling about the baseball cap. "Your husband and I were discussing gift bags," he said in amusement.

The deputy's eyes smoldered. "I'll see what I can do about your budget. I guess it is reasonable—at least, the computers are. But those fancy cooling jackets, that's a hefty price tag."

Baxter could not believe his good fortune. Because of a fluke, the deputy was negotiating with him. Seizing the opportunity, Baxter refused to budge on the jackets. His stance became rigid.

"I'll make sure I recommend everything in your budget," the deputy said finally. "I'll call you first thing next week."

"Thanks," Baxter said, both flummoxed and amused at the turn of events.

The deputy's wife looked at them suspiciously. Then her eyes lit up in reluctant admiration of Baxter's handsome features. He recognized the look.

"Nice jacket," she said.

Baxter smiled. "I won't keep you from your husband any longer," he said.

The deputy touched his wife's elbow. "Let's go."

Baxter now considered the night a success. The deputy would recommend his budget all because of a baseball cap. Baxter intended to thank the gift bag committee profusely.

He wanted to thank Carla too. He loved hanging out with her, enjoyed her company immensely—even without the booty. But he was getting tired of so many elements of the TiTi invading their lives. Maybe, he needed to quit while he was ahead. He was going to have a long talk with Frank too. He loved Frank and tolerated his love of wild women. But Mimi was becoming more than Frank could handle. And there would always be the shadow of Gutter Joe. He was slime incarnate.

CHAPTER 22

Carla was glad she worked at the fitness center. It was the perfect place to exercise and lift her spirits. She could let out all her frustrations on the equipment. She and Baxter couldn't seem to find a rhythm in their relationship. He was backing off from seeing her again. He said he was tired of Mimi's behavior, and he almost wanted to kill Gutter Joe. Carla had done her best to calm him down about Joe. "Let the arson investigation do him in," she had insisted. "He's not worth ruining your life." She had diffused Baxter's anger at the time.

When Carla told him she couldn't abandon Mimi, Baxter claimed he understood, yet she hadn't seen him for weeks now. She missed him and yearned for his company. Now that she was ready to give up the booty, he had pulled back from her. She even had dreams about screwing him. A couple of times, she was so disappointed when she awakened to find that his hardness inside her was all a dream.

Carla shook her head sadly. Who was she kidding? Maybe, Baxter wasn't the one for her. She wished she could run into him at work, but after that first day he visited, he seldom came to the fitness center. Carla knew his walking in that day was not a coincidence. He admitted that he learned about her new workplace from Mimi and Frank.

In some ways, Carla was relieved that Baxter exercised at his fire station rather than the center. Their relationship was so new, and so was her job. She needed no distractions. Baxter would always be a distraction until she no longer felt butterflies in her stomach whenever she saw him.

She was getting tired of this back and forth with him. Maybe their relationship was doomed, and she needed to face it. They had such a good time together, but something always interfered. Carla wasn't a very religious person, but she certainly believed in a higher power. She closed her eyes and prayed for some sign that her knight in fireman's armor was indeed the one for her. She refused to continue like this—the longing, the aching. She prayed for some immediate sign that Baxter was the right one.

Carla opened her eyes and waited. She laughed at herself for expecting some sudden revelation. She looked up to see Oscar watching her. He was definitely not the sign she wanted. Oscar was one of the personal trainers on staff. He was a handsome man around Baxter's age, but he was always sniffing around. He was a hound by any definition, and he let Carla know every chance he got that he was always available for her. He was sneaky with his advances, and he never let Jasmine, the manager, catch him. Jasmine didn't play when it came to sexual harassment. She'd initiate dismissal proceedings immediately if she found anyone on her staff harassing other staff or patrons. Carla figured Jasmine must have been harassed herself to battle it so openly.

Carla enjoyed working under Jasmine. She was beautiful, smart, and very self-assured for her thirty years. Jasmine wasn't a hater. At first, Carla wasn't sure how their work relationship would progress, especially since Jasmine was young enough to be her daughter. But Jasmine proved to be a very fair, competent manager. She allowed Carla to advance quickly. Besides Carla's basic duties at the front desk, Jasmine was allowing her to sign up new members at the center. Carla was still in the training phase, but Jasmine appreciated her skill in recruiting new members.

Jasmine suddenly flew out of her office, agitated.

"What's up?" Carla asked.

Jasmine lowered her voice, not wanting everyone around the front desk to hear. "My boyfriend always does this to me. We make plans, and he comes up with something else. He won a trip to Cabo San Lucas this weekend—in a poker game. Can

you believe it? Now I've got to rearrange everything to go with
him."

"How awful," Carla teased. "You don't have to go."

"Yeah, right," Jasmine said. She stopped. "What are you
doing this weekend?"

Carla sighed. "Besides working—probably nothing."

"Oh, good. I've got a cabin in the mountains, a timeshare. I
have to use it this weekend, but I can't go now. You think you
and your boyfriend might want to go? I'll arrange it so you can
switch weekends with somebody."

Carla perked up. "I'd love to. Let me check with him. Even
if he can't, I'll get somebody to go with me," she said in case
she had to save face.

As soon as Jasmine retreated to her office, Carla pulled out
her cell phone to send Baxter a text. She was a little nervous.
What if he turned her down? Was he really her boyfriend? She
truly wanted things to work out between them. Well, she could
always take her nieces if Baxter didn't want to go. Carla took
a deep breath and sent him a text.

CARLA: Hi, Baxter. Wanna get away this weekend? I got us
a cabin in the mountains.

Her stomach fluttered as she hit "send." This might be the
true test of whether or not they had a relationship. Carla
looked down at her cell phone. No response. She tried to busy
herself at the front counter. She refreshed her computer
screen, then checked in a group of clients. Still no word from
Baxter. Carla was starting to fidget. Regina, the young smart
ass who had tried to stop Carla from getting hired, stood at the
counter too. She observed Carla suspiciously.

"What's up? You make a mistake or something," Regina
smirked.

Carla tried to sound lighthearted. "Everything's fine."
Baxter, please text me back, she thought. *Don't embarrass me
in front of Regina.*

Right on cue, he responded.

BAXTER: Do we have to babysit Mimi and Frank?

CARLA: Nope. Just us.

BAXTER: Great! Say when and where.

That was all the sign she needed. Carla looked up towards the heavens and gave thanks. She turned to Regina, beaming. "Everything's great. Thanks for asking."

Regina's face fell in disappointment at Carla's sudden elation.

"Hope things are good for you too," Carla continued. She really meant it. She was on top of the world and wanted everyone to be happy, even Regina.

CHAPTER 23

Carla floated on cloud nine. She was giddy with excitement. They were almost near the cabin in Big Bear Lake, California, in the San Bernardino Mountains. It was about a three-hour drive northeast of Los Angeles along a myriad of highways, starting with the 10 East. Baxter pushed his Honda hybrid fast, but less maniacally than usual. She hoped she was exerting some influence on him. She enjoyed the ride. Baxter had brought a flash drive of great music with him. It contained from smooth jazz to hip-hop and a few country sounds. He even played some New Orleans jazz music that made her party in her seat. As they snaked through the mountains, Carla beheld a stunning view of tall pines trees surrounding a sparkling blue lake. The mountains around them were breathtaking, yet foreboding.

Carla enjoyed city driving herself. She was not a long-distance driver, but she loved being a passenger. She recalled the fun she had when she was a teenager, and her father took the family on various road trips. They drove to the beach and the mountains. They drove to South Carolina once to visit relatives in Cross Keys. While Carla sometimes missed her friends on these road trips, she never wanted the drive to end. She could ride forever with her mother, father, and little Natalie, who was just a toddler then. It seemed that all the family's cares dissolved on their road trips.

After Carla graduated from high school, she stopped accompanying her family on road trips because her parents fought with her about dancing in the strip clubs. They didn't want Carla setting a bad example for Natalie. Her parents lectured over and over again that they had not raised her to be a stripper. Her mother argued that just because Carla had lost so much of her hair in high school was no reason to seek attention in strip clubs. Finally, Carla moved out into what she thought would be total freedom.

She partied, enjoyed plenty of sex, and got high. But the longer she danced in the clubs, the more she experienced verbal, physical, and psychological abuse at the hands of the patrons, owners, and bouncers. Because of her body and her manner of dressing, Carla was forced to take a number of self-defense courses. Every now and then, she tried leaving the clubs and working in an office, but her plans never materialized because of sexual harassment or boredom.

Well, she certainly wasn't bored now as she and Baxter pulled up in front of the cabin. They could relax and cuddle up the whole weekend and maybe do some hiking. Carla jumped out of the car and inhaled the clean, fresh mountain air. The cabin itself looked ruggedly impressive on the outside. It was rustic dark wood with a deck, railing, and high stairs. A few deer scampered off among the trees as Baxter got out of the car. She and Baxter both smiled and watched the deer scurry off.

Baxter opened the car trunk and started unloading bags of groceries. They had stopped at an upscale grocery store on the way to the cabin. He had told her to get what she wanted, and he'd pay for it. In the grocery store, he had trusted her judgment. Now he frowned. "Why'd you buy all this stuff?" he asked.

"So we'd have something to eat," Carla answered patiently. She hoped this cabin retreat was a good idea. The man of her dreams had been a little cranky ever since they started the trip. She was doing everything in her power to avoid arguing with him. She planned to make the best of their weekend.

The inside of the cabin was more modern than it looked on the outside. Carla and Baxter both roamed around and examined the rooms. The furniture was plush and stylish. There was a big, plump couch in the living room and striking prints of landscapes on the walls. The couch faced a big fireplace and a faux sheepskin rug. Carla couldn't wait to screw on the rug. Her panties heated up just thinking about it. She remembered the three bedrooms. She and Baxter could screw in each one of them too. She was ready to jump him now, but she had to take care of one thing first.

"Baxter, I need to study for a few hours," Carla said.

"Study? You started that course already?" Baxter asked, annoyed.

Carla nodded.

"Can't you study another time?"

"I've got to be certified if I want to advance on the job. I've never gone to college, yet I'm supposed to learn all this stuff in twelve weeks. The course covers kinesiology and physiology. I've got to keep up with the studying since I haven't been to school in so long."

"You should have told me that before, and maybe, we could have come up here another time."

"Oh no," Carla said. "I didn't want to give this up. It's okay. I'll find a way to squeeze in my studying."

Baxter was still fuming. Carla couldn't understand why he was being so irritable. He was usually good-natured. He hadn't even tried to sneak a feel of her legs or butt.

"Why are you acting like this?" Carla snapped.

"I've been up all night."

Baxter hated to appear short-tempered, but he felt tense and tired from fighting a fire the night before. What he thought would be an ordinary combustible fire, escalated because somebody had created a makeshift crystal meth lab in a vacant building on the west side. He and his crew ended up bringing in a HazMat team to help extinguish the fire. Not only did he direct his crew, but he worked side by side with them as well.

Carla was sorry she snapped at him. Her baby had been firefighting all night. He was entitled to be grumpy. They had started their trip later than planned because of the fire. She was extremely grateful to Baxter for his service. But he needed a nap, she decided, so she could get her studies done. Before he could resist, she grabbed his hand and led him over to one of the dining chairs.

"Not now. I don't feel like sitting down," he growled.

"For a minute," Carla persuaded him. "I'm going to give you a massage so you can relax?"

"Do you know how to give a massage?" he challenged.

"We'll see," Carla countered.

When he finally sat down, she began massaging his neck and shoulders. He was stubbornly defiant like a kid. "This is not going to work," he said.

"Give me a few more minutes," Carla coaxed. "If it doesn't work, I'll stop. But at least, give me a chance."

He gradually succumbed to her touch as Carla continued to knead the muscles in his neck and shoulders. She massaged softly at first, then increased the pressure. She didn't tell Baxter, but she was just learning how to do a massage. So she improvised and used a little of what she had learned already in combination with what she had experienced. She tried to mimic the motions she remembered from those quickie chair massages at the mall with her face down and buried in a cushion. She recalled surrendering completely a few times to the nimble fingers of a mall masseuse. She hadn't experienced many longer, regular massages because she could never seem to find the time.

"Ow," Baxter grumbled.

"You're tight in there, baby. I'm trying to loosen you up a bit."

Carla kept massaging away. She went deeper, then pulled back. Baxter's resistance waned. He relaxed under her fingers. She used her touch to calm him down. She loved touching his neck and shoulders. He was so buff. They were going to have a good time this weekend, she decided.

"You feeling better?" Carla asked in a soothing voice.

"A little." He refused to yield completely.

A lot, Carla thought. She could definitely feel the tension easing out of him. She kept massaging, enjoying the feel of him.

"How are you feeling now?" she asked.

Baxter didn't respond. Carla bent over him and realized that he had fallen asleep.

She smiled and massaged a bit more until she realized that he was nodding so hard that he might fall out of the chair.

It worked. Carla beamed triumphantly. Her baby could take a nap, and she could get her studies out of the way so they could enjoy the rest of the weekend.

Carla coaxed Baxter out of the chair. He was heavy, but she let him lean on her anyway. Finally, she got him in bed in the master bedroom. Somehow, she managed to tug his pants and work boots off and pull the covers over him. Before he totally succumbed to sleep, he managed to say, "I'm sorry if I was a little grumpy."

Carla kissed him gently. "It's okay."

Then he was knocked out.

"Yes!" Carla raised a victorious fist. She had everything she wanted—Baxter sound asleep in her bed and time to study while he slept. Then they could put all their cares aside and have a ball.

The next morning, Carla was up bright and early. She hummed to herself and looked out the kitchen window as she made breakfast. The sun streamed into the kitchen through the tall pine trees surrounding the cabin. The sky was crystal clear, and the birds were noisy, vying for nature's attention. The weather was perfect for cuddling. It was unseasonably cool even though it was early summer.

Carla wasn't a great cook, but she did know how to make breakfast. She had cooked some turkey bacon and was letting it drain on a paper towel. She turned down the fire on the grits, then popped open a bottle of extra dry champagne that was inexpensive, but left no headache. She used to order the same champagne for the TiTi from time to time and serve it as the house bubbly for the few patrons who ordered it. Ready to pour the champagne, she pulled out some orange juice and found a crystal pitcher that she could use to make mimosas. After mixing the mimosas, she pulled out some eggs, spinach, mushrooms, tomatoes—the works—to make omelets.

She could hear sleeping beauty rousing in the bedroom and bathroom. Finally, he entered the kitchen.

"Why didn't you wake me up last night, Carla?" he said accusingly.

She picked up the spatula for the eggs. "Brother, I will beat you down."

Baxter started laughing. "Okay, okay. But I thought you were going to wake me up."

"I tried at least three times," Carla said emphatically. "The fourth time, I gave up. I made sure you were breathing and left."

Baxter smiled smugly. Carla could almost see the wheels spinning in his head. Yes, she had tried everything in her power to wake him up. She had gotten all her studying done and was feeling extremely horny, but Baxter was knocked out. That last time she went to wake him, she felt guilty because he was sprawled out all over the bed, totally lost in sleep.

Carla realized right then that she was on her own for Friday night. So she simply enjoyed the cabin and explored every room. She sat out on the deck for a while in the crisp night air. Then she came back inside, read, and watched television. The experience was so new to her. When she worked at the TiTi, she had never known much of a life outside the club. And she had never met a man she cared for the way she cared for Baxter. She had thoroughly enjoyed her Friday night even though he was asleep in the bedroom.

Baxter's eyes lit up as he looked around the kitchen. On the island countertop, Carla had set out tableware for breakfast. She had bought fancy disposable plates and cutlery along with paper napkins that complimented the colors in the plates. An enchanting bouquet of multicolored roses sat on the countertop as well. The faux arrangement rivaled many real bunches he had seen. Baxter was truly humbled and impressed by Carla's efforts. She had set a magnificent breakfast table. The smell of grits and bacon made his mouth water.

"Wow!" he said admiringly. Then he became contrite. "I'm sorry if I was a little crabby yesterday."

Carla smiled in understanding. "It's okay. I know you were tired."

Baxter strolled over and stood close to her. She could feel the heat from his body. He leaned over and gave her a chaste kiss on the forehead. "Let me finish washing up. I'll be right back," he said and headed for the bathroom.

Carla felt cheated. Was he playing games with her? She thought he would have given her a lustier kiss than that.

As Carla and Baxter ate breakfast in the high countertop chairs, their shoulders rubbed together in intimate camaraderie. Baxter was playing quite the gentleman, Carla decided. Too much the gentleman. Well, if he wanted to play cat and mouse, she'd be happy to oblige. Sooner or later, she knew they'd be tumbling all over the sheets. She felt hot between the thighs at the thought.

"You get your studying done?" Baxter asked.

"Yes, I did," Carla said with a self-satisfied smile.

"All of it."

"As much as I intend to do this weekend. I don't know if I'll ever be able to finish all of it or even keep up. I'm trying, Baxter, but this course is kicking my ass. I've got to know the BMI formula. I'm supposed to know target heart rate formulas. I'm supposed to know all the bones in the body. I've got to know the agonist muscles, antagonist muscles."

Baxter stared at her in amazement, impressed and proud.

Carla continued. "I'm supposed to know the difference between fast glycolytic muscle fibers and slow oxidative. I can barely pronounce half the shit."

Baxter winced for a moment.

"You got a problem with me cursing?"

"Well . . . ."

"Get over it, Baxter. Sometimes I curse. I worked at the TiTi. You curse, don't you?"

"Alright, alright. You made your point," Baxter acknowledged. "Wow. I didn't know you had to study all that for your certification. I remember some of that stuff from my courses years ago. You know all the pulse monitoring sites?"

"That's easy," Carla said. "The temporal, carotids, radial, and . . . ." She couldn't remember the last one.

"Brachial," Baxter finished for her.

Carla rolled her eyes at him. "Showoff."

He laughed. "No, baby. It's my job. But I feel for you. Hats off to you."

"I had no idea I had to learn all this stuff to become a fitness trainer. Can I be honest with you?"

Baxter nodded and waited.

"It would be so much easier to go back to work at the TiTi. I was the manager. I know how to do that."

"You gave me a great massage. You got a knack for this fitness work," he said encouragingly.

Carla laughed at the reference to the massage. Yes, she put Baxter to sleep with that massage so she could study, but she was still horny.

"Thanks for the motivation," she said finally. "But there's so much to learn in this course. I'm the oldest in the class."

Baxter shrugged. "So."

"Suppose I do all this studying and don't pass the test?"

"Suppose you do?" Baxter responded.

"I hate to say this, but sometimes, I'm a few seconds away from going back to my old life," she said with a snap of her fingers.

Baxter was firm. "It's your choice if you want to go back to the TiTi—if that's what makes you happy. But our thing is over if you do. I told you, I'm not Frank. I can't deal with that shit, the way men talk about you, the way they look at you."

"I was the manager, and it's still a decent living."

"Then go for it. Disappoint me and Mimi and your niece— little Brittany. That's her name, right?"

"Don't do that, Baxter."

"A lot of people are rooting for you, Carla."

They ate the rest of their meal in brooding quiet. When they finished, Baxter offered to help clean up, but Carla declined his offer. Baxter definitely didn't argue with her.

He plopped down on the couch. "I'm going to watch the basketball playoffs. You want to watch with me?"

"Later. I need to take a walk. Clear my head."

Baxter nodded in understanding.

Carla went back to the bedroom and later returned in a red plaid shirt with one edge fashionably tucked into her jeans. The jeans were not as snug as she usually wore them. She wore tan hiking boots. Baxter realized that she had gone all out for this trip. He was both touched and amused.

Carla bristled at his amusement until he spoke. "You are by far the loveliest lumberjack I have ever seen."

Carla couldn't help but smile at the compliment. It was a special moment between them. "Thanks," she said and slipped on a light jacket. She headed for the door.

"Don't go far. I need to be able to see you when I come to the window."

"You're fucking kidding, right?" Carla said.

Baxter's face was firm. "No, I'm not. Watch the language."

"I'm a grown woman."

"I still don't want you walking too far by yourself. I'm pretty sure it's safe up here, but just in case, I need to see you when I come over to the window. Humor me, will you?"

Carla fumed. In her younger years, she would have cursed him out from head to toe. She didn't care how fine he was. "You know, before this weekend is over, I'm going to kick your ass," she told him.

"Dream on, girl," Baxter responded.

Carla was forced to smile. "I'm still going to kick your ass," she said and left.

He laughed at the thought.

Carla walked laps along a pathway in front of the cabin. She threw rocks into the stream that ran alongside the cabin. She looked up and saw Baxter watching her from the window. He waved. She couldn't believe it. He was checking up on her as though she were a kid. A part of her was extremely flattered by his concern, but another part of her felt rebellious. He didn't want her to go back to the TiTi. He didn't want her to take a walk. She was not going to let him control her life.

Before long, Baxter came outside in his sweats and a jacket and joined her. He reached for her hand and held it as they walked.

"A commercial came on?" she asked.

He grinned.

They walked in companionable silence for a while. "Look, Carla," he said. "I'm not trying to tell you how to live your life."

"Yes, you are," she said.

He looked her in the eye. "I want you to be happy. But not at the TiTi."

Carla sighed. "I hear you. I don't want to go back. But sometimes, I feel a little overwhelmed by all the changes in my life."

"That makes sense. But I'm here. I'll help you in any way I can."

She kissed him on the lips. He was still dispensing chaste kisses.

"What do you want to do this evening?" Baxter asked.

"Dinner and dancing," Carla responded without missing a beat.

"Dinner and dancing?" Baxter's face fell. He wanted to relax and simply chill. Then he saw how excited she was. He rose to the occasion. "Where to? Is there someplace special up here you have in mind?"

"Yep."

He waited for her to elaborate.

Carla's eyes danced playfully. "Our cabin. We got a nice dinner and some wine. We can get dressed up and dance in the living room."

Baxter's face lit up. He liked the idea. They could dine in the cabin and dance a little. After that, he had big plans. He had no intentions of falling asleep early tonight. He kissed her lightly again. He knew she wondered why he wasn't rubbing his hands all over her the way he wanted. He was getting a kick out of teasing her. "Going back to the game," he said. "You want to join me?"

Carla nodded. She shivered a little. It was a beautiful crisp day, but chilly. Baxter put his arm around her to ward off the chill. Together, they walked back to the cabin.

CHAPTER 24

Carla dressed carefully in the master bedroom. She was trying to keep Baxter from seeing her. She wanted them to meet in the living room all dressed up for their night of dinner and dancing. She had coaxed him into one of the other bedrooms so that he could finish watching the game and she could prepare for their party. She was excited and wanted to surprise him.

She wore a hot black mini dress that sizzled. The dress had a high neckline, but it was sheer from the collarbone to just above her nipples. The back was sheer all the way down to her butt. She wore her red satin slingbacks with the sexy heel, but a heel she could dance in. She planned to have a good time tonight.

In the living room, Baxter strolled into an assault on his senses. He was already dressed for the party. He surveyed the kitchen island. The vibrant multicolored roses still graced the countertop. All of the foods were set out on the island in colorful thermal dishes. He lifted some of the lids and sniffed the aroma of Indian curry dishes, with chicken and salmon. The array of food also included samosas, creamed spinach, rice, naan, and chutney. There was baklava for dessert.

Baxter turned his attention to the dining room and marveled at the red roses on the table that looked genuine. He realized that Carla had removed them from the kitchen island arrangement and transferred them to the table. In lieu of a tablecloth, she had crisscrossed two colorful strips of African fabric and anchored them with the vase of faux roses. Candles added a soft, flickering ambience to both the dining room and the living room. A bottle of red wine, ready for opening, graced the table. For the place settings, she had used more of the fancy paper plates and napkins from earlier. The wine goblets, placemats, and flatware were all set artfully and meticulously. Baxter was bowled over.

Carla put the finishing touches on her makeup. She wondered if she should add a bit more lipstick even though she would soon be eating it off and Baxter would later be kissing it off. She decided to add more lipstick anyway. Instead of one of her curly afro wigs, she decided to be more of a vamp and wear a soft black straight wig that hung down to her shoulders. She finished dressing and headed for the party.

Carla entered the living room to total silence. She looked around, quite pleased with her handiwork, but where was Baxter? She checked the bedroom where he was supposed to dress. She checked the other rooms. She looked out the window and didn't see his car. The cabin seemed so empty without him. She opened the front door and stepped outside into the cool evening air. She called out, but there was no response. She lingered for a moment, then went back inside.

Carla knew there had to be a reasonable explanation. Where could he have gone? Why would he leave in the first place? She tried to ignore thoughts of Gutter Joe harming him. But she couldn't. She prayed that Baxter was safe.

Carla looked out the window, dread starting to engulf her. Was her exquisite weekend going to be destroyed? She shook off her fear and rearranged the warming dishes on the countertop. Then she heard the doorbell ring. She flew to the door. She almost fainted in relief.

Baxter stood grinning with a colorful gift bag in his hand. His car was back. "May I come in?" he said.

Carla pulled him inside and hugged him frantically. "You scared me."

He held her and calmed her. "Sorry. Didn't mean to scare you. But I couldn't come to the party empty-handed. You set up everything so nicely. I had to bring you something." He held out the bag to her.

Carla opened it and pushed aside the delicate tissue paper

to reveal a beautiful Black rag doll in a bright yellow dress. The doll possessed a beautiful face and a saucy spirit. Her chin-length curly hair resembled sisterlocks. Carla gasped in delight. She loved the doll.

"I found a gift shop not far from here," Baxter said. "I didn't know what to get you. Then I saw the doll. Her dress reminds me of you at the ball."

Carla felt a sudden rush. Her insides were starting to tingle both from gratitude for the doll and relief over Baxter's safety. Seductively, she leaned into Baxter, but he held her at arm's length in admiration.

Carla looked like a dream come true, Baxter thought. Her dress was hot, so hot that he was glad his pants had room in the crotch area. He realized that he was going to be hard all night. He was thrilled. He couldn't remember the last time he felt like this.

Carla delighted in the play of emotions on his face. He looked so handsome. He had taken some time with his appearance as well. He wore tapered gray pants with a slight sheen. His satiny black T-shirt gently defined the length of his torso, a perfect shirt for dancing and caressing. She was glad that she had worn at least a thong so she could enjoy the meal without messing up her dress should any secretions escape.

"Wow!" was all Baxter could say as he stared at her and their surroundings.

"I can't cook like my mother, but I can set the table," Carla said. She hung the doll over the mantelpiece and stepped back in appreciation.

Baxter gestured all around him. "Thank you, baby. This is awesome. That's why I had to run out and get you something." He kissed her.

Another chaste kiss, Carla noted. So Baxter still wanted to play games. *Let the games begin,* she thought.

With a gleaming red manicure and lots of flourish, Carla began transferring food from the kitchen onto their plates. As she sashayed around the table, wiggling her hips, Baxter squelched the urge to stick his fingers up her dress and inside her canal. He wanted to slide his fingers in and out, then along her clit and make her moan. The way her ass moved, he figured she wore a thong. Later, he would push the thong aside and stick his fingers in and out until she was sloppy wet. But that was for later. For now, he would clamp down and pretend that Carla's wiggling her ass all around the table did not faze him.

Carla looked for signs of a tent pole forming in his pants, but she had to admit, he was playing cool, calm, and collected. She brushed her butt up against him as she finished filling up their plates. He smiled pleasantly, but seemed not the least bit affected. Carla wasn't used to this kind of response from him. She was almost ready to plop down in his lap and let him slide in and out of her as much as he wanted to. She imagined his kisses all over her breasts. She felt her breath quicken. She put the serving dish down and stepped away from him.

Baxter was so glad when she went back to her corner of the table. He'd have to go easy on the wine for now. He needed a clear head to help him get through dinner and a few dances without hiking her dress up and sliding his hardness inside her.

Throughout dinner, they smiled and shared small talk. By candlelight, Carla looked even more ravishing to Baxter. Some of her lipstick had come off, giving her a softer look. Her breasts were almost spilling out of the sheer top of her dress. He found it amazing that her nipples didn't show. He imagined her shapely legs under the table in her red high-heeled sandals. He should have feasted his eyes on her legs more. The sexy sheen of her red pedicure only heightened his desire. He was tempted to crawl under the table and kiss her legs all the way up to her soft spot. Then he would lightly and teasingly lick her clit. He shook his head to clear it and forced his thoughts elsewhere. He hoped he could make it to the dancing. The swelling in his slacks was more rigid now.

Carla heard his breath catch in his throat. She smiled smugly. She guessed the effect she was having on him. So he wasn't immune to her charms after all. She wanted to crawl under the table to see the tent pole stiffening in his pants. She wanted to cup the pole in her palm and warm it. Then she wanted to unzip his pants, pull his dick out, then kiss and lick it all over until he pushed her away so he wouldn't come.

Neither of them ate much dinner since other appetites were more pressing. When they finished eating, Carla cleared the table. Baxter made a feeble offer to help, but Carla laughed him away. This was fine with Baxter. He wanted to check out the fireplace and queue the music up for their dance party. Excitedly, he hooked up his iPod to the sound dock system in the cabin. He was having a good time with Carla. He needed this.

Carla quickly rinsed the serving dishes, then stacked them in the dishwasher. She put the remainder of the wine on the island countertop. She refilled their wine glasses and offered one to Baxter. He took a sip, then put it down. He pulled her out on the dance floor. He had moved the coffee table out of the way to give them more room for dancing. He had also pushed the sheepskin rug away so they could dance freely on the hardwood floors of the cabin. The fireplace awaited them for later.

First up on Baxter's queue was "Candy Rain" by Soul For Real. Carla sprang into action when the song came on. "Wow, I remember this. I love this song," she said. It was a nice mellow dance song with plenty of soul. A blast from the past, it was a classic. They both danced freestyle to the music. It was a good choice to get their party started.

Then the music tempo increased. Carla and Baxter were really jamming now. They were both good dancers who loved to dance, although Carla had the upper edge. Even though it was cool outside, Baxter opened the window since things were steaming up. They rocked all over the living room dance floor with total abandon.

Then Frankie Beverly's song, "Before I Let Go," pulsated from the speakers. Baxter let go like nothing Carla had ever seen before. He danced his butt off. Carla could do nothing with him. They had danced to the song before, but Carla never remembered him dancing like this. He cut her up on the dance floor. Carla was slightly miffed since she was supposed to be the dancer. While she held her own against him, he loved the song so much that his dancing was superb. He was a big guy who moved with ease. He could almost shake and gyrate as well as she could. Carla decided that she would take him down a peg or two when the time came.

When the song was over, Baxter smiled humbly. "That's my jam," he said and tried to downplay his talent.

Carla simply tolerated his smile. She did not want to be patronized. Though it was all in fun, she'd get him back.

They continued to party, enjoying the time of their lives. Baxter had uncorked a second bottle of wine. They danced to more tunes with Baxter holding his own against Carla's liquid moves. She had to admit that Baxter was a worthy partner. They brushed up against each other and engaged in a little dirty dancing every now and then. But for the most part, they danced apart with free-flowing moves and gyrations that could have landed them in dance music videos. Carla lunged very low a few times and marveled that Baxter was right there with her.

"You got some great music," she told Baxter. He grinned proudly and kept right on dancing. Then a clear recording of "Tighten Up" by Archie Bell and the Drells pulsed through the iPod.

"Oh, shit!" Carla exclaimed. "My parents used to dance on that song."

"My mom too," Baxter announced, laughing.

Baxter rocked to the tune, but Carla was in her world on this one. The beat was difficult for the latest dances so Carla improvised a mix of the old and the new. She borrowed steps from her parents and blew Baxter off the dance floor. He tried to keep up with her, but she was moving so wild and fast that for a moment, he stopped dancing and watched. Carla kept moving. She didn't waste a moment of the song. She dipped, shimmied, and bounced with total abandon. Baxter tried again to match some of her moves, but Carla was all over the place. She smiled at him when she realized that she was a few steps away from wiping him off the dance floor.

"That's *my* jam," she said when the tune ended.

Baxter chuckled. "Touché."

The next tune up was "The Men All Pause" by Klymaxx.

Carla and Baxter both rollicked on the dance floor. Carla strutted and posed to the song as Baxter made the requisite "woofing" sounds. They gyrated and dipped. Baxter's shirt was becoming slightly damp. Then a funky mix of hip-hop tunes played. Carla moved in closer to Baxter. She stood a breath away from him, then turned and twerked. Baxter started laughing, but he still held back. She turned around to face him again with very little space between them. He touched her waist lightly and moved with her, but when she edged closer, he pulled back. Carla smiled and enjoyed the thrill of the chase. She rubbed her breasts against his chest. Baxter still struggled to maintain his wits.

The tempo of the music slowed to "Not a Bad Thing" by Justin Timberlake. Carla's heart flipped when Baxter started singing to her. He had a great voice, a rich, distinctive baritone. She couldn't believe how well he sang and that he was singing to her. His voice reminded her of the late Paul Williams of the Temptations. She was now more enamored with Baxter than ever. She was trapped between love and lust for him.

Then "Between the Sheets" by The Isley Brothers played. Baxter suddenly twirled her into him. Carla laughed, ecstatic. Though he pulled her close, he still teased and held her loosely. She could feel the steam rising between them. Every time she tried to move in closer to him, he held her at bay. Carla simply wanted to lean against him and feel his hard body.

"Stop teasing." Her voice was hoarse.

Baxter finally pulled her tight against him. He was hard and throbbing. "Is this what you want?" he said.

"Yes," she moaned compliantly.

He lifted her a little higher so that he planted himself right against the mound between her legs. Carla reveled in the feel of him. He started kissing her neck then down to her breasts. His kisses seared through her dress. Carla wrapped her arms around his neck and pushed deeper against him. She never wanted to let go. He released her slightly. Carla whimpered in protest until he did what he wanted to do the whole night. He rubbed his hands all over her butt, then slid his fingers under her dress. He pulled her thong aside and slipped his finger inside. He pushed his finger in and out until she was soaking wet. He resisted the urge to slide his dick in right then and there.

Carla's legs trembled. Baxter held her close as they danced to another slow tune. Carla thought her legs would buckle she was so hot. But Baxter held her upright. He edged her closer to the sheepskin rug and pulled it away from the corner. They stood on top of the rug, still dancing. Carla slipped her shoes off, and Baxter went under her dress again. He slid his finger in and out and massaged her clit. He rubbed his finger back and forth over the tumescent bud. Carla totally let go. It felt so good. They sank to the rug.

Baxter lifted her dress and pulled her panties down. He gave her a deep kiss on the lips. He twirled his tongue around hers. He lay on top of her as she writhed and moaned beneath him. He kissed her breasts again and fondled them through the delicate transparency of her dress. He intended to touch every part of her. He turned her over and caressed her back. His fingers trailed from her neck to her hips. He rubbed her butt and slipped his finger inside her from the back. He found her clit and stroked it soothingly.

Carla was like putty in his hands. He turned her over and kissed all the way up from her red pedicured toenails to the tops of her thighs. Then he kissed the juicy, throbbing swell between her legs. He licked very lightly at first, making Carla writhe in pleasure. Then he licked more insistently as he put his finger back inside. Carla could only moan and cry out. She was completely at his mercy as he massaged every fiber between her legs.

Before she went over the edge, she pulled his head away and up to her lips. She kissed him, enjoying her taste on his mouth. She reached down and stroked his rock hardness. She inched down until the hard outline of his organ was a whisper away from her lips. She kissed it through his pants. She felt it throb even harder. It scorched through his slacks. She still continued to kiss and stroke. Baxter was moaning now. Carla buried her face in his crotch, then slowly unzipped his pants. She released the pole that begged greedily for her touch. She blew on it, kissed it, then placed it in her mouth. She slid her lips softly up and down his shaft until it was bone hard.

Baxter moaned loudly now. He pulled her up against him and rubbed his hardness against her softness. He rolled her over on her back and pulled her dress up higher above her waist. Carla helped him slide his pants down. They never managed to get his shirt off nor her dress. When Baxter pushed inside her, they both moaned passionately. He lay still for a moment to force his body under control. Then slowly, he began to move. The feeling was exquisite for both of them. Carla arched her body up to meet his. He stroked in and out as Carla coated him with wetness. He pushed deeper, and Carla opened her legs wider to envelop him.

They lay stroking, sliding, and gliding until Baxter was sloppy wet from her juices. He gave her one last thrust that made them both cry out in escape. Carla came all over him, and he spilled himself inside her.

When their heartbeats normalized, they pulled apart. Carla laughed weakly and kissed him. Baxter kissed her back.

"You still want to do platonic?" he grinned.

"Oh, no," she purred. "I want to do it again."

"Give me a minute," he said.

He shut the window and lit a fire with one of the logs in the fireplace. After he closed the fire screen, he returned to Carla. He was hard again. They took off all their clothes and made love. Carla was ravenous with him, drawing him deeper and deeper inside her. Baxter was more than happy to accommodate her. She mounted him. Over and over, she slid up and down his engorged hardness. The slurping sounds of their bodies further fueled their lust. Their moans and groans only intensified their feelings.

As the fireplace crackled, Carla and Baxter were consumed by their own flames. She opened up wide to him, and he filled her insides completely. Their bodies slapped against each other, further igniting their passion. In total abandon, they stroked and rode each other until they both cried out into the night.

* * *

Carla shifted herself on top of Baxter. She kissed him affectionately. "Enjoying your weekend?" she asked.

"Most definitely," he said as she snuggled against him.

Carla felt giddy and drained. She relaxed in his arms. "Where'd you learn to dance like that?"

"Vincent Conrad," he said without hesitation. "Good ole Vincent."

"Who's he?"

"Vincent was like a stepfather to me for a while. He was one of my mother's first boyfriends. My mom got pregnant with me when she was nineteen. My father acted like a jerk and split. Eventually, my mom met Vincent. He was cool and loved to party. He could get down on any song."

Carla rolled off Baxter and lay beside him. She smiled and played with the rich, tight curls of his hair.

"Vincent told me I had to learn how to dance if I wanted to impress the girls," Baxter chuckled. "So I learned how to dance. Fortunately, I had the rhythm."

"What happened to him? "You still keep in touch?"

Baxter shrugged. "He got somebody pregnant. I think he kind of broke my mom's heart. She dated a lot after Vincent, even got married in her forties, but she didn't love that guy the way she did Vincent. She's divorced now and a confirmed bachelorette."

"You never kept in touch with him?"

"He taught me how to play basketball. I mean, we did a lot of things together. He fit in perfectly with me and my mom, but when he got some girl pregnant, that was the end of the relationship for my mom. I tried to keep in touch with him, but he married the woman he got pregnant. She didn't want me around. Vincent never stood up for me. So I moved on the way my mom did."

Carla kissed him in support, but Baxter pulled away slightly. "I'm okay. That's life. I learned a lot from Vincent. He taught me about being a man, even though he didn't act like one around his wife."

"How long was he in your life?"

"From the time I was around five to twelve."

Carla kissed Baxter's forehead. She couldn't resist coddling him. "That was a long time."

They were both quiet for a while, engrossed in their thoughts.

Carla broke the silence. "What made you so strong?"

Baxter smiled warmly at her and kissed her cheek. "Thanks, baby. Well, I got a lot of help from my teachers, coaches, guidance counselors." He chuckled. "My mom was a pretty good dad. She didn't take no shit from me. She enrolled my ass in every sports team you could think of and the church choir too."

"That's where you learned to sing?"

"Yeah, had no choice."

"She's a strong woman."

Baxter nodded. "Yep. She's a good woman."

Carla wondered when she would get to meet his mother. *In time,* she told herself. She snuggled against him and rose higher. She nestled his head against her breast. He resisted at first to show his independence and that he needed no nurturance.

"Lie still," Carla told him. She couldn't believe it when he stopped resisting. She smiled to herself.

As they cuddled together, the flames from the fireplace flickered and danced, engulfing them in a warm coziness. The light from candles softened the ambience as well. Carla didn't want the night to end. She intended to resist sleep for as long as she could. She wanted to savor the feel of Baxter lying against her breast. He had left the blinds open slightly in the living room so that slivers of moonlight slipped through and further enhanced the mellow, seductive glow in the room. Carla would always remember the beauty of this night.

Between her legs, the longing emerged again. As if he could feel her heat, Baxter lifted himself off her breast and moved up beside her. He was hard again and poked her thigh. Then he fit himself snugly between her legs and rested against her clit. He was hot and slippery now. Carla relished the feel of him. He tried to glide inside her, but Carla kept him anchored against the swelling bud between her legs. She slid all over his firmness. He was becoming more insistent now as he tried to enter her.

"Stop fucking with me," he murmured against her mouth. His lips and breath were hot.

Carla whispered huskily. "You really want me to stop fucking with you?"

"No, baby," he said and pushed his pulsating hardness inside her. "You can fuck with me all night."

"Like this?" she asked, swallowing him up inside her.

"Any way you want," he said. "Just don't stop."

"I won't," Carla said and rolled over on top of him. She rode up and down his shaft with slow, steady movements. She caressed her breasts and popped one in his mouth, then the other. She slid up and down his thickness faster when Baxter grabbed her butt to guide her juicy ride. Carla bent over and kissed him. She plunged her tongue into his mouth and rode to unbridled ecstasy with Baxter's greedy hands all over her breasts and butt. Then he flipped her over and rode to ecstasy himself.

CHAPTER 25

The next morning was Baxter's turn to cook. He had already prepared most of the food when Carla entered the kitchen. Dressed in soft, clingy loungewear, she glowed with hardly any makeup on. Baxter smiled.

Carla smiled back. She felt like a "freshly fucked fox," an expression her mother's friend used back in the day, whenever the woman had a good night with her boyfriend. Carla and her friends were usually sent outside to play whenever the woman came to visit and spout her hilarious, X-rated comments.

"Feels good in here," Carla said. Baxter had lit the fireplace in the living room, and the kitchen was warm from his cooking.

Carla pulled out one of the high chairs from the kitchen island. She stopped suddenly and doubled over in laughter. Baxter turned around in surprise, then realized why she laughed. He had on a soft white T-shirt and black pajama bottoms. The back of the pants was totally sheer. Carla could see his butt through the fabric. "Where did you get those pants?" she laughed.

He smiled. "My tribute to Prince. I found them online. Thought you'd get a kick out of them."

"I certainly do," she said. She climbed down from the chair and felt his ass through the sheer fabric. "Nice."

He moved away from the stove. Carla lifted her heels up and pressed against the hardening bulge in his pants. Then she reached into his pants and stroked him lightly. She heard his intake of breath.

"Alright," he warned. "If you want breakfast . . . ." His voice was becoming hoarser.

In one swift motion, Carla bent down and pulled his manhood out. She kissed it and gave it a tight squeeze. Then she walked away and went back to her chair.

"Carry on," she said.

He grinned. "I owe you one."

Carla observed that the tent pole was rock hard at attention. She delighted in the knowledge that she had totally distracted him. She had destroyed his rhythm in the kitchen, and he was trying to get it back.

Baxter was torn between cooking breakfast and hauling her butt up on the kitchen counter and pushing inside her. Carla smiled at him in amusement.

"Do you want to eat or not?" he asked.

Carla laughed. "Yes, I do. I'm hungry."

Their eyes met over the double entendre.

Carla dipped her fingers into the fried potatoes that were sitting in a ceramic warming bowl on the island. "These are good. Uh . . .," she hesitated.

Baxter raised his brow.

"They're a bit oily."

Carla hopped up from the stool and grabbed a paper towel. She lined a new bowl with the towel and transferred the potatoes to drain the oil.

"Perfect," she said. "This is beautiful, baby."

He frowned.

"I'm looking out for us," Carla said lightly. "Don't you want to grow up to be big and strong?"

"I already am," he said with a smile.

Carla stopped teasing him and allowed him to finish cooking breakfast. She was impressed with the fare. He set out salmon cakes, grits, potatoes, and pancakes. He had also mixed a batch of mimosas. She felt ravenous, but she had to be honest with him. "We can eat like this today since we're just having fun. But that's quite a few starches, Baxter. Can we get something green in there next time?"

"Next time," he sighed resignedly.

She rose up and kissed him across the counter. "Not trying to tell you how to cook, but we both need to stay in shape."

"You're right, Miss Killjoy," Baxter said and started fixing her plate.

Carla laughed and poured mimosas.

They sat side by side, arms touching from time to time as they ate.

Carla devoured everything on her plate. "The food was good."

Baxter smiled at her validation of his cooking. "Glad you enjoyed it."

"Oh, I'm going to hate to go home."

"Me too. But we still have the rest of the day. You want to watch the game with me?"

"Sure. You keeping those pants on?"

Baxter grinned. "Just for you."

Carla felt a warmth in her loins as she thought about lounging around and watching the game with him. "You know what else I want to do?" she asked.

"What?"

She leaned over and whispered. "I want to fuck in every room in this cabin."

Her lips against his ear made his pulse quicken. He kissed her. "We can do that."

They watched the game together, then at half-time, they stroked, fondled, and caressed each other until the game resumed.

Eventually, Baxter forgot about the game and decided that it was time to give Carla her wish. On the sofa, he slid his fullness in and out of her a few times and gave her an extra stroke for good measure. Then they engaged in a marathon bout of wild abandon all throughout the cabin. Baxter carried her over to the kitchen countertop and glided in and out of her before proceeding to the next room.

They moved through the rest of the cabin with Baxter's fingers inside her, probing and stroking, then feather touching her soaking wet clit. She stroked his balls, licked his erection, then rode on top of it. She came several times throughout the house as Baxter hung in there and appeased her passion.

They ended up in the master bedroom. They had already exploited the guest bedrooms and the bathrooms. They stayed longer in some rooms than others, but the goal was to get at least a few good strokes in every room.

By the time they landed on the bed in the master suite, Baxter stroked her hungrily, fondled her nipples, and grabbed her hips. As he inserted himself deeper into her canal, Carla stuck her tongue in his mouth and caressed his butt. They were both sloppy wet and plunging into the abyss of release. Unable to hold back any longer, they both shouted and clung to each other as spasms rocked their bodies.

On Monday morning as they drove down the mountain back to the real world, they were both pensive. Though sated, they were a little tired and disappointed that their weekend retreat had ended. Baxter drove quietly, immersed in thought.

"What's up?" Carla asked.

He patted her leg. "I'm sorry the weekend is over. I had a nice time, Carla. This was one of the best weekends I've ever had. Thanks for inviting me."

Carla beamed. "You're welcome. I had a great time too."

Baxter sighed. "But now it's back to reality. Back to Mimi and Frank—and Gutter Joe."

Carla wrinkled her nose in distaste at the mention of Gutter Joe. Yet she knew they had to deal with the elephant in the room.

"You know he's trying to get to you and to me when he supplies Mimi with drugs," Baxter said. "That messes with Frank's head, and it definitely fucks with mine. We need to get Joe out of the way."

"What do you mean by that?" Carla asked warily.

"He needs to go."

"I'm not sure what you have in mind," Carla said, alarmed. "Joe's not worth it. You've got your career, Baxter. You don't want to lose everything that you've built because of him. He's a fucking punk."

"That's why he's gotta go. I don't plan to look over my shoulder for the rest of my life because I flattened him out. I might have to call on some of my law enforcement buddies."

"You don't think he's got cop friends? I'm so sorry I got you involved in this."

Baxter's face was grim. "That's why you need to stay away from that place."

Carla nodded. While Baxter's comments may have been a product of Monday morning blues, she realized that he had been thinking about Joe for a while.

"Let me talk to Mimi," Carla said. "See if I can help her."

"Good luck. She's got some serious issues."

"The arson investigation—how's that going?"

"It's going nowhere," Baxter said.

"I'll investigate myself."

Baxter smiled warily. "How are you going to do that?"

"I don't know, but I will." She reached over and caressingly touched his hair.

"I don't need you to protect me," he said.

Yes, you do, Carla thought. Joe was vermin. Baxter probably had no idea how low Joe could sink. "Please, Baxter, don't do anything that you'll regret for the rest of your life," she entreated. "Promise me."

Baxter's face was unyielding. "We'll see."

"Please don't do anything foolish."

"I don't plan to do anything foolish, only what's necessary."

Carla's stomach churned. She turned the radio on to the news station then turned it off. All the negative news stories didn't make her feel any better. She inserted Baxter's flash drive. It made them both feel better and uplifted their spirits. They rode the rest of the way home chatting lightly and listening to the music on his drive.

Once they arrived at Carla's apartment, Baxter helped carry her luggage inside. He was tempted to stay. He liked her place. She had a flair for decorating. Her condo was sunny and bright. Colorful posters and art decorated her walls. The floors were hardwood, covered with vibrant rugs. A tan, overstuffed couch invited him to sink into it and fall asleep since he still felt lazy from all their lovemaking over the weekend. He noticed an African fertility mask hanging on one of her walls. He remembered the mask from the Pan African Arts Festival they attended. He had offered to buy it for her, but she wanted to pay for it herself. The mask worked well in her living room.

He was forced to admit that he was becoming more enamored with her each day. He liked her spirit and independence. She wasn't a gold digger. Now if she would just keep away from the TiTi. He looked around again and resisted the urge to stay. They hadn't made love in her place yet because she had insisted on a platonic relationship. Well, the past weekend shattered that. He relished the thought of spending more time with her.

He gave her a lusty kiss goodbye. "I'll be back," he said in his Terminator voice.

Carla laughed and returned the kiss. They embraced for a while, both sensing each other's thoughts about all the wicked things they could do in her apartment. Then he finally released her.

"Thanks for rolling with a sister," Carla said.

"Thanks for letting a brother roll."

Carla smiled from ear to ear.

CHAPTER 26

Brittany and Tiffany ran around the patio in excitement. Natalie shot the girls a warning glance. Carla couldn't blame her nieces. They were having a good time, and so was she. She had told Baxter that she wanted to host a summer barbecue at his house. He liked the idea. They agreed on a small gathering. Almost everybody had arrived.

Baxter had invited his crew, and Carla had invited hers. She had extended an invitation to her sister and her nieces, and they had eagerly accepted. Natalie was thrilled that Carla had attracted a new man in her life and had graduated from the TiTi. Even Russell, Natalie's ex, had arrived. Russell's girlfriend was attending some other affair so he decided to join Natalie and his daughters for the day. Carla figured Russell was also curious about Baxter.

Carla enjoyed playing hostess at Baxter's house. Nestled in Baldwin Hills, the house was solid and roomy, with an earthy palette that included lots of tans and browns. The furnishings were a bit heavy for Carla's taste, but she liked the house. It simply needed a woman's touch. In time, she'd offer some suggestions.

Baxter's house presided over an impressive skyline and majestic hills. At night, city lights sparkled in the distance. Carla's nieces were awed by the view. Even Stephanie, the pre-teen, lost her cool and ran around the house with her little sisters.

Baxter sat at a long patio table, laughing and talking with his crew. Percy manned the barbecue grill. He had brought his date, Teddy, with him. Carla remembered her from the charity ball. She seemed to hold Percy's attention. Carla was grateful because it meant Percy ogled her less.

Once out on the patio, Carla's nieces were itching to jump into the pool.

"Go for it, girls," Natalie said, realizing that she couldn't contain their excitement any longer. Baxter had a big, beautiful pool that everybody could fit into.

Tiffany, the five-year-old, dove in first. "Yes! It's heated."

Brittany, the six-year-old, followed right behind her, then surfaced above water. "It is heated. We can stay in here all day."

Their older sister, Stephanie, held back. She sat beside Carla and Natalie on one of the lounge chairs.

"Get in, Stephanie," Natalie urged.

"I will, Mom," Stephanie said. But she made no move towards the pool, after running around Baxter's house with her sisters like a three-year-old. Now she played demure for the lifeguard, who was a handsome teenager and too old for Stephanie. Carla and Natalie smiled in amusement.

Baxter walked over to the pool area and poured on the charm. "The five beautiful Hepburn girls."

Brittany and Tiffany giggled. Even Stephanie momentarily forgot her infatuation with the lifeguard and grinned. Natalie succumbed to Baxter's charm almost as much as her daughters did.

"Everybody okay?" Baxter asked.

"Oh, yes," Tiffany said, playing in the water. Brittany was too busy swimming underwater to respond.

Baxter checked with the lifeguard. "You got everything covered?"

"Yes, sir," the lifeguard said.

Baxter focused his attention on Carla. "You okay?"

Carla stood up and brushed his lips lightly with a kiss. Though Baxter conducted himself honorably in front of the girls, she still tasted the hunger in his kiss. She tried not to melt.

"I'm fine," Carla said.

Baxter turned to Natalie. "Hop in."

"Oh, I will," Natalie smiled, still impressed by Baxter's charm.

Baxter turned to Stephanie, the pre-teen. Carla realized that something about Stephanie affected him. When he first met Stephanie, Carla saw a play of emotions on his face that she couldn't fathom. She was determined to ask him about it later.

"You're not jumping into the pool?" Baxter asked Stephanie.

"I am—in a minute."

Baxter looked from Stephanie to the lifeguard. "Uhm," he said in understanding. "He's too old."

Carla and Natalie tried to stifle their amusement. Stephanie rolled her eyes in embarrassment. Baxter tried to soften the blow. "Ten years from now, he won't be too old."

"That's right," Natalie agreed.

Baxter headed back to the patio table. "You ladies coming to join us?"

"We'll be over soon," Carla said.

When he was out of earshot, Natalie spoke. "Girlfriend, did you luck up."

Carla started giggling. "I know. I can't believe it." With Baxter, she enjoyed a different style of life. She had missed out on a number of things when she worked at the club. All she did was work, party, and fend off the lechers. She hoped that was all behind her.

The caterer Baxter hired for the occasion signaled to Carla. "Let me go see what she wants," Carla said.

Natalie rolled her eyes playfully. "Yes, go check on your staff."

At first, Carla was worried frantic about how she could host a summer barbecue, work at the fitness center, study for her certification, and do meal preparation for the party. Her mother would have pulled off the feat nicely, but Carla needed help. Fortunately, Baxter was accustomed to relaxing at his parties. He believed in hiring help. He told Carla to pick the caterer of her choice.

Mimi and Frank arrived just as Carla approached the caterer. Mimi stopped her in mid-stride. They hugged warmly, bouncing around like kids.

"You look good, chica," Mimi said.

"So do you."

Mimi was still beautiful, but the drugs were starting to diminish her looks. Carla realized that Mimi was doing heavier drugs. She intended to have a talk with Mimi later even though she knew Mimi would act hardheaded and resistant.

"Hi, Frank," Carla said.

Frank was starting to look a little haggard, trying to keep up with Mimi. He was still blond, buff, and handsome, but his kind eyes had lost some of their luster.

Frank hugged Carla, then headed over to Baxter and Percy. Natalie joined Carla and Mimi. Natalie's greeting to Mimi was a cool one. Natalie considered anyone working at the TiTi to be a negative influence.

Mimi dismissed Natalie's attitude and was as exuberant as ever. "Good to see you, Natalie. It's been a long time. You ready to apply at the TiTi yet?"

"Never," Natalie said drily.

"Never say never," Mimi said, unperturbed.

She ran over to the pool and stuck her toe in. "Wow. It's heated," she squealed in delight. Carla's nieces watched Mimi in fascination as though she were a reality star. "Ah, Stephanie, Brittany, and Tiffany," Mimi said and gave them a dazzling smile. She matched their names with their faces. They were impressed with the beautiful, ethereal goddess Mimi embodied. "I'll be joining you girls soon," Mimi promised. They watched her in wonder as she headed back to Carla and Natalie. Carla was still trying to work her way into the house to check with the caterer.

Then loud-mouthed Earl, the young rookie, arrived. He greeted everybody boisterously and waved to Carla's nieces. The girls watched him, too, fascinated by his liveliness.

Earl walked over to the patio table where Baxter introduced him to Russell, Natalie's ex. Earl looked around the patio. "Everybody's in couples," he said to Baxter.

"Everybody's not in couples," Baxter replied.

"Where are your sons?" Earl asked Percy.

"They had something else to do, man."

"You mean I'm stuck here with infants in the pool and a bunch of old fogies—not you, Teddy," Earl said. "I'm not staying long."

Baxter laughed. "Man, these old fogies will kick your ass."

Frank joined in. "Don't make me come over there and prove it."

Percy brandished the barbecue tongs. "We'll toss your ass in the pool."

Teddy laughed. She seemed quite at ease with their bantering.

"Nah. You the one need to jump in that pool and cool off," Earl said, laughing at Percy. "Look at you, sweating and everything." He turned to Baxter. "When you gonna learn how to grill?"

"I know how to grill."

"Yeah, but you always got Percy doing it. We ain't at work."

Everybody was laughing heartily at Earl.

"That manly man barbecue stuff is not for me," Baxter said with a shrug. "Since Percy likes to grill . . . ."

"Hey, there's an art to it," Percy said proudly.

"I'm sure the captain is glad you feel that way." Earl was still in high gear.

Then Jasmine, Carla's boss, arrived with her two young nephews. Carla ushered them into the patio. Immediately, the boys' eyes lit up at the pool.

Earl's eyes lit up at Jasmine. "Uh, oh," Earl said.

"I thought you were leaving," Baxter said.

"Nah, not yet. I'm just getting comfortable." Earl was still eyeing Jasmine.

Baxter decided to give Earl fair warning. "That's Carla's boss. She's got a boyfriend. I think she's engaged."

"Let her tell me," Earl grinned. "I got this." Earl stood up, on a mission.

The rest of the table cracked up.

Russell rose to his feet and strolled over to the pool to hang out with Natalie and his daughters.

"About time he went over and checked on 'em," Percy said.

Baxter shook his head in agreement. But the rest of the table was still focused on Earl, who made a beeline over to Carla and Jasmine.

Carla saw him coming. "What's up, Earl?" she asked warily.

"Who's this lovely young lady?" Earl turned his attention to Jasmine. "I was all set to leave until you walked in."

Carla had to hand it to him. He was hitting on Jasmine hard, but at least, he was upfront about it. Carla introduced them. "Jasmine, this is Earl, one of Baxter's cohorts."

They laughed.

"Cohorts, is it?" Earl asked.

"Roadies, homies," Carla expounded. "Earl is one of Baxter's crew."

Earl shook Jasmine's hand. He playfully addressed her nephews. "Who are these guys?"

Jasmine smiled. "My nephews. They wanted to hang out with me today."

Carla decided to give Earl a warning. "Jasmine's fiancé couldn't make it."

Earl reached for Jasmine's hand and raised it. A big, beautiful diamond sat on her engagement finger. "That's a sparkler, alright." Earl smiled, but seemed unaffected. He took his time releasing Jasmine's hand. Carla watched in amazement as there seemed to be some current flowing between Earl and Jasmine.

Carla attempted to shut the current off. "Let me show Jasmine around. Introduce her to everybody."

"Fine," Earl said. Then he addressed Jasmine. "I'll be here. I'm not going anywhere." He smiled at Jasmine's nephews. "I see the little guys are ready to hop in the pool."

"I'm not little," the oldest nephew said. "I'm five."

Earl laughed. "Right, man. You're old. You too," he said to the youngest one.

The youngest nodded. "Yep, I'm four."

Earl laughed hard now. "Alright, guys. I'll meet you in the pool later. See how bad you are."

Jasmine laughed and allowed Carla to usher her away.

* * *

Carla and Mimi lounged around the pool. Natalie and Russell talked nearby. Jasmine was getting her nephews ready for a swim. Baxter and the rest of the crew, along with Teddy, sat at the big patio table, laughing and clowning.

Carla observed it all. She was pleased with the way things turned out. Her nieces were in high spirits as they watched Natalie and Russell talking and laughing by the pool. Carla noted rays of hope in the eyes of her nieces, although Stephanie, the pre-teen, was still more concerned about the handsome, young lifeguard than anyone else.

Carla turned to Mimi. "What's up, girl?"

"Where's the liquor?"

Carla laughed. "Baxter doesn't want to put anything out until after everybody's finished swimming." She was glad Baxter made that decision. Mimi seemed to be sober for a change.

"I've been trying to give up the drugs and the liquor. But it's so hard," Mimi said.

Carla patted Mimi's arm. "You can't do it by yourself. You may need a program."

"I'm always gonna get high. Sometimes, I wish Frank would just let go and let me do my thing. I love him, but I'm no good for him. I just want to fly high."

"You been flying high for quite a while now. Time to give it a rest."

"I know, but . . . ." Mimi's eyes fixed on Carla's nieces in the pool. "I wish I was that age again—the little ones," she clarified. "Not Stephanie's age. By that time, I was on my own."

Carla stifled a shudder at the thought. She observed her nieces. She was so glad they lived a sheltered life. They were having a ball in the pool and enjoying innocent fun.

She noticed the lifeguard was beginning to pay more attention to Stephanie. Brittany and Tiffany noticed it too. They giggled.

Princess Tiffany smiled at the lifeguard. "How old are you?"

Brittany pointed to Stephanie. "She's eleven."

Stephanie was horrified.

"Damn, you're my little sister's age," the lifeguard sputtered.

Stephanie was definitely busted. Brittany and Tiffany laughed their heads off. Stephanie shot them furious glances. Carla and Mimi pretended not to notice, but they were definitely amused. Carla decided it was time to jump in the pool and rescue Stephanie from embarrassment. "Come on, Mimi. Let's dive in. This is better than rum and coke."

"Might as well," Mimi laughed.

They both removed their cover-ups and dove into the pool. Their playful enthusiasm was infectious.

Baxter jumped to his feet. He shook the patio table.

Earl laughed. "Aw, you act like you've never seen a woman in a swimsuit."

"Man, be quiet," Baxter said and headed over to the pool.

He wanted to play in the water with Carla in her peach-colored bathing suit, cut low in the front and back. It was stunning against her skin. Instead of a wig, she wore a wide colorful headband that wrapped around a ponytail piece.

Mimi's bathing suit was white with a plunging neckline. Frank jumped to his feet to join her.

Soon everybody started peeling off clothing and heading for the pool. Teddy thought she left Percy and Earl at the grill, but they trailed behind her, waiting for her to reveal her assets.

Male eyes feasted on the swimsuits. Natalie turned heads too. She was subtler with her curviness, but still filled out her suit in all the right places. Teddy was a big-boned woman who carried her voluptuousness like a badge of honor. Jasmine represented the well-toned body of a fitness expert. She joined her nephews who were already splashing in the pool.

Baxter jumped into the water. "Look at all these lovely women in my pool." He stopped Frank and Russell before they could enter. "It's time to go, guys. I got things covered." He signaled to Percy and Earl too. "Bye. Go home. All the men go home." Jasmine's nephews were staring, wide-eyed.

Baxter put them at ease. "Y'all can stay."

Frank and Russell laughed and dove in. Percy and Earl peeled off their clothes and joined everyone.

Carla was ecstatic. Everybody was in the pool. She swam over to Mimi. "You okay?"

Mimi nodded and started swimming the length of the pool, creating her own lane. She swam hard, trying to bury her demons in the water.

Everybody was having a good time. Even Stephanie was having fun in the water and overcoming her infatuation with the lifeguard. The kids laughed and played and splashed water on the adults, until Natalie and Russell started splashing back. Earl splashed the kids too. The lifeguard sprang to full alert. He was obviously enjoying himself, but he was watching everybody too.

Baxter checked with the lifeguard. "You got it?"

The lifeguard nodded his head in assurance. "Yes, sir."

Baxter floated over to Carla. "You look great, baby."

"A minute ago, you were ready to ditch me for all the women in the pool," she teased.

He pulled her close. "Never."

"Yeah, right."

Brittany and Tiffany swam beside them and giggled.

For the rest of the day, they were all in good spirits, swimming, eating, and lounging by the pool. Mimi's edginess mellowed after her laps. Earl sat beside Jasmine, admiring her bathing suit and the curvy form under it. Her nephews played in the water with Carla's nieces.

Earl noted that Jasmine was no longer wearing her diamond. "You took it off to swim?"

Jasmine nodded at her empty ring finger.

"That's a lot of responsibility," Earl remarked.

"You mean the ring?"

"I'm talking about the ring and the engagement. How do you feel about it?"

Jasmine appeared at a loss for words. "I'm happy. I really am," she said finally. "I love him."

"Good. Now tell me how you really feel."

Jasmine burst out laughing. "I do love him, but I'm scared shitless."

Earl laughed with her. "Alright, now you're talking. I hear you. I'd be scared too. I know I'm not ready."

Carla and Baxter heard the laughter. They were still in the pool with the kids.

Carla frowned. "She's engaged."

Baxter grinned. "They're adults. They're only talking."

Baxter glided her around in the water. Carla couldn't resist putting her arms around him. He looked good in his swim trunks.

"I've got big plans for you later," she said and rubbed against him.

"Can't wait," he responded. He was about to give her a hearty feel when he saw the kids snickering at them. "You see how your aunt is always pulling on me?" he grinned.

CHAPTER 27

So far, so good, Carla thought. Everybody seemed to enjoy the food. She served the traditional fare of barbecue ribs, chicken, hamburgers, and hot dogs that Percy had grilled. They also ate grilled salmon, shrimp, and vegetable kebobs, along with scrumptious baked beans, potato salad, and a hearty tossed salad. Carla had picked the caterer specifically because they boasted wholesome ingredients with low sugar and salt. Judging by the way everybody ate, Carla figured she made a good choice.

At the big patio table, Baxter and Earl huddled in a corner, talking in low, hushed tones. Earl's face was more solemn than usual.

"What's up?" Baxter asked.

Earl's diction and stance became more businesslike. "I hear Willy is coming back."

"Well, you knew that was a possibility."

"Yeah, but I like it at the station, Captain. I don't want to transfer."

Baxter's face was impassive. "Seniority ranks. That's how it works."

Earl tried to conceal his disappointment. "I know, and I respect that, but I work my ass off for you. I don't want to leave and go to another station."

"What do you expect me to do?"

"Tell me I don't have to transfer."

"You don't have to transfer."

Earl held his breath. "I don't?"

Baxter nodded, amused. "Willy is going back East to be closer to his parents."

A broad grin spread over Earl's face. "You mean it, Captain? I can stay?"

Baxter smiled proudly at Earl. "We'd love to have you. You're an asset to our station."

Earl jumped to his feet and hugged Baxter. "Wow! Thank you, cap. I don't know what to say."

"That's a first. I can't believe you don't have anything to say."

Earl suddenly whooped and hollered with glee. He raced over to the pool and jumped in with such force that water splashed everywhere. The kids were back in the pool. They laughed hilariously at Earl.

"I'm going to make you fill up my pool," Baxter shouted.

"I can stay!" Earl shouted. "I don't have to transfer."

Princess Tiffany gave Earl a doe-eyed look. She found him fascinating. Exhilarated, Earl played like a kid in the water. He splashed all the kids and ducked Jasmine's nephews. Tiffany was even more impressed with him.

"No goo-goo eyes over me," he teased Tiffany. "Hey, Russell. Tell your daughter she's too young. When she's twenty-one, she can look me up. No, not twenty-one." He turned to Tiffany. "At 12:01 a.m. on your twenty-second birthday, you can look me up if I'm still available."

Princess Tiffany wore a quizzical expression. Natalie and Russell and everybody around the pool started laughing. Earl continued to splash in the pool like a kid.

"You sure we want him at our station?" Percy joked with Baxter.

"Earl's just having fun. He's not too far removed from being a kid himself," Baxter said. "He's come a long way. I'm very proud of him."

Percy and Frank nodded their heads in agreement.

When Earl finished playing in the water, he told the lifeguard, "You can take a break, man. I got you covered."

"You certified?" the lifeguard asked in surprise.

"Yes, I am. The captain makes sure we're certified even though we're not in the Lifeguard Division. He makes us go to seminars on everything. I can fix a truck. I can do ballet. I can set bones. The only thing I can't do is open heart surgery—yet."

"Yet," Frank chimed in. "We'll probably do a seminar on that next year."

"Nah. Six months from now," Baxter responded.

"You know everybody calls you, Mr. S&M, right?" Earl ribbed.

Baxter laughed. "So I heard."

At the mention of "S&M," adult ears perked up around the pool.

Earl laughed. "Mr. Safety Man, y'all. That's why we call him Mr. S&M."

The women lounged around the pool with the kids. Baxter and the men sat at the patio table. The hard liquor was out now since most people had finished swimming. The guys had imbibed a drink or two and were feeling more expansive. They razzed Earl, and he definitely reciprocated. From time to time, he glanced over at Jasmine.

"You better let her alone," Baxter cautioned. "You know she's got a man."

"Take your butt over to the TiTi if you want a woman," Percy joked. "Do like your captain and Frank."

"Mind your business, man," Baxter laughed.

"Nope," Earl said. "You'll never catch me over there. I'm scared of those women." He turned to Russell. "You ever been to the TiTi."

Russell chuckled, but didn't say anything.

"Stay away from that club," Earl said. "You see how messed up the captain and Frank are. The captain's nose is so wide open, you can run a train through it. And don't even get me started about Frank."

Frank's laughter was good-natured and genuine. "You're not going to be satisfied until I come over there and put you under the table."

Baxter laughed. "I'll help you, Frank. We'll dig a real big hole under the table and stuff his ass in it."

Russell laughed with them. Then he leaned forward and looked directly at Earl. "You told my baby girl at 12:01 a.m. on her twenty-second birthday, she can look you up?" Earl braced himself. He didn't know what to expect. "Then you don't know Tiffany," Russell continued. "At 12:02 a.m., my baby will come looking for you."

Everybody at the table howled.

"Oh, shit," Earl said. "In that case, I better have my fun while I can." He headed over to Jasmine and her nephews.

Carla intercepted him. "Where you going, Earl?"

"Over to see your boss." Earl politely walked past Carla and sank down beside Jasmine.

Carla watched him, fuming. But Jasmine was all fluttery-eyed and smiling. Carla strode over to Baxter to recruit his help. Only Baxter and Percy relaxed at the table now. Everybody else had scattered.

Baxter saw her coming. He and Percy shook their heads and laughed. "Baby, what you doing?" Baxter said. "They grown folks."

Carla disagreed. "Talk to him, Baxter."

Baxter and Percy were still amused. "Why don't you talk to *her*?" Baxter replied. "I mean, she's the one who's engaged. He's single. Plus, she's older than he is. I don't see him twisting her arm."

Percy was still cracking up. Carla narrowed her eyes at both of them. Baxter's eyes still twinkled with laughter. "Come sit down on my lap, so we can discuss it."

Carla was really ticked with him now. "Sit on your lap? Are you serious?"

But Baxter and Percy were still clowning with her. Carla turned away in a huff, then headed straight back to Baxter and plopped down on his lap. "I'm here. Now what?"

Baxter was stunned. Percy got up from the table, laughing his head off.

"Uh . . .," Baxter stammered.

"Surprised you, didn't I?" Carla asked.

"Yeah," he chuckled. "But now that you're here, let's talk. Why you worried about them? Let them—"

"She's going to be married."

"She knows that."

"It's not right."

"Now, Miss TiTi. Don't go getting sanctimonious on me."

Carla sighed and eased up.

Baxter shifted them more comfortably. "Didn't you tell me how your boss looks out for you, how she lets you advance? You're a beautiful woman. I'm sure a lot of women give you a rough time. But Jasmine is secure enough not to do that. You want to blow it? You got a cool boss."

Baxter made perfect sense, Carla decided. *What was she getting so worked up about?*

"The only person you should be worried about is—" Baxter began.

"I know—me," Carla said.

"No," Baxter corrected her.

Carla looked puzzled.

"Me," he said. "I should be your only priority."

They both burst out laughing. Baxter was glad to see her lighten up.

"You having a good time?" he asked.

Carla nodded and hugged him.

"That's all that matters." He paused for a moment. "Would you do that to me if we were engaged?"

The question caught Carla totally off guard. "Of course not."

Baxter studied her expression. "You don't know for sure."

"Would you do that to me?" Carla countered.

"I don't think so," Baxter responded honestly.

"You don't think so?"

"I hope not."

They were both pensive for a moment. Carla decided not to force the issue. Baxter made some good points. She was crazy about him, but their relationship was still so new.

"Maybe, Jasmine is just scared," Baxter said.

Carla nodded in agreement. She decided right then and there to mind her own business. After all, she was no saint herself. But she didn't think she could ever cheat on Baxter if they were engaged.

To Carla's delight, hours later, everybody was still having a good time. It was early evening. Mimi was relatively sober although she had imbibed something, Carla determined.

Baxter had turned DJ now, and music poured from portable speakers hooked up to an iPod. Baxter started out slow and played "Let Me Make Love To You" by The O'Jays. He pulled Carla close, and everybody else followed suit—Mimi and Frank, Percy and Teddy. Earl jumped at the chance to pull Jasmine close. The kids grinned and snickered. They mocked the slow dancing until Natalie and Russell got up and danced on the classic love song. Carla's nieces suddenly appeared wide-eyed and hopeful. Stephanie dismissed her crush on the lifeguard and watched her parents.

Then the music tempo turned upbeat. A few hip-hop songs, sanitized versions, boomed from Baxter's speakers. Then "Blurred Lines" got everybody on the dance floor, including the kids. Carla, Baxter, and Mimi were in their milieu since they loved to dance. But everybody else held their own on different songs. Janet Jackson's "Control" had all the women rocking. The guys didn't stand a chance. But Kendrick Lamar's rap song, "I Love Myself" got all the men moving. Even Earl and Frank, who weren't the greatest dancers, rocked to that one.

Then "Wobble" pumped through the speakers. Everybody line danced behind Princess Tiffany. The princess led her entire court on the dance floor. She kept Earl right beside her. Even the lifeguard fled his post and joined in.

Next up was "Blow the Whistle." Carla and Mimi sprang into action. This was one of their TiTi songs. They tried to tone it down at first, but their exotic dance experience took over. All eyes couldn't help but lock on Carla and Mimi. Then six-year-old Brittany threw off all inhibitions and joined them. She matched them gyration for gyration and twerk for twerk. Brittany's moves acted like a shock of cold water on everybody. Carla and Mimi instinctively pulled back and reined in their dancing. Natalie eyed them smugly.

Everybody was a bit subdued now. Carla tried to laugh it off. "What am I going to do with you, Brittany?" She pulled her niece aside. "You can't dance like that. People get the wrong impression."

"You dance like that," Brittany said accusingly.

"I'm an adult. You're not. Besides, I don't do that anymore. I just got a little carried away today." Carla paused. "I don't want you dancing like that, Brittany. It's not good. It's not safe. Do you understand me? I'm not playing." Carla didn't care if Natalie heard or not, but apparently, Natalie was content to let Carla handle this one.

Baxter took over as host, trying to divert attention away from Carla and her niece. "There's still plenty of food, everybody. Y'all want dessert?" People started eating again and scattering about. Percy and Teddy forgot about everyone and continued to dance. Mimi was still focused on Carla and Brittany.

Russell came over to rescue his daughter. He handed Brittany his cell phone. "Take some pictures. Show your aunt how good you are with the camera."

Brittany refused to budge.

Carla's eyes lit up in surprise. "Come on, Brittany. I didn't know you take good pictures. Let's see some."

Brittany snatched the camera. "Okay. I'll show you. Smile," she instructed Carla and Russell. She snapped the picture without preamble. She aimed the camera at Jasmine's nephews and took their pictures. She snapped the lifeguard.

Carla raced over to Brittany and examined the pictures. Carla's face fell in dismay. They were awful. They were crooked. One was blurry.

Brittany read Carla's expression and smiled smugly.

Russell wasn't happy about the pictures either. "You can do better than that."

"Whenever you're ready, Brittany. I'd like to see some good pictures," Carla said.

"I'm better at dancing."

"You're a great dancer," Carla agreed. "But I don't want you dancing the way you did earlier."

Natalie observed with judgmental eyes. "Oh, hush up," Carla said before Natalie could comment. Carla patted Brittany's braids and walked away, allowing mother, daughter, and father time to sort things out.

Mimi rushed over to Carla and laughed conspiratorially. "Your niece could dance at the club."

Carla shook her head and frowned. "That's what I'm afraid of. That's why you need to get away from there," Carla insisted.

"She's not my niece," Mimi said defensively.

"You know what I'm saying."

Mimi sighed. "I don't know what else to do, and I like my independence. I can't live off Frank. I got some pride."

"Look at what the club life is doing to you. You're high right now."

"No lectures. I'm trying. I really am. I'm going out to the car, sober up for a minute."

Carla sighed. "Okay, Mimi."

Carla was relieved when Mimi came back to the patio, seemingly refreshed. But then she deteriorated rapidly right before Carla's eyes. Mimi began talking loud and staggering. The kids watched her with curiosity.

"What's the matter with her?" Tiffany asked.

"She's not feeling well." Carla tried to reassure the kids that everything was fine.

Frank steadied Mimi on her feet and started voicing his farewells. Carla's face expressed disappointment.

Mimi turned to Carla and apologized. "Sorry. He gets some good shit."

"Who?"

Mimi didn't say anything.

"That fucking Joe," Carla guessed. She lowered her voice. "He'll destroy you. What about Frank? Do you want to mess up everything with him?"

Carla's words no longer registered with Mimi. Frank stabilized her enough to walk out with as much dignity as she could muster.

Baxter didn't say anything, but Carla could easily guess

what he was thinking. Everybody else tried to regroup and continue the fun. But Mimi had been such a lively, vivacious presence that everyone missed her. The kids seemed a little sad.

Carla and Baxter kept the food and music flowing, but the party momentum dissipated. Then Russell received a text. He started expressing his farewells and easing towards the door.

Natalie snapped her fingers. "You're leaving just like that? As soon as she calls, you come running."

"Don't start," Russell warned. "She got back earlier than expected. Hey, I've been with the girls all day."

Surprisingly, Natalie didn't push the issue. "Whatever," she said. "Girls, come hug your father."

Though disappointed that he was leaving, Stephanie and Princess Tiffany hugged him warmly. Russell picked Tiffany up. "Damn, girl, you gettin' big."

Tiffany giggled and hugged him tighter.

"Can't pick you up, big girl," he told Stephanie. The pre-teen was fine with that. She kissed him on the cheek, but Russell bent over so she could hop on his back. She did and laughed uproariously as her father gave her a piggy back and pranced around the patio. Everybody laughed, but Natalie smirked as Russell tried to atone for his leave-taking.

Brittany refused to budge from her spot. She stood beside Baxter.

Russell tried to win her over. "Come give daddy a hug."

Brittany remained rigid and unyielding. She planted herself firmly beside Baxter and leaned against him. He gently tried to coax her forward, but Brittany wouldn't budge. Baxter felt as though he parried against rock solid Percy on the basketball court. He gave up on coaxing her any further.

"Oh, that's the way you want to act?" Russell asked.

Brittany maintained her stance. Russell waved goodbye to everyone and left anyway.

Brittany still leaned against Baxter. Instinctively, he picked her up. She put her head on his shoulder and cried. "Your daddy loves you," Baxter said. Carla smiled as she watched

Baxter comfort her niece. He turned to Stephanie and Tiffany. "You girls okay?"

They nodded, but their faces were more somber now that their dad was gone.

"You want to spend the night?" Baxter said. "I got some good scary movies."

The girls lit up. Tiffany started dancing around. Brittany lifted her head off his shoulder, so he put her down.

Baxter looked at Natalie.

"Not too scary," Natalie said finally.

"Yeah, not too scary," Stephanie echoed.

"And you?" he grinned at Carla.

"I don't do scary movies at all."

"I'll protect you," he said.

Carla simply raised an eyebrow.

"Guess I'll be leaving," Natalie said. She started gathering her bags and sifting through the girls' bags. "I think they got enough underwear and stuff."

"Don't worry about it," Carla said. "We'll come up with something."

"I might have some things they can wear," Baxter offered.

Carla looked at him suspiciously.

He grinned and shrugged.

Carla realized she had a few questions for Baxter. While she was glad her nieces were spending the night, she had wanted to talk with him and enjoy a little hanky-panky later. Oh well, they could still have a little fun between the sheets, just not with their usual abandon.

After Natalie left, Carla commented to Baxter, "Wow. You must have really made an impression. She usually doesn't let her girls spend the night anywhere."

Baxter smiled in amusement. "Natalie's been texting her butt off since she got here. She's got a new man."

Carla was surprised at the announcement. She remembered Natalie texting, but she hadn't given it a second thought. She realized Baxter was right. His wisdom this evening was starting to exasperate her. She should have guessed that her sister had met someone. Natalie was very much alive and sexy. The tables had reversed. Carla had become the prude of the day. Once again, Carla resolved to live and let live. She felt slightly hurt that Natalie hadn't confided in her, but she was sure Natalie would divulge something soon.

Carla threw her hands up. "I guess I need to get my head out of the clouds. Stuff has been bypassing me all day."

Baxter nodded and grinned.

Carla mock punched him. "Know it all."

Jasmine started gathering up her bags with Earl's help. Her nephews were running around the patio with Brittany and Tiffany, squeezing in every ounce of play they could rally. Stephanie watched in amused boredom. Her lifeguard had left so there was no one to pine for. She reached for her cell phone now that Natalie was gone.

"Don't get carried away with the phone. You know how your mom is," Carla admonished.

Stephanie nodded absently. "She uses hers all the time now."

Carla refused to debate. She spoke to Earl. "You leaving too?"

Earl grinned. "Yeah, probably. I'll walk Jasmine and her nephews out to the car."

As Jasmine gathered her nephews, Carla lowered her voice to Earl. "So you charmed my boss and my little niece."

Earl smiled. "It's been a good day."

"I'll say," Carla answered.

Baxter and Percy came over and joined them. Earl hugged Baxter. "Thanks for everything, cap."

"You're welcome. Stay out of trouble," Baxter teased.

Earl started laughing. "I'm gonna walk Jasmine and her nephews out and go from there."

"Take your ass home, man," Percy laughed.

Carla and Jasmine hugged and said their goodbyes.

Of the guests, Percy and Teddy were the last man and woman standing. They hung around laughing and talking with Carla and Baxter for a while longer.

Before they left, Teddy pulled Carla aside. "Not much you can do until Mimi is ready."

Carla sighed heavily. "I'm not giving up on her."

"That's admirable. But watch yourself."

Carla was surprised at this display of support from Teddy. Perhaps, Teddy no longer considered her a rival. Maybe, Percy finally paid more attention to Teddy's butt than Carla's. Whatever the reason, Carla noticed that Teddy had dropped her guard. She and Teddy were starting to talk more.

A brief flicker of sadness crossed Teddy's face.

"You know somebody on drugs too?" Carla inquired.

"I have a younger sister. She's . . . . I don't know if we'll ever be able to get her back. She's out there."

Carla nodded in understanding.

"That's why I'm saying, don't get your hopes up about Mimi."

Carla's face was determined. "I'm not giving up."

"Okay," Teddy smiled sadly.

"You ready?" Percy said to his date. He was slightly drunk and feeling no pain.

"Who's driving?" Baxter asked.

"Me," Teddy said firmly.

Baxter started howling. "You're letting Teddy drive? Maybe, y'all should spend the night too."

"She drives like Baxter, hell on wheels," Percy revealed to Carla.

"Damn," Carla said. "You want me to drive you home?"

Baxter and Teddy narrowed their eyes at her. Percy seemed amused.

Carla couldn't help but laugh. She rolled her eyes. "Oh, come on."

Everybody eased up and said their final farewells.

Brittany and Tiffany fidgeted in the background. They were ready to see the horror movies that Baxter had promised.

After Percy and Teddy left, Baxter addressed Carla's nieces. "Y'all ready to hang?"

Stephanie put her cell phone down. "Yep."

"I'm sitting next to Baxter," Carla announced.

CHAPTER 28

Carla was relieved that the movie Baxter chose wasn't as gruesome as she expected. Still, his state-of-the art sound system rattled her nerves because everything sounded so real. The girls' eyes were glued to the television. Stephanie hid behind her hoodie from time to time as she watched the movie. Mr. Safety Man was immersed in the movie also.

"Everybody okay?" Carla asked.

"This one's not too bad," Tiffany said absently. Everybody else dismissed Carla and kept watching the movie.

Baxter gave her a patronizing hug.

They had all fallen asleep in front of the television after a busy day, topped off with a scary movie. Carla awakened and gathered everybody up, including Baxter.

Wide awake now, he gave her a lusty kiss. "Meet me in my room after you get the girls in bed."

Carla's insides stirred, and her lower body warmed. She kissed him back and let him brush up against her breasts.

Carla looked down at her sleeping nieces and smiled. She had finally gotten them into bed. They were knocked out from a long day. She tiptoed over to the door.

"Where you goin'?" Tiffany asked groggily.

"I'm going to my room," Carla answered.

"Can you sleep in here with us?"

"I told y'all not to watch that movie."

Tiffany didn't say anything, but her eyes held a plea. Carla couldn't resist. She had to comfort her niece. She also didn't want the princess to fully awaken.

Carla kissed Tiffany on the cheek and sat on the edge of the bed. Tiffany relaxed and fell asleep. The other girls seemed to relax deeper into slumber also.

Barely breathing so as to avoid disturbance, Carla remained seated on the edge of the bed. She couldn't wait to join Baxter, but she wanted to make sure Tiffany was sound asleep. Gingerly, Carla rose to her feet and tiptoed to the door.

Baxter waited for her in the hallway. "What took you so long?"

Carla started giggling. Baxter was all over her. He was cupping her breasts and butt as though he couldn't get enough.

"I had to make sure Tiffany was asleep," Carla managed between kisses. "The movie scared her. I told you—"

"It wasn't that scary. She'll be fine," Baxter murmured against Carla's lips.

They were edging down the hall towards his room. Carla was soaking wet around his fingers. Baxter was ready to pull out his stiffness and give her a quick stroke in the hallway. Then Princess Tiffany came out of her room, shivering in fear.

Carla and Baxter quickly regrouped and rearranged their clothing.

"Can you spend the night with us, auntie?"

Carla sighed, but her niece looked so distraught. "Sure," Carla said soothingly.

The princess fixed her gaze on Baxter. "You too. Can you come in here with us? You can sleep on the floor."

Carla started laughing. "Of course, he can."

Baxter entered the room, carrying a T-shirt for Carla and pajama bottoms for Stephanie. "Want to make sure everybody is covered up before I settle down."

Carla knew he wasn't happy about sleeping on the floor. She grinned. "That's what you get for letting them watch that movie."

Baxter grunted and left the room. He came back with an inflatable mattress that he put on the floor near the door. He made up his bed swiftly and plopped down on it.

Carla wore the T-shirt that he had given her, and Stephanie wore the pajama bottoms. The T-shirt gingerly grazed Carla's butt.

Baxter's eyes devoured her in the shirt. "Let me find you some pants so I can get some sleep."

"No. I'm good."

Carla then proceeded to prance above him as she tucked her nieces in. Baxter could see her butt and panties under the shirt. Her panties rode up over the swell of her butt. Carla lingered longer than necessary above him.

He was forced to laugh. "Alright, baby. Knock it off."

"What?" she asked innocently and spread her legs this time.

Baxter moaned and rolled over on his stomach on the mattress.

"Looks like you've risen six inches," Carla teased.

"No. Thirteen."

She laughed and bent over him. She pressed her lips to his ear and whispered. "I'll let you stick all thirteen inches inside when the girls leave."

Baxter groaned in longing.

Before Carla hopped into bed with the girls, she announced, "Okay. Nobody kick me."

Her words fell on deaf ears. Stephanie and Brittany were back to sleep, and Tiffany was more concerned about the boogey man. "Can anybody get in the door?" she asked with big eyes.

"No, Tiffany," Baxter reassured her. "All the doors are locked, and nobody is getting past me. I'm right here with you."

Tiffany settled down after that. Carla was still in a teasing mood. Before climbing into bed, she bent down over Baxter and kissed him good night. She pressed against him and felt his butt.

"Alright," he warned.

Soon everybody fell asleep.

* * *

The next morning, the kids sat around the breakfast nook while Carla and Baxter prepared food for them. Baxter cooked the turkey bacon and sausage. Carla diced vegetables for the omelets and cooked the grits. Stephanie sliced some potatoes that Carla intended to steam with broccoli and spices.

Carla liked Baxter's kitchen. It was one of the brightest, coziest places in the house. The nook itself had been remodeled with light-colored wood and plump cushions. Brittany and Tiffany loved sitting in the nook as they talked about their friends and school escapades. They seemed to be enjoying themselves.

After Stephanie finished slicing the potatoes, she sprawled out leisurely with her sisters. Carla smiled at them, then shook her head. She sported a swollen lip, compliments of one of her nieces. A flailing arm had hit her during sleep.

Baxter kissed the swelling and ran his tongue over it. "You'll live," he chuckled.

Princess Tiffany interrupted. "If you both only like to cook breakfast, who's going to cook dinner?"

Carla and Baxter pointed to each other.

"He is."

"She is."

They both grinned at each other like lovebirds.

Tiffany rolled her eyes. She was back to her fearless self again. Carla was glad. Baxter seemed relieved too.

Stephanie, the pre-teen, smiled at her aunt and Baxter. But Brittany's eyes held a different look. "I wish my mom and dad acted like you two," she said wistfully.

Carla didn't know what to say at first. "Your mom and dad love you all very much," she said after a pause.

"My mom does, but not my dad," Brittany replied.

Baxter chimed in. "Yes, he does. Look at how he came over and hung out with you girls yesterday. Your aunt tells me he does a lot of things for you."

Brittany refused to be mollified. "He doesn't love us, or he wouldn't leave."

"Don't say that. Your daddy is crazy about you."

"Do you have kids?" Tiffany asked.

Baxter hesitated. "I have a daughter," he admitted.

Carla stopped in her tracks. This was news to her. He told her he didn't have any children.

Baxter looked at her apologetically. "I had a daughter a long time ago. I was nineteen. She's in her twenties now."

Carla was still digesting his words.

"Is that why you look at me funny?" Stephanie asked. "Does she look like me?"

Baxter nodded. "She probably did when she was eleven."

"Where is she?" Tiffany pressed.

Baxter took a deep breath and stood tall. "I don't know."

"You left your daughter too?" Brittany asked accusingly.

"No. Her mother left me."

Carla and her nieces were all wide-eyed and attentive.

"I'm not going into a lot of details. It's grown folks' talk." He turned to Carla. "I'll tell you about it later."

Carla merely nodded.

"I'll say this," he continued. "I love my daughter—very much. I'm sure your daddy loves you more than you realize."

Baxter's words seemed to soothe the girls as they allowed his words to sink in. Brittany's defiance melted.

Tiffany shifted to another concern. "What about Earl?"

"What about him?" Baxter asked, amused.

"Should I call him when I'm twenty-two?"

"You probably won't. By then, you'll both be moving in different directions."

"You don't know Tiffany," Stephanie laughed.

"You're just mad because the lifeguard wouldn't talk to you," Tiffany shot back.

"Oh, he would have," Stephanie said confidently, "if I was older."

Carla and Baxter both smiled at each other in amusement.

Tiffany nudged Brittany. "You want them to see it?"

Brittany shrugged in response.

"What?" Stephanie asked. Then she remembered and nodded.

Tiffany left the kitchen and came back with Brittany's cell phone. Tiffany expertly scrolled through her big sister's phone.

"Here it is," Tiffany said. She held out the phone to Carla.

Carla looked at the picture on the screen and gasped. She fought back tears. Baxter was surprised at her display of emotion. She usually played hard ass. He had never seen her cry. He looked over her shoulder at the picture.

"You took this, Brittany?" Carla asked.

Brittany nodded and smiled.

The picture captured Carla and Mimi rising at the same time from the deep end of Baxter's pool. Brittany had captured the grace and fluidity of their bodies as they rose from the water. They looked like mythical goddesses—Carla in the peach-colored bathing suit and Mimi in white. Carla's skin gleamed a rich chocolate brown, while Mimi's gleamed a light golden tan. Water glistened on their faces.

Baxter was stunned by the picture. "Wow, Brittany."

She smiled, slightly embarrassed.

Carla was speechless. She finally wrapped her arms around Brittany. "My goodness. You made us look fantastic. Nobody has ever taken a picture of me like that. You're an artist, Brittany. You've got a gift. You've got to send me that picture. Wait until I show Mimi. She'll love it."

Brittany smiled in satisfaction. "I still wanna dance," she reminded Carla.

"Not that dancing you did yesterday," Carla warned.

Brittany's mouth formed a stubborn line.

"There are all kinds of dance forms. You can do African dance, ballet, modern. Or you can study photography and take pictures. Tell her, girls," Carla urged.

Baxter studied Carla and her nieces. They fascinated him. Brittany was embracing a pre-stripper phase. Stephanie was discovering boys. And Tiffany was the most precocious five-year-old he had ever met. Along with their aunt, they were a complex bunch of women. He couldn't remember the last time he had been around so many females. He had to admit he enjoyed their company. They kept him on his toes. And they all had that Hepburn butt, even little Tiffany. He shook his head and laughed to himself. The young men who hooked up with Carla's nieces had better be strong, resilient young men.

The girls were dressed and ready to go home or so Carla thought.

"I don't want to go home yet," Tiffany protested.

Her two older sisters joined in. "Neither do we."

Carla and Baxter glanced at each other. They were ready to drop the girls off. They had some unfinished business to conduct. Carla wanted to know about his daughter, and Baxter wanted to indulge between the sheets.

Princess Tiffany's eyes sparkled with a devilish twinkle. "I want to see Pop-Pop."

Carla stiffened. "Not today."

Tiffany pressed. "Aw, I want to see him."

Stephanie and Brittany held their breaths and remained silent.

"Some other time," Carla said.

"He told mom he had gifts for us."

Brittany supported her younger sister. "He did say he had gifts."

"Your mom can take you," Carla suggested.

"Okay," Stephanie capitulated. "But we know why you don't want to see him."

Baxter watched Carla curiously. She seemed tense.

"Who's Pop-Pop?" he asked.

"My father," Carla answered. She turned to the girls and tried to lighten her tone. "Mr. Baxter has met enough family for one weekend."

"Pop-Pop doesn't like her to dance. They fight about it," Tiffany blurted out.

Baxter's brow shot up. "Really?"

Carla turned around firmly to Tiffany. "That's enough."

"I'd like to meet him," Baxter said. "He sounds like a good man."

"If I wanted you to meet him, you wouldn't want to," Carla sighed in exasperation.

"Probably," Baxter grinned. "Okay, girls. Let's go see Pop-Pop. The day is still young."

The girls were thrilled. Carla simply shook her head in amazement. "I might start fighting with Pop-Pop," she warned.

"Play nice, auntie," Princess Tiffany said.

CHAPTER 29

Carla, her nieces, and Baxter energized the nursing home as they strode through its antiseptic hallways. They were dressed in shorts and jeans and brightly colored tops. Residents smiled as they walked past.

Aaron Hepburn's eyes lit up at the sight of the lively group entering his room. He wheeled himself over to his daughter and granddaughters.

The kids hugged him. "Hi, Pop-Pop."

Carla kissed him on the cheek. "Hi, Dad."

"You came back," Aaron said. He looked Baxter up and down. "You the fireman?"

"Dad!" Carla protested.

"Yes, Sir. I am," Baxter replied.

"Baxter Rose, right?" Aaron didn't wait for a response. "See," he winked at Carla. "I remember sometimes." He returned his attention to Baxter. "You the one got her to give up stripping? Haven't seen her in years. When she finally did visit, I knew she met somebody."

"I keep telling you. I wasn't stripping. I was managing the club."

"Same thing," Aaron replied.

Carla took a deep breath and avoided a response.

"You must be the one with the fire truck collection," Aaron said.

Carla rolled her eyes in embarrassment. Her father was revealing everything she had said about Baxter during her last visit.

Aaron wheeled over to the glass case containing his

miniature car collection. Baxter was right behind him. Carla noted that all the cars were still there. Russell had threatened to kick ass if any more of Aaron's cars disappeared. Apparently, his threat still worked.

Aaron's ten cars, ranging from his 1962 Corvette convertible to his old-model Buicks, were all gleaming in the case. He cheerfully opened it.

Baxter immediately scooped up one of the 1940s Buicks. It was a teal blue Roadmaster with a white hard top and big white-walled tires. "Wow," he said and held it up in admiration. "1949 Buick Riviera, right?"

Aaron smiled in appreciation. "You bet." He opened one of his dresser drawers and pulled out a 1959 pink Cadillac Eldorado with the big fishtail lights and white-walled tires. He pulled out two more identical cars. All three possessed shiny pink bodies with cream-colored interiors and cream-colored convertible tops that were folded down. Aaron lifted the convertible top on one of the cars and snapped it in place. "Voilà" he smiled. Then he presented the Cadillacs. "For my granddaughters," he said.

All eyes were spellbound by the miniatures.

"These are our gifts?" Tiffany squealed in delight.

"Yep," Aaron answered.

The girls fingered the cars in awe and, of course, snapped the convertible tops off and on.

"Now be careful. They're pretty sturdy, but if they break, that's it," Aaron said in warning.

The girls' faces beamed. Baxter coaxed Stephanie to part with hers so he could examine it and flip the top up and down. Carla was glad they came to visit her father. Aaron seemed very alert and pleased with his granddaughters' reactions. He seemed to like Baxter. Carla's earlier wariness with her father had dissolved.

"I've got to show you some of my fire truck collection," Baxter said excitedly. "I'll bring some with me next time."

"You coming back?" Aaron asked.

Baxter refused to commit. "That depends on your daughter."

The girls grinned. Carla sucked in her breath and stood taller. "We're just getting started, Dad. Don't scare him away."

"He's not scared," Aaron said. "Just thinks he is."

Baxter shook his head and smiled.

"Wish your mom were here to meet him. About time you met somebody decent."

Carla tried to squelch rising anger. "Okay, Dad."

"I remember when your mom and I first met. We couldn't keep our hands off each other."

The Cadillac girls listened intently now.

"You know it's not just about sex, right?" he said to Baxter.

"Dad," Carla protested, "the girls are here."

Carla's nieces tittered.

"I hear you, Sir," Baxter said.

"Damn, how I loved that woman," Aaron said. He became thoughtful, then his eyes started to glaze over.

"Dad?" Carla felt frustrated. But her father had retreated into that private space of his.

Baxter was surprised at how quickly Aaron tuned them out as if he had a stopwatch in his head.

Carla sighed. "Okay, girls. I guess it's time to go. You ready?" she asked Baxter.

He nodded, a bit unnerved. "Good night, Sir," Baxter said.

"I don't think he can hear you," Carla said.

"I can hear him, Natalie," Aaron responded.

Carla swung around to see if he was teasing, but Aaron's eyes held that distant gaze. He really did think she was Natalie. The girls were a little disconcerted too. They tried to bring him back to their world, but he kept smiling in his own.

They looked at their cars, then hugged him anyway.

"Does he have Alzheimer's or dementia?" Baxter asked when they left the nursing home.

Carla shrugged. "They don't know what he has. He's been going downhill for fifteen years, since my mom passed. A perfectly good, strong man wasting away because he can't cope."

"Don't be so hard on him," Baxter said.

"It's so frustrating," Carla responded. She noted her nieces' somber attitudes and tried to placate them. "Your mom can take you to see him again when he's feeling better." She grabbed Stephanie's car and held it up. "These are cool cars."

"Are you going back to see him?" Stephanie asked.

"We'll all go back," Carla said. "Where to, girls? Ready to go home?"

Carla figured they were ready to return to Natalie to show off their cars.

Once inside his house, after they dropped off the girls, Baxter was all over Carla. She stopped him in mid-feel. "You have a daughter?"

"Yes," he said weakly.

"You told me you didn't have any children."

"I know. In a way, I don't."

Carla waited for him to continue.

He hesitated, then let out a deep breath. "I was young and dumb and loved the ladies. I got this girl, Alana, pregnant, and we moved in together. She was so jealous and spiteful. She upped and took the baby away."

Baxter sat down on the couch and waited for Carla to join him. Carla remained standing. Before she got sidetracked by his charms, she wanted him to finish his story.

Baxter smiled wryly. "We named the baby, Zoe. She was a wonderful baby, and she came from me."

Carla tried to smother a pang of jealousy.

"I loved that tiny little girl, but not Alana. So I started messing around. I was wrong, but I was only nineteen, younger than Earl." He stared unflinchingly at Carla. "I was still a good dad, but Alana started hounding me, accusing me, even when I wasn't doing anything. Then one day, she left and took the baby with her." He paused for a moment. "Zoe was seven months old. I've been looking for them ever since. It's like they disappeared off the face of the earth. I almost made contact once. Alana has a sister. But it never happened."

Carla was glad that he was finally being honest with her, but she still felt that he withheld something. "Why couldn't you tell me this sooner?"

Baxter shrugged. "We never got around to it. So much has been happening between us."

"But you told me you had no kids."

"I don't really have a kid I can see. It's a sore spot with me."

Carla sat down beside him. "Any other secrets?"

"I have no other children."

Carla believed him, but she still felt that he was holding something back. She was determined to pry it out of him at some point.

For the rest of the evening, Baxter was quiet and moody. He kissed her affectionately a few times, but he didn't try to make love to her. Carla pulled out her books and tried to study for her certification exam, but she couldn't concentrate. Baxter said he had some paperwork to do, but he ended up putting it aside. They were both restless. They tried watching a mind-numbing action movie together, but Baxter seemed preoccupied. Talking about his daughter had put him in a funk that he couldn't seem to shake off.

When they went to bed, neither of them felt like having sex. They both tossed and turned. There was still something unsaid hanging in the air.

Carla sat up in bed and turned on the light. "You'll feel better when you finish the story."

Baxter still lay on his side with his head turned away from her. "I told you everything."

"Not everything."

"There's not much to tell."

Carla caressed his shoulder and smoothed his hair. He finally sat up beside her.

"I messed around on Alana. I didn't love her. Then I met somebody who knocked my socks off—Isabel." Baxter paused for a moment. "I told her about Alana and the baby, and we decided to tread slowly at first. Isabel was a few years older than I was. I brought little Zoe by her house one time. Zoe laughed and played with her."

Carla listened without comment.

Baxter sighed. "I decided to leave Alana, but I knew she would probably keep me from seeing the baby. So I started looking into how we could share custody. She found out about it and snatched Zoe from me before I could even figure it all out."

Carla still remained silent. She wanted to hear everything.

"I did move in with Isabel," he continued, "but our relationship was strained because I was always searching for my daughter. It became one big, ugly mess. The only thing that kept me sane was work. I poured myself into it. You can get a lot of overtime in the Fire Department. Isabel left me eventually, and I couldn't blame her." He stopped and looked at Carla. "I've got my issues, baby. That's why I'm a little anxious about getting involved."

"Are you still looking for your daughter?" Carla asked.

"Always. I'm on social media. I've hired investigators. But nothing happens."

"I remember one time Mimi said you were traveling. Is that why?"

"Sometimes, it's for work. Sometimes, it's to find Zoe."

"What if you never find her?"

"I'll deal with it."

Carla didn't know what to say. She certainly understood his need to find his daughter, but at what cost? "How does this affect us?" Carla asked.

"I enjoy your company. I have fun with you, but things seem to work out better for me if I don't get too serious."

"Is that a cop out?"

"Don't know."

Carla decided not to press the matter. At least, she no longer felt that he was hiding something from her. She was sorry in a way that she had probed. Before his revelations, she was content to live in her world of roses and lilies and knights in shining red armor. She was content to embrace the thrill of new romance and turn a blind eye, however brief, to reality.

Carla switched off the light. She realized they certainly couldn't solve all their problems in one night—if ever.

Baxter slid down in bed beside her. Carla was glad to see that he no longer appeared so restless. They still seemed to have lost their mood for sex.

"Thanks for sharing," Carla said.

He merely nodded. As he rolled away from her, his hand brushed against her butt. That one little touch caught them totally by surprise and inflamed them. The longing they had squelched because of her nieces took over. A fire spread below her belly. Baxter rolled back over, his erection poking against her.

Carla let out a sultry laugh. "Uh, oh."

Baxter's voice was husky in her ear. "Now you can share with me."

Carla let him grind all over her butt. His thickness poked between her cheeks. He still wore his undershorts, and she wore her panties. He reached down and massaged her clit through the silk fabric of her panties. With his other hand, he lifted her satin nightshirt and played with her nipples. Carla moaned and pushed against him.

"I love fucking you, baby," he said against her ear.

"I love fucking *you*," she said, turning her head and sticking her tongue in his mouth.

Carla's juices soaked through her panties. But Baxter wouldn't slide them off. He continued to massage and probe the pliant flesh between her thighs. The wetness seeping through her panties only served to arouse him. Then he pulled the crotch aside. He fingered her freely now. His finger glided smoothly back and forth as he stroked her and inserted his fingers.

Carla squirmed and rode all over his fingers. She couldn't wait until he pushed himself inside. Finally, he opened up his shorts and slid his hardness easily into her from the back. Carla gasped from the sheer pleasure of it. She pressed down harder on him as their bodies slapped against each other. Baxter greedily pushed into her with wild abandon. Carla let him ride as he wished. She kissed him again as he rode her from the back. She could feel him reaching a crescendo. She slowed him down and climbed on top of him. She cupped her breasts in his face.

Baxter buried his head in her breasts and sucked hungrily. He clasped her butt in his hands as she glided freely up and down his thickness. She kissed him and moaned loudly. He filled up every part of her hot, throbbing insides. She clung to him, ready to pour herself all over him. Baxter turned her over on her back. He stroked and thrust until she came all over his pumping organ. He stuck his tongue in her mouth, then filled her canal with his own hot stickiness.

When their breathing subsided, they both fell asleep like babies.

The next morning, even though it was Monday, Carla felt radiant and happy. She sensed a new intimacy with Baxter. His kisses were warmer. She smiled to herself as she dressed in her leggings and tank top for work.

Baxter was dressed in his black uniform and captain's badge. Carla smiled, feeling proud of him.

"What are you grinning at?" he asked.

"Nothing," she responded demurely.

Baxter noticed her tight leggings and the top. He pulled her into his arms. "Don't you know it's Monday morning?"

"I'm starting to like Monday mornings." She pressed against him. "I had such a great weekend."

"Glad you did," he smiled.

Carla could feel him hardening. "We need to get to work."

But Baxter was being silly and playfully devouring her with kisses.

Carla protested. "Stop, we're going to be late."

"No problem. You can work for me. Just a little quickie," he coaxed.

"I didn't give you enough last night?"

"I want more," he said against her lips. Baxter then proceeded to fondle her in all the right places. Carla tried to ignore the growing warmth in her loins. She capitulated as the fire spread between her thighs. He peeled off all her clothing, and she stripped off his.

They enjoyed a sexy morning romp, made sexier because they should have been on their way to work. Carla wrapped her legs around him and devoured him. Savoring each delicious stroke, they forgot about everything. Then they cried out in release.

CHAPTER 30

Carla's breath caught in her throat as she remembered Baxter's touch from the day before. She smiled dreamily. Then she remembered to compose herself because she didn't want any display of passion for Baxter to be misinterpreted by Wendell.

She and Wendell were truly history. Yet, there was certainly a feeling of nostalgia as she walked through the TiTi. She wore a pair of skinny jeans and a loose top, a drastic departure from her previous skin-tight, barely there attire. She felt strange and out of place. The only women in the lounge tonight were the strippers, dancers, and waitresses, all scantily clad. Carla sighed and looked around. Only months had passed since she worked at the TiTi, but it seemed like a lifetime.

As Carla headed over to Mimi's table, most of the dancers greeted her warmly. A few of the new dancers didn't know who she was, nor did they care.

A hand reached out and patted Carla's butt. She swung around.

"What you doing here dressed like that?" the man said.

Carla recognized him as a nut case who had hounded her in the past. But she had always kept him at bay and so did Wendell's henchmen.

Carla stopped nut case in his tracks. "You know I don't play that shit. I will fuck you up. My boyfriend will fuck you up, and you know what Wendell's guys will do."

The man gave her a feeble laugh. "Hey, I just wanted to know what you been up to."

Carla dismissed him. "Now you know."

She realized why she had left the TiTi. Some guys were decent, but a lot of them showed no respect. You had to zigzag your way through the club in order to avoid gropes, feels, and "accidental" pokes. True, she missed the attention she received at the club. Even as manager, she had commanded notice. But now she preferred the attention she got from Baxter, her family, and her new lifestyle.

After Carla chatted briefly with a few patrons she remembered, she worked her way over to Mimi's table. There were only a few guys at the table. A couple of them greeted her curiously. They wondered about her new life. Carla returned their greeting and let them wonder.

Mimi wore a tiny silver G-string, pasties, and spike heels. Her eyes registered surprise when she saw Carla. To the men's dismay, Mimi cut her dance short and stepped off the stage. She tried to cover herself with her hands, then defiantly, gave up and let it all hang out.

Carla was forced to laugh at Mimi's defiance. But the fact that Mimi even attempted to cover herself up was a welcome gesture to Carla. It meant that Mimi was starting to examine her ways.

"What's up, chica? Aren't you a little overdressed?" Mimi's voice was distrustful. She led Carla over to an empty table in a small alcove where they both sat down.

"I came to visit you," Carla said.

"You can visit me at my apartment."

"I wanted to come here. See what's up."

Mimi sat up taller and flaunted her nakedness. To Carla's relief, Mimi appeared sober. She was still a beauty, but even sober, her looks were hardening.

"You can go now," Mimi said. "I don't need you to check up on me. Frank is enough."

"We love you, Mimi. We're concerned."

Mimi's eyes glistened for a moment. Then she pulled herself together. "I need a job, and this is all I know how to do. I don't want to live off Frank. That would drive me out of my mind. Like I told *him*, deal with it."

"I'm not giving up, Mimi. You've got too many talents. You're sober now, but for how long—for the rest of the night? How are you going to avoid Joe?"

"I'll do my best to keep away from him. I feel stronger." Mimi paused. "I'm trying to sort things out. I don't want to act like I did at your fiesta. But I've got to do it my way."

"I hear you, but you make us all upset when you get so high."

"Don't rub it in my face."

Carla shrugged. "Okay. But if you want to walk out of here right now, just like that," she said, pointing to Mimi's almost naked body, "I'll take you away from here and help you get yourself together."

Mimi's eyes watered again. "Thanks, chica. But I got it."

"If you say so." Carla rose from the table. "I'll still keep checking up on you."

"You leaving already?" Mimi's voice held a note of disappointment.

"No need to stay. I came to get you."

"I'm not ready to go yet."

"Okay. Then I'll go check Wendell out for a minute."

Mimi eyed Carla suspiciously. "There's nothing he can do."

"Can't I visit an old boyfriend?"

"Does Baxter know?"

"Who's going to tell?"

Mimi smiled wryly.

Carla bent over and hugged her. "Call me."

Mimi nodded. Her eyes turned playful. "You want to join me for my next show? We'll draw plenty of guys over here. You need some tip money?"

Carla smiled. "No, I don't."

"Prude," Mimi said.

Papers were still stacked high on Wendell's big oak desk, but to Carla's surprise, the rest of the office wasn't as cluttered as she expected. It was definitely a man's office. The mixed-media collages of famous boxers still adorned his walls and added an eclectic sense of style. Carla was glad she had insisted that Wendell buy the collages.

Wendell's eyes feasted on Carla. She looked respectable, but sexy. Her jeans weren't as snug as she usually wore them, but they still hugged her body. Her blouse fell softly over her breasts.

"The prodigal daughter returns," Wendell said.

Carla laughed. "Yeah, right."

"So what brings you my way?"

Carla sighed. "Mimi."

"She seems okay tonight," Wendell said.

Carla frowned at him.

Wendell shrugged. "I keep telling you, she's a grown woman. She's not a kid anymore. If she wants to fuck up and get inebriated every night, that's her decision."

"She's doing more than drinking. Heard she's getting a little help from Gutter Joe."

Wendell nodded. "If it wasn't Joe, it would be somebody else."

"Come on, Wendell. Help us out."

"I am. I give her a table, and I don't charge her much to rent it. I don't take a lot of her tips. She's lucky I even let her work here. Yeah, she could go someplace else, but she'd be dead in a minute, the way she likes to get high. Somebody would haul her ass off and dump her someplace after they finish with her."

Carla winced at his words.

"Hey, you know what I'm saying is true. I don't know why she don't cohabitate with that boyfriend of hers. He should grab her ass off the stage, take her home, and lock her up. Do us all a favor."

"It doesn't work like that, Wendell." Carla wanted to punch him, but she almost agreed with him.

He chuckled. "Yeah, you're right. But I don't know what to do with Mimi. And the guys still love her."

"How's it going with Joe as your new business partner?"

"He'll always be a problem until I can pay off the loan. I've been saving money, and I hit big in Vegas. Soon, I'll buy him out, walk away, or kill him."

"He's not worth going to jail for."

"Maybe."

"That's not your style, Wendell."

"It should be. Then he would've been dead a long time ago."

Carla knew that killing a man wasn't how Wendell operated. That's why she'd always felt loyal to Wendell. He had protected her, and he was fairly decent to everybody else. Of course, he was no saint, and she imagined Wendell had committed a number of shady acts to keep his business afloat. In the early days with Wendell, she had stumbled across a few late-night meetings he held with his cronies, but she had made a swift retreat and exited quickly before she heard anything.

In a way, Wendell was like a former husband. She would always feel a certain loyalty to him. They had gone through good times and bad times together, and he had provided shelter from a perilous industry. Wendell had a heart. It could be his downfall in dealing with Gutter Joe. Somehow, she had to figure out a way to destroy Joe. His presence threatened too many lives.

"It could be worse for Mimi," Wendell said. "I give her as much protection as I can, but the only way she can get rid of Joe is to stop doing drugs or run off with that crazy boyfriend of hers. He must really love her."

"We all love Mimi."

Wendell grinned. "But not like that."

Carla shrugged and grinned with him.

Wendell's eyes burned through her clothing. "You look good enough to eat, Rae. How's fire boy treating you?"

"He's good."

"No, I asked how he's treating you."

"I'm treating her fine." Baxter entered Wendell's office. His eyes were hard. Carla held her breath. Wendell tensed.

"I came here to see about Mimi," Carla explained quickly.

"I know," Baxter said. His manner became more accommodating.

Wendell loosened up a bit.

"Why are *you* here?" she asked Baxter, perplexed.

"Same as you. Came to see about Mimi. Let me walk you to your car."

"Suppose I'm not ready to leave?"

Baxter's stance was inflexible. Carla decided she didn't want to have a big argument with him in front of Wendell. Baxter sensed her acquiescence. Before they walked out, he turned to Wendell. "I'll be back. Let's talk."

Wendell didn't appear very receptive. Finally, he shrugged. "Sure. I don't have all day."

Baxter nodded, then escorted Carla through the club and past Mimi's table.

"See you later, Mimi," Carla shouted as they left. Mimi barely acknowledged them. Without missing a step, she kept right on dancing. Carla figured Mimi was pissed with everybody for interfering in her life.

Baxter was pissed too. He displayed it in the parking lot. "You come to Wendell before you come to me?"

Carla shook her head. "No. I wanted to see Mimi for myself, and then I wanted to see if Wendell . . . ." Her words trailed off.

"You went to see Wendell about Gutter Joe," Baxter finished for her.

Carla sighed in frustration. "I'm trying to keep you out of this, Baxter. That's all I'm trying to do. I was putting my feelers out. See what I can do."

"You need to let me handle it."

Carla's eyes bore into his. "I've got to help Mimi, and I have to get rid of Joe. I don't want you involved."

"It's too late. I am involved."

Carla's head was spinning. "I can't deal with this right now, Baxter. My test is coming up. Let's go to my house. You can relax while I'm studying. We'll figure out what to do with Joe eventually."

Baxter's stance was rigid. "Go home and study. I'll check with you later."

Carla knew better than to argue with him.

He held her car door open and kissed her absently. "Hop in. Talk to you later." His manner was still unbending as she started her car. Before she took off, he said, "Next time, come to me. You can talk to me about anything."

"Apparently not," Carla ventured. "I'm trying to talk to you right now."

Baxter didn't say anything. He waited for her to drive away. Carla finally shifted into gear, wishing she could be a fly on the wall when he talked to Wendell.

"Leave my girl alone," Baxter said bluntly. He and Wendell faced each other squarely.

Wendell smirked. "She came to me."

"I'm not talking about that. I'm talking about that comment you made. Yeah, I'm treating her right."

Baxter saw the play of emotions on Wendell's face. He knew that Wendell considered him either dumb or crazy.

"You in my domicile," Wendell said. "I could have my guys rip you to pieces. I ain't Gutter Joe. I don't fall down that easy."

"Neither do I," Baxter said.

Wendell smiled warily. "You got balls, fire boy."

"Don't call me fire boy." Baxter's tone was cold.

Wendell glared at him. "You know, I think you are one maniacal mother fucker. The only reason I let you get away with this shit is that you rescued my Rae from that fire. That's the only plausible reason."

Even with the tension between them, Baxter repressed a wry smile. He remembered Carla joking about how Wendell could mix all kinds of slang, profanity, and polysyllabic words in one sentence.

Wendell guessed the reason for Baxter's half-smile. "Nothing wrong with me trying to improve my vocabulary," Wendell said. He looked Baxter right in the eye. "Don't you ever come in here and tell me what I can and can't verbalize to your girlfriend."

"I just did."

Baxter braced himself for Wendell's reaction. He watched Wendell struggle to suppress his anger. Any minute, Wendell could strike, but Baxter realized he wouldn't. Wendell knew he'd have to fight hard to take Baxter down.

Unexpectedly, Wendell laughed. "Man, you must be out of your fuckin' mind." He then went over to his liquor cabinet, grabbed a bottle of bourbon, and poured two glasses. "Rather than kill you, I'm going to offer you a drink."

Baxter was forced to grin. "Sure. Not a big one."

Wendell proffered one of the glasses. They both sat down.

Baxter relaxed a bit as the dark liquor with its woody flavor slid down his throat. "What can we do about Joe?" he asked finally.

"The same thing I told Rae. Nothing—unless we kill him. You think you got the heart to do that?" Wendell challenged.

Baxter felt himself bristle every time Wendell said, "Rae" or "my Rae." Yet Baxter knew that Carla had a past just as he did. Still, he hoped the bourbon would make him relax and not have the reverse effect of provoking him to smash Wendell's face. Baxter took another sip. So far, he felt the tension easing out of him, but he didn't know for how long.

He put his glass down. "I don't want to kill anybody, but I can't think of anyone who deserves it more."

"Me neither. But that's what it's gonna take."

Baxter didn't say anything.

Wendell spoke. "He's my silent partner. Got his hooks into my bar without me even knowing it. So yeah, I'd love to see him dead. But I'm not ready to kill him—yet. If you want him dead, you have to do that yourself. Or maybe get some help from your cop buddies. Remember, he's got cop buddies too." Wendell paused. "Whatever you do, I don't think you got the stomach to kill him."

"I'm in the business of saving lives, not destroying them."

"Then why you come here? What you expect me to do?"

"Wanted to see what I'm up against," Baxter said earnestly.

"You up against a lot. You knocked him down in front of his boys. You always gonna be on his hit list. He'll get to you vicariously through Mimi, Frank, and Rae, one by one, until he finally decides to take you out himself."

"Thanks for the rosy picture."

Wendell shrugged. "You asked."

Baxter suddenly felt that the weight of the world loomed heavy on his shoulders. He wondered what he had gotten himself into.

CHAPTER 31

Baxter was hungry. He'd been on the go all day. In the morning, he had played basketball with Percy and some of the crew. Then he had met some of his investment club buddies for lunch. He tried to convince them that autonomous, solar-powered vehicles were the future.

After lunch, he had run a few errands, visited his mother, and now he was ready to enjoy his Saturday evening—without Carla. He missed her, but his talk with Wendell had made him seriously contemplate his future with her. He was always going to be looking over his shoulder with the Gutter Joe shit hanging over his head. Mimi might always do drugs, and Frank would always try to bail her out, literally and figuratively. And Carla would forever try to save Mimi. Baxter wanted a simpler life with Carla, but that didn't seem possible under the circumstances.

His stomach growled. He stared into the window of a new restaurant that just opened in the Crenshaw area of LA. One of his investment buddies had mentioned the place. It was called Toast and Cream, a soul food restaurant with southern style cooking and upscale dining. He preferred not to dine alone, but he was determined to put a little distance between him and Carla. He was starting to feel deeply for her, and he didn't want to become even more involved only to discover that too many obstacles stood in their path.

Baxter peered into the window of the restaurant. The furnishings were art deco with a mauve and black palette. Then, he heard a female voice call out behind him. "Where have you been hiding?"

Baxter turned and faced Simone. A teasing smile played across her features.

"Been busy," Baxter answered.

"You alone?"

"Yes, I am," Baxter responded. Simone looked hot as usual in a simple sheath dress and strappy sandals. The dress, with its beautiful colors, conformed to her curves. Her long, thick hair was pulled back from her face. Baxter's eyes paid tribute to her beauty. Then he suddenly felt a pang of guilt as he thought about Carla.

Simone sensed his guilt, but she forged ahead anyway. "You're alone. I'm alone. Let's have dinner."

Baxter held out his arm. "Let's do it."

Simone laughed and grabbed his arm.

Baxter knew he should have turned and walked away immediately from Simone, but he allowed her to take over. He was hungry, and he didn't want to think. They were lucky. Even though the restaurant was almost full, Simone found a table for them in a quiet, dimly lit alcove. Baxter smiled at Simone's self-assurance. He always liked her confidence, although sometimes, he felt she could be a little pushy. Still, she possessed almost everything he wanted in a woman. Her major flaw was her insecurity around other women. But tonight, it didn't matter. He simply wanted to eat, relax, and avoid thinking about Carla. He'd let everything unfold on its own tonight.

"So what's up?" Simone asked.

"I've been on the go all day and decided to eat. One of my buddies told me about this place. I figured I'd check it out."

"Yeah, I heard about it too. I was supposed to meet a girlfriend here, but she had to cancel. But you know me. I decided to come anyway. Nothing can keep a good woman down."

Baxter laughed appreciatively. That was Simone. She had no problems entertaining herself. She was smart, witty, and poised. So far, his Saturday night was turning out better than he anticipated.

He liked the restaurant. Some of the art represented artists

from the Harlem Renaissance period. There were a few
Archibald Motley prints of lively jazz club scenes along with a
Jacob Lawrence print from his Harriet Tubman series. Baxter
also recognized a sensuous black and white print of a mother
and child by Elizabeth Catlett.

After the waitress brought their wine, Simone elevated her
glass in toast. "To friendship renewed."

Baxter didn't quite like the sound of the word "renewed,"
but he loved to toast. He lifted his glass. "To friendship."

"Who's been keeping you busy?" Simone asked.

Baxter shrugged.

"Who is she?" Simone pressed.

"Somebody I've been seeing for a while now, but there are
some issues."

"Is she the same one you were involved with the last time
you raced out of my apartment?"

Baxter merely nodded.

"Want to talk about it?"

"Not really."

A jealous look crossed Simone's face. "How'd you meet her?
What does she do?"

"She's a former dancer—an exotic dancer." Baxter waited
for Simone's reaction.

"I see. Is that the problem—being a former stripper?"

"You know what? I don't want to talk about it right now. I
came out to relax and have fun."

But he had stoked Simone's curiosity. "Is she beautiful?"
Simone asked.

"More exotic looking." The words escaped before he had a
chance to stop them.

"Makes sense. She's an exotic dancer, right?"

Baxter bristled. "I meant her looks, not her profession. She's
not a dancer anymore."

"What does she do now?"

Baxter knew he should have kept his mouth shut. Now
Simone would pester him with a million questions. He noticed
a beautiful young woman leaving the restaurant with her

girlfriends. Without thinking, Baxter gave her a cursory glance. Simone caught him. She frowned.

"What?" Baxter asked. "Stop it with the insecurity, Simone. I'm having dinner with you, and I want to enjoy it. If I glance at a woman every now and then, it does not mean that I want her more than you."

He didn't want to compare Simone to Carla, but he couldn't help himself. Yes, he did look at a pretty woman on occasion, but Carla didn't hassle him about it. She took it in stride. Besides, he never meant to appear disrespectful. He tried to be careful about that. But with Simone, he always had to restrict himself. He could never glance at another woman nor express his appreciation of her beauty, talent, or whatever asset she possessed because Simone would badger him about it.

He decided to halt her badgering. "Right now, all I want to do is eat. I'm hungry."

Simone shrugged. "I was simply curious about your girlfriend."

"I don't know if she's my girlfriend anymore."

Simone's face radiated with a smile. "Good."

When their food arrived, Baxter plunged in and ate with relish. He had ordered the smothered chicken with onions and gravy. It also came with yams, kale, and warm couscous bread with whipped honey butter. He wanted smothered pork chops, but decided against it. He could picture Carla's raised eyebrows if he ate any red meat. He shook his head and tried to dismiss thoughts of her.

He stared at Simone in the soft flickering candlelight from their table. His manner softened. "I like you, Simone," Baxter said, "but you've got to give me space to breathe. Lighten up."

Simone looked up, then glared at him. "You might want to tell her to lighten up."

"Could I speak with you for a minute?" Baxter heard Carla's voice. He turned, shocked to see her standing above him. Her face was stony. "Now please." Her voice was insistent.

Baxter pushed his plate away and stood up from the table. Simone rose too.

"Excuse me for a minute," he told Simone.

Baxter stepped aside with Carla. He was at a loss for words, but Carla had no difficulty speaking.

"In my younger years, I would have kicked both your asses," she said, "but I'm learning. I suggest you leave right now before I revert to my old ways."

Baxter looked over at his plate and started to protest.

"Get a doggy bag," Carla said. "Otherwise, I'll turn that whole damn table over, and you won't have any food at all."

Baxter was ticked off. He was still hungry, and he liked the restaurant. He could not believe his misfortune. But he could tell by Carla's stance that it was time for him and Simone to leave. He didn't want to create a scene and possibly read about it on the Internet. He saw Natalie in the background. He smiled weakly at her. She nodded impassively. Both sisters were dressed in skinny leg pants and heels. They looked gorgeous. Baxter wished he were with Carla instead of Simone. He'd have more fun. He felt torn. Carla would always have his heart, but he didn't want to keep toying with Simone's feelings. Nor did he want to continue subjecting himself to baggage from Carla's past.

Baxter finally acquiesced. "We're leaving."

"Please don't linger," Carla said and walked over to Natalie. They waited in line for a table.

Baxter faced Simone. "Let's get out of here."

Simone's temper flared. "I don't believe this. Why do we have to leave?"

Baxter tried to placate her. "We can find someplace else to eat."

"I'm fine right here."

"I know, but I don't want any hassles."

"That's your girlfriend?"

Baxter nodded.

"Why would you invite me to dinner if you knew she was going to show up?"

"I didn't formally invite you to dinner. And I certainly didn't know she was going to show up. Let's go," Baxter coaxed.

The manager quickly assessed the situation and brought over their checks. In brotherhood, he gave Baxter a sympathetic nod. Simone, however, wasn't as accommodating. Daggers shot from her eyes at both Baxter and Carla.

With their checks paid and their doggy bags in tow, Baxter quickly ushered Simone out of the restaurant.

Simone flipped when they stepped outside. "I'm through with you, Baxter. It's over between us. That was so lame."

"I'm sorry, Simone. I didn't plan this. I had no idea—"

"She's a stone-cold hoochie. You know that, right? Once a hooker, always a hooker."

"She's not a hooker."

"Oh, that's right, she's a former stripper. Same thing," Simone stated flatly.

Baxter refused to argue. "I'll walk you to your car," he said.

Simone stared at Baxter accusingly. "You really like her, don't you?"

"We're not having this conversation. I said, I'm sorry."

"I guess there's no accounting for taste. You want a hoochie, with tight pants and plenty of makeup, then you got it. I bet she's dumb as hell. She'll bring you down."

A fog surrounding Baxter suddenly evaporated. "Actually, she lifts me up. I'm fortunate to know her. She's a smart, beautiful woman. Thanks for helping me see that."

Simone's mouth hung open. "Fuck you both. You deserve each other."

"Thanks," Baxter said and headed to his car. Simone had helped him see a lot of things. One thing was certain, Simone would never change. He understood her anger tonight, but he never understood her badgering him about other women. He was through with her whether he had blown it with Carla or not.

Carla and Natalie had picked a table away from the window. Carla didn't want to see Baxter leave with another woman. She found it heartbreaking and infuriating.

Natalie laughed and put down her menu. "I see he hightailed his butt out of here."

Carla smiled half-heartedly.

Natalie reached out and patted her hand. "Not sure why he was with *her*, but he's still crazy about you."

"He has a hell of a way of showing it."

Natalie shrugged. "He's smitten with you and afraid of it."

"Smitten? You've been reading too many romance novels."

"No, I haven't."

Carla sighed. "I'm heartbroken, Natalie."

"Don't be. He wants you, not her. Talk to him. Find out what's up before you start jumping to conclusions." Natalie's face turned into a devilish grin. "Girl, you didn't give him no time to explain. You just kicked him out of the restaurant. That's my big sis."

Carla actually smiled now. "I guess I should have at least let him explain."

"Oh, I'm sure he will." Natalie raised her wine glass to Carla. "Congratulations on finishing that course."

Carla raised hers. "Thanks, Natalie. Yeah, I'm finished, but I still have to wait for the test results."

"You'll do fine, Carla. I'm so glad you're away from that club life.

Carla refrained from comment. She didn't want to explain how difficult the exam was. Nor did she want to admit that she might have driven Baxter away with all the fallout from the TiTi. Carla decided to put her best foot forward even though her heart was breaking over Baxter and so much was riding on her passing that exam. She smiled, drained her glass of wine, and ordered another before her meal came. She ignored Natalie's raised eyebrows.

Baxter drove around for a while before finally stopping in front of Carla's building in West Hollywood. He had gone home and tried to relax, but that hadn't worked. He needed to talk to Carla, explain to her that he didn't intentionally plan dinner with Simone.

Carla had changed into one of her favorite house dresses after she arrived home. The dress was a beautiful rose color. It was short and swirled loosely around her hips. She knew she could have gotten away with wearing the dress in a club, and she would still have attracted her share of men. Sadly, the only man she wanted to engage tonight was Baxter, but she had caught him with another woman. She was also tired of his pulling back whenever elements of her past arose and presented a challenge. She wished he'd make up his mind.

Her body steamed beneath the dress. She wore no panties, nor a bra in case Baxter showed up with a good explanation. She wanted to slide the moist heat between her thighs all over his heat. She hadn't seen him for a while. But he had antagonized her.

Baxter pressed Carla's intercom.

Carla heard the buzzer. She prayed it was Baxter so they could straighten things out. She rushed to answer, then paused. She didn't want to appear too eager. She waited.

Baxter felt a bit unsettled. What if Carla hadn't gotten home yet? Suppose she simply refused to answer. He inhaled deeply and pressed again. Still no answer.

Carla decided to make him press the buzzer once more. The third time would be a charm. She hoped he wouldn't leave, but she'd take her chances.

Baxter was determined now. If she was home, he was going to tell her ass off. If she wasn't home, then he was going to park himself outside her building and wait.

He pressed the intercom again insistently.

Carla's voice finally filtered through. "Yes?"

"You know it's me," Baxter answered.

"What do you want?"

"You."

"Act like it."

"Let me up, and I will."

Carla buzzed him into the building. Moments later, he stood outside her door and waited impatiently. She took her time opening the door and finally ushered him in. She had slipped on a pair of low-heeled, sparkly mules.

He forgot about his annoyance as his eyes locked on her dress. "That's a pretty color on you."

"Thanks," she said warily.

He had changed clothes too. He appeared more relaxed in

low-hanging jeans and a soft white T-shirt that skimmed over his chest and shoulders. The shirt accentuated his warm brown skin and amber eyes. Carla tried to ignore the rising heat below her waist. Baxter still had some explaining to do.

Baxter was more than ready to explain, until his x-ray vision scanned over her dress. She wore no bra, and he was fairly certain she wore no panties. The thought intrigued him. He narrowed the distance between them.

Carla stepped back. "Don't you have something to say?"

He was still staring at the rose-colored dress against her chocolate skin. Her wig was soft and curly. The cleft in her chin invited him to kiss it. Her big dark eyes glowed with intensity.

"I did have something to say, but it all escapes me now," Baxter admitted.

"Let me help you out." Carla headed towards the bedroom with no invitation in her eyes.

"Where are you going?" Baxter asked.

"I'm going to change. You seem more concerned about my dress than our conversation."

"No, I'm not. I'm concerned about what's under the dress."

Carla turned around and tried to stifle a smile. "Can we hold an intelligent conversation or what?"

"Yes, we can. But no need for you to change."

Carla folded her arms. "Talk."

"I hung out all day with my buddies, then my mom. I got hungry. I decided to check out that restaurant. It's a new one. And I ran into her."

"Who is she?"

"Her name is Simone."

"You invited her to dinner?"

"No, not formally. I ran into her outside the restaurant, and since we were both alone, we decided to have dinner together."

"Did you plan to leave with her?"

Baxter didn't know how to answer. If he told the truth, Carla might kick him out, but he was determined to get under that dress. He wanted to salvage his Saturday night. Plus, he liked her apartment. It was cozy and comfortable with hardwood floors, thick rugs, and that tan overstuffed couch. She had some nice art.

He liked the haunting black and white lithograph called "New Year's Eve" by Marion Greenwood. It showed a disillusioned young couple all dressed up at a table replete with liquor, cigarettes, and party favors. The picture was a moody piece, and Carla loved it. She said she bought it from an old flame years ago. Baxter appreciated her taste. She offered him more sanctuary than she realized.

He sighed. "I thought about going home with Simone," he finally confessed. "I mean, you and me—there's always some shit we have to go through with that fuckin' Gutter Joe hanging over our heads. And you seem determined to save Mimi."

Carla smiled wryly. Maybe, she should have threatened to change her clothes in the past when she wanted him to open up.

"Mimi, the TiTi—is that why I haven't seen you in a while?" Carla asked.

Baxter nodded. "After I talked to Wendell, I realized that asshole Joe is not going anywhere unless I put him underground. That's not what I do. I save lives."

"That's why I don't want you involved. Joe will get what he deserves. Trust me."

"But I am involved."

"Are you? You keep running away from me. Make up your mind. Do you want to be with me or not?"

"I'm here, right?"

"Then accept the fact that I come with some baggage right now. Mimi means to me what Earl means to you. She fought to make you find me after that fire. I can't let her waste away without putting up a fight. I can't let her succumb to somebody like Joe. I make no apologies. If you're going to walk away from me, you might as well do it now."

"No, I don't want to walk. I just want a clean slate."

"We'll have it—in time. But let me figure out how to handle Joe. I know I can. I've never been afraid of him."

Baxter's jaw clenched. "Oh, I'm not afraid of him."

"I know that, Baxter. But I've worked around him. I know him. I'll come up with something where nobody gets hurt, but him, if it comes to that."

Baxter didn't appear very convinced. "We'll see."

"Please."

"Okay for now," was all Baxter would concede.

They stared at each other. Then Baxter confidently plopped down on her couch.

"Don't get comfortable," Carla said. "You still have some explaining to do. Did you go home with Simone?"

"Nope. She's bad news, too insecure. Even if I hadn't run into you and Natalie—I guess Natalie thinks I'm a real jerk, right?"

"Possibly."

Baxter frowned at the thought, then continued, "Even if I hadn't seen you tonight, Simone's not for me."

Carla squinted her eyes playfully. "A likely story."

"I knew her long before I met you. I've had plenty of chances to get serious with her. You know, you got my heart, girl."

"But you did think about going home with her."

"What do you want me to do? You want me to leave?" Baxter grabbed his jacket and headed for the door.

Carla's mouth fell open. She couldn't believe that he would get up and leave like that, not when the heat was still spreading between her legs. She ran after him and jumped on his back. He managed to turn around and scoop her up, laughing. "Got you, didn't I?"

Carla melted in his arms. She kissed him hungrily, then managed to subdue her passion for a moment. "I don't want to see you with another woman."

"You come to me from now on, instead of Wendell," he responded.

"Okay," Carla agreed. She finally surrendered to the heat of Baxter's touch, but his hands suddenly stopped exploring beneath her dress.

"I need to run down to my car," he said hoarsely.

"Now?"

"While I can," he grinned. "I got you something a while back—a present for completing your course."

Carla's passion waned. She felt pressured by him and Natalie. "Yes, I finished the course and took the test. But that test was very hard. I thought I knew the BMI formula inside out. Weight in kilograms divided by height in meters, but I forgot—"

"You forgot to square the meters, right?"

Carla glared at him.

Baxter laughed. "I still remember some of that stuff."

"Then I mixed up the muscle fibers—the Type IIx with the Type IIa . . . ." She stopped complaining.

"You got me on some of the muscle fibers," Baxter admitted. "I bet you passed the test though. Let me go down to my car. Be right back." He kissed her and left.

Carla sighed and prayed that she passed the test. She felt reasonably certain that she did, but she didn't want to disappoint anybody.

When Baxter returned, he carried a colorful gift bag. Carla couldn't help herself. She squealed in delight. Her heart skipped a beat when she noticed a small velvet pouch inside the bag. She thought of jewelry.

"Close your eyes," Baxter said.

Carla complied, but her mind raced. *Was it a ring?* She was crazy about him, but neither of them was ready yet. They still had a few things to iron out. What if he proposed? How could she resist? Carla's heart raced when she sensed him go down on his knees. Her own knees felt weak. She didn't know what to do.

Carla felt Baxter's fingers fasten something delicate around her right ankle. Instinctively, she opened her eyes

"I didn't tell you to open yet," he said.

Carla stared down at the exquisite gold chain around her ankle. A feeling of relief seized her, followed by a pang of regret that the chain wasn't a ring. She squelched both feelings and held her leg out. The chain gleamed around her ankle. Small diamonds were sprinkled around the chain. Carla gasped. It was beautiful and sexy. Trust Baxter to think of a gold and diamond anklet as a gift. Then he rose, pulled out a small box of gourmet chocolates from the bag, and offered them to her.

Carla laughed and hugged him. "The perfect size. I don't have to feel guilty about eating them. You're wonderful. I'll take that test over and over again for these gifts."

Baxter smiled, pleased with himself.

Carla continued to stare down at her ankle. The chain sparkled against her skin. This was better than a ring and sexier. "Does this mean we're chained together?" she teased.

"Yep," he responded.

Carla entwined her arms around his neck and backed into the door, pulling him with her. He dropped to his knees and kissed her legs from ankle to thigh. Her legs quivered. Beneath her dress, he kissed higher and rested his lips against the swelling mound between her legs. Carla's breath quickened. Baxter continued to kiss between her thighs. She opened her legs wider when he stuck his tongue out and licked her. He licked back and forth, exquisitely the way she liked. His hands cupped her butt. He was creating all kinds of luscious sensations. She arched her back so that he could lick deeper. Then she felt his finger slide inside her. She moaned aloud as his finger and his tongue competed for her clit. He stuck a second finger inside. Carla was soaking wet from his probing fingers. He wiped his fingers all over her butt, then rose and kissed her.

Carla could feel his hardness vibrating against her. She peeled down his zipper, jeans, and shorts. She lifted her dress and let him glide back and forth against her wetness. She reached down to guide him inside her, but he continued to stroke her clit with his throbbing flesh. He held her locked against him and pulled her away from the door over to the sofa. He kept his hardness fastened against her the whole time. When they finally landed on the couch, he slid inside Carla and rode back and forth.

"You feel so good, baby," Carla moaned.

"All for you," he said and stroked deeper. He hiked her dress up higher around her waist, and pulled the spaghetti straps of her dress down over her shoulders. He bared her breasts. He fondled her nipples until they were rock hard. Carla rolled over on top of him, pushed her breasts in his face, and rode him hungrily. She slid off him and cupped his fullness in her hands, wiping off some of the juiciness as she stroked him firmly. Baxter moaned, giving in to the moment. Carla bent down and opened her mouth to engulf him. His moans were loud now. She slid her tongue up and down his shaft as it stood at attention. She licked faster and harder until Baxter pulled her up.

"What you doing to me, girl?" He kissed her and rolled on top of her.

By now, he was so hard and rigid inside Carla that she was ready to explode. When he palmed her breasts and grabbed her hips, she unleashed everything within and exploded all over him. Baxter let go, too, and splattered inside her. They both panted and groaned until the slick, juicy explosion subsided.

Carla laughed weakly and kissed him when it was over. "That was the best gift of all," she said against his lips.

He grinned. "Glad you liked it. I've got more gifts for you." He took his shirt off and removed her dress. Then he pulled her to her feet, and they headed back to the bedroom.

On their way, he said. "We gotta do it in your kitchen."

"Yeah." Her breath quickened at the thought.

CHAPTER 32

Baxter and his team surveyed the fire damage to an abandoned warehouse that had been used as a meth lab. Afternoon sunlight forced its way in patches through cloudy and broken windows of the structure. Baxter and his crew had put out a similar fire in another warehouse months ago, the night before he and Carla had gone on their cabin trip. Baxter was now forced to conclude that he and his crew had an arsonist on their hands, one who set up meth labs, ignited them, and moved onto the next lab.

Baxter and Percy stood inside the front of the warehouse in their turnout gear, all sixty pounds of it. Their gear consisted of thick yellow-striped coats and pants, as well as helmets, axes, hand tools, and the air tanks they carried on their backs. They still wore gloves, but had raised their visors after approval from the HazMat team. As Baxter examined their water-soaked surroundings, he felt confident that they had extinguished the fire. They were in the overhaul phase, checking out walls and ceilings of the structure to make sure the fire had been totally suppressed. Baxter was grateful that, aside from the meth lab, there wasn't much else in the warehouse to catch fire, except discarded wooden shipping crates.

Baxter spoke to Percy. "This was a lot like that other warehouse fire. I think we got an arsonist on our hands."

Percy nodded. "Yeah, a fucking meth dealer who likes to set fires."

"Somehow, I think this is connected to the TiTi fire," Baxter said.

"Why? Because of the accelerants they found at the TiTi?"

Baxter nodded. "Yeah. Somebody deliberately added that excess turpentine."

"You think Gutter Joe?"

"Yeah, I think he's connected. But we have to prove it. I'm going to take a look around, see if I come up with something for the arson team."

"Why don't you wait until we get more crew here?" Percy suggested.

But Baxter was already investigating the front of the warehouse, looking around with his flashlight for charred personal effects, tools with fingerprints, anything that might be left by an arsonist. "It's going to take a while before those guys get here. Go check on everybody. Make sure everything's okay. I'll join you in a few minutes."

"Captain, I know we're a little short-staffed, but you don't have to do this. I don't want to leave you in this area alone. You know that's not protocol."

"I'm only going to poke around for a minute."

Percy hesitated. "Let's wait until we get more crew."

Baxter's stance was firm. "I'll be fine. Everything's solid here. Go check on the crew."

Percy shrugged. "Yes, sir," he said reluctantly.

Baxter began inspecting the perimeter of the cement floor near the entrance of the building. With a probe, he sifted through wet, blackened debris, hoping to find some seemingly insignificant item that would provide a major breakthrough. Cautiously, he advanced towards what appeared to be the remnants of a wallet. As he lifted his flashlight, the floor shifted and vibrated beneath him. "Shit," he muttered and tried to backtrack. But the floor shook, and part of the front wall started to loosen. Baxter raised his arms to protect himself from the crumbling wall. Then the floor suddenly crashed beneath him as he plunged into an abyss of ashes, concrete, and darkness.

Baxter couldn't believe his misfortune. All he wanted was to find some kind of clue that would incriminate Gutter Joe legally. He had this nagging suspicion that Joe was involved in all three fires.

As Baxter reached for his breathing apparatus, the floor beneath him began creaking and opening. He found himself falling again, only a few feet this time, but deeper into the belly of the warehouse basement. As he fell, the walls and slabs of concrete flooring around him tumbled as well. Baxter swore. He should never have ventured along the perimeter by himself. He knew better. He should have listened to Percy.

Fortunately, he hadn't lost his face mask and the air tank on his back. He sat up, lowered his face visor, and plugged in the air hose to protect himself from inhaling dust and fumes. He searched for his flashlight and his radio amid the mounds of debris on the floor, but he was unable to recover them. He decided to try again after his eyes grew more accustomed to the darkness. No sunlight from anywhere ventured through the concrete and ash surrounding him.

He knew Percy and the rest of the crew must have heard the loud noise from the front structure collapsing. He dismissed any doubts about his crew finding him. They would get him out of here very soon, he prayed. He didn't have much space to move about, and he knew the huge chunks of debris surrounding him were very unsteady, so was the dirt floor of the basement. He could barely afford to shift his weight around without causing more sinking. An unforgiving slab of wall restricted his left leg and forced him to turn his leg sideways so that his foot wouldn't jut into the fallen wall. Miraculously, the rest of his limbs felt okay. He thought about Carla as he tried to rotate his ankle in tiny circles to keep the circulation going.

He had been talking to her on his cell when the dispatch alarm sounded. That was not the first time she had heard the alarm while they talked on the phone, but she seemed more unnerved by it this time. She had asked him to text her that he was alright as soon as he got a chance. He had managed a brief text to her when they extinguished the fire. But the first moment he got, he would call her and let her know he was fine. Damn! All he had to do was follow protocol, and he would never have found himself in this predicament. Percy probably wanted to kick his ass for being so hardheaded.

The moment Percy stepped to another area of the warehouse to check on the rest of the crew, he heard the commotion at the front.

"Captain!" he yelled. He heard no response. Percy grabbed his radio. "Mayday! Firefighter down!"

Instinctively, Earl charged forward. Percy grabbed him and pulled him back. "What you doin'? You wait for orders."

Earl looked torn. He wanted to follow procedure, but with the rashness of youth, he wanted to plunge in and rescue Baxter.

Frank was obviously torn, too, but he had no doubts that Percy was in charge. "Your call," Frank said.

"You come with me," Percy addressed Frank and several other crew members. "Earl, you wait for backup and keep everything running smoothly."

Earl looked bewildered. "You leaving me in charge? I want to get the captain out."

"I'll get him out. You follow orders and direct everybody. Stay in touch with the command center. Frank will radio what we need." Percy pulled Earl aside. "Now man up, boy!" he ordered through clenched teeth.

Earl's eyes flashed with anger, but he started barking orders the way he had seen Baxter do during an overhaul phase. Percy turned around to check on Earl. Satisfied that Earl was handling matters properly, Percy cautiously advanced to the front of the building with Frank and a few other crew members.

Adrenaline pumping, Earl went outside and directed the paramedics, but he steered clear of the press. He ordered other crew members to work with the police and widen the perimeter for the second crew when they arrived.

At the front of the warehouse, Percy and Frank tested the standing wall and the rest of the floor that had not collapsed. They carried ropes, ladders, flashlights, shovels, and axes. Percy surveyed the gaping hole in the floor. He and his crew extended a rope ladder into the sinkhole for entry and exit.

Using the ladder, Percy descended into the hole, trying to avoid any protruding edges of cement he encountered. He signaled for Frank to follow. Together, they descended deeper into the chasm. They both wore face masks and thick gloves for protection. The rest of the crew roped down shovels and poles for digging through the debris.

Illuminating the darkness with their flashlights, Percy and Frank dug and probed through the fragments around them as they searched for Baxter. With determined faces, they tested, poked, and shoveled relentlessly.

"He's gotta be in here," Percy said, trying to reassure himself and Frank.

Frank started to explore and lift some of the broken slabs of concrete flooring. Percy joined him immediately, heaving chunks of concrete aside with his tools and his gloved hands. Still, they had no luck.

Frank swallowed nervously. Percy was unyielding. "We'll get him out," he said through his mask.

Pacing back and forth never worked for Carla. She always felt that she had to do something more constructive with her energy. If she worried about something, she usually put on some music and danced, or she took a walk, or she housecleaned. Now that she worked at the fitness center, she exercised on the machines, or she took a class to eliminate her stress. Of course, when she wrapped her legs around Baxter, that always eliminated stress.

But now, she found herself pacing back and forth in her living room because she didn't know what else to do. She had left work early because she hadn't heard from Baxter. He had sent her a text.

BAXTER: M ok.

But that text was sent hours ago.

She was on the phone with him when the dispatch buzzer sounded. It was not the first time a fire alarm interrupted their conversation, but for some reason, she felt a rush of anxiety this time. Maybe, she suddenly comprehended the real dangers of his job. All she wanted now was some sign that he was safe and sound. She checked her cell phone again to make sure it worked. She dialed the number to her bank, and a recording kicked in. Her phone definitely functioned.

She paced some more. The thought occurred to her that she would have to develop a way to deal with Baxter's fire calls. She couldn't afford to take off from work every time she felt anxious. She couldn't do that to herself, nor to Jasmine who was a great manager. For her own sanity, Carla knew she had to figure out a way to dismiss the worry she felt over Baxter's safety. She decided to take a walk and clear her head.

Carla walked at a brisk pace in the mall. She usually loved to shop, but today she didn't feel like shopping. Instead, she wandered aimlessly in and out of boutiques. She felt guilty that she had left work early, yet here she was roaming around the mall.

"Rae! Rae Hepburn!" a voice shouted.

Carla swung around. Only contacts from her stripper days called her "Rae." Carla saw a very pretty, brown-skinned woman in a green cotton tunic and pants that resembled a nurse's uniform. The woman laughed when she realized that Carla didn't recognize her.

As they moved closer, Carla shouted in delight. "Gigi Jones!"

They hugged warmly.

"It's Gina now."

"Oh, is it?" Carla teased. "Well, look at you. Are you a nurse?"

Gina beamed and nodded. "Can you believe it?"

Carla hugged her again. "I'm so happy for you."

"I've come a long way, thanks to you," Gina said.

Carla hesitated. "Really?"

"You did a lot for me. You were the only dancer at the club who wasn't jealous or crazy."

"They were jealous because you were beautiful. Still are," Carla added. "I see you still got that body. You must work out." Carla pulled out a business card. "I'm a fitness trainer now. I'm waiting for my certification results before I take on clients. But I'll know my score soon."

"I may take you up on that." Gina's eyes rested on Carla. "You look good, Rae. Or is it Carla?"

"It's Carla."

"So we both got out of the rat race."

"Kicking and screaming, girl. I still miss it a little."

"That's because you had Wendell watching your back."

"Up to a point. But I had to look out for myself, you know. Some of those guys, they were filthy creeps."

Gina shuddered. "I remember. But Wendell always had your back, and you had mine. I really appreciate it. I'm glad we both moved on. How's that real young girl?"

"You mean, Mimi? She's not so young now. I mean, she's young, but not for dancing. She's got some issues."

"Keep talking to her. Don't stop."

Carla smiled warmly. "Thanks, Gina. It's good to hear you say that. I refuse to give up on Mimi."

"Who's the man in your life now? You still with Wendell?"

"Wendell is history. I met a fireman. He's really cool. That's why I'm out roaming the mall. I'm worried. He got an alarm call this afternoon, and I haven't heard from him."

"I'm sure he's okay," Gina said soothingly. "Y'all exclusive? You practicing safe sex?"

Carla lowered her eyes and dodged the question. "You seeing somebody?"

"Was. It didn't work out. But I'll meet somebody. Glad you met a nice guy. Get tested, girl," Gina said. "So y'all can really get into each other. No lectures. Just the nurse coming out."

"I hear you," Carla said. "Well, I need to get back to my worries."

Gina laughed.

"You got my card," Carla said.

"I do. I'll give you a call," Gina responded.

Carla was glad to be out of the hot seat. Of course, Gina was right about the testing, but right now, the only thing Carla cared about was hearing from Baxter. She checked her phone again. Still nothing from him.

* * *

Baxter's spirits soared when he heard movement above him. He knew his crew would find him. He didn't have much air left in his breathing apparatus. He lifted his mask and shouted several times so they could hear him, but he received no response. He decided to conserve his energy and wait until the sounds of his crew were more audible, then he would yell his ass off. He was tired of the confined space.

Almost an hour had passed, but it seemed so much longer. He continued to play mental games and think of how he intended to wrap Carla in his arms the moment he broke out of this concrete hole. He refused to let doubt creep in. He had too much to live for. He knew Percy would find him. He hoped very soon. He was still able to rotate his ankle to keep the circulation going in his left leg. Other than his left leg being restricted, he felt only a little stiffness and soreness throughout the rest of his body.

Percy and Frank dug feverishly now. More of the crew had descended into the hole with them. Everybody dug tenaciously. But still no sign of Baxter. Percy halted the operation for a moment. He tested various sections of the floor around him and listened to see if he heard anything.

"He's gotta be here," Percy said. He grabbed a probe and poked through more concrete. He removed his air mask. "Where the fuck are you, man?" he shouted. Frank and some of the crew found themselves chuckling at Percy's rescue call. It eased some of the tension.

Percy continued to prod until he found a soft spot. He and Frank started carefully pushing away chunks of debris. "Reveal yourself, mother fucker!" Percy shouted. Frank and the rest of the crew were openly laughing now.

Then they heard Baxter shout back, "It's captain. Reveal yourself, Captain."

Everybody laughed louder and heaved sighs of relief. Percy continued to clear the opening. Frank and the rest of the crew dug with him. Finally, they saw Baxter below them, surrounded by mounds of rubble and concrete. Percy eased down into the hole where Baxter was confined. The opening was small and unstable. The floor creaked beneath Percy's weight. He signaled for Frank and the rest of the crew to halt so as not to disturb anything and cause further collapse. Percy poked and probed through more rubble. Then with his big frame, he started pushing bigger chunks of concrete away so that he could rescue Baxter. Frank edged beside him, and they both cleared away more detritus. Finally, they heaved away the slab of concrete that pinned Baxter's left leg in one spot. The crew above dropped the rope ladder further down into the enclosure.

Percy and Frank lifted Baxter to his feet. "Play time is over, Captain," Percy said.

All three laughed and hugged. "Thanks, my brothers," Baxter said gratefully.

"You hurt? Anything broken?" Percy asked.

"No, I'm feeling okay. My left ankle is a little sore, but other than that . . . ." Baxter's voice trailed off. He looked up and smiled at the rest of the crew above him. "Thanks, guys."

"Aye, Captain," they said.

When the second crew arrived, Earl dispatched some of them as backup to the crew inside the building. He directed others to check the stability of the exterior front, especially where the wall had collapsed.

The moment Baxter and Percy emerged from the building, Earl raced over to them and grabbed Baxter in a bear hug. Baxter hugged him back.

"You okay?" Baxter asked.

Earl was so overcome with emotion that tears slid down his cheeks. "Yeah, I just tried to set up everything the way you do."

"You did great, Earl. I'm proud of you." Baxter released him. "Now man up."

Earl quickly regrouped and stood at attention. Percy and Frank watched with approval.

Percy spoke. "You did good. I just wanted you to focus."

Earl nodded in understanding. Frank gave him a thumbs up.

"Carry on," Baxter instructed.

Earl stuck his chest out proudly. With a slight limp, Baxter departed and headed over to the paramedics.

Carla dragged herself through the lobby and up the stairs to her apartment. She had finally gotten a text from Baxter. But that was a while ago.

BAXTER: C u soon.

Carla still sensed there was something wrong. She longed to hear his voice to erase her fears. With heavy footsteps, she turned the hallway corner leading to her apartment. She stopped in her tracks. Baxter stood outside her door. He was out of uniform and wore a pair of casual slacks and a soft sport shirt. He looked so handsome to her, but he looked tired. She ran to him ecstatically. Her prayers were answered. He lifted her off her feet and kissed her.

After Carla managed to get the front door open, Baxter closed it behind them. She noticed he walked with a slight limp.

"What happened?" she asked in alarm.

"I'm fine," he said calmly. "My ankle's a little tender." He lifted the left leg of his trousers and revealed the elastic bandage wrapped around his ankle. He grinned. "Had a fall."

"What kind of fall? I haven't heard from you. Talk to me."

"Stop worrying, baby. The floor gave way, but Percy, Frank, and the rest of the crew, they got me out, and Earl handled everything like a champ."

Concern spread across Carla's features as she tried to digest his words.

"I'm okay," Baxter said. "Another one of those warehouse fires."

Carla frowned. "A meth lab?"

He nodded in confirmation.

The wheels spun in Carla's head, until she realized Baxter was almost asleep on his feet. She led him to her bedroom and pushed him down on the bed.

"Relax," she grinned. "My intentions are honorable. You need some rest."

"Good," he smiled. "I'm exhausted."

Carla helped him remove his shoes, trousers, and shirt, then she rolled back the covers so he could slide under. She hugged him tight and kissed him hard. He hugged her back, then immediately fell off to sleep. Carla kissed his forehead and caressed his hair. She felt elated that he was safe and in her care. She knew he came straight to her after the fire. Thrilled, she sat on the bed and watched over him protectively. Then she hung up his clothes and left him alone in the bedroom so he could sleep undisturbed.

The next morning when he awakened, Carla lay beside him. She opened her eyes. Baxter kissed the cleft in her chin.

"Sleep well?" he asked.

She nodded. "Did you?"

"Very well." His dick stood at early morning attention.

Carla slid away from him. "Only a quickie, baby. I can't be late for work because I left early yesterday, worrying about you. I'll make it up to you this evening," she promised. Then her eyes danced mischievously. "You want to conserve energy and shower with a friend?"

Baxter required no further invitation.

In the shower, they explored each other's bodies, teasing and tantalizing.

"I'm so glad you're okay," she said, kissing him. "You had me worried."

"No worries. I'm here now," he said. He kissed her neck, then her breasts. He licked her nipples until they stood as rock hard as he was. Water cascaded all over their bodies, adding to their pleasure. He slid his hands all over her breasts. He rubbed her favorite spot and felt it harden against his fingers. He pushed her against the shower wall away from the water. He turned her around and penetrated her from the back. He used one hand to cup and massage her breasts, and the other hand to stroke her clit as he rode her from the back. He slid her under the water again.

Carla gasped in pleasure. He always knew what to do. She felt so good with his hands all over her as he slid in and out of her from the back. She pressed her butt against his groin so he could push in deeper. She felt her canal muscles grip him with every thrust. She turned her head to kiss him. While his tongue plunged into her mouth, his maleness plunged deeper inside her. His hands roamed boldly all over her body. He grabbed her ass and slapped it a few times, then he went back to fondling her breasts and nipples. He returned to her clit and simply let his finger and the water work magic, all the while assuaging his dick.

They both moaned as their bodies slapped under the water. Carla turned around and slid her soaking canal right on top of his shaft.

"Fuck me good, baby," he said.

Carla lustily obliged. Baxter held her arms up against the shower wall as he stroked from the front, unimpeded. With tongues and bodies locked, they managed a few more good thrusts before their insides burst with gratification. As they peaked, they moaned and groaned without censure.

When it was all over, a guilty look crossed Carla's face. "How's your ankle?"

"Oh now, you're concerned," he laughed.

She kissed him and laughed against his lips. "I forgot about your ankle."

"So did I," he said. "It's not bad. It feels much better."

He gave her one last lusty feel from her breasts to her butt before he released her.

"You're so nasty," she said, arching her back and pressing against him.

"You too," he chuckled.

Baxter and Carla lounged in bed with breakfast trays over their laps. Carla had fixed them savory omelets with cherry tomatoes on the side. Toast and orange juice completed their meal. She had transferred some fresh flowers from her dining room table and placed them on the trays. She smiled as Baxter ate heartily.

"Eat," he said.

But Carla simply wanted to watch him. "I'm so happy you're safe," she said.

Baxter kissed her forehead. "Glad you feel that way. That's what kept me going while I was in that hole."

Carla sat up straighter. "What hole?"

Baxter was ready to kick himself. He tried to keep the dangers of his job out of his romance life. "Nothing," he said.

"You know what, Baxter? Let's make a pact. You talk to me, and I promise not to worry. You don't have to tell me everything. Just some things."

Baxter looked doubtful. "Okay, but I don't want you stressing out."

"Deal." Carla waited for him to elaborate about the hole. "Well?" she asked when he wasn't forthcoming.

"I fell into a hole when I should have known better. The floor caved in under me."

Carla gasped.

"See. That's why I didn't want to tell you."

Carla calmed herself. "Sorry. Finish telling me."

"You sure you can handle it?"

Carla steeled herself. "Yes."

"I was looking around to see if I could find some clues and didn't realize that the floor was weak in one area. It seemed fine when we tested it, but part of the wall and the floor collapsed."

"What were you looking for?"

"Any kind of clues."

Carla guessed immediately what he was searching for. "You think Joe set the fire?"

Baxter nodded.

"You think he was behind the other warehouse fire?"

"Yeah, and the TiTi. I'm trying to find some evidence that ties him to those fires so we can get him the fuck out of our lives legally."

"I keep saying this, and I know you don't believe me, but I'm going to kick him out of our lives."

Baxter sighed. "Okay, Carla. Whoever gets him first."

They ate for a while in silence.

"How long were you in the hole?" Carla asked.

"About an hour."

"You were by yourself?"

"My crew was right there to rescue me."

Carla let out an involuntary shudder. Baxter was right in not wanting to tell her. She didn't want to hear anything more about it. She didn't want to picture him alone in a hole. One day, she might have to kill Gutter Joe if that's what it took.

Baxter sensed her concern and switched the subject. "Eat your breakfast, baby. I'm ready for dessert," he said and fingered a nipple that popped out of her nightshirt.

"I have to go to work, Baxter. I don't have banker's hours like you do—twenty-four hours on and twenty-four hours off. Or whatever your hours are."

Baxter laughed. "You know I don't have banker's hours. But I'm sure you got a few minutes for me," he said, kissing her shoulder.

"I'm gonna lose my job hanging with you."

"I'll take care of you. I got investments," he teased.

"Good. You'll need them if you keep making my pussy wet."

In response, his dick almost toppled over the tray. Carla laughed at him.

CHAPTER 33

Baxter pulled up in front of his mother's house in Atwater Village on the northeast side of Los Angeles. He hopped out of the car with a beautiful bouquet of perfect yellow roses. He rang the doorbell of her quaint Spanish-style house. It was hot outside. Lillie opened the door in a long, summer dress with a thigh-high split up the side. Baxter had to admit his mom was still in great shape. He thought the slit was a bit high, but she still had the curves to get away with it.

Lillie didn't speak. She simply grunted at him and turned away coolly. "I'm in the back," she said, barely looking at him. She led him towards the patio.

Baxter stopped her at the kitchen. He held the roses out to her. "Don't you want to put these in a vase first?"

Lillie narrowed her eyes at him, but finally stared at the roses and couldn't resist a smile. "Is this a bribe?"

"It's to let you know that you're still my heart."

"Apparently not. You went to that hussy first. You always come to me after a big fire."

"Doesn't mean that I love you any less than I did before. Come on, Mom. She's my girlfriend."

"We'll talk about that."

Lillie finally took the roses from him and pulled out a large crystal vase. She spread the roses out in a beautiful array, then set them on her dining room table. The roses immediately brightened up the room. Her décor was eclectic like Carla's, but the similarity stopped there. Lillie managed to blend modern, antique, flea market, and designer furnishings in a way that defied interior design logic, but somehow worked. An expensive, emerald green couch anchored her chic hodgepodge of furniture.

Lillie stepped back and surveyed the contrast of the roses against her décor. A smile beamed across her pretty face. She hugged Baxter and quickly brushed away tears.

Baxter held her tightly. "I love you, Mom. That hasn't changed." He released her.

Lillie nodded. "I know. At least, you called and sent texts. I suppose that counts."

"And I'm here. I came to hang out with you," Baxter said.

"Let's go out back. I put some ribs and chicken on the grill."

Baxter hesitated.

Lillie waved her hand. "I know you don't eat ribs any more, but I've got plenty of chicken. I grilled some vegetables too. Made a salad, kebobs, all kinds of healthy stuff since you're watching what you eat now."

"I pretty much eat the way I used to. I just don't eat red meat anymore. I always tried to eat healthy."

His mother snorted. "Not as healthy as you do now, with that new girlfriend of yours."

Baxter shrugged. "When I eat better, I feel better."

"I guess I'm going to have to meet this hussy sooner or later."

As soon as he entered the patio, Baxter sniffed the aroma of barbequed chicken and his mother's homemade barbeque sauce. He picked up a kebob of peppers, tomatoes, onions, mushrooms, and chicken. He downed it.

"Stop calling her a hussy, Mom," he said after he finished. He grabbed a couple of paper plates and handed one to Lillie so she could go first.

"No, you eat."

Baxter loaded his plate with barbequed chicken, corn on the cob, green salad, potato salad, deviled eggs, and more kebobs.

"How's the barbeque sauce?" Lillie asked as she prepared her plate. "I changed some of the ingredients—less sugar and salt. But I'm still not telling you what I put in my sauce."

"You can tell me. I'm not going to tell anybody. I don't cook."

"I'll leave you the recipe in my will."

Baxter shook his head and laughed. "People and their barbeque sauce. Why don't you leave me the recipe now so I can make some money from it?"

"It's in my will, Bax."

They sat down at the patio table and ate heartily.

Baxter complimented Lillie. "I love the sauce, Mom."

She nodded appreciatively. "Thanks. It's good, isn't it?" She paused and stared directly at Baxter. "You must be really serious about this woman."

"Carla. Her name is Carla."

"You sure it's not the sex?"

Baxter chuckled. "I hope not. I like her, Mom. I enjoy her company. I like her family too."

"So I guess I'm the only holdout. Guess I would be since she's marrying up, not down."

"Whoa. Who said anything about marriage?"

"I guess the apple doesn't fall far from the tree on that one. Just because marriage didn't work for me doesn't mean you have to feel that way."

"I know, but marriage is a major commitment."

"Hope I haven't ruined you, Bax."

Baxter simply smiled at his mom, but didn't say anything.

Lillie sighed resignedly. "I hope Carla doesn't go back to working in that club. You already told me the problems Frank has with her friend."

"Carla's different. She's working at a fitness center. She'll be a certified trainer soon. She's really working hard to leave the club life behind."

"Yeah, but when you work in those strip clubs, somebody's always going to remember. What are you gonna say when some guy calls her a slut or a ho?"

"You mean before I knock him down or after?" Baxter said firmly.

Lillie slapped her thigh and laughed proudly. "At least, I ain't raise no pussy."

"Mom!" Baxter protested.

"I'm glad you're not a pussy. I didn't put you in all those self-defense classes for nothing."

Baxter shook his head and smiled warily.

"What about children? I want grandkids."

Baxter held up his hand. "Who said anything about kids?"

Lillie smiled knowingly. "Baxter, you got a thing for this woman. But she probably can't give you any kids."

"I already have a kid. For that matter, my kid might have kids—your grandchildren. Zoe is in her mid-twenties now."

Lillie sighed. "You may never see her again, Baxter, nor her kids. I think you set yourself up for—"

"Are we going to have this conversation again?"

"You're right. It's your life. So what about kids for you and Carla?"

"That's probably not going to happen, but she's got great little nieces. I know you'd enjoy them. And there's always Earl. You know he's going to have kids one day."

"But they're not my full-blooded grandchildren."

Baxter frowned at his mom.

"Sorry. I know Earl is like a son to you."

"He's like a son to you too," Baxter said.

Lillie chuckled. "He's a feisty young man. Wonder what his kids will be like." Lillie paused and reflected for a moment. "I wanted so much for you, Baxter. I wanted you to go to college. I wanted you to get married and have children. I wanted . . . ." She stopped. "I know, I know. It's not what I want. It's what you want. And I have to say I'm very proud of you and what you've accomplished. I couldn't be more proud of you if you had gone to college," she admitted. "But grandchildren with your blood would have put the icing on the cake."

"There are other ways of experiencing grandkids."

Lillie got up and kissed his forehead. "You're right. But I'll meet Carla when I'm good and ready."

CHAPTER 34

The waters of Santa Monica Beach, despite their murky reputation, almost sparkled blue. A white expanse of sand stretched clear ahead and blended with the ocean and a cloudless sky.

Carla inhaled deeply. It was a hot Friday, a perfect day for the beach. "This is a good spot," she said.

Baxter plopped their bags down on the sand and began setting up the umbrella. Carla watched him and smiled.

"Don't I get any help?" he asked.

"Oh, I think you're doing a fine job, my strong muscle man."

Baxter simply grunted and continued to anchor the umbrella in the sand.

Carla spread out the blanket and unfolded a chair. She felt like a little kid. She was excited to play in the water and lounge in the sun the whole day. She loved the beach, but when she worked at the TiTi, she seldom had time to appreciate it. After working late, then sleeping late, by the time she got to the beach, she had only a couple hours left before sunset. Then there was the issue of getting someone to accompany her. Her nieces would have been perfect, but Natalie often made excuses that the girls had other plans. Carla knew it was because she worked at the TiTi.

As for male companionship, she could barely remember the last time a man had escorted her to the beach. Men loved hanging with her at the club, but the ones she liked didn't want to commit to activities with her outside the TiTi. She couldn't get Wendell to go either. He hated the beach. It restricted him, interfered with his hustling. Wendell's primary passions were clubs, bars, and sex and how to make money off them. While he didn't pimp his dancers, he wasn't averse to their turning tricks every now and then, provided he got a cut.

Carla had met a few nice men at the club who worshipped the ground she walked on and would have taken her anywhere, but she didn't feel the same towards them. She had tried to muster up some feelings for one of the guys who came to the club mainly to visit her, but she had to get high to stomach him. At that point, she decided she wasn't about to become a junkie simply so she could have a man. She just might have to remain single all her life.

Yet here she was at the beach with a man who thrilled her. Less than a year ago, she could never have imagined this.

Baxter removed his t-shirt and sank down on the blanket in his shorts. They hung low and loose, a neon orange with a dark blue horizontal stripe. He looked hot, especially since he had trimmed down after Carla tactfully admonished him about some of his eating habits. She didn't have to do much coaching, though, after he started seeing and feeling results. Since he exercised almost as much as she did, she had coached him primarily on his food choices. He had a tendency to eat too many starches and fried foods.

Carla's eyes danced. "You look like a hunk."

He grinned. "Flattery will get you everywhere. Now your turn." He tugged lightly on her cover-up.

Carla removed the long wrap skirt she wore and revealed her swimsuit. It was a cobalt blue, cut high on the thigh. Horizontal strips anchored the plunging neckline in the front and back. The strips exposed her bare skin underneath. Carla had found the suit at one of those odd little boutiques where she often shopped.

The owner carried few-of-a-kind items, and she delighted in finding things for Carla. Sometimes, the woman carried great pieces. Other times, Carla couldn't find anything. She had to visit the store often to catch some of the unique standout items.

She was eternally grateful to the woman and patronized her

often. Unfortunately, Carla realized that she needed to cut back considerably on her shopping if she wanted to stay afloat financially. Money was tighter since she couldn't rely on the managing income, tips, and commissions that she earned at the TiTi. Her fitness center earnings reflected a big pay cut, and she had spent a nice chunk of money for the certification course. Carla took a deep breath and refused to worry about anything for the rest of the day as she sank down on the blanket beside Baxter.

His eyes were glued to her bathing suit and the flesh beneath it. "That's a nice suit, baby. Your blue matches my stripe. Good choice," he said, lightly caressing her thigh.

Carla couldn't believe the tingle she experienced so quickly from his touch. She kissed him on the lips.

"You want to leave already?" he asked.

Carla laughed. "Are you kidding? We just got here."

"Just checking." He looked around the beach and smiled. "This is great—a nice way to relax."

"So you're okay we didn't go somewhere more secluded?"

"This works fine," he assured her.

They both soaked in the sights and sounds around them. Baxter threw a ball back to a little Asian boy who had tossed it in their direction. He was about three and ready to toss it again until his mother stopped him and grabbed the ball. Carla and Baxter smiled, amused by the little boy.

Carla pulled out a tube of sunblock lotion.

"Want some help?" Baxter asked.

Carla rolled over. "Sure."

Baxter squeezed lotion onto her back. He massaged under the strips of the V-neck and down to the top of her butt.

Carla started laughing. "I don't need that much."

He still kept rubbing. "Want to make sure you're protected."

Carla noticed a sudden rise in his shorts. She felt a quickening in her own loins. She took the sunblock from him. "Let me do you."

He laughed. "Right here? In front of everybody?"

"Roll over," Carla said and began massaging the lotion onto his back. He totally surrendered to her touch.

"That feels good," Baxter said lazily.

"Glad you like it." Carla continued to rub. "How are your investments coming along?"

He sat up, excited. "I told you about the solar-powered car company, didn't I?"

Carla nodded and smiled.

"I went ahead and moved on it. We'll see how it goes. I think it's going to be a big industry. How are *your* investments rolling?"

Carla looked puzzled.

"Your investment in you," Baxter clarified.

Carla ceased rubbing the sunblock lotion on him. "Stop it. You don't have to psyche me up about staying away from the TiTi."

"I know," he said apologetically. "Hear about your certification test?"

"I'll know soon." She hesitated. "I'm thinking about going to college. I love the fitness field. I might major in it. Makes good use of my energy."

Hallelujah! Baxter thought. She really was putting the TiTi behind her. Down the road, he might have to return to school to keep up with her. He looked forward to the challenge. She was a fascinating woman.

"I'm not sure whether I want to major in kinesiology or business," Carla continued. "That kinesiology stuff is hard."

Baxter smiled at her, pleased. "I'm sure you'll figure it out."

"You know, I certainly don't miss that boring data entry job at Natalie's office, but I do miss walking across the lobby with my heels clicking. I know that sounds silly."

"Okay, Dorothy," Baxter teased.

"I want to run a fitness business with all kinds of products. I want to have an office in a big building so I can click my heels in the lobby."

"Things are changing. You might be working from home."

"Then I'll click my heels on the way to meetings."

"Good stuff you're talking."

Carla opened a tote bag and pulled out a colorfully bound proposal. She offered it to Baxter. "Since you like to invest."

Baxter held up his hand in warning. "I like to invest in new technology and the environment."

"And you seem to be doing great. You got a knack for it. You said so yourself."

Baxter was still reluctant. "We got a good thing going, Carla. Let's not mix it up with business."

Carla's face fell in disappointment. "Could you look at it, please?"

Baxter sighed and finally took the proposal from her. "I'll look at it later. Let's go play in the water." But he started leafing through it anyway. "Shoes? Do you know how difficult it is to sell—"

Carla stopped him in mid-sentence. "Do you know how difficult it is for mature women to find stylish shoes that aren't ten inches high? There's a major market out there, and I intend to tap it. It's a fitness issue."

Baxter flipped through more pages. "You wrote this?"

Carla nodded and smiled.

"Who did the graphics and the illustrations?"

"I did the illustrations. Mimi did the graphics and layout. She's great on anything with the computer, social networking, you name it."

"Is that why Frank acts so stupid about her?"

"I guess."

They both started laughing.

Baxter was impressed. Carla amazed him. She had illustrated pumps, boots, and strappy sandals. "You did some nice illustrations. But shoes go out of style."

"Not those. My shoes are hip and classic. Doesn't matter when I get the funds. Those shoes won't go out of style. I might have to update them a little."

"Okay. I'll go through your proposal later. I might even mention it to my mom. She's my silent partner on some things."

Carla raised an eyebrow.

"She's an accountant," Baxter explained. "She went back to school and got her degree. That's why she gives me a rough time about not getting mine."

"When am I going to meet your mom?"

Baxter jumped up from the blanket and grabbed her hand. "Soon. Come on, let's go play."

"I want to meet her, Baxter," Carla said firmly.

"You will."

Carla decided not to press the issue. It was a gorgeous day, and she wanted to enjoy every minute of it. "Fine. I'll race you." She caught Baxter totally off guard and dashed to the water. He didn't stand a chance. She could really sprint. "I beat," she laughed gaily when he caught up with her.

"You cheated," Baxter said and playfully lifted her up.

Carla and Baxter bounced around in the water like kids. Carla body surfed and rode the waves, while Baxter dove into them. Discretely, he found a few accidental ways to feel her butt and her breasts as they played in the water. He was ready to brush up against her hard when the little Asian boy came over to play with them.

Carla laughed as Baxter walked the toddler over to his mother. Moments later, the little boy was back beside them. Baxter finally decided to surrender to their newfound friend, and all three of them played in the water.

The little boy's mother threw up her hands. "He likes you," she said. The boy's father shook his head and joined them.

After more than an hour, Carla decided it was time to get out of the water for a while. "I'm going back to our spot," she said to Baxter.

He was still in play mode with the little boy and his family. "I'll be there in a few," he said, then lowered his voice. "Keep it warm for me."

"I will," she laughed and headed back to the blanket.

Carla sat basking in the sun. She gazed out at the water and the swimmers. Her swimsuit was almost dry, and she had applied more sunblock lotion. She checked her cell phone. A half hour had passed, and she didn't see Baxter in the water. She looked around the beach in both directions and still didn't see him. A slight pang of anxiety hit her. But she reassured herself that Baxter was a strong swimmer, and he probably decided to take a walk or a run along the beach. Once he returned, she'd tell him that in the future, he should let her know his whereabouts.

Carla put her cell phone away and reveled in the moment. The Asian family was back on their blanket. The little boy smiled at Carla as he played in the sand, building his own version of a castle. Carla smiled back and waved to him. She gazed around again, reveling in the crashing of the waves along the shoreline and the squawking of the sea gulls. She sniffed the air appreciatively and settled into the beach chair. She grabbed her headset and a magazine. She was in her world.

After a while, Carla gave up on reading the magazine. Even the music from her headset wasn't soothing. Forty-five minutes had passed and still no sign of Baxter. She was trying not to worry. But the moment he returned, she intended to let him know how she felt about his going off and staying away for so long. Again, she reassured herself that maybe he had taken a run along the beach. That could take about an hour. She'd give him a few more minutes before she sounded the alarm.

Damn, she had finally gotten over that last scare when he fell through the floor and had to be rescued. Fortunately, his ankle had healed in no time. Now she had to worry about him at the beach. She tried hard to dismiss all thoughts that he might be in danger. She didn't know what she would do if anything happened to him. She could no longer picture life without him. They were getting along so well now. Could fate be so cruel as to snatch him away?

After an hour, Carla got up from the blanket. She went over to the Asian family. The little boy was delighted.

"Have you seen my boyfriend?" she asked the boy's parents.

The wife pointed. "I think he went in that direction."

But Carla didn't see anyone wearing neon orange shorts. She thanked the boy's parents and asked them to watch her things while she searched for Baxter.

Carla proceeded over to the lifeguard station. "Have you seen a tall black man in orange shorts? You know those day-glow shorts? He's a fireman," she added, hoping it would make

Baxter a top priority. He had told her that the beach lifeguards were members of the Lifeguard Division of the Fire Department.

The lifeguard was a very athletic blond woman. "I saw him about thirty minutes ago. He was running over in that direction." She pointed in the same direction that the little boy's mother had indicated.

Carla hesitated for a moment. The lifeguard immediately reassured her. "We've had no incidents in this area. Everybody's accounted for, and no other station has reported anything. Your guy seemed fine when I saw him. He was jogging."

Carla breathed a sigh of relief, but she still decided to check with the next station. She wished she had tracked Baxter's movements when she got out of the water. Trying not to panic, Carla approached the second lifeguard, a young man. He basically repeated the same thing the first lifeguard said—everybody was accounted for.

After trying a third station, Carla headed back to the blanket in case Baxter had returned while she was gone. Her spirits perked up when she caught a glimpse of a man in neon orange shorts walking in the distance, but as he drew closer, she knew it wasn't Baxter.

Carla plopped down on the blanket, defeated. Her beautiful day, spoiled. She tried to squelch the rising panic. Was Gutter Joe involved—first the fires, now this? She would never forgive herself if Joe caused Baxter any harm.

She wrapped her arms around her knees and rocked back and forth. Her eyes scanned the distance, searching for Baxter. She checked the time again. An hour and twenty minutes had gone by. She knew there had to be a reasonable explanation for Baxter's absence. She knew he'd appear soon. She would wait a few minutes, then ask for help.

Carla couldn't sit still any longer. She sprang to her feet and decided to walk in the direction where Baxter had gone. First, she retrieved her wrap skirt and tied it around the umbrella. She wanted to make sure she knew how to get back to their spot. The colorful skirt swirled and fluttered around the umbrella pole like a flag. Carla then took off, searching for Baxter. The Asian family appeared worried, too, as she passed them. Carla squelched another wave of panic.

Baxter knew Carla was going to kill him when he got back. He raced along the beach towards Lifeguard Station 26. He was glad he remembered the number. Of course, he always noted landmarks and signs to help him with directions. That was his job.

After Carla had left him in the water, he had taken a walk that turned into a longer jog than he intended. On his way back, a lifeguard was racing towards a teenage boy and his sister in distress in the water. Baxter felt obligated to help. The lifeguards were part of the Fire Department. He dove in immediately with the lifeguard and rescued the boy while the lifeguard rescued his sister. As soon as Baxter laid the teenager on the beach, he administered CPR to get the boy breathing again. Baxter was elated when the boy choked up water from his lungs and started breathing naturally. All the boy's vital signs returned to normal. His sister fared better and breathed normally from the moment of her rescue.

Baxter heaved a sigh of relief that the teenager and his sister were safe. They were lucky. Events didn't always turn out so well. He himself could have had problems with the rescue since he wasn't as strong a swimmer as the lifeguard. He made a mental note to swim more.

After the rescue, the lifeguard, the parents, and a host of others thanked Baxter profusely. He accepted their thanks graciously, but reminded everyone that he was doing his job. Now he realized that his job might land him in hot water with Carla. A few more lifeguard stations to go, and he would be back on his blanket with Carla. He jogged faster in her direction.

Baxter saw Carla searching frantically for him along the beach. She appeared so distraught. Finally, she turned and saw him racing towards her. He closed the distance between them.

"Where have you been?" she shrieked. She started pounding

on his chest hysterically. "I've been looking all over for you." Tears streamed down her cheeks.

Baxter grabbed her fists and tried to calm her. "It's okay. I got caught up in a rescue."

People along the beach began staring at them. An older lady got involved and addressed Carla directly. "You okay, miss? Is he harming you?"

Carla was still crying hysterically. Baxter pulled her close. He didn't want to create a scene. "She's fine," he told the lady. "She got a little upset because she thought—"

"Let her tell me she's okay." The woman was getting louder now.

Baxter was losing his patience. The day hadn't turned out as planned. He was totally unprepared for Carla's waterworks and the woman's interference. "Baby, would you please tell her you're okay?" he said to Carla a little harsher than he intended.

Carla was still crying, yet trying to nod at the same time.

"She doesn't look like she's okay," the woman said.

Baxter was forced to agree. Carla was having a meltdown. He understood the woman's concern and realized that he was in a delicate situation. "Carla, can you please pull yourself together so we can get away from this woman?" Baxter said.

As Carla struggled to force her emotions under control, a new bout of sobbing overtook her. Baxter couldn't understand it. He didn't know what to do, and a small crowd was forming. He couldn't believe it. He hugged Carla against him as she continued crying against his chest. The woman's stance was becoming more emboldened now.

Tired of the woman's meddling and the curiosity of the crowd, Baxter did the only thing he could think of. He lifted Carla off her feet and carried her away from the crowd. "It's okay," he said soothingly as Carla tried to stop crying and pull herself together. Baxter felt more in command now as he carried her back to their blanket. It didn't matter that the fucking hot sand burned his feet so long as his baby was okay. He hugged her closer to him.

Then he heard a different woman's voice shouting from the crowd behind him. "When you put her down, you can come back and get me." Baxter was forced to smile. He guessed it was the leggy woman in the black bikini. He could hear snickers from the crowd.

"Tell that witch," Carla sobbed, "I'll kick her ass when I get myself together."

"That's my girl." Baxter laughed and kissed her wet cheek.

When they finally neared the blanket, the first thing he saw was Carla's colorful cover-up, tied to the pole of the beach umbrella. It fluttered in the wind and welcomed them back with undulating swirls. He noticed the Asian family appeared relieved to see them. The little boy watched them curiously. Baxter lowered Carla gently to her feet. Her tears had subsided. She seemed more in control.

"I didn't mean to freak out like that," she said apologetically. "I don't know what came over me."

But Baxter could tell the waterworks were starting up again. He didn't know what to do. He felt at a loss for words. He had never seen her cry like this. He sank down on the blanket and pulled her down beside him.

Carla blinked back more tears. "I thought something happened to you. I was so worried."

"I'm fine," Baxter said. "I was trying to tell you that I took a quick run and ended up rescuing a kid in the water."

Carla nodded. "I knew there had to be an explanation. But I still haven't gotten over that warehouse fire where the floor caved in."

Baxter lifted her chin. His eyes were steady. "I'm a first responder. It's what I do. If I see somebody in distress, I have to respond. You can't go to pieces every time you think I'm in danger. If I'm worried about you, it's harder for me to focus on my job. That can cause serious problems for me."

Carla simply nodded.

Baxter slipped behind her, his arms encircling her waist, his legs surrounding hers. "I plan to be around a long time. But anything can happen. That's the kind of work I do. You're going to have to get used to it."

"I know," Carla said.

"I want to retire soon and start a new chapter. Do some

community work, focus on my investments. But until I do," he said, pausing to let the words sink in, "I need you to be strong and have faith."

"I am strong. I don't know what got into me today."

"If anything happens to me, I want you to go on with your life. Meet somebody new, live and enjoy."

Carla nodded, but she couldn't imagine life without him.

Then Baxter stared her straight in the eye. "But absolutely no Percy."

Carla suddenly felt amused.

"I mean it," Baxter said. "No Percy."

Carla fell out on the blanket, laughing.

"I'll come back and haunt the shit out of both of you," he said.

Carla was still rolling in laughter.

Baxter smiled. He was happy to see her laugh. "You got that?" he asked.

"Tell that to Percy."

"No, I'm telling you."

Carla still found it funny that if anything happened to Baxter, he didn't want her involved with Percy. "What about Wendell?" Carla teased and sat up.

"Don't push it, baby."

She smiled in amusement.

"I guess Wendell's not too bad. He did look out for you," Baxter finally admitted. "But I don't want you going back to the club life."

"That's over with," Carla said. Then she posed a question. "Suppose something happened to me, would you ever consider Natalie?"

Baxter smiled. "Your sister's good-looking. She doesn't have your spunk though." Then he quickly dismissed the idea. "Nope, no Natalie. I'd have to deal with Stephanie, Brittany, and Tiffany. That's a wild bunch."

Carla laughed in understanding. She was glad he had ruled out Natalie. "I don't want to think about anybody else for either of us," Carla said, positioning herself in front of him again. She leaned back against his chest.

"Then let's enjoy the moment," Baxter said. He stopped, then hesitated. "I want to make sure you're okay. You've gone through a lot since I met you—the fire at the TiTi, Mimi, a new job. That's why I mentioned counseling before. Talk with somebody. Put things in proper perspective. Your whole life has turned around. And . . . ." His voice trailed off.

"Go on," Carla urged.

"There's your father. If anything happens to me, I don't want you wasting away like that," he finally said. "Maybe, if you talk with someone, you can prevent it."

Carla pulled away from him and turned around. "I don't need counseling, and I won't allow myself to get like that. Don't flatter yourself."

Baxter realized he had struck a chord that Carla didn't appreciate.

She threw up her hands. "I got upset today because like you said, this is all new to me. Maybe, it's my hormones. I mean, what the fuck, I still get my period."

"Counseling wouldn't hurt. Just a conversation with somebody. I've done it."

Carla jumped to her feet angrily. "I'm fine. I don't need it. Thanks, but no thanks." She turned to face the beach. "I need to take a walk. I'll be back in a few minutes."

"I'll go with you," Baxter said.

"No. I want to walk by myself. Clear my head."

"Fine. Then I'll walk behind you. But wherever you go, I go. I don't want any more problems today."

"I'm going by myself. I'll be right back." Carla stormed off, without turning around. She sensed Baxter walking behind her. She kept going and tried to ignore him. She knew he was watching her ass.

She turned around. "Come walk beside me."

He smiled. "That's okay. I'll stay back here. I know you want to be by yourself."

"You just want to look at my ass," Carla said. She raised her fists and adopted a boxing stance. She closed in on him and started mock punching him. Her fists were flying. He laughed so hard he couldn't defend himself. Carla continued swinging at him. She deliberately held back from punching him hard. He finally grabbed her wrists and pulled her close.

"You want me to put you over my knee, like in that book?" His voice deepened with desire.

"I dare you," Carla taunted.

He picked her up and hauled her over his shoulder.

"Stop," Carla laughed. "Put me down."

He did. But he made sure that his maleness brushed against the front of her as he put her down on her feet. Carla wrapped her arms around his neck and kissed him hungrily. He held her tight and kissed her back. They stood locked in each other's arms amid the heat of the sunlight and the sparkle of the ocean. They shut out everybody around them.

When they finished kissing, they held hands and walked along the beach. Carla stopped abruptly and turned in the opposite direction. "Let's go this way. I want to kick that witch's ass."

Baxter tried to suppress a smile. "Who?"

"You know who—that smart ass in the little bikini. I saw her watching you. I bet she's the one who wanted you to carry her."

Baxter feigned innocence. "I don't think I noticed her. You know I only have eyes for you," he said smoothly.

Carla snickered. "Yeah, right."

They walked in silence for a while, basking in the sunlight and each other's company.

Carla finally spoke. "We are exclusive, right?"

He looked at her and nodded. "We are."

Carla cleared her throat and hesitated.

"What's up?" Baxter asked.

"I ran into a friend of mine the other day. She used to work at the club."

Baxter tensed for a moment.

"She's a nurse now. Would you believe it? She got out of stripping too."

Baxter's chest heaved in relief. "Sounds like she's a good influence."

Carla narrowed her eyes at him. "I don't need her influence."

"I know, but the more the merrier."

"Oh, stop worrying. I don't want to go back to the TiTi." She hesitated again.

"What's up? Talk to me."

"We should do HIV testing," she said, finally broaching the subject.

Baxter raised an eyebrow.

"That's what Gigi says. I mean Gina. She's the nurse. We should make sure everything's okay so we can really get into the relationship."

A chuckle escaped Baxter's lips. "Okay. Makes sense."

Carla made perfect sense, he decided. He was supposed to be "Mr. Safety Man," but he had thrown caution to the wind with her. The testing was a good idea. He was glad Carla was attracting better influences.

He squeezed her hand as they headed towards the blanket. "I'm starved," he said.

Once they reached their spot, Carla plopped down and opened a cooler. She grabbed some paper plates and dished out hefty servings of a pasta salad that contained shrimp and crabmeat. Baxter nodded appreciatively. She pulled out a mixed green salad and slices of French bread. She and Baxter ate voraciously. They barely came up for air. Once the feeding frenzy ended, they both laughed at how famished they were.

"You okay now?" Carla asked.

"Yeah, thanks, baby," he said.

After they ate, they lounged on the blanket the way they had planned to earlier in the day. Then they went out in the water again for a while. They looked for their little toddler friend, but he played with another kid his age. The two little boys were both engrossed in hauling buckets of sand from one point to the next.

Carla and Baxter played without him. Eventually, they got out of the water and waited for the sun to set. Baxter sat behind her again, his arms draped around her waist. Carla leaned against him. As he talked, she loved the way the timbre of his voice reverberated through her body, from her back to her chest. She giggled.

"What's so funny?"

"Your voice vibrates right through me."

"Oh, yeah? You want to feel some more vibrations?"

Carla could feel him hardening against her, but their little neighbor had returned.

"What happened to your friend?" Baxter asked the little boy. "Don't you want to go play with your buddy?"

Carla howled in laughter. "It's okay. You can hang out with us," Carla told the little boy.

Fortunately, his father came to the rescue. He scooped up the little boy and tossed him in the air as they returned to their own blanket.

"I guess no touchy-feely for us with little hardhead around," Baxter laughed.

Carla shifted and sat beside him. She leaned close. "I would love to have carried your babies," she said wistfully.

"Me too," he answered. "A little late for that, don't you think?"

"Not in today's world."

Baxter's eyes grew big.

Carla chuckled. "Don't get your panties all bunched up. I can satisfy my maternal instincts some other way. Besides, there's so much I want to do. I feel like I've been cooped up forever in the TiTi. I want to go to school. I want to start a business. Maybe, we can adopt down the road."

Baxter started squirming. "Uh, I've already got a daughter and maybe even grandchildren somewhere." He hated to dampen her spirits, but he had to be honest. "Since you've come into my world, I don't search for them as much, but I never know what's going to jump off."

Carla sighed. "I understand."

"Until we figure things out . . . ." Baxter's words trailed off. "Maybe, we could get a dog down the road."

Carla was pleased to hear him talking long term. "Not a big dog, a small dog," she said.

"A small dog is okay, but not too small. I'm a big guy. I don't want to walk down the street with some one-inch dog on a chain."

Carla burst out laughing. "Okay, baby."

Shoulder to shoulder, they fell silent, reveling in the sunset. A glorious blend of pastels streaked the sky. Baxter kissed her hand. Carla caressed his cheek. The day was turning out to be marvelous after all.

When the sun finally slid beneath the horizon, Baxter rose from the blanket. "I thought we could make out a little, but I see we still have company." He nodded over at the little boy and his family.

Carla smiled. "That'll teach you."

"So where to, young lady?" Baxter inquired.

Carla stood and stretched lazily. "I don't know, but I'm not ready to go home yet."

Baxter reached for his cell phone. "I've got an idea. Let me check with a buddy of mine."

Carla started packing things up as Baxter talked on the phone. His face lit up after he finished the conversation. "I've got a little surprise," he said.

"I'm ready," Carla responded.

They finished packing up and headed for the car.

CHAPTER 35

Carla twirled around in the living room of one of the most beautiful beach houses she had ever seen. It sat high up along the sands of Malibu Beach. The living room was off-white and tan with stark, clean lines. A soft cashmere throw embellished the couch along with pillows in rich geometric patterns. The floors were polished concrete, covered with expensive rugs. Bold splashes of color radiated from abstract art. Carla thought she recognized a Kandinsky painting. She remembered an umbrella with a pattern replicating one of his works that she had seen years ago in a gift shop.

She had never been overly fond of ultra-modern furniture. She found it bland, stiff, and impersonal, but not the modern furniture in this living room. It was both elegant and inviting.

Floor-to-ceiling windows provided a spectacular view of the beach and the swirling ocean as it swallowed up the sand during the evening tide. Waves danced vigorously against the rocky cliffs jutting out in the distance. The sounds of the crashing, foaming waters along the shoreline provided music to Carla's ears.

She squealed in delight. "My goodness. Whose place is this?"

Baxter smiled, pleased. "A buddy of mine."

Carla threw her hands up. "He lets you come here whenever you want?"

"Not exactly. But yeah, whenever it's available, I can come by and hang out. He gives me the code so I can drive in and pick up the key card wherever he hides it."

Carla remembered Baxter punching in the code to enter a gated driveway off the Pacific Coast Highway.

"How do you know him?" Carla asked. She was still amazed by all the luxury surrounding her.

"I did him a favor," Baxter responded.

"What favor?"

Baxter shrugged humbly. "I helped him out."

Carla knew she wasn't going to get anything more out of Baxter. Had he rescued the owner of the house? she wondered. "Will I ever get to meet this guy?" she asked.

"Probably."

Carla had a million questions. "How come we never came here before? How long have you had access? Why didn't you tell me—" She stopped.

Baxter smiled and shook his head. "I don't come here often because I don't want to wear my welcome out. Besides, I've got my own house with a nice view, thank you very much. This place is my motivation to buy my own beach house. I only come here on special occasions."

"Am I your special occasion?" Carla asked with a sly grin.

Baxter grinned back. "Maybe."

Carla stepped closer to him and savored the moment. She kissed him softly. "This is a great way to top the day."

"We've had a crazy one so I figured we could come here and unwind."

"How long can we stay? I should have brought more clothing."

"You're fine," Baxter said. "We're only staying overnight. I've got to give it back in the morning."

"Then, we better get busy." She grabbed Baxter's hand and led him out a sliding glass door onto a deck. They descended the stairs and headed for the beach.

"You didn't get enough of the beach yet?" Baxter asked, laughing.

"Not like this."

They walked along the beach under a softly darkening sky. The stars were starting to unveil. A tiny sliver of moon peeped out and formed a perfect crescent.

Carla gazed up and smiled. "A new moon. I love a new moon. Means there's more to come. I love the full moon too, but it makes me a little sad. I know it's going to waste away."

"Then I'm glad it's growing. We don't want you to be sad," Baxter teased.

"You want me to beat you up again?"

"You can do whatever you want now that little hardhead isn't around."

They both started laughing. Carla squeezed his hand tighter as they continued to stroll along the beach. Her colorful wrap skirt swirled and opened, revealing her legs. Baxter's eyes danced in admiration. The wind picked up for a moment, making the skirt twirl against his legs too.

Carla laughed. "You want to get under my skirt?"

"Oh, I intend to."

Delaying gratification, they continued strolling along the beach with Carla's skirt whipping around their legs. They had flaked off most of the sand from their skins and still wore their bathing suits. Baxter's trunks protruded in the front. Carla glanced down and smiled. She stepped closer to his side, allowing her skirt to flutter even more against him. She heard his sharp intake of breath. Then he removed the soft hoodie that covered the top of her bathing suit.

"You cold?" he asked.

"No. I'm fine."

"Yes, you are fine. I want to look at you."

His eyes devoured her cleavage in the bathing suit. He caressed the strips across the front and back. Carla's insides tingled as Baxter explored her exposed skin between the strips of cloth. His arm slid down to her waist, just above the swell of her butt. His fingers traced the high cut of her suit along the thigh. Then his fingers lightly skimmed between her legs for a moment. Carla's breath became ragged. She arched her body against his fingers, but he teased, then retreated.

Carla reached down to massage the neon orange protrusion of his shorts. She caressed his hardness through the cloth of his trunks. He was rock hard in her hands. They resumed walking again, punctuating their stroll with probing, titillating fingers.

Finally, Carla dropped down on the sand and kissed the jutting outline of his trunks. Her hot breath inflamed him. He pulled his stiffness out and pressed it against her lips. Carla's mouth engulfed him greedily. She stopped sucking for a moment and pulled his shorts down so his maleness could spring free and clear. Baxter moaned and groaned as she buried her head in his crotch and sucked long and hard. She twirled her tongue around him. The more she sucked, the hotter her insides grew.

Baxter pulled her to her feet. His unrestrained fullness pressed wantonly against her. He kissed her lips, her neck, the tops of her breasts. He freed one breast, then the other and fondled her nipples until they grew rigid. He buried his head in her breasts and sucked until she moaned and arched against him. He eased her swimsuit down to her waist and kissed down to her navel. Then he slid down in the sand and kissed from her ankles to her thighs. He buried his head between her legs and breathed hot and heavy against her pulsing flesh. His kisses burned through the fabric of her bathing suit.

Carla felt exquisite sensations coursing through her loins. He slid the crotch over and slipped his finger inside. Carla gasped from the pleasure of it. Then he removed his finger and licked it. He stood, removed her skirt, and eased her swimsuit off. They stood butt-naked under the glowing sliver of moonlight.

To savor the night, they walked naked along the sand. For every few steps they took, they explored and groped each other with hungry, insistent fingers. Their kisses devoured each other until they were both panting. They retrieved her skirt and fell on top of it in the sand. Then Baxter lowered his head between her legs. Carla moaned and opened wider for his tongue. She lay back, gazing up at the stars as Baxter twirled his tongue around the bloom between her thighs. Her insides quivered with pleasure as he inserted a finger, then slid it in and out as he licked her.

"That feels so good, baby," Carla moaned. She sat on top of him and slid herself all over his thickness. He was bone hard inside her. Not wanting to explode yet, she lifted herself off him, stroked him, then slipped his shaft into her mouth and sucked wantonly. Baxter groaned and guided her head as she sucked away. Then she stopped sucking and rode him up and down as her juices slushed over his hardness. His hands played with her breasts and butt as they fucked shamelessly in the sand under the eavesdropping stars. Their bodies rocked with such delicious sensations until Baxter couldn't stand it any longer. He flipped Carla over and plunged deeply into her. She swallowed him greedily between her legs.

As the waves slapped against the rocks and the beach, their bodies slapped against each other. Baxter rode to his heart's content until they panted and shouted in ecstasy under the cover of a blue velvet night that only intensified their pleasure.

As their heavy breathing subsided, they both laughed weakly.

"You okay?" he asked.

She hugged him. "Yeah. I could stay here all night."

"We can go inside, you know."

She squeezed his dick. "Looking forward to it."

They continued to lie on the sand, wrapped in each other's arms under the coverlet of stars and the crescent of moonlight. After a while, they rose from her skirt and headed back to the house. Carla wrapped the skirt around her bare bottom and slipped her hoodie over her bare breasts.

Knowing she was naked underneath, Baxter became aroused again when he saw her skirt flutter open. His dick started to protrude. Carla laughed at him. He wore his hoodie and nothing else. She reached down and massaged him. He responded immediately and grew harder. They stopped for a minute to kiss and fondle. Eventually, they climbed the stairs to the deck. Still wanting to relish the night, they leaned against the railing and stared at the frothy shoreline. Then Baxter moved behind her and entered her from the back. He grabbed a handful of her butt and pushed in deeply. He kissed all over her neck and played with her tits. Carla wanted to enjoy the night forever. She pushed her butt even tighter against him as they stood locked together on the deck. Then Carla slid off his hardness. Before he could protest at the loss of her pulsating warmth, she backed him onto a patio bench, lifted her skirt, and straddled him. She pushed him back against the table and slid up and down his shaft until they both kissed, moaned, and groaned in sheer abandonment.

"Damn, baby," Baxter said when it was all over and his breathing returned to normal.

"You having a good day?" Carla asked huskily.

"The best," he said.

They showered and found some chicken pot pies in the freezer. Carla heated them up and added the leftover salad from their cooler to round out the meal. Baxter uncorked the bottle of white wine they never had a chance to drink earlier. They sat languidly at the marble kitchen island, staring out the window. The high chairs were bone white leather and chrome. Carla was bewitched by the beauty of the place and the pleasure of Baxter's company. They ate leisurely, consuming the opulence of the night.

"Your birthday's coming up soon. What do you want for your birthday? A tie?" Carla teased, breaking the silence.

"A lap dance," Baxter replied, without missing a beat. "A formal one with all the trimmings."

Carla burst out laughing. "A lap dance? And here, I've been trying to get away from that. I thought you don't want me to dance anymore."

"Not at the club, but you can dance for me."

"You never had a real lap dance before?"

"Nope."

"Are you serious? All this time, I thought . . . . You a virgin?" Carla asked, amazed.

"I never thought of it like that, but I guess."

Carla stared at him in disbelief.

"I don't hang out in strip clubs much," Baxter said. "I never felt comfortable with some dancer grinding all over me. I could never let go."

Carla was the ultimate stripper, and in her heyday, she had performed plenty of lap dances. But she suddenly felt a little shy about giving Baxter a lap dance. She thought he was going to ask for a more traditional birthday present.

Baxter saw the play of emotions on her face. "You asked me what I wanted."

Carla nodded. "I guess I wasn't expecting a lap dance."

"What do you want for *your* birthday?"

"The Art Biennale or FESPACO," Carla said firmly.

"The Biennale? Isn't that the arts festival in Venice?"

Carla grinned mischievously. "Art from all over the world."

Baxter's eyes grew wide. "Or FESPACO? That's the film festival in Burkina Faso."

Carla's grin broadened.

"Whoa! Those are big trips—honeymoon trips."

Carla ears perked up. She observed him intently.

"I meant . . . what I meant to say was," he stammered, "those are expensive trips."

Shit, Baxter thought. He was ready to kick himself. He couldn't believe he said, "honeymoon." Carla looked like the cat that swallowed the canary. Well, he had no intention of being the canary. "All I meant was that either one of those trips is a big-ticket item," Baxter said, trying to extricate himself from a slip of the tongue.

Carla decided to let him squirm as her insides danced with glee. She tried to suppress a smug smile.

"You know what I meant," Baxter said. "If you want those kinds of trips, I might have to send you back to the TiTi," he joked.

"You asked me what I wanted for my birthday, and I'm not going back to the TiTi."

"How about if I give *you* a lap dance?" Baxter laughed.

"No, that's what you want. I'll make it a good one. I'll give you the best lap dance you could ever imagine," she said huskily and waited for his reaction.

Baxter smiled in anticipation. Carla figured his dick was probably doing leaps and bounds at the thought. It was. She cupped it in the palm of her hands and tugged gently. His breath caught in his chest.

She smiled. "I'll come up with something special for your birthday."

"What about now?" he asked.

"You finished eating?"

They slid off the high chairs and made their way to one of the bedrooms. The beachfront view from the bedroom was even better than from the kitchen. They lit a few candles and watched the light dance along the walls. The candlelight illuminated the sundress that Carla now wore. She started to remove it, but Baxter stopped her.

"Keep it on," he said softly as he watched the flickering candlelight illumine her nakedness under the dress.

She moved sultrily in front of the fluttering flames so that he could see even more. Eventually, they fell into each other's arms, fondling and probing again. Insatiably, they fucked all over the house until they retreated in exhaustion to the bedroom.

CHAPTER 36

Carla and Gina, the former stripper-turned-nurse, lounged at a restaurant happy hour in Century City on the west side. They both had ordered sweet cocktail drinks. They lifted their glasses for a toast.

"Congratulations on passing your test, girl," Gina smiled.

Carla beamed from ear to ear. "Thanks, Gina. Congratulations to us both on finding new careers."

"I'll drink to that," Gina said and sipped heartily.

Carla was floating on cloud nine. She had passed her exam and completed her CPR class which was a part of the certification. In a few weeks, she'd receive her Personal Trainer Certificate. She was now drumming up business and creating her own client base. She could train clients privately or at the fitness center. She and Jasmine had worked out a deal. Gina might become her first client.

Carla smiled. What a difference a few months made. She had charted a whole new path. Natalie and the girls were so proud of her. She planned to celebrate with them too.

Baxter planned to take her out to dinner so they could celebrate. He suggested they meet up at the happy hour, after she and Gina had a chance to talk. He liked her shoe business idea too. Because it was uncharted territory for her, he wanted her to think seriously about how much time and energy she would have to expend. Carla didn't know what to do. So many doors had opened up for her, and she still wanted to attend college. She suddenly had this thirst for all the opportunities she had missed when she worked at the TiTi. She knew she was all over the place, but she didn't care. In time, she'd focus.

Right now, she simply wanted to bask in the knowledge that plenty of adventures awaited her. The sky was the limit.

"We've come a long way, Gina," Carla said expansively.

"Yes, indeed," Gina laughed.

They became more relaxed as their drinks started taking effect.

"So you got a new job, a new man," Gina said. "Tell me about him. Nope. You don't have to tell me. I can see it in your face, in your eyes. You're fucked up over him."

"Is it that obvious?"

Gina shook her head. "Yes, it is."

"He rescued me from that fire at the old TiTi."

"Damn."

"I know. It's deep."

Gina hesitated for a moment. "Make sure you're not confusing gratitude and love."

"I don't think so. He's a really cool guy. You'll meet him. He's going to stop by here and take me to dinner. He wants to help me celebrate my certification."

Gina nodded, impressed. "I envy you, Carla. You know how hard it is to find a good man?"

Carla gave Gina a high five. "Tell me about it." Carla felt so exhilarated that she wished everybody well. "You'll meet somebody," she told Gina. "He's out there."

They continued sipping their drinks and people watching.

"You've convinced me," Gina said eventually. "I'll be your first client, and we'll go from there. Maybe, you can come to my job and offer classes."

Carla shook Gina's hand. "Thank you, girl. You don't need a lot of work. I'll help you firm up a bit, spice up your routine. You'll get a man," Carla teased.

"I'm going to hold you to it."

They ordered a second round of drinks and talked and laughed about their days at the TiTi. They joked about Wendell and his growing polysyllabic vocabulary, laced with every curse word imaginable.

Gina suddenly gasped. "Is that him? Damn, girl. He's fine."

Carla turned around. Baxter strode towards them in a pair

of black jeans and a blue and white pin-striped shirt that graced his broad frame. He carried a dark jacket over his arm. As usual, he looked so handsome to Carla. Her face broke into a smile when she made eye contact with him.

"Yep, that's my baby," Carla confirmed with a giggle. "Ain't he fine?" she mumbled quickly before he reached them.

"I was just about to ask Carla if you had a brother," Gina said, when Baxter reached the patio railing. He bent down and kissed Carla chastely on the lips. In one lithe move, he climbed over the railing and joined them. Both women laughed.

"Gina, this is my sweetheart, Baxter." Carla was all smiles as she introduced him.

Baxter grinned at Gina as they shook hands. "Sorry. No brothers. But I've got plenty of buddies," he said.

"Well, that's a start," Gina responded.

Baxter was pleased that Carla was associating with someone who had found a constructive life after stripping. He hoped Carla would continue her association with Gina, either as a friend or a business contact. He was relatively sure that Carla was finished with the club life, but he figured good influences never hurt. He guessed that Gina was probably in her early forties, possibly late thirties. It was hard to tell these days. She was a pretty woman with a nice body, not as stunning as Carla, but he imagined Gina turned plenty of heads in her stripping days. She attracted attention now in her pencil slim skirt and silk blouse. She wore killer heels.

"We're going to dinner to celebrate Carla's certification. You want to join us?" Baxter asked Gina.

"No thanks. I'll let you two hang out. I've got a few things to do."

"You're quite welcome to join us," Carla said.

"Thanks, but I really need to get going."

"We can all hang out some time," Baxter offered. "I'll bring one of my play brothers along."

"Only if he's as fine as you," Gina teased.

"He's almost," Baxter replied with a grin.

"Did I tell you how modest my baby is?" Carla interjected with a laugh.

Baxter liked Gina's confidence. She and Carla both knew how to flirt and talk with men. He guessed it was from their club days. Baxter ordered a quick drink to be sociable, and all three left after he finished.

"You get a chance to click your heels today, Dorothy?" Baxter asked.

Carla's face lit up in response. From the happy hour restaurant, they walked over to the Century City mall. Carla wore moderately high heels and a wrap dress in a print pattern of blues, mauves, and golds. Instead of a loose skirt, her wrap dress was slim and fitted. The V-neck of the dress plunged just enough to arouse curiosity.

Baxter enjoyed walking with her over to the mall. Her heels clicked, and she turned heads along the way.

Inside a trendy restaurant in the mall, Carla and Baxter ate a leisurely dinner. The whole area had undergone a facelift, and there were plenty of diners surrounding them. Carla had ordered the roasted salmon and crushed potatoes. Baxter ordered southern style shrimp and grits. He had already devoured his appetizer and salad.

"I like Gina. I think she's a good influence," Baxter said.

"I'm a good influence on her," Carla countered.

Baxter elevated his wine glass. "Yes, you are. May your accomplishments continue."

Carla smiled and quickly forgave him.

"So you got your first client today?" Baxter asked.

"Can you believe it? I passed that test just in time," she said cheerfully.

Baxter thoroughly enjoyed her good spirts. He couldn't help but compare her to Simone, who would have been so jealous that she would never have introduced him to an attractive client, let alone allow the client to compliment him. Simone would have quizzed him all night. But Carla was secure with herself. She never tried to restrict his freedom. She was starting to captivate him more and more. Yet he didn't want to lose control.

After they finished eating, while Baxter pondered over

dessert, Carla checked her text messages. "I haven't heard from Mimi in a while," Carla said. "I sent her a text earlier, and she hasn't answered. She usually responds right away."

Baxter lowered his eyes for a moment. Carla's heart beat faster. "What's up?" she demanded.

"I don't know, but Frank hasn't heard from her either. I think she's pulling away from him."

"Why didn't you tell me this sooner?"

"I thought you were keeping in touch with her."

Carla gestured at their tony surroundings. "I knew this was too good to be true." Abruptly, she jumped up from the table and almost knocked over their glasses.

"Calm down, baby. I'm sure there's a good reason you haven't heard from her."

"I could wring her neck sometimes," Carla said and sank back down in the booth. She stared at Baxter apologetically. "I've got to see her. Make sure everything's okay. I'll check back with you later." She leaned over and kissed him. "Thanks so much for dinner."

Carla was stunned when Baxter didn't offer a word of protest.

"Okay," he said. "You going over to the TiTi?"

Carla nodded. She suddenly felt a sense of dread.

"I'll drive you over," he insisted.

"I'll be fine, Baxter. Just take me back to my car."

"No, I'll take you over to the club."

Carla's eyes were insistent. "Please let me go by myself in case it's a girl thing. I'll text you the moment I get to the TiTi and the moment I leave."

Baxter finally agreed. "Okay." His face broke into a smile. "I guess you'll bring me dessert later?"

Carla smiled slyly. "Oh, you want dessert?" She pointed to the menu. "Let's get the waiter back so you can order."

"Very funny," Baxter said. "Keep the dress on. I'll unwrap it for dessert."

Carla rose from the table, bent down, and kissed him. "Cool."

* * *

Carla's heels thudded instead of clicked at the TiTi. The carpet dulled her heels. The darkness of the club and the neon lights sealed her in a vacuum that she wanted to escape. Still, she was on a mission. She headed straight over to Mimi's table. She breathed a sigh of relief when she saw Mimi dancing. Wendell intercepted her before she could reach Mimi.

"Look at you. Aren't you a vision of comeliness?"

Carla was forced to smile. "Thanks, Wendell."

"No, I mean it. You look good. Your face has softened. Some of them hard lines have dissipated."

"Gee, thanks."

"You know I don't mean no harm. I see a change in you. This ambience don't seem to suit you anymore." Still Wendell couldn't resist. "But if you want to come back and do a show, I'll hook you up, especially now. You really look good, Rae. You ain't got many more dancing years left, you know."

At first, Carla felt a sting from his words until her eyes dropped unintentionally to his bloated belly. At that moment, Carla knew she could have delivered a serious blow to Wendell's ego, but she chose the high road and refrained from comment.

Guessing her thoughts, Wendell was sufficiently chastened and embarrassed. "I'm just saying you might as well take advantage of that physiology you got going and do one more show."

Carla shook her head and laughed at him. "Give it up, Wendell. I'm not interested."

Wendell persisted. "Come on, be honest. Doesn't the entertainer in you miss performing, even a little bit?"

"A little," Carla finally admitted. "But I don't miss the environment—the guys pawing all over me and the lewd, vulgar comments."

Wendell shrugged. "Goes with the territory. What do you expect?"

"I expect more now, and I get it."

"When you're ready to throw fire boy to the curb, let me know. We complement each other, Rae. I got a new hostess, but she don't hold a candle to you. Come back any time you want. You need a place to sleep, my bed is always ready to accommodate you."

Carla was tired of Wendell's bullshit. She changed the subject. "How's Mimi doing?"

"Check her out. She seems fine. She's working harder than usual, but that's good."

"Alright, Wendell, catch you later." She walked away without giving him time to respond. She could feel his eyes boring through her back.

"I like that dress, nice and professional," he called out.

Carla nodded and kept walking. She was thrilled when she reached Mimi's table. Mimi appeared stark sober for a change. Her eyes shone bright and alert and full of her usual rebellion. When Carla sat down at the table, Mimi shook her butt in front of Carla just to be a smart ass.

"Girl, I'll come up there and kick your ass," Carla said, half-joking, half-threatening.

"Get on up here, chica," Mimi taunted. "Come on, one last time. You know you want to dance. Show 'em what you got."

The guys at Mimi's table fixed their gazes on Carla. She remembered a couple of the men. They started egging her on. Carla almost felt tempted, but she refused the bait. She did miss performing for the guys and titillating them to a frenzy. But she didn't miss the way some of them ogled her now. She could feel their eyes scalding through her dress. One guy kept bumping his leg into hers. Finally, he reached out and put his hand under her dress and stroked her thigh.

Carla kicked his chair over, and he fell to the floor. He lay in a sulking, fuming heap at her feet. Mimi and the whole table laughed. The man's eyes narrowed in anger and embarrassment, but he quickly picked himself up off the floor.

One of Wendell's henchmen walked over, amused. "You alright, Rae?"

Carla nodded. "I got it." She turned a withering glance towards the offender. "If you want to sit at this table, don't touch me again."

The man decided to leave instead. Carla smiled to herself as he departed. Her fitness training was really paying off. She stared at the other guys around the table. They realized they weren't getting any action from her so their eyes returned to Mimi. Carla suddenly felt out of place at the TiTi. The encounter with the man reaffirmed her commitment to a different life. She had no tolerance anymore for disrespect from the patrons. She wished Mimi would hurry up and finish her routine.

Mimi did a series of bumps, grinds, and twerks that made the guys salivate. She climbed the pole and encircled her body all around it like a wanton gymnast. She held onto the pole and spread her legs wide in the air. Every guy at the table wanted her to mount their own poles. Mimi capitalized on their lust until they had stuck enough bills in her G-string. Then she ended the dance and stepped off the table.

Carla and Mimi had moved to a side table. Mimi was now scantily clad in a silver mini dress and silver stilettos. The dress gave her a gorgeous raunchiness that turned men's heads even though she had finished dancing. Her eyes looked clear for a change.

"What's up, girl?" Carla asked. "You didn't return my text."

"I forgot my phone, and I didn't have time to go home for it. You know I always text you back."

Carla breathed a sigh of relief. "Okay." She observed Mimi carefully. "You sober?"

"I'm trying, chica."

Carla nodded, impressed. "I hope you keep it up."

"You give the shoe proposal to Baxter?"

"Yes, I did."

"What did he say?" Mimi was anxious for a response.

Carla shrugged her shoulders. "Well . . . ."

Mimi's face fell. "I think it's a good idea," she said defensively.

Carla decided to tease her a little longer. "Just because we think it's a good idea—"

"Yeah, yeah," Mimi interrupted in disappointment.

Carla finally stopped teasing. "Baxter feels it's a good idea too." Her words took a moment to fully register with Mimi.

"He liked it?"

"Yep. He loved your graphics and the layout."

Mimi glowed with pride. "Wow. Thanks, Carla, for giving me the chance."

"No, you helped me. That's why you have to get away from this." Carla gestured around the room.

"I'm trying to. I've been going to a few NA meetings."

"You have?" Carla said in a voice filled with hope.

"Don't get all excited. I'm just checking things out."

"You still seeing Frank?"

"You know I'm crazy about Frank, and I know he loves me. But I'm trying to clear my head. I need to get clean on my own without Frank. I'm trying to quit the club. I've been working my butt off, putting money aside so I'll have something to live on when I leave. I don't know what kind of job I can find."

"Mimi, with your skills, you can do anything you want with computers and social networking. And don't forget our shoe business. You can do all the PR and networking for that."

"Yeah, but that's going to take time. I need money right away for when I leave here."

"What about Teddy, Percy's girlfriend?"

"What about her?"

Carla's voice rose in excitement. "She does PR. You could intern with her or see if she'll pay you something."

Mimi's face was wary. "I don't know, chica. Teddy don't play. I have to step right when I go to her. I really want to be clean when I ask her for a job."

"What about that other woman at the charity ball? She works in PR too. You got her card."

Mimi appeared overwhelmed. "Hold it. One day at a time. I'll contact both of them when I'm ready."

Carla was so excited to get Mimi out of the TiTi that she was ready to carry her out. But Mimi was right. One day at a time. Mimi had to do it her way.

"Okay, however you want to do things," Carla said finally.

Mimi nodded in gratitude. "It's hard for me. I like getting high. I like being clear-headed too, but I miss getting high. Every day is a fight."

"That's why you gotta walk away from here, Mimi. Does Joe know you're trying to get clean?" Carla asked suspiciously.

"Fortunately, he doesn't come around anymore. Nobody's seen him for a while."

"Good. Then hurry up and get away from here. I can give you some money now."

Mimi started laughing. "Slow down, chica. You act like you the one on speed."

"I want you to split from this place while you can."

"I don't need money right now. I'll let you know if I do. But I'm trying to do this for myself, nobody else."

"Okay," Carla conceded. "But this is definitely not the best environment to get clean. Joe's a filthy snake."

"I know, but he ain't been around. I'm just trying to make a little more money, and then I'll be on my way, before he shows up. But it's not about Joe now. It's about me."

"I'm proud of you," Carla said.

Mimi smiled warmly.

CHAPTER 37

Carla glanced at the clock on her bedroom night table and picked up the pace. She slipped on a glittery G-string and attached sparkly pasties over her nipples. Then she entwined a strappy satin slingshot on top. The bikini-like slingshot formed a halter neck and tied around her waist, barely covering the pasties and the G-string. The scandalous contrivance meandered all around her torso, exposing her curves.

For her next layer, Carla stepped into a strapless black mini dress that was sheer from top to bottom. The halter neck of the slingshot meshed with the dress. Carla next clasped the beautiful gold and diamond chain that Baxter had given her around her ankle. She felt a bit jittery, yet excited. Baxter was on his way over to her house for his birthday lap dance. It was a beautiful, end-of-summer evening, and Carla had opened her windows to welcome the breezy twilight air.

She glanced around the bedroom. Everything was in order, except her vanity with its tons of makeup spread all over the top. But she could never get that in order. Still, she managed to make the vanity look like elegant chaos with its contrasting lipsticks, blushers, and eye shadows covering the glass top. Her plump bed was dressed for the occasion with satin sheets and a comforter she had found on sale. Bold flashes of color streaked through the cream-colored quilt like an abstract painting. The comforter was feminine enough for her, but not too frilly for Baxter to lie under. She was impressed with her good find.

Throughout the bedroom, she had placed candles in

strategic spots for sensuous lighting as nightfall advanced. A thick woven area rug with golden flecks covered the shiny oak floor and provided a chic coziness. The yellow-attired rag doll that Baxter had given her presided over her dresser with its legs crossed. It fell right in place with her décor.

The intercom rang. Carla smiled to herself. Baxter was a little early, but she wasn't surprised. He was all excited for his lap dance. Carla entered the living room and buzzed him in when she heard his voice.

In record time, he stood in her apartment, wearing a fitted black shirt and stylish gray slacks that hung low on his hips. He wore a big grin on his face.

Carla kissed him lustily. "Happy Birthday, Baxter."

The short sleeves of his shirt accentuated his arms. She rubbed her hands over his chest in the fitted shirt. She looked forward to sitting on his lap. He kissed her in happy anticipation.

Carla laughed at him. "Hold your horses. I'm almost ready, running a little late." She pointed to the coffee table. "But there's wine you can uncork, and there's a cheese tray."

Baxter smiled in appreciation at the nicely arranged tray of fruit, cheese, and crackers on the coffee table. "Thanks, baby," he said and kissed her again.

A small vase of flowers adorned the table as well. A larger bouquet graced the dining room table, and Baxter noted the candles dispersed throughout both rooms. Carla had even decorated one of the dining room chairs with a colorful metallic balloon which read, "Happy Birthday," in big gold letters. She had tied the streamers to the back of the chair so that the balloon floated up high.

Baxter's face broke into a devilish grin. "Is that my dance chair?"

Carla merely smiled. Baxter put his arms around her from the back. She was barefooted and wore a short satin wrap-around that covered the sheer dress underneath. He pressed against her butt. Carla could feel his growing erection. "Hurry up and get dressed," he urged. He started caressing the satin of her robe. "You look fine like this. Just put some heels on."

Carla pulled away from him. "I will, but I want to put on more makeup and slip on a dress."

"Let me catch you before you put your lipstick on," Baxter said and plunged his tongue into her mouth. Carla realized Baxter was operating on full steam for his birthday celebration. She let him feel her up a little, then eased away from him and headed back to the bedroom. If she didn't pull away from him now, she would never get a chance to finish dressing.

"I'll be back in a few minutes," she said.

Swiftly, she headed to the bedroom to put the finishing touches on her makeup. The intercom buzzed.

Baxter strode back to the bedroom. Carla was still in her satin robe. "You expecting somebody? On my birthday?" he added.

Carla laughed. He was like a little kid. It was all about his birthday. "Somebody probably buzzed the wrong number," she said.

The intercom buzzed again. Baxter walked out into the living room and pressed the button. "Who is it?" he asked firmly.

"It's me, Gina. Do I have the right apartment? I'm trying to reach Carla. I was in the neighborhood."

Baxter suppressed a frown. "This is Baxter, Carla's boyfriend. I'll let you up." He buzzed her in, then he quickly headed back to Carla's bedroom. "It's Gina," he announced. "She said she was in the neighborhood. I let her in. She's your new client, right?"

"Yeah, but I hadn't planned on training her today."

Baxter's eyes lingered on Carla's dress. Gauzy black silk now layered the sheer, skin-tight dress underneath. Carla was glad that her wrap hadn't opened earlier and given Baxter a preview of the seductive layers beneath her flowing chiffon. That might have spoiled things.

Baxter continued to stare at Carla's enticing layers. "Get rid of Gina as soon as you can," he said.

Carla laughed. "I will. Now let me finish up and put on some jewelry."

He caressed her leg. "I see you're wearing my anklet."

The doorbell rang. "Hurry up," Baxter said, "so we can get rid of her."

"Answer the door. I'll be right out."

Baxter opened the door for Gina. "Hi, how are you?" he said and ushered her inside.

"Ah, I remember. Carla's handsome boyfriend."

Baxter smiled. "Thank you. Carla will be out in a minute. Have a seat. You want some wine?"

Gina looked around and observed the snack tray, candles, and flowers. Then she saw the birthday balloon.

Baxter chuckled. "It's my birthday. We're celebrating."

Gina dropped her tote bag beside the couch and sank down. "Well, I won't stay long, but I will have some wine."

Baxter reacted graciously and uncorked the wine. He poured a glass for Gina. He hoped her visit would be short. He liked her. He thought she might make a good friend for Carla. But he was ready to commence his birthday celebration. He hadn't planned on company. Of course, Gina was pleasing enough to the eye in her mini peasant dress. The gold colors of the leopard print enhanced her caramel skin. The dress was belted at the waist and loose, but not loose enough to hide her shapeliness. She wore black and gold ballet flats that matched the dress. She wasn't quite as long and leggy as his Carla, but she was a very pretty woman.

Baxter forced his mind away from Gina's legs. He had eyes only for Carla if she would just bring her butt out of the bedroom. He was about to head back and get her, when she appeared.

"Hi, Gina." Carla walked over and hugged her. "How are you?"

"Fine. I happened to be in the neighborhood so I thought I'd stop by for a minute." She pointed to the glass of wine in front of her. "Didn't realize you were celebrating Baxter's birthday."

"No problem. We have the whole night to celebrate," she smiled chidingly at Baxter.

He smiled patiently at Carla, but he gave her a firm glance when Gina wasn't looking.

"I won't stay long," Gina said. "I'll have a glass of wine to help you celebrate, then I'll be gone. But look at you. You look great, girl."

Carla was the center of attention in her full makeup, black chiffon dress, and black satin high-heeled sandals. She wore her long, straight sexy wig. Her fingernails and toenails gleamed a vibrant red, the result of a flawless manicure and pedicure. Rhinestone earrings dangled from her ears and almost matched the gold and diamond chain around her ankle.

Baxter felt incredibly lucky. "Wow. You look awesome," he said.

"Yes, you do," Gina concurred.

Carla smiled demurely. "Thanks."

Gina swirled around in her best modeling stance. "What about me?"

"You look lovely too," Baxter said, surprised by her straightforwardness.

"You always look good, Gina," Carla agreed.

Baxter had a chance to study Gina's curves. He had to admit her dress was sexy though understated. It flowed softly over her body. He'd have to introduce her to one of his friends.

"What can I say? I'm here with two beautiful women on my birthday. Doesn't get any better than this," Baxter grinned. "We need music." He cued some jazzy music on Carla's iPod. It flowed through the speakers and heightened the ambience.

"And food. We need food. Let me heat up a few things. It'll only take me a couple minutes," Carla said.

"Oh, no," Gina protested. "I don't want to interfere with your party."

"No, stay for a while." Carla dismissed Baxter's piercing eyes.

"You sure?" Gina asked.

"Positive." Carla picked up a wine glass from the coffee table and held it out so that Baxter could fill it. He resigned himself to a delayed lap dance and obliged. Carla headed to the kitchen.

"You sure I'm not interrupting your party?" Gina asked when Carla was out of earshot.

Baxter smiled wryly. What could he say? *Yes, you're messing up my birthday night.* Instead, he said, "Not a problem, Gina. We've got plenty of time to celebrate."

"You sure?"

"Absolutely."

Gina relaxed more and settled into the couch. Baxter sat on the opposite end.

"I love Carla's place," Gina said. "It's so cozy and elegant. She knows how to add all the right touches." Baxter nodded in agreement. The wine was making Gina more demonstrative. She reached over and touched Baxter's thigh. "And she definitely found a nice guy." She shifted her hand up higher on his thigh.

Baxter's eyes widened. He moved his leg away and rose from the couch. "Let me check on Carla and see if she needs any help," he said and excused himself. He did not want Carla walking out of the kitchen and seeing Gina's hand on his thigh. That would ruin his whole night.

When he entered the kitchen, Carla was pulling a small tray out of the oven and examining it. "Almost ready, baby. I've got broiled lobster tails, stuffed crab cakes, oysters, a salad. We're going to have a good time."

"How well do you know Gina?" Baxter asked, his voice low. He was glad Carla's kitchen was off to the side so that Gina couldn't hear him.

"I've known her for years. We worked at the club."

"I mean, how well do you really know her?"

"How well do we really know anybody?" Carla asked. She stopped and stared at Baxter. "What's up?"

Baxter took a deep breath. "I think she likes me."

Carla looked puzzled.

"I think she's trying to hit on me," he clarified.

Carla stared at him. "Wishful thinking, maybe?"

"Everything okay? Need any help?" Gina called out.

Carla stuck her head out of the kitchen. "Almost done. We'll be out in a minute."

She returned to Baxter. "You sure she's trying to hit on you? I've known her off and on for a long time. She's cool. I never had any problems with her. You sure you're not misjudging her? I mean, you're the one who said she's a great influence."

"I know what I said, but I'm not so certain now."

Carla looked Baxter straight in the eye. "Are you telling me I can't trust you with my friends? Do we have trust issues here?"

Baxter sighed. "Of course not."

"Well, prove it. I'll be out there in a minute."

"Baby, this is my birthday. All I wanted was a lap dance. You didn't have to get all dressed up and serve anything special. I wanted a quiet evening, just the two of us. First, it took you a while to get dressed. Now you're cooking."

"I'm not cooking. I'm heating up a few things that I ordered especially for tonight. You'll get your lap dance, okay? Now go out there and entertain our guest, and I'll let you know when everything's ready. Your birthday is very important to me, but so is a relationship with a client whom I consider a friend. You wanted me to broaden my horizons, right?"

"Right," Baxter mumbled and left the kitchen.

In the living room, Baxter changed the music tempo to upbeat party sounds. Not because he wanted to, but because he felt it might change Gina's mood. He plopped down in the armchair instead of the couch. Gina smiled in amusement.

"You're a nurse, right?" Baxter was doing everything he could to stay out of trouble.

"Yes. I've been a nurse for a while now, almost ten years if you count my training." She leisurely held out her glass for Baxter to refill.

He walked over and poured more wine for her, but he kept his distance.

"When I was a kid, I used to line up my dolls and operate on them. That vision always stuck with me. But somewhere, I made a fast turn and started dancing. I'm so glad I got out when I did. I'm glad Carla's out too."

Baxter unwound a bit, pleased by the revelation.

"Carla's a good woman," Gina said. "She told me your relationship is exclusive. I told her to get tested."

Baxter didn't know whether to tell Gina to mind her own business or to thank her.

Gina saw the play of emotions on his face. "Nobody likes to talk about this shit, but it's important."

"I know," Baxter admitted. "We both got tested. You practice what you preach?" he asked.

"I certainly do. I'm in the health field. But at the moment, I'm not in a relationship. That's why I asked you if you had a brother."

Baxter always liked people who were direct with him, but this woman was a "bold, brazen hussy," a term his mother sometimes used. "I'll introduce you to one of my buddies," he said. He felt this was probably the best way to protect himself.

"Can't wait," Gina said halfheartedly. She got up and stretched. Her mini dress rose higher. She walked over to Baxter and patted his chest. "You know, you're the one I really want." She quickly sank down on his lap and pushed her hip between his legs.

Baxter gulped and froze. At any moment, Carla would come out of the kitchen and catch him. Yet he wasn't the aggressor. He lifted Gina off him and headed to the kitchen. He heard Gina giggling behind him. He didn't care. He was not going to let Gina ruin his relationship with Carla. He and Carla were finally on a roll. Gina was not going to spoil things, nor his lap dance. Carla would have to ask her to leave.

Baxter raced into the kitchen, determined to remove himself from an incriminating situation.

"Oh great. Perfect timing," Carla said. "Everything's ready. Take the wine out first. I know the other bottle is almost empty by now."

"Listen to me," Baxter said, eyes wide. "She's hitting on me hard."

Carla looked down at his trousers. He was definitely aroused.

"She's hitting on you, or the other way around?" Carla asked accusingly.

He faced her, unwavering. "She's hitting on me."

Something in his tone resonated with Carla. She sighed. "You want me to go out and talk to her?"

"Yes, and ask her to leave."

Carla half-smiled. "You're serious, aren't you?"

Baxter didn't budge. "Yes, I am."

"Fine. I'll go out and talk to her. I don't believe this. You know how hard it is to get good clients, let alone friends?"

Baxter remained steadfast. He stepped aside so Carla could lead the way. She grabbed her wine glass and drained it. Baxter waited. He was determined not to venture into the living room without Carla. He didn't care if he was being a punk or not. He was not going to have his birthday or any other night with Carla ruined.

Carla entered the living room, fortified by the wine. Baxter followed her. Gina sat innocently on the couch with her legs crossed. She sipped her wine.

Carla hesitated, then cleared her throat. "Uh, Gina."

Gina turned without flinching.

"Baxter feels that you're trying to hit on him."

"Are you serious?" Gina asked.

Carla nodded. Her stance was firmer now. "Yes, my baby says you're hitting on him—hard."

Gina rolled her eyes and jumped off the couch. "The only thing hard is your dick," she said to Baxter. "Tattletale. Hiding behind momma's apron strings."

Baxter's mouth fell open in shock.

Gina walked over to him right in front of Carla and kissed him square on the lips. "Happy Birthday," she said sweetly.

Then Carla laughed wickedly and kissed him. "Happy Birthday, baby."

Baxter froze and held his breath. He looked from one to the other. He blinked his eyes to make sure he wasn't dreaming. "I can touch you both?" he asked huskily.

Carla grinned and kissed him again. "Think you can handle it?"

Baxter wasn't sure. He was certainly up for the challenge, but he couldn't believe this was really happening. He hesitated, hoping the rug wouldn't be pulled out from under him. He sought reassurance from Carla. "You're saying it's okay?"

"Yes," she grinned mischievously.

Baxter decided to test them both. He kissed Gina fully on the lips. When Gina responded and Carla didn't protest, he proceeded further. He caressed Gina's breasts and hips. She arched against him.

Carla stopped him before he went any further. "A few ground rules," she said. "Gina already knows the rules." Carla headed to the kitchen and signaled for him to follow. "Come on, let's talk," she said.

Baxter was putty in her hands. He followed Carla into the kitchen, but not without sticking his hand up her dress and giving her butt a tight squeeze. Carla smiled and let him have a good feel.

"This is a one-time thing," she began. "I thought it would be something different for your birthday."

"Oh, this is definitely something different. You're not afraid that me and Gina . . . ."

Carla's faced transformed into a crafty smile. "She's moving out of state."

Baxter's face registered surprise and gradually, acceptance. "Well then, we better not keep her waiting."

"In a minute. I want to make sure we understand each other. I don't want any disrespect after this. No repeats of the first time we had sex, and you shunned me afterwards. If you can't handle this maturely, let me know, and we'll stop now."

Carla figured she was wasting her breath. Baxter's pants jutted straight out. His dick had taken over. He'd tell her anything now. Still, she wanted him to heed her warning. "I mean it. I don't want any stupid shit after tonight," Carla said.

Baxter looked her straight in the eye. "I can handle it. You don't have to worry about my feelings changing after tonight."

Carla nodded. "Fine."

Baxter kissed her. "Wow! What a birthday. Sorry I complained earlier."

"So you don't think I took too long to get dressed?"

He cupped her butt in his hands and licked the tops of her breasts. "No, you look so good."

Gina came into the kitchen to join them. Baxter's breath quickened. She had transformed into an erotic vixen. The mini peasant dress hung off her shoulders now and exposed the top swell of her breasts. Something sheer and red peeped beneath the new neckline of the dress. She wore sexy red spike heels and had adorned herself with more jewelry and makeup. Her hair hung down around her shoulders.

"Y'all finished discussing your ground rules? Think you can do us both?" Gina asked boldly.

Baxter pulled her over and cupped her butt too. He kissed her breasts, then let his tongue explore hers. "No problem. I can do you both," he said, coming up for air.

He went from one to the other, grinding his dick against them and fondling them. "Y'all both gonna give me a lap dance?"

"Yes." Carla's voice was hoarse as he pressed against the swelling mound between her legs. Then he went back to grinding all over Gina.

CHAPTER 38

Carla stifled a yawn as she tried to register a new client at the fitness center. She was tired. She hadn't gotten much sleep due to Baxter's birthday party the night before. She wished the client would make up her mind. Carla knew it was too good to be true that the woman would so agreeably decide to join EveryDay Fitness with no hassles.

Carla had watched the client walk straight to the counter and ask to join. Carla figured it would be an easy sign-up that wouldn't require much persuasion. She needed an easy day. But the client was having second thoughts about joining, specifically about having an automatic deduction coming out of her bank account. So the client began wavering and changing her mind about whether to use a debit or a credit card.

Carla smiled patiently. "Whichever card you prefer."

"I want you to know that even if I use a credit card, I pay my cards off at the end of each month. I don't like to keep a balance," the client said.

"I understand," Carla said supportively. "If you want to use a credit card—fine. If you want to use a debit card—fine." She refused to engage in a lengthy bout of indecisiveness with the client. On another day, she would have welcomed the challenge, but today she was tired.

Oscar, her co-worker, approached. He was always sniffing around Carla like a hound. Normally, she would have given him a firm glance, warning him to back off from her and her clients. But today, she decided to let him intercede. Oscar was always fishing for an opportunity to show his manliness around her.

"What's up, girls?" Oscar's face morphed into a charming smile.

The client brightened. She was in her forties, about the same age as Oscar. She was a perfect candidate to join the center since she was starting to develop a middle-age spread around the waist. Oscar pounced upon the opportunity to show Carla how to coax the woman into membership.

He flexed his biceps and his pecs. "Don't you want to build strong arms and muscles?" he asked playfully. In response, the woman broke into an admiring grin. Even though Carla knew he was a hound, Oscar came across as a grassroots, good-looking guy to the client.

"Oscar is one of our personal trainers," Carla explained. "Either I can work with you, or he can work with you." Carla made a sweeping gesture. "Or any one of our trainers can help you."

"So what's it going to be, young lady?" Oscar asked the client in a smooth voice. "We'll get you in tip-top shape. Won't take much. Just need you to sign so we can get started."

The woman sighed and stared at Oscar dreamily. "I guess I'll use my debit card. I don't know why it took me so long to figure it out."

I don't know why it took you so long either, Carla thought.

Oscar gave Carla a smug smile and moved on to another patron. When Carla finished recruiting her client, she grudgingly thanked Oscar.

His eyes roamed up and down her body. "What's up with you today? You usually rope in clients with no problem."

"I'm a little tired today, but don't push it," Carla warned. "My thanks to you doesn't mean anything more than that. Got it?"

"Got it," Oscar said. He still wore a complacent smile.

Carla wanted to wipe the smugness off his face, but then she thought about Baxter's birthday party the night before. Arousal began to overtake weariness. She, Baxter, and Gina had made the most of the night.

* * *

After all the fondling and groping in the kitchen, all three of them finally reached the living room. Baxter had become so excited that he had to calm himself down. Carla was aroused too, and Gina was all over Baxter, pressing against him and allowing him to touch her everywhere. To slow themselves down, they wined and dined lightly on the food Carla had heated. But Baxter still couldn't keep his hands off the women.

Carla pulled out his birthday chair with its balloon jutting high and firm, like his dick. She and Gina positioned the chair in the middle of the living room. Then they lit the candles, played some sexy music, and began Baxter's birthday show. Both of them circled and gyrated in front of him as he sat in the chair. Everyone was still fully clothed in an effort to extend the pleasure of the night. Carla cupped her breasts in her hands and offered them to Baxter whose breath flamed hot all over them. She massaged her whole body in front of him as he reached out and touched. Certainly not wanting to neglect Gina, he reached out and caressed her too. Gina pushed her breasts in his face and turned her butt to him and allowed him to touch her freely. Then the women stepped away from him and continued massaging themselves, bumping and grinding to the music.

With her butt facing him, Gina sank on top of him, pressing against his hardness. He held her butt with one hand and her breasts in the other as she bent over and rotated all over his thickness. She finally lifted herself off him after turning around and sticking her tongue down his throat, then she let Carla have a turn with him. Carla sank her butt against him, too, and pushed and circled as he gripped her against his hardness. She leaned over and gave him as much butt as he could handle. She turned around and straddled him, legs wide open, and did more bumps and grinds. When she got up, she ran her hands lightly over the stiff protrusion in his pants. Gina joined her, but Gina's fingers were more insistent. Baxter moaned and reached to unzip his pants. They both pulled away from him.

"Not yet," Carla chided gently.

"We still have a show to do," Gina promised.

Baxter forced himself under control.

"You okay?" Carla teased.

He nodded his head, deliriously anticipating their next moves.

Gina untied the belt of her dress so that it flowed freely around her. The dress was both demure and sexy. Her bare shoulders and cleavage gleamed golden in the candlelight. Baxter stuck his hand up her dress, and Gina stood with legs open so he could rub and massage wherever he wanted. Then she lifted the dress high above her hips so that he could have a better view. She teased him with a few gyrations. Then with an expert move, she hiked the dress up over her head and exposed a strapless red mini. It was totally sheer and showed a red satin G-string and shimmering pasties underneath. The dress was latticed on the side to show her breasts and hips. She stood directly in front of Baxter, then turned around and twerked. She faced him again with her crotch in his face. Baxter obliged and kissed her crotch through the sheer red dress. He stuck his tongue out and wet the dress and the red satin G-string. Gina moaned and finally pulled away from him.

It was Carla's turn. She swirled around in her dress and made it flutter around her hips. She sank down on Baxter's hardness and let the chiffon skirt surround them. She pulled the dress down off her shoulders and exposed a bit of the black tight dress underneath. The strings of the slingshot were exposed too. Baxter was drunk with passion and matched all of her grinding moves. He licked the tops of her breasts.

Then Carla lifted herself up and pushed the dress all the way down to display the short tight dress underneath in its entirety. She stepped out of the cloud of chiffon at her feet and raised her arms overhead in abandon. She danced a breath away from Baxter. His nostrils flamed over her crotch. He kissed it and licked through the material. He reached his hands up and fingered her breasts through the sheer fabric of the dress. He rose and sucked the pasties through the gossamer sheerness. He sank to the chair and tried to pull Carla on top of him, but she moved away.

Then Carla and Gina both danced before him in their tight, sheer minis, displaying their bodies from all angles. They wantonly paraded themselves in front of him. They pulled out chairs and sat wide-legged, teasing and tantalizing him. They opened their legs wider when he got up from his birthday chair and buried his head between their legs, moving from one to the other. He stood up with them and floated his hands all over their bodies through the sexy sheerness of their dresses.

When he returned to his chair, Gina slithered her red dress down to her ankles and kicked it away. She wore nothing more than her satin G-string and glittery pasties. She circled her hips in front of him as his manhood skyrocketed to the moon.

Carla finally slid her sheer dress down to the floor to reveal the brazen, strappy slingshot crisscrossing her body. Baxter reached his hands out and greedily cupped her breasts and ass. He fondled the strings of the slingshot, then kissed and licked all over her exposed flesh. Carla finally pulled the string around her waist and unraveled the scanty covering. She shimmied and shook in her thong and pasties as the candlelight played over her gleaming chocolate body.

"You enjoying the show?" Carla asked.

Baxter moaned and slid his finger inside her G-string. He pulled his finger out and licked it. Carla bent down and kissed him, twirling her tongue around his.

"Where are my manners?" he said huskily and drew Gina over to him. He slid his fingers into her G-string and twirled them around. He pulled his fingers out and put them in Gina's mouth. She sucked greedily.

Passion overtook all of them as Baxter continued to tease and fondle their swollen breasts and clits through their pasties and G-strings. Carla and Gina finally removed their tiny coverings and danced naked in front of him. They rubbed their clits, then stuck their fingers in his mouth. Baxter sucked heartily. Intoxicated with desire, Gina buried her head in his lap and kissed his hardness through his pants. Carla started kissing it too. They finally unzipped his pants and pulled them off along with his shorts, allowing his throbbing organ to spring free.

Baxter held his breath as they stroked their hands up and down his hardened length. Carla kissed his dick and popped it into her mouth. She let her tongue play all over the head. She held it out to Gina who licked hungrily. Baxter was in his world as their heads bobbed up and down on his thick erection. He pushed them away for a moment so he wouldn't come. He wanted the night to last forever.

Gina was tired of waiting. She plunged her breasts into his mouth, straddled him in the chair, and sank her pulsing canal all over his hardened flesh. She helped him lift off his shirt as she encircled him greedily in her soaking heat. She rode him up and down, turned around and let him ride her from the back. Baxter buried himself inside Gina. He reached out and pulled Carla close. He played with her nipples and fingered her clit. She opened her legs wide as he stuck his fingers inside her as Gina rode him.

Carla moaned in pleasure as Baxter stroked her insides with his fingers, all the while holding Gina's butt atop his dick. Finally, Gina slid off him and let Carla take over. Carla slipped right over his dick. Their bodies slapped as Carla opened wider to him. His teeming organ was still wet and warm from Gina's juices.

"Do me some more," Gina said unabashedly. She stuck her pussy in Baxter's face so he could expertly lick her up and down. She writhed and moaned as Baxter slid in and out of Carla.

Carla turned around so he could push in from the back. He stimulated her clit, then held her ass while she slid up and down. Immersed inside her, he went back to licking Gina until all three fell out on the floor, kissing, licking, and stroking. As they lay side by side on the carpet, Baxter pushed his dick inside Carla, then into Gina, then back again. They took turns on top of him on the rug, content to ride his dick as he wantonly explored their bodies. Ecstatically, he stroked and accommodated their every whim.

He turned them over on the carpet and penetrated them

from behind. He went from Gina to Carla, then Carla to Gina. He licked and sucked their clits and stuck his fingers in their pussies as they lay side by side. They fucked like this for a while until Carla could hold back no longer. The next time Baxter stuck his turgid column inside her, she exploded with a loud moan. "Happy Birthday, Baxter!" she said, quivering against his lips. They held like that for a moment.

Then Baxter pulled out and went back to stroking Gina. "Now I've got you to myself for a while," she said.

Baxter didn't know how much longer he could hold out. He buried himself deeper into Gina, and she opened up completely. They grunted and stroked for a while as Carla lay content. Finally, Gina screamed, "Happy Birthday!" as she came up and down Baxter's shaft, and he filled up her canal. When it was over, all three of them lay panting and sated.

Carla felt so satisfied that she didn't know if she could come anymore. But Baxter and Gina revived her passion when all three moved to the bedroom. Gina decided to make the most of her night with Baxter. She and Baxter fucked more leisurely now on the plump cushioned platform built into the recess of a wall.

Carla gradually became aroused again as she watched the candlelight flicker over their bodies on the cushion. Gina rode his dick until she climaxed all over him. Then Baxter slid out of Gina and pulled Carla down on the cushion. He pumped in and out of Carla until she found her insides exploding again. With a loud moan, Baxter exploded, too, as they peaked in unison.

In the middle of the night, Carla woke up, engulfed by a fire between her thighs. She turned and saw Baxter sliding in and out of Gina from the back. Savoring every moment, he had his fingers between Gina's legs and the other hand all over her breasts. When he saw that Carla was awake, he stared at her lustily and pulled out of Gina. He turned Carla around and entered her from the back. He stroked and fondled as Carla covered him with her slippery warmth. Gina smiled and watched. She grabbed Baxter's hand and coaxed his fingers to her clit.

Finally, they lay sated and exhausted. *What a party,* Baxter thought. He kissed Carla affectionately, hoping to dispel any crazy ideas she might have that he didn't care for her. Carla kissed him back.

CHAPTER 39

Carla sipped her margarita with relish. It was the perfect way to top her workday. She put her drink down and glared at Oscar, daring him to "accidentally" bump her leg again.

Oscar heeded the warning. "Hey, we're in close quarters."

He was right about that. She and her co-workers enjoyed happy hour at a Mexican restaurant where everyone huddled shoulder to shoulder at the table. Since Carla was one of the first to arrive, she had avoided sitting next to Regina, the young smart ass at the fitness center. But Oscar had plunked down right beside her. Carla had sighed in resignation as Oscar took his seat.

The small group had assembled to celebrate Jasmine's impending wedding. Carla decided "impending" was the word because the celebrant had not shown up yet to her own gala. While they waited for Jasmine to arrive, everybody eagerly snatched a few minutes on their cell phones. They knew that as much as Jasmine loved her phone, she did not tolerate phone distractions during happy hour if you wanted to remain on her good side. Jasmine insisted that cell phone use be kept to a minimum at work and social gatherings.

Carla loved working for such a grounded young woman. But exactly where was Jasmine? The table was starting to liven up without her as everyone sipped their drinks and put away their phones. Carla quickly sent off another text to Mimi to check on her. She hadn't heard from Mimi for a few days, and Baxter had mentioned that Frank was fed up with Mimi.

Finally, Mimi sent a text back.

MIMI: K.

Carla assumed that "K" meant Mimi was okay. Carla decided to stop by the TiTi after she left Jasmine's party. She was going to wring Mimi's skinny neck. Taking a deep breath, Carla put her cell phone away and decided to enjoy the evening. She'd worry about Mimi later. Carla finished her drink and excused herself from the table.

As she headed for the restroom, Carla regarded her surroundings. The restaurant boasted traditional calla lily prints by Mexican artist, Diego Rivera. There were also self-portrait prints of Frida Kahlo hanging on the stucco walls. Dark red floor tiles gleamed underfoot while rustic wooden beams anchored the ceiling. It was a big place, but with softly lit, cozy alcoves. Carla enjoyed coming to the restaurant with her co-workers. While she was forced to admit that she sometimes missed the TiTi, she enjoyed working at the fitness center more. She was spreading her wings and broadening her horizons in a way that she could never have done at the TiTi. If only she could get Mimi to leave.

Carla halted in her tracks before she reached the restroom. At the end of the bar, Jasmine sat sipping a drink and texting. Carla walked straight over to her, indignant. "Care to join us?"

"I'm sorry," Jasmine apologized. "I needed to send a few texts, and I didn't want to do it at the table."

Carla stared at Jasmine's half-empty glass.

Jasmine smiled guiltily. "I figured I'd have a drink too."

"Why not drink with us? I mean, you are the guest of the party."

Jasmine sighed and shrugged. She removed her handbag from the stool beside her and motioned for Carla to join her.

"Shouldn't we go hang with everybody else?" Carla asked. Then she noted a mixture of emotions on Jasmine's face. Carla sank down on the stool. "What's up?"

Jasmine started to fidget. She put her phone away and sipped her drink. But she made no effort to speak.

Carla sighed. "You don't want to get married?"

"I think so. I don't know," Jasmine admitted.

"So our little happy hour is putting some pressure on you."

Jasmine nodded.

"Well, we're not the only ones putting pressure on you. You've sent out invitations. You got the reception hall—"

"He won the reception hall in a poker match."

Carla laughed. "Didn't he win that Cabo San Lucas trip? That's how me and Baxter went to the cabin."

Jasmine nodded and smiled.

"Wow, Kenny wins some cool stuff."

"He does."

"But you're concerned about his gambling, right?" Carla asked.

"Right. He's cut back considerably. I read him the riot act because he loses too."

"Well, if you feel he's got things under control, what's wrong?"

"I really don't want him to gamble, but it's okay sometimes. But I'd prefer that he gamble for money. Instead, he plays for trips, boxing matches, football games, reception halls. You name it. Odd stuff." Jasmine rolled her eyes.

"You must admit. He's pretty unique."

"Yes, he is," Jasmine acknowledged.

"And you say he's cut back. That's a good sign." Carla paused. "Do you love him?"

"Yes," Jasmine answered without hesitation.

"Then what's the problem? You've worked out the gambling. He's rich, he's handsome. He's got the ideal job in hotel and restaurant management. What more do you want?"

"My freedom. When I'm with Kenny, it's wonderful. When I'm by myself, it's wonderful."

"He seems to give you plenty of space. He's not a possessive guy."

"I know. I guess I'm used to running my own life and not having to consider someone else all the time."

Carla shook her head and laughed. "Then I don't know what to tell you, girl. I hear you." Carla found herself groping for some resolution. She remembered the summer barbecue and the attraction between Jasmine and Earl. Jasmine had never spoken about whether or not she slept with Earl that night. For some reason, Carla never pressed the issue.

"Can you see yourself waking up to Kenny day after day?" Carla asked.

"Yes."

Carla was afraid to voice the next question. Maybe, that was the problem. "How's the sex?"

Jasmine became distracted by a text on her phone. She rapidly shot off a response. Carla wondered if Jasmine was avoiding the sex question.

"Sorry about that," Jasmine said. "But I've been waiting for that text." She put her phone down and sipped her drink.

Carla wondered if she should drop the sex issue since it didn't seem that Jasmine planned to answer.

Jasmine ended the suspense with a grin. "I heard you. The sex is fine. No complaints."

"Girl, you scared me for a minute," Carla chuckled. "What about babies? Do you want to have his babies?"

Jasmine perked up. "I'd love to carry his babies."

Carla hopped up from the barstool. "Then grab your drink and take your ass over to the party. I'll be there in a minute."

After Jasmine left, Carla wondered about her own relationship with Baxter. They were still going strong, hot and heavy. But would she eventually want more from him? He still maintained his aversion to the "C" word—commitment. Well, now was not the time to worry about it, she thought. She simply planned to have fun at Jasmine's prenuptial celebration. Nothing else mattered at the moment.

When Carla returned to the table, Jasmine mouthed a "thank you." Carla nodded and ordered another drink. The drinks were flowing freely. Jasmine was the life of the party. Oscar watched Carla and Jasmine curiously. Carla quickly deflected his curiosity. "Did you miss me?" she asked.

"Don't start nothing you can't finish," Oscar warned.

Carla heeded his advice. Abruptly, she stepped away from him and circulated around the rest of the table.

Carla was still a little tipsy when she walked into the TiTi. Her spirits were high. She and her co-workers had thoroughly enjoyed Jasmine's party. She decided not to wring Mimi's neck after all, just make sure Mimi was okay.

Carla looked down at herself and smiled. She fit perfectly into the TiTi's atmosphere. She wore the black leggings required of her job, but she had added a bit of pizazz for Jasmine's party. Her leggings were faux leather in the front. Instead of the fitness center T-shirt, she wore a black tank top with skinny straps that crisscrossed her back. Her high-heeled booties and lightweight tan jacket completed the outfit. All she needed was some sparkly high heels, and she could have jumped up onto one of the stages and did a few bumps and grinds on the pole. Then she could peel her leggings down and flaunt her lacy bikini panties. Carla smiled. The margaritas in her system made it all seem appealing until a slimy character started following her around, blatantly ogling her ass.

"You one of the dancers? Where you goin'? I want to sit at your table."

Carla swung around on him and caught him grabbing his crotch. "I'm not one of the dancers," she stated flatly. "Do I need to get security to show you outside?" She looked him straight in the eye without flinching. He glared at her for a moment, checked out Wendell's bouncers, and decided he didn't want to tangle with them. He quietly proceeded to a table where a young woman actually danced.

Carla stifled a victorious smile and headed over to Mimi's table. Another girl danced there instead. Carla stopped one of the dancers who walked towards the dressing room. "Have you seen Mimi?"

The dancer lowered her eyes. "Nah," she said and quickly moved on.

Carla's heart raced. Her instincts told her something was wrong. She headed towards Wendell's office, but one of his henchmen intercepted her. He was a new guy. "If you looking for Wendell, he's not here. He's out of town."

An expression of dismay crossed Carla's face.

"I'll tell Wendell you stopped by when he comes back," the henchman offered.

"I'm looking for Mimi."

"Uh, there's the hostess over there." He pointed to a buxom woman in her thirties. She didn't have Carla's curves, but she had huge breasts and fantastic legs. She was tough-looking, and her eyes didn't miss a beat.

Carla strode over to her. "Where's Mimi?" The hostess stared Carla up and down jealously. Carla dismissed the woman's reaction and waited.

The hostess rolled her eyes. "Who knows? Probably somewhere gettin' high. She done started back up again."

Carla could feel her temper rising. The hostess seemed pleased. She obviously felt some rivalry towards Carla.

"Sometimes, Mimi comes to work. Sometimes, she don't," the hostess said.

Carla knew she was getting nowhere with this woman. She pushed past the hostess brusquely, not caring about the consequences.

"Hey, I'm only trying to give you the information you asked for."

"Thanks a lot." Carla hurled the words over her shoulder sarcastically.

She felt agitated and uneasy. Nobody wanted to tell her where Mimi was. Carla stopped in mid-stride and sent Mimi a text. She waited briefly for a response and received nothing. Carla exited the club and headed for the parking lot. She ignored the leers and jeers from some of the guys departing the club who thought they could wheedle her into their cars and take her home.

In the parking lot, Carla realized her high had evaporated. She no longer felt tipsy. Instead, she felt a sense of foreboding. She hoped Mimi was okay. Maybe, she should have checked on Mimi more often. But only a few days had passed since they last communicated. Besides, Mimi was a grown woman. Yet deep down, Carla knew something was off.

Suddenly, Carla realized someone was following her. She heard the click of high heels behind her. She turned and saw the young dancer she had previously asked about Mimi. The young woman kept her eyes downcast. Carla hoped the young dancer showed more guts in the club, or she'd never survive the TiTi.

As the young woman passed, she quickly slipped Carla a note. "That's the address to the trophy den. Pull up beside me at the corner," the young dancer said in a barely audible voice. Then she strode past Carla without missing a step. Carla resisted the urge to run after the young woman, and she resisted an even greater urge to open the note.

Inside her car, Carla unfolded the note. It listed an address to the trophy den. The den was supposed to be a place where Gutter Joe kept his valuables and trophies of his criminal exploits. Nobody ever seemed to know exactly where the den was located, but now, Carla had the address in her hand. She swallowed in dread as she turned her engine on and drove out of the parking lot behind the young woman.

At the light, Carla lowered her window. The young dancer lowered hers. "Mimi's there with Joe and his men—if she's still alive. She's strung out, in really bad shape. Nobody wants to help her. Everybody's scared of Joe. Wendell's out of town at a funeral."

"You sure Mimi's at the den?" Carla didn't want to believe it. She held the note up. "You sure about the address?"

The young dancer gave Carla an exasperated stare. "You think I'm lying about this? You know Gutter Joe. And you know Mimi." The traffic light changed. "I gotta go," the woman said and drove off. Carla decided the young woman might be a perfect fit for the TiTi after all.

Carla's heart sank. She didn't know what to do. She could call the police, but Joe had some of them on his payroll. And she didn't want Mimi going to jail for doing drugs or forced into some seedy halfway house. She certainly didn't want to involve Baxter. While he might contact the police himself, there was a strong possibility that he might act like a hothead and take matters into his own hands. Baxter could risk losing everything he worked so hard for. Carla thought about Frank and his love of guns. In no way could she involve Frank. That might mean a gun battle that Baxter could easily be drawn into.

Carla pulled over to the curb and turned off the engine. She exchanged her heels and lightweight jacket for sneakers and a red hoodie that she kept in her trunk. She transferred her purse to the trunk. She stuffed ID, money, keys, and cell phone into her pockets. She was glad she wore leggings and a tank top. She could maneuver easily in them if necessary. She still wasn't clear on what to do, but she knew she had to help Mimi. She owed Mimi.

Moments later, Carla found herself driving towards downtown Los Angeles to Gutter Joe's hell hole. She stopped and parked in the Mid-Wilshire district, midway between West LA and downtown. She rushed into a convenience store in a mini mall and grabbed a chocolate bar. Natalie had advised her to eat a square of chocolate before she took her fitness trainer exam. Her sister said that once the chocolate kicked in, it would help Carla think clearly. Natalie's advice had worked. Carla hoped it still worked. Now more than ever, she needed to think clearly, and what a pleasant way to do it.

While quickly devouring the chocolate bar, Carla hailed a cab. Though the light beamed on the rooftop, it passed her by. Carla wished she had downloaded one of those taxi apps onto her phone, but she had never needed them, and now, she didn't have time. She wanted to hop back into her car and drive downtown, but she couldn't afford to take the risk that Joe or one of his men might recognize her car. She had to wait for another cab or download an app. She didn't know what to expect when she arrived at the den, but she couldn't abandon Mimi.

Carla hailed a second cab. This one stopped.

"I'm finishing up," the cabbie, an olive-skinned man with jet black hair, told her. "Where to?"

Carla gave him an address that was in the heart of downtown, not far from the arts district. But unlike the arts district, the trophy den was in a neighborhood untouched by any gentrification whatsoever.

The cabbie's eyes bulged. "You know where you goin'? That's a rough hood, a druggie hood." He had a slight foreign accent. He noted Carla's curves in the leggings and the hoodie.

"What? You a hooker or somethin'? My shift is almost over. You wanna go have a drink?"

Carla wanted to curse him out, but she knew that wouldn't get her downtown. "Please, sir," she said, feigning the most polite tone she could.

The cabbie was unimpressed. "I'm not going down there. Now if you wanna go have a drink?"

"Please." Carla's eyes locked with his.

The cabbie sighed in irritation. "I'll take you down there, but I'm not waiting. You understand?"

Carla nodded and hopped in the back seat. "Thank you."

As they neared the address on the note, Carla asked the driver to slow down. The neighborhood was one of the bleakest and sleaziest she had ever seen. Dirty white stucco apartment buildings co-mingled with drab gray warehouses. Because it was a weekday night, the neighborhood was dark and quiet. Carla saw a few petty drug dealers on the street, plying their wares when certain cars stopped, but other than that, the street wasn't heavily populated. Carla didn't know if this was to her advantage or not.

"Stop right here," Carla ordered as they passed a dark, desolate alleyway.

"Here?" the driver asked, dumbfounded.

"Here," Carla said and paid him the fare. After she exited the cab, she unzipped the hoodie and intentionally gave him a profile of her contours. "If you come back for me, we can have that drink," she invited.

The cabbie looked around nervously to make sure he was safe. Then he relaxed a little and pulled out a business card. "Call me when you're ready. I'll try to come back and pick you up."

"Thanks," Carla smiled sweetly. She felt genuinely relieved. She'd figure out how to worm her way out of the drink with him later. For now, at least, she might have a ride out of this wretched neighborhood. Carla shivered when the cabbie took off and left her standing in front of the alley. She zipped her hoodie back up.

CHAPTER 40

Carla slipped into the darkness of the alleyway. She tried to blend into the night as much as possible in her black leggings. She hoped her red hoodie didn't attract attention. Her heart pounded. Maybe, she shouldn't have eaten the chocolate. Maybe, she shouldn't have come here at all. What was she thinking? How could she expect to rescue Mimi from Joe and his thugs? Baxter would have a fit if he knew she was standing in one of the seediest neighborhoods of downtown. What if Mimi wasn't here? They might have moved her. But if there was any possibility that Mimi was inside the den, Carla had to help. She surveyed the neighborhood and looked down the alleyway behind her. *Think!* she told herself.

Venturing out of the alley, she inched closer to the address on the note. She stopped and hid beside a raggedy, decrepit apartment building. Joe's trophy den was the next building over. It was not as bleak and rundown as the other buildings on the block.

Carla began to hear the sounds of men's voices coming out of Joe's building. They became louder, breaking the silence of her terrified thoughts. Carla took a deep breath and peeped out of her hiding place. She saw a group of men coming out of the trophy den address. They were laughing and talking.

One of them hiked his pants up and patted his dick. "We had a good time tonight."

Carla's breath caught in her throat. She stuck her head out a little further. She recognized Gutter Joe among the men. In the dim street lights, he looked even paler than she remembered. She shuddered when she thought about what he and his men might have done to Mimi. Carla slid back into the obscurity of her hiding place. A mixture of rage and pure, unadulterated fear churned in her stomach. She placed a hand over her racing heart to steady it. She prayed for a miracle to yank her out of the mess she had gotten herself into. She wasn't ready to die yet. She had finally met the love of her life, so had Mimi for that matter. They both had so much to live for, yet she couldn't think of a way out of their plight. She peeped out of her hiding place again and focused on Joe.

He pulled one of his henchmen aside. "Come right back. I got stuff to do. I don't want to leave her alone."

The henchman nodded.

He and the rest of Joe's minions got into their cars. The cars were neither flashy nor excessive. Carla figured that not even Gutter Joe could keep the junkies away from extravagant cars in this neighborhood.

She sighed in relief when Joe's men took off. Perhaps, this was the miracle she prayed for, but she had to act quickly. She watched Joe enter one of the first-floor apartments. She waited a few minutes. Then she approached the door. She rang the bell, but no one answered. She took a deep breath and rang the bell again. A knot formed in her stomach. Finally, she heard someone come to the door. Then it opened.

Carla stood face-to-face with Gutter Joe. With his reddish hair and hazel eyes, she still tried to figure out whether he was black or white. He reeked of depravity. He looked over her shoulder and surveyed the street around her. He leered. "I know you didn't come here by yourself."

Carla's mouth felt like parchment. "I came to pick up Mimi."

Joe whistled in amazement. "You dumb bitch, come and get her." He opened the door wider and yanked Carla inside. His lanky body belied his strength. He slammed her against the wall so hard that she literally saw stars. Her ears rang. A cold fear coursed through her veins. Joe stared her up and down, licking his lips in anticipation. "Oh, we got two of you now. See if that asshole fire boy still wants you when we finish with you."

A sudden calm engulfed Carla. Her head cleared. She knew

it was kill or be killed. She didn't want to die, but she would definitely do her best to take Joe with her. With deliberate fanfare, she yanked a picture off the wall. She brandished it as a weapon, aiming at Joe's head.

He laughed cruelly. "I ain't one of those yokels in the club who you think you can whip."

Joe reached for the picture to snatch it from her. He left his crotch exposed. Carla gave him a debilitating kick with her sneakers that sent him to his knees. Pure hatred seethed in his eyes, but he refused to moan. He tried to reach out and subdue her, but Carla was driven by a fury that she had never experienced. She delivered another brutalizing kick to his groin, harder than the first one. She packed so much rage, strength, and adrenaline into the blow that she knocked him out flat on the floor. Then she took the picture and smashed it over his head. As further insurance, she grabbed a pole lamp standing in a corner and brought it crashing down on his legs in a series of bone-crunching blows. Joe lay dazed and immobilized from her assault.

"Mimi!" Carla raced through the apartment, searching. Outside a bedroom, she heard Mimi's weak voice. "In here, chica."

Carla flinched when she entered the bedroom. Mimi lay naked on the bed on filthy, stained sheets. The room smelled of sex, semen, and desperation.

Carla found some of Mimi's clothes and tossed them to her. "Put these on."

Mimi started crying. "Thanks for coming to get me, chica." Her words were slurred, and she made no effort to budge.

"Get up, Mimi. We have to go. They'll kill us both." Carla snatched Mimi to her feet. She winced at Mimi's breath. Mimi's eyes were bloodshot. "Sober up. We gotta move," Carla ordered.

Mimi finally started to dress. Her movements were slow and lumbering. "Don't be mad at me."

"I'm not mad at you. Let's go."

When Mimi finally stood dressed, she wobbled in high heels.

"You can't wear those shoes," Carla said.

"Joe kidnapped me from the club. This is all I got."

"Take them off," Carla said. She held Mimi up and tried to remove the heels. "You'll have to walk barefoot."

"No. I'm not walking out of here without shoes. Give me some dignity."

Carla knew better than to argue with her. "Then you better walk in them, Mimi."

Mimi nodded and stood straighter. Carla held her upright to steady her.

"What'd you do with Joe? How'd you get past his men?" Mimi asked nervously.

"I had to knock Joe out. But we don't have much time."

As they progressed towards the front door, Mimi's eyes darted around the room nervously when she saw Joe sprawled out on the floor. She shrank in fear as he started regaining consciousness. He sneered at her.

Mimi suddenly went berserk. "You mother fucker! You fucking slimeball," she shouted at Joe. She kicked him right in the groin with her shoes. Joe doubled over in pain. But Mimi kept kicking him—in the stomach, in the chest. She took off a high heel and slammed it into his head. Joe's blood splattered onto Mimi.

Carla flinched at the onslaught. She grabbed Mimi and pulled her off Joe. "Let's get out of here, Mimi!"

"No, wait!"

Carla watched incredulously as Mimi ran back to the bedroom. "Are you out of your fucking mind!" Carla shouted and ran after her.

Mimi emerged from the bedroom with a locked metal case about the size of a large tool kit. She slammed it against Joe's face. "Some of his trophies," she explained to Carla. "I've got 'em now, mother fucker," she snarled at Joe. She tried to give him one more blow, but Carla, operating on pure adrenaline, forced Mimi away.

"Let's go," Carla ordered.

"I've got to pee," Mimi said.

Carla couldn't believe her ears. Her insides were quaking. "Pee outside, Mimi. Please let's go," she implored.

Mimi lifted her disheveled, glittery mini dress and pulled down her thong. She urinated right in Joe's face. Carla's mouth hung open. Mimi wiped herself on Joe's shirt. "Okay, I'm ready," she said.

Carla's jaw dropped.

"What?" Mimi said. "You don't know what they did to me."

Mimi's arms and legs were bruised. There was a cut above her eye. Carla looked down at Joe. Stunned and brutalized to a pulp, he still managed to glare at her coldly.

Carla matched his glare. Then she and Mimi fled the apartment.

Outside Joe's den, Carla and Mimi reeled from the magnitude of what they had done. They stood shivering in the alley, both from fear and the cool night air. Carla knew Mimi had to be cold in her skinny-strapped dress. Mimi rubbed her hands up and down her arms to warm them. Carla was tempted to run back into the apartment and grab any covering she could find.

Mimi stopped her. "Don't. I'm fine."

Carla retrieved her cell phone and the cabbie's business card from her pocket. She took off the hoodie and wrapped it around Mimi's shoulders. "We can take turns with it, but we won't be out here long," Carla said hopefully. "Sit, Mimi." Carla lowered Mimi to the ground beside the metal trophy box. Mimi didn't resist.

Carla dialed the cabbie's number. "I'm ready when you are," she tried to make her voice sound seductive.

"Tell them to hurry," Mimi said in the background.

The cabbie's voice rose suspiciously on the phone. "You by yourself?"

Carla still tried to keep her voice seductive. "Just a girlfriend with me. The more, the merrier. We're ready to go now."

"Get yourself another ride." The cabbie hung up in Carla's ear.

"Mother fucker," Carla swore in frustration. She turned to Mimi whose eyes were big and hopeful.

A black Mercedes, older model, advanced towards them, then slowed. Carla's heart pounded. She prayed it wasn't one of Joe's men. Her eyes widened. A woman was driving the car. As the driver became visible, Carla's mouth fell open. She recognized Percy's girlfriend, Teddy. What was she doing in this neighborhood? Carla wondered. Then she remembered Teddy's sister was on drugs. Teddy mentioned it at the barbecue at Baxter's house.

Whatever the reason for Teddy's sudden appearance, Carla didn't question it. She accepted it as a blessing from the heavens. Her prayers were answered. She heaved a sigh of relief and hailed Teddy's car. Teddy stopped for a moment. She noted Carla's wild eyes and gestures. Then she noticed Mimi all disheveled in the alleyway. Teddy lowered her eyes and pretended not to see them. She kept on driving down the street. Carla stood there, stunned. She quickly ducked back into the alley.

"That was Teddy, wasn't it?" Mimi guessed.

Carla swallowed. She didn't want to scare Mimi. "I don't think so. Whoever it was, they didn't stop."

"No, that was Teddy. That bitch. Her sister lives over here. She's a druggie."

"I don't think it was Teddy. I can't imagine her leaving us like this."

"I can," Mimi said and buried her head between her knees.

"We'll get out of here," Carla said determinedly. *But how?* she wondered. She resigned herself to the fact that the cabbie wasn't coming back. Neither was Teddy. She couldn't call Wendell. He was out of town. Besides, those days were over. Baxter would have a fit if she called Wendell for help. She still didn't want to call Baxter. Any minute now, Joe's men would return. They'd do their best to kill Baxter if he showed up. She thought about the police again. But suppose the ones on Joe's payroll intercepted the radio dispatch? Carla had no choice. She had to flag down any driver she saw, careful not to flag down any of Joe's men.

Carla turned her attention back to Mimi. "You okay?"

Mimi lifted her head and nodded.

"I'll get us out of here," Carla said.

"You should have left me, chica. You should have just let

them use me up and put me out of my misery. I can't seem to get it right." Tears rolled down Mimi's cheeks.

Carla sank beside Mimi and hugged her. "Don't say that. We're going to get out of this mess."

Mimi looked doubtful. Carla didn't have time for doubt. They had to get moving. But Mimi appeared so forlorn. Carla held her tighter.

"This could be our last hug," Mimi said.

Carla realized that Mimi might be right, yet Carla didn't want to die. She had found a good man and a whole new lifestyle. For that matter, Mimi had a found a good man if she could just straighten up. Carla rose to her feet with renewed vigor. She scrolled through her cell phone contacts. No name popped out. She certainly didn't want to involve Natalie.

"I'm going to flag down a car," Carla said. "Maybe, the police if I see them."

"Be careful you don't pick the wrong car. Any second, Joe's men will come back," Mimi warned. "Oh, chica, I'm so sorry I got you into this. If you want to leave me, I understand."

"Stop it, Mimi. That's not going to happen," Carla said harshly.

She stepped from the alley. A dark, late model car approached. Carla's breath caught in her throat. Instinctively, she knew it was one of Joe's men. He pulled into the driveway alongside Joe's building and drove to the back. Carla assumed there was a parking lot entrance behind the building. She caught a glimpse of Joe's henchman. She remembered him from earlier. He was a big guy. Her heartbeat thumped in her chest. She knew once he entered Joe's apartment, all hell would break loose. He'd come looking for Carla and Mimi with a vengeance.

Carla wondered if she should run to the parking lot, surprise him, and try to subdue him. There was an empty wine bottle in the alleyway. She could crack him in the head with it, but Carla realized that her hatred of Joe fueled her fearlessness of him. She didn't feel the same towards this man. That would be the chink in her armor. She didn't want to press her luck. With mounting trepidation, Carla waited for the fallout once he found Joe. Minutes passed. She swallowed.

Then a miracle occurred. Teddy swiftly drove up and lowered her window.

"Get in!" she exclaimed.

Carla swung into action. She lifted Mimi and the metal box off the ground. She pushed Mimi into the back seat of the car and jumped in beside her. Teddy took off like a bat out of hell.

Joe's henchman flew out of the apartment with a gun in his hand. Teddy floored the engine and sped off, stretching the distance between them and the gunman. Shots rang out. Something hit the back of Teddy's car. The unruly sound of gun metal clanked against car metal. Carla ducked and pushed Mimi down with her. Teddy kept driving at breakneck speed. She raced through a maze of streets in downtown LA.

Carla and Mimi finally sat up in the backseat. Mimi's eyes suddenly twinkled. "Next time I want to commit suicide, I'll just ride with Teddy."

All three women laughed.

"You got Baxter beat," Carla added.

They still looked over their shoulders, praying that none of Joe's henchmen suddenly drove up behind them.

Carla's eyes met Teddy's in the rearview mirror. "Thanks, Teddy."

She simply nodded and kept driving.

CHAPTER 41

Baxter and Percy headed towards their cars in the parking lot behind the fire station. It was after midnight and still dark. "Go home and get some rest," Baxter told Percy.

"I intend to. Y'all working me too hard. I don't need all this overtime."

Baxter laughed. "Join the club."

Suddenly, Teddy drove into the lot. She pulled right in front of them, parking haphazardly and taking up two spaces.

"You leaving your car here?" Baxter asked Percy. "She giving you a lift?"

"I hadn't planned on it." Percy grinned. "What can I say? She can't get enough of me."

Baxter smiled to himself. He was glad it was Teddy who couldn't get enough of Percy and not Carla. "Well, you better tell her to slow down on this lot," Baxter said.

Teddy jumped out of the car, a bundle of nerves. Percy's amazon woman, though gorgeous, appeared wide-eyed and disheveled. The jacket she wore over her slacks was carelessly flung over her shoulders and ready to fall to the ground. Her hair looked wild.

Baxter sensed a major problem. So did Percy.

"What's up, Teddy?" Percy asked. "You look like you saw a ghost."

Teddy swallowed. Percy's eyes were drawn to her car under the lights of the parking lot.

"Is that a bullet hole in your trunk?" he asked in alarm. Percy started to fuss. "You been over your sister's neighborhood again. Don't you know how dangerous it is over there? We've been through this before. You can't help your sister until she's ready."

Percy was really upset. Baxter felt like an intruder. He tried to tactfully interrupt. "I'll let you two talk," he said and stepped away.

"No!" Teddy's voice cut through Baxter like a knife, stopping him in his tracks.

Frank strolled out of the fire station and walked towards them. "Good night. Good morning. Whatever. I'm beat. Hey, Teddy, how you doing? Good to see you." Frank immediately noticed the hole in Teddy's trunk.

"Is that a bullet hole?" Frank asked in amazement. He finally noticed Teddy's agitation.

"Something you want to tell us?" Baxter demanded.

Percy held up his hand. "Give her a minute."

Frank's face turned ashen. "It's Mimi, isn't it?"

Teddy nodded. She turned to Baxter. "And Carla. I took them to the hospital."

Baxter felt like the ground was caving in under his feet. He planted himself firmer in his boots.

"I don't think Carla was hurt. But I think Mimi's in bad shape," Teddy blurted out. "I tried to reach you," she said to Percy. "Carla told me to come get you," she told Baxter.

He and Frank appeared shocked.

"I can drive everybody over to the hospital," Teddy offered.

"I'll drive," Percy said. "I don't think you need to drive right now, Teddy."

Baxter and Frank each hurried to their own cars. "No, man, you drive too slow." They almost said in unison.

"I'm driving," Percy insisted. "You're all too upset."

Frank was becoming frantic. "I don't give a shit who drives! Let's go."

Moments later, Percy drove, and Teddy sat beside him. Percy patted Teddy's hand soothingly. Baxter and Frank rode in the back seat, impatient to arrive at the hospital.

Mimi lay in bed in a white hospital gown. An IV tube snaked into her arm and dripped fluid into her veins. Carla sat by the bed. The doctor, a young Latina in her thirties, stood typing some notes into the computer in Mimi's room. She patted Mimi's hand and left.

"Shit, chica. What am I gonna do?"

"You'll do fine, Mimi."

"What the hell am I gonna to do with a baby?"

"You don't have to keep it."

"I don't want to get rid of any more."

Carla nodded. "I understand."

"But I'm a junkie!"

"Not if you want to raise your baby."

"What if the baby isn't healthy? It's not like I live a nurturing life."

Carla smiled wryly. "No shit."

Mimi rolled her eyes and became sullen.

Carla leaned forward. "Listen, they're still doing tests, but so far, the doctor thinks the baby is okay. You're incredibly lucky."

"I am?" Mimi gestured to her surroundings and the IV tube in her arm.

"Yes, you are." Carla paused. "You know who the father is?"

Mimi lowered her eyes. "I hope it's Frank, but I don't know for sure. Joe was giving me some good shit. Sometimes, I had to do things I'm not proud of even before he kidnapped me. At least, it can't be any of the guys this past week," Mimi ended in a small voice.

"What about Gutter Joe?" Carla ventured.

"That sick fuck!" Mimi exclaimed. "He couldn't get it up. He liked to watch. That's all his sick ass could do."

Carla heaved a deep sigh of relief. She didn't know how she could muster up affection for any of Joe's offspring.

Mimi chuckled. "I'd do the abortion myself if I thought it was Joe's baby."

Carla chuckled too. "I hear you."

They both became silent. Carla's face turned into a wistful smile.

"Don't, chica. Don't envy me. Be glad you don't have nothing to tie you down."

Carla smiled sadly. "I wish I could have had Baxter's baby. I never thought about babies until I met him."

"You can still have them," Mimi said. "They're doing all kinds of fertility things now."

"Nah. I waited too long. I'll just have to stick close to my nieces."

"You can help me raise my baby."

"I'm not big on babysitting."

"Help me out," Mimi said.

"I will. Right now, let's hope the baby is healthy." Carla hesitated. "What are you going to tell Frank?"

"I don't know."

"You've got to give up the drugs now, Mimi. You've got a kid to raise. You can go back to school. You're so good with social media. There are all kinds of programs."

"It's going to be hard to give up the drugs," Mimi said honestly.

Carla squeezed her hand in encouragement. "I know. But you can do it."

Baxter and Frank rushed over to the nurse's station. Baxter addressed the nurse on duty. "We're here for Carla Hepburn and Mimi Hernandez."

"Are you relatives?" the nurse asked.

"Boyfriends," Frank said.

The nurse cleared her throat. "Uh, let's see what we can find out." She addressed a second nurse who approached. "They're here for—"

"Can you give us any information on Carla Hepburn and Mimi Hernandez?" Baxter asked, impatient. Frank paced back and forth.

"The doctor will be coming out soon," the second nurse said.

Baxter pressed further. "Can you at least tell us something?"

"You for Carla Hepburn?"

Baxter nodded and held his breath.

"She's okay. She'll be out soon."

Relief flooded over Baxter. Frank was ready to burst.

"You for Hermione Hernandez?" the nurse asked Frank. His eyes bore into the nurse's. "The doctor will be coming out to talk with you, sir," she stated.

All the color drained from Frank's face.

"It shouldn't take much longer," she assured Frank and left.

"Let's go sit down," Baxter suggested. "Give them a few more minutes before we raise hell."

When they entered the waiting room, Percy and Teddy were already there. Frank refused to sit down. He continued pacing. Finally, he sank into a chair and buried his head in his hands. "I shouldn't have stopped seeing her. Maybe, this wouldn't have happened."

"You did good, Frank," Baxter said. "You stuck by Mimi. But after a while, you had to protect yourself. Nobody can blame you for that."

"Maybe I should have tried a little harder," Frank responded.

"Don't beat yourself up. You've been through a lot with Mimi."

Percy nodded in agreement. Teddy kept quiet. Frank didn't want to be placated.

Baxter's heart leapt for joy when he saw Carla walking down the hallway towards them. Impatient, he and Frank had abandoned the waiting room. Carla carried a metal box shaped like a tool kit. Even tired and drained, she still attracted attention. Baxter sprang forward and covered the distance between them in long strides. He gave Carla a bear hug when he reached her. She sank against him in welcome relief. They held onto each other. Then he kissed her.

Baxter suddenly noticed blood stains on her hoodie. "You okay?" he asked, concerned.

Carla nodded. "I'm fine."

"How's Mimi?" Baxter asked.

"Where is she?" Frank interrupted impatiently. "I thought the doctor was coming out."

"The doctor's with her now. I'll show you where she is," Carla said sympathetically.

Percy and Teddy stood in the background. Carla greeted them warmly. Then she handed the metal box over to Baxter. "I'll be right back. Let me show Frank where Mimi is."

Baxter took the box and stared at it curiously.

As Carla and Frank drew closer to Mimi's room, Frank halted for a minute. He appeared agitated. Carla noted that Baxter still remained in the hallway. Her expression coaxed him back into the waiting room so that Frank could have more privacy. Percy and Teddy went back into the waiting room as well.

Frank appeared as though he had been through hell during the last hour. "I want to know something before I go in there," he said to Carla.

"Sure, Frank."

"Is she pregnant?"

Carla wasn't prepared for the question. "Why don't you go in and talk to Mimi?"

Frank's eyes were desperate. "I need to know before I go in there."

"I think you need to talk to Mimi about . . . ." Her words trailed off.

Frank was unyielding. He wanted an answer.

Carla nodded. "Yes, she's pregnant."

Frank took a moment to digest Carla's words. "Is it Gutter Joe's?" he asked.

"Please go talk to Mimi."

"I'm asking you. Is there any possibility it's Joe's?"

"Frank, please."

"I've been through all kinds of shit with Mimi. I'm crazy about her. But as much as I love her, if that baby is Joe's, I can't stay with her. I'll do anything for Mimi, but not that. I can't raise his kid. I might as well leave right now. Keep on going. No need for me to even go in there and see her."

"You would walk out right now?" Carla asked.

Frank's face was firm. "Yes."

"Damn, Frank. That's cold."

"I put up with a lot from Mimi."

Carla was tempted not to tell him anything, to insist that he go in and see Mimi. But she had never seen Frank like this before. He despised Joe almost as much she did. She couldn't risk his walking away before Mimi had a chance to defend herself.

Carla sighed heavily. "It's not Joe's."

Frank still looked doubtful, his torment in plain view.

"It's not Joe's," Carla said firmly.

"Thanks." Frank walked lighter now. He no longer followed Carla's lead. He took off down the hallway and found Mimi's room on his own.

"Everything okay?" Baxter asked when Carla entered the waiting room.

She lowered herself wearily beside him. "Mimi's a little battered, but she's okay. They may keep her for a few days."

Baxter pointed to the metal box. "What's this?"

"I don't know. I couldn't get it open. Mimi thinks it's something that could incriminate Joe." Carla could tell that Baxter and Percy were itching to break the box open.

Baxter squeezed her thigh. "You sure you're alright?"

"Positive."

Assured that Carla was okay, his voice rose in anger and frustration. "Why the hell would you go over there and try to rescue Mimi by yourself? All you had to do was pick up the phone. Call me. Text me. Do you know what could have happened to you both?"

Carla stole a glance at Teddy. They smiled in understanding. Neither Baxter nor Percy cracked a smile, but fortunately, they were still consumed with curiosity about the contents of the box.

"Frank's going to be a while," Baxter said to Percy. "Let's go down to your car and see if we can get this thing open."

Percy jumped at the chance. They eagerly departed.

Carla was relieved when they left. She didn't feel like arguing with Baxter about why she didn't solicit his help. Now she could focus her attention on Teddy. She noticed that Teddy fidgeted uncomfortably.

"Thanks for coming back for us," Carla said.

Teddy toyed with her jacket. "I should never have left you in the first place." Her eyes averted Carla's.

"That's all behind us, Teddy. You don't have to worry about me and Mimi saying anything." Carla smiled. "Girl power honor." Teddy smiled too.

"We're just glad you came back," Carla continued. "You risked your life to help us. You could have been shot. Without you—" Carla shuddered. She didn't want to think about it. She went over and hugged Teddy.

Frank appeared unexpectedly in the waiting room.

"Everything okay?" Carla asked.

"Mimi's asleep. I need to run home and get some clothes. I want to be here when she wakes up."

Carla nodded. "Okay, Frank. I'll keep an eye on her."

Frank turned to leave, but Carla stopped him. "How are you getting home?"

"The guys are downstairs waiting for me."

Carla wondered if they planned to go over to Joe's den and exact vengeance. Had she saved Mimi only to put their men in jeopardy?

"Come right back, Frank," Carla admonished. "And please tell Baxter and Percy not to do anything stupid."

Frank raised his brow.

"We did what we had to," Carla said in defense.

"I'll tell them," Frank said and left.

Carla wasn't convinced.

Hours later, after she and Baxter had picked up her car and dropped it off at her condo, they rode to his house. Fortunately, he drove at a somewhat moderate speed. Carla had enough of daredevil driving for a while. She felt drained and wiped out. She simply wanted to crawl into bed and sleep, with or without Baxter.

They were both irritated with each other. He was still angry with her for endangering her life and not seeking his help. She was angry with him because he, Percy, and Frank had returned to the hospital hours after they left with no plausible explanation for their delay. They claimed they were trying to open the metal box. Carla knew it didn't take them hours to open a box that her nieces could have pried open in minutes.

Carla supposed she would have to accept his explanation. At least, he was safe and sound beside her. Baxter reached out and touched her knee affectionately. Carla was surprised to feel a tiny stirring within her core. Her anger dissipated.

Inside Baxter's house, Carla felt safe and protected. It had been a long, rough night. Immersed in thought, she stared at the glorious view of the city through Baxter's big bay window.

Baxter was on his cell phone listening attentively. He hung up and expelled his breath. "We found a tape in the box you gave me," he said. "Some kind of surveillance tape. It ties Joe to one of those warehouse fires. We can probably connect him to the fire at the TiTi as well," Baxter continued. "Before it's all over, we should be able to link him to a number of fires he set to eliminate his rivals. I didn't want to tell you until I was sure."

A flood of relief washed over Carla.

Baxter's eyes narrowed. "That still doesn't let you off the hook for going over there."

"I'm glad I went," Carla said. "I know it wasn't the smartest thing to do, but it worked. I got Mimi away from Joe, and he's going to jail."

Baxter hesitated. "Uh, if he ever gets out of the hospital."

"I had to defend myself." The words tumbled from Carla's lips.

"You did all that to Joe by yourself?"

"How do you know what I did?"

"I heard about it," Baxter said.

Carla searched his face. She didn't care if he was telling the truth or not. She just wanted to go to bed and sleep. But his eyes still probed hers intently.

Carla sighed. "I had to knock Joe down to make sure he didn't get back up. And Mimi . . . ." Carla suddenly felt very emotional when she tried to imagine what Mimi had gone through. "Mimi lost it—after all they had done to her. She went off on Joe. Don't tell Frank," Carla entreated.

"I won't," Baxter said.

"How do you know Joe is in the hospital?"

Baxter shrugged. "I told you. I heard about it. He and one of his bodyguards—they're both in the hospital."

"The guy who shot at us?"

"I guess." Baxter was being evasive.

Carla sighed heavily. "We didn't do that. We didn't touch his bodyguard. Somebody else did that."

Baxter nodded.

Carla didn't want to know any more. "Baxter, can we please put this behind us? I told you we'd get rid of Joe, and I think we have. After the hospital, he's going to prison."

Baxter pulled her close. "Okay. It's behind us for the most part. There's still the arson investigation." He stopped. "I'm so glad you're safe, baby."

Carla leaned against him and clung to his strength. She refused to cry, but the tears squeezed out anyway and rolled down her cheeks, wetting Baxter's shirt. He continued to hold her close and calm her with his embrace.

"I'm okay now," Carla said and pulled away from him. "I'm so tired. Let's go to bed. I have to go into work later. I need at least a few hours' sleep."

"You've been through a lot. Maybe you should take the day off."

"I can't. Jasmine is out. Her wedding is this weekend—which reminds me. You're going, right? You never told me."

Baxter responded on a completely different tangent. "What happened with Teddy?"

"What do you mean?"

"I get the impression something happened when she picked up you and Mimi."

"Teddy saved our lives! Mimi and I might both be—" Carla frowned. "You still haven't answered my question. Are you going to the wedding with me or not? I asked you a while ago. And every time I ask, I don't get a straight answer."

Baxter put his arm around her shoulder and guided her towards the bedroom. "You're right. Let's go to bed. We can discuss this later."

Carla pulled away from him. "No, I want to discuss it now. Are you going to the wedding with me or not?"

"Why are you getting so worked up about this?"

"Answer the question."

Baxter sighed heavily. "No, I'm not."

"You're not?" Carla asked incredulously. "Why?"

"I don't do weddings," Baxter said simply.

Carla's patience snapped. "Oh, get over yourself. I'm not asking you to marry me. I'm asking you to go to a fucking wedding."

Baxter's eyes held a warning. "I think we've both had a long night. We can discuss this later when we're feeling refreshed."

Carla refused to budge. "Refreshed, my ass. I want to know why you don't do weddings."

"It's nothing major. I don't do weddings. They make me uncomfortable. The single women want to know if I'm attached, and everybody else wants to know why I'm not married. I feel so awkward at weddings."

"I'll be with you. I'm your date."

"I'm not going," Baxter said firmly.

"I don't believe this shit."

"Watch your language."

"You're lucky. In my younger days, I would have cursed your ass out. This is the most ridiculous thing I've ever heard. You don't want to go to a wedding with me. Jasmine invited us both. She came to our barbecue."

"I like Jasmine. I think she's cool. I'll pay for the gift. You can get her anything you want."

"But you're not going to the wedding?"

Baxter refused to yield. "Nor reception."

Carla studied him. "Is it because you think something happened between her and Earl after the barbecue?"

Baxter looked offended. "Of course not. That's their business. That's forgotten about."

"What is it then?"

"I'm not going, that's all."

Carla was starting to breathe fire. "Is it because of your birthday party and Gina? Do you think less of me now? I notice a change in you lately. I can sense it. Did my helping Mimi turn you off that much? I mean, what the fuck is it?"

Baxter could feel his blood pressure rise. "It's none of those things, dammit. The birthday party was one of the best nights of my life. And I'm proud of you for rescuing Mimi even though I think it was a fucking crazy thing to do. You told me you were going to take Gutter Joe down, and you did. I'm glad you're in my corner. I know you got my back—always."

"So you just don't go to weddings?"

Baxter shrugged. She finally got it. "Right," he said.

"Take me home."

"Now?" Baxter asked, dumbfounded.

"Now," Carla insisted.

"Aw, come on. Don't go home like this. Stay with me. We'll talk later." He tried to soften her up. He brushed his fingers along her chin.

"Please take me home," Carla said.

They rode in silence thick enough to slice with a knife. Through the early morning traffic, Baxter drove more like his old self to aggravate her. Even so, when he pulled up in front of her building, he leaned over and tried to kiss her to make amends. Carla eluded him and jumped out of the car. She was still angry.

She swung around to him. "Still kicking and screaming like a kid—right, Baxter? I finally understand you don't want any commitment whatsoever. The 'C' word fucks with you. I keep trying to reassure you that I don't want to tie you down, that I don't want any commitment either. But you know what? I do want to get married somewhere down the line. If you don't want that, I respect your feelings. I think you're silly, but I have to respect your feelings. Now that I can admit what I want, we may have to go our separate ways. I don't want to force anything on you."

On that note, Carla walked away. Baxter stared after her, speechless. She was so brazenly honest. He hated to see her walk away, but he couldn't stop himself from watching the rhythm of her butt as she walked. He squelched the stirring in his loins.

He jumped out of the car and tried to inject a touch of humor to lighten things up. "Won't you come back and tell me how you really feel?"

Carla whirled around furiously. There was no trace of humor whatsoever on her face.

Baxter sighed and stepped back into his car with mixed emotions. He didn't want her to go, but he wasn't backing down. He dreaded going to weddings—no exceptions. Besides, he needed to reassess his feelings about her. She was wrong about the birthday party. He would always remember that night. In no way did it lessen his feelings for her. That was the problem. He was becoming too enamored with her. When Teddy told him that Carla was in the hospital, his whole world came crumbling down.

Carla filled an empty space in his heart. She was beautiful, fun, and so alluring. Their sex life was great, and they were still riding high off the birthday party. But suppose something bad ever happened to her. He felt so violent when he thought about Gutter Joe hurting Carla. He wanted to bash Joe's head in and clean up the pavement with him. Baxter realized that if he didn't learn how to reign in his emotions, he would be devastated if Carla disappeared from his life. They shared so many interests, and he loved her spirit of adventure. Now that she was out of the TiTi, they embraced a whole new world together.

But he had to wrest control of his feelings before they got out of hand. He still wanted to date her, but he had to keep things in proper perspective so he could enjoy his life without commitment. He hoped Carla would see things his way. They could date and have lots of fun, but they needed to pull back a bit. Otherwise, as she declared, they might have to go their separate ways.

CHAPTER 42

Carla pressed the chiffon of her skirt down to cover her legs more. It was September and still warm like summer. She sat beside Oscar in the church as they waited for the wedding to begin. She sat at one end of the pew, and smart-mouthed Regina sat at the other end. Oscar had maneuvered himself between them, closer to Carla.

Regina had smirked when Carla entered the pew alone. Carla tried to ignore her and dismiss the fact that Baxter would not be attending. Carla felt torn. She was pissed at Baxter, but she missed him, too, even though it had only been a few days since they argued about the wedding. He had become such a major part of her life. Yet she might have to walk away from him.

She had asked Natalie for advice. Her sister told her, "You deserve to have what you want. If he can't go to a simple wedding with you, then you don't need him." But then Natalie turned around and said, "However, he's a good man. He's generous. He takes you out all the time. The kids love him. And he's definitely not hard on the eyes."

"Whose side are you on?" Carla had asked in irritation.

"Yours," Natalie had answered unconvincingly.

Carla decided her sister was no help at all.

"You okay?" Oscar asked with probing eyes. He seemed to have slipped closer to Carla in the pew.

She shifted further away from him. "I'm fine."

"You don't seem like it."

Mind your business, Carla thought. But it wasn't really fair to take out her frustrations on Oscar. At least, Oscar had no problem sitting beside her at a wedding. How she wished he were Baxter. Could she really live without Baxter? Maybe, she should accept the fact that he didn't want any commitment. Natalie was right. Baxter took her anywhere she wanted to go— other than weddings. Their sex life was great. She still wondered if the birthday party was a good idea. Maybe, that's why he was pulling back from her. She could never tell with him. One minute, they were the perfect couple, and the next minute, he was pulling away from her for whatever reason. She supposed she could get used to the roller-coaster relationship they had. He definitely thrilled her. She'd call him after the reception and see if he wanted to hang out.

"Where's your boyfriend?" Oscar asked.

"He had to work," Carla said.

"He couldn't take off for your boss's wedding?"

Carla bristled. "You know he's a fireman."

"He's a captain, ain't he? He couldn't rearrange his schedule?"

"Mind your own business, Oscar."

He shrugged. "If I had a girlfriend as fine as you, I'd go anywhere with her."

"Where's *your* girlfriend?" Carla shot back.

"Who said I had one?"

Carla stared hard at him. Oscar finally confessed. "I see somebody from time to time. You can't expect me to wait on you forever."

"So where is she?"

"She's coming to the reception," Oscar admitted.

"But not the wedding."

"She had to work."

"You're sitting here flirting with me, and you're going to hook up with your girlfriend at the reception?"

"What do you expect? I can't get any play from you."

Carla realized he had a point.

Oscar saw an opening and seized it. "After today, we can both ditch our partners. I swear I'll treat you right. You'll never have to worry about me not showing up."

True, Oscar had shown an unabashed interest in her ever since she started working at the fitness center. However, Carla was under no illusion about his true motives. Part of his ardor was the thrill of the chase. Still, she knew Oscar liked her. He was a good-looking guy and in great shape. Maybe, she should give him a chance. If only she could stop comparing him to Baxter. But Oscar fell short. She couldn't imagine him kissing her the way Baxter did. And Oscar was shallow, although so was Baxter at times like this. Still, all things considered, Baxter possessed a lot more substance.

Damn, Baxter had spoiled her. But she might have to give him up cold turkey. She refused to settle for crumbs when she could eat the whole loaf. She decided not to call him after the reception. She'd have to get used to living without him. He was not going to dictate the terms of their relationship. She wanted more than he was willing to give, and she refused to compromise. She had compromised enough.

Strengthened by her new resolve, Carla's usual impatience with Oscar vanished. She knew even if she and Baxter didn't work out, Oscar was not the one for her. She'd meet somebody to love, or she'd enjoy life by herself.

Oscar sensed that his window of opportunity had passed. He lost patience. "What you gonna do? Wait around for Big Daddy forever? He don't want you."

Carla saw a side of Oscar that she knew existed all along. Regina was starting to notice. Carla decided to nip Oscar's tirade in the bud. "You and I are only co-workers—nothing more."

Oscar still smarted. "I'm here for you right now. Where is Big Daddy?"

"Sorry I'm late," Baxter said.

Oscar was stunned. Carla swung around, mouth open. Baxter planted a kiss on her parted lips. He stood dressed to impress in a tan suit and a black open-necked shirt. The suit brought out the amber of his eyes. Carla stared at him like a love-struck schoolgirl.

"Slide over," he said.

Carla decided to mess with him. She refused to budge.

Baxter smiled. "Girl, you better move over. Don't embarrass me and leave me out in this aisle."

Carla smiled coyly, then slid over. She still didn't give him much room. She loved pressing close to him.

"Give me some space, baby," he grinned.

Carla finally gave him enough space. She tried to keep a straight face, but she felt like a giggly little jellyfish in his presence. Her heart was doing leaps and bounds for joy. She hadn't been to a wedding since one of her cousins got married a long time ago. Her heart danced with glee now that Baxter had shown up. She now understood why some women became absolutely foolish over their men. Carla's face beamed into a smile. Regina snorted at the other end of the pew.

Baxter was pleased with Carla's reaction. Though he still didn't care for weddings, he was glad he had shown up for his Carla. He rested his hand on her thigh possessively and leaned over to Oscar. "Thanks for amusing my girl until I got here."

Oscar barely nodded in response.

Carla stifled a laugh. She knew Oscar was pissed, but she also knew that he didn't want to tangle with Baxter, who was taller and bigger and probably ready to flatten Oscar for acting like a jerk.

Baxter's eyes fastened on Carla's dress. "Oh, you fancy, huh?"

Her dress was a flowing chiffon skirt with a fitted bodice in a beautiful berry red. She had draped a shawl over her shoulders. Baxter realized why. The whole back of the dress was out, and the skirt was well above the knee.

"Isn't that dress a little short?" he asked.

Carla's eyes twinkled. "A little."

Baxter shook his head and smiled. He was pleased she wore the gold and diamond anklet he gave her.

Carla snuggled against him. She was in her world. The sky was the limit. Baxter sat beside her, Mimi was safe, and Gutter Joe was going to survive—in prison. Everyone could sleep better at night, knowing Joe was behind bars.

Carla finally noticed the beauty of the church with its high cathedral ceilings and stained-glass windows. The floor was marble and the pews were solid oak. A white carpet had been rolled down the aisle for the bride.

"When's this thing going to start?" Baxter asked.

As if on cue, the groom and his best man came out from a side door and stood at the altar. They wore formal black and gray, but Kenny, the groom, wore a longer jacket.

Then everybody stood up as the organ music began and the procession of bridesmaids, ushers, ring bearer, and flower girl entered the church and strolled down the aisle. It was a large wedding party.

Carla felt giddy with excitement as the first chords of "Here Comes the Bride" played. Then Jasmine came into view with her father guiding her down the aisle. Jasmine was gorgeous in beautiful white lace that showed just enough cleavage in the front and enough skin in the back to conservatively tantalize. Instead of the normal bride demeanor, Jasmine greeted various attendees as she marched beside her father. Kenny smiled and watched proudly as his bride strolled towards him.

Then Jasmine noticed Carla and Baxter. She stopped beside them. "You made it," she said to Baxter.

"Couldn't miss it," Baxter said.

"You look lovely," Jasmine told Carla and hugged her.

"You're stunning," Carla said.

"Y'all ready for the reception? We're going to really party. I'm glad you're here, Carla. So glad we work together. This is my girl," she said to Baxter.

Carla and Baxter were both starting to squirm. Jasmine needed to pick up the pace. Her father was trying to nudge her forward. Kenny was shifting from one foot to the other at the altar.

"You better get down that aisle. Everybody's waiting, including the groom," Carla said with raised eyebrows.

"I'll get there," Jasmine said. "This is my day. I want to savor it. I see these weddings where the bride is so stiff and barely acknowledges anybody. I don't want to be like that on my day."

"We still got to move it along," Jasmine's father said.

"Yes, you do," Carla coaxed in a whisper.

Jasmine finally stepped away, only to stop a few pews down the aisle and talk to other attendees. She hugged them and greeted them too. Almost everybody in the church ceased breathing. Kenny was still shifting uncomfortably at the altar as he waited for his bride to join him. Jasmine's father was at a loss for words. Her mother got up and signaled for Jasmine to keep moving, but Jasmine still held court and talked to relatives and friends as she progressed forward. Kenny decided it was time to fetch his bride. He stepped off the altar and walked down the aisle. Jasmine's father threw up his hands and released her. Together, Jasmine and Kenny walked the bridal carpet to the altar. Everyone in attendance clapped.

Baxter couldn't resist smiling mischievously. "You think I should have brought Earl?"

Carla tried to keep a straight face. "Stop it, baby."

But Baxter couldn't stop grinning.

The minister brought down the house when he said, "We are gathered here today for one hell of a wedding."

The whole church erupted in laughter.

When the wedding was over, Jasmine glowed on Kenny's arm. Together, they held court with family and friends as they exited the church. Carla imagined it was the longest leave-taking by a bride and groom she would ever witness. Kenny had learned to follow the lead of his bride and savor the experience as well.

Baxter turned to Carla, thoroughly amused. "I don't know why I fought you on this wedding. I should have known hanging out with you is never dull. This is the best wedding I've ever been to."

Carla laughed.

"You riding with me to the reception?" Baxter asked.

"Sure," Carla said.

"Why are they having the reception all the way down in Rancho Palos Verdes. It's so far away from the church?"

Carla sighed and evaded the question.

"What?" Baxter asked. "You can tell me. After this wedding, nothing's going to surprise me."

"Kenny won the reception hall."

"You're kidding." Baxter howled with laughter. "That's how we got that cabin because he won that trip, remember?"

Carla tried to hush him. "We're still in church, baby."

Baxter laughed all the way outside.

With the top down, Carla and Baxter rode to the reception in his Thunderbird convertible. Carla's hair remained in place because of the assortment of women's scarves he kept in the glove compartment. She no longer chided him about the assortment since she felt more confident about her status with him, especially after today. Regardless of whoever came before her, she was the one who had gotten him to attend a wedding. She refused to gloat, though, because they still needed to resolve some things.

For now, though, she was perfectly content to enjoy the rest of the day with the man who swelled her heart. "How Far is Heaven?" by Los Lonely Boys played from Baxter's speakers. Carla decided that she was already in heaven, riding with Baxter to Jasmine's wedding reception with the top down. He kissed her hand when he noted the radiant smile on her face.

Carla bubbled with excitement when they stepped into the reception hall. She glanced around. Kenny had done well. It was a huge hall with a carpeted marble staircase which everyone descended to enter the reception area. There were balconies scattered about and a courtyard that hosted musicians who played soft jazz and classical music. In the center of the reception hall, a fountain rippled with fruit-flavored sparkling punch. There were two bars, one on each end of the hall. A DJ had set up his music station at the edge of the dance floor.

Baxter held Carla's hand as they explored the courtyard and balconies. On one balcony, they stood mesmerized by a splendid view of the Pacific Ocean frothing against the Palos Verdes Hills and bluffs. As Baxter inhaled the opulence of nature's sparkling blue ocean and emerald green hillsides, he told Carla, "I need to take lessons from Kenny."

"I'm sure he loses too," Carla said in warning.

Baxter looked around at all the glorious surroundings. "I'll take my chances."

Carla smiled and shook her head.

Baxter tried to pull her close and nibble on her neck when no one was looking. He seemed to love her dress. His fingers caressed her bare back on occasion, and she could tell he was itching to reach under the chiffon of her skirt and give her a quick feel. She eluded him with a giggle as the wedding party descended the stairs.

The carpeted marble staircase provided a magnificent entrance for the bridal party. The bridesmaids and maid of honor wore flowing lilac gowns with a Grecian effect. The bridesmaids wore their straps off the shoulders. The maid of honor wore a totally strapless gown. The lilac of their dresses contrasted well with the gray and black tuxedos of the groom and his party. With Kenny escorting her, Jasmine presented an enthralling picture when she descended the staircase in her beautiful white lace gown. Everybody clapped in appreciation as the bridal party completed its entrance.

After menu choices of prime rib, lobster, broiled salmon, and baby rack of lamb, the guests were ready to party in earnest, Carla and Baxter included.

"Did he win the catering too?" Baxter teased.

Carla laughed. "Behave yourself."

Since they both loved to dance, Carla and Baxter were definitely not shy on the dance floor. The bride and groom had danced, and father and daughter had danced. Carla and Baxter, along with some of the other guests, had danced with the bride and groom as well.

The DJ, a young, flamboyant gay male, danced at his station as he played a mix of old and new school. When he played "Curious (About Your Loving)," a Midnight Star song from the 1980s, Carla and Baxter hopped out on the dance floor and led the way.

"You remember this song?" Carla teased. "Weren't you in elementary school?"

"I used to party on this song with my mother and her

boyfriend. You must have been in your thirties then," Baxter laughed.

"Not hardly," Carla corrected him. "I was a budding teenager who could dance her ass off. I'll show you."

Carla proceeded to strut her stuff on the dance floor. Not to be outdone, Baxter laughed and kept pace with her.

Jasmine's father hopped out on the dance floor with his wife. "Grown folks' music," he said. He and his wife were thoroughly enjoying their daughter's wedding, despite its unusual start. The DJ played another oldie, "Weak At The Knees," by Steve Arrington. Then he played a sanitized remix of the rap version of the song. The dance floor was filled with young and old alike. Carla and Baxter danced their asses off. Carla performed some mild twerking, but she kept it low-key for the wedding reception.

With heads bobbing and booties shaking, sideliners watched from the perimeter. Carla never understood why some people shimmied on the sidelines, but wouldn't step out on the dance floor. It was okay, she decided. She and Baxter danced enough for all of them.

Carla was enjoying the time of her life with the man she adored. She wanted the reception to last forever. Then the DJ played the love song, "Don't Let Go" by En Vogue.

"That's my song!" Carla exclaimed. Baxter was already encircling her waist to pull her close. Carla sank against him and started singing. She knew her voice wasn't the greatest, but it wasn't the worst either. It was a difficult tune to sing. But Carla loved the song and modulated her voice low enough that she sang almost perfectly in Baxter's ear. She switched back and forth between the chorus and the lead. The DJ couldn't have played a more appropriate song, Carla decided.

Baxter was starting to squirm as Carla sang the lyrics in his ear. Essentially, it was a song telling him how much she cared and to get his act together. Every time he pulled slightly away, Carla pushed in closer and sang with even more fervor. Eventually, Baxter stopped resisting and allowed Carla to sing her heart out to him.

When the song was over, Carla didn't know what to make of

things. Baxter looked at her and made no comment. His eyes were guarded. Carla didn't care. She was having the time of her life, and she wanted him to know it. Let him squirm. She refused to apologize for her feelings.

"You okay?" Carla asked, stifling a smile. "You want to discuss the lyrics?" She laughed fully now.

"No, I don't, Miss Smarty Pants. I'm here to enjoy the wedding."

Carla's eyes still danced with mirth.

Baxter kissed her on the forehead. "I'm stepping out of the hot seat right now. I'm going over to talk with the groom. See if Kenny can give me some tips on playing poker."

Carla's mouth hung open in dismay. "Oh, please don't let him know I told you about the reception hall."

Baxter grinned. "I won't. I'll get him to tell me about it, then ask him to teach me how to play better poker."

"Maybe, you should stay here with me. Stay out of trouble."

"Bye," Baxter said and headed towards Kenny.

Carla headed over to some of her co-workers. Oscar watched her every move as she joined the group. Ignoring his unbridled gawking, Carla introduced herself to Oscar's date. The woman reacted suspiciously. Carla gave up and decided that she preferred to deal with Regina rather than Oscar and his date. Jasmine came over and joined them. As the bride, she truly enjoyed her status as belle of the ball. In no time, everybody in their group was laughing, talking, and drinking. They teased and reminisced about work escapades. Oscar's girlfriend loosened up and became friendlier. She even became expansive enough to line dance with Carla and the rest of the group. Of course, Oscar insinuated himself beside Carla as he danced between her and his girlfriend.

Carla glanced around for Baxter. He seemed to be enjoying himself on the other side of the room. He danced with several women, but from time to time, he would gesture and point to Carla as his date. Carla smiled broadly.

Then the wedding coordinator began to assemble Jasmine and all the single women for the bouquet toss. At first, Carla declined, but then she figured she might as well. She'd be thrilled if she caught it, and inwardly, she'd gloat if Baxter squirmed.

"You better get out there, girl." Jasmine lured Carla out on the floor.

Baxter made his way back and stood on the sidelines. He smiled and shook his head. "Let somebody else catch it," he shouted playfully. The women chided him, but the men laughed.

Carla was now determined to catch the bouquet. She positioned herself slightly off center in the crowd of women jockeying for the bouquet. She carved enough space for herself to avoid flailing, overzealous arms. Twice, Jasmine teased and pretended to toss the bouquet. Finally, she hurled it high over her shoulder. There was a mad scramble by the women as it flew in the air. Carla jockeyed into position so that the bouquet sailed right in her direction. She jumped up to grab it, but a more ruthless adversary snatched it away. Carla was miffed at first, but she laughed it off good-naturedly.

"You're safe!" she shouted to Baxter in a voice reminiscent of a dancing reality show host.

Everybody laughed.

Baxter hugged her. "Good girl."

Next was the garter toss. With delicate fingers, Kenny caressingly removed the garter from Jasmine's thigh. Fueled by good food and libations, the crowd laughed and cheered. Then Kenny urged all the single men out on the floor to catch the garter.

Baxter refused to move.

"Don't you want to get out there?" Carla cajoled.

"No. I'll stand here and watch."

Carla frowned. "Come on, it's a simple garter catch."

Baxter lowered his voice for Carla's ears only. "Hey, I think I've been more than accommodating. But no garter catch."

Carla sighed and folded her arms across her chest.

Baxter capitulated. "Okay. I'll get out there and catch the damn thing. And I don't want to hear any complaints when I push it up as high as I can on the lady who caught the bouquet."

"We'll deal with that if you catch it," Carla teased.

"Okay." Baxter walked out on the floor in defiance.

Kenny laughed at him. "That's the spirit!"

The single men crowded behind Kenny on the floor. Not to be outdone by Jasmine, Kenny faked a few throws as well. Baxter stood relaxed and poised to catch the garter. Kenny tossed it high over his shoulder. Baxter sliced his way through the crowd, reached up, and caught it. He turned and smiled smugly at Carla. She was forced to laugh.

For the grand finale of the garter ceremony, Carla stood front and center as the woman who caught the bouquet sat in a chair and Baxter knelt down and inched the garter up her leg.

"I'm right here, baby," Carla said.

Everyone howled with laughter.

Baxter took his time sliding the garter up the bouquet catcher's leg, then thigh. Carla wondered just how far he was going to push things, but then he stopped at a decent point, took the appropriate pictures, stood up, and walked over to Carla. "You satisfied now?" he asked.

Carla smiled in relief. "Now see that wasn't so bad, was it?"

Baxter merely shrugged. Then the music started back up again, and Carla and Baxter found themselves out on the dance floor with other partners. Carla enjoyed herself, secure in the knowledge that Baxter was leaving with her. When the DJ played Frankie Beverly's "Before I Let Go," Carla was almost glad that somebody else danced with Baxter. That was Baxter's song. Nobody could outdo him on the dance floor. Plenty of women tried, but he beat everybody. He signaled to Carla, but she evaded him. He mouthed the word, "punk," to her when she wouldn't dance with him. Partying at his music station, the young DJ danced almost as well as Baxter to the song, but in the end, Baxter outdid him too. Carla laughed as her baby kicked ass on the dance floor, even on Beyoncé's version.

As the reception was winding down, Carla looked around for Baxter. He was the center of attention in a small group of women. One of them was the bouquet catcher. She was a buxom woman in her late thirties. She definitely took her bouquet catch and Baxter's garter catch seriously. Baxter appeared to be having a good time. Carla headed over to the group.

Baxter looked up and saw his beautiful Lady Killjoy on her way over to fetch him. He decided to beat her to the punch. He excused himself from the ladies and headed towards her.

Carla frowned when they stood face-to-face. "Did you tell Miss Garter Belt that you're spoken for, or do I need to tell her?"

Baxter laughed. "No, that won't be necessary. Do I need to go over and pulverize Oscar?"

It was Carla's turn to laugh. "You having a good time?" she asked.

Baxter shrugged. "So, so."

"So, so, my ass. I thought you didn't like weddings."

"I didn't . . . until I met you."

Carla was astonished. "What about Gina?" she blurted out.

Baxter smiled. "What about her? You're all I want. The birthday party was fun, but a little rich, don't you think? It's not something I want to do all the time. Maybe, every ten years."

Carla laughed. Whether he meant it or not, she didn't care. She simply wanted to be with him.

Baxter led her out on the dance floor. The DJ was slowing the pace and preparing everybody to leave. He played Kem's "Share My Life." Baxter pulled Carla in his arms. He began singing to her in his rich baritone voice. At first, Carla thought he simply liked the song, but then she realized that he was really serenading her. Carla held her breath. Maybe, it was all wishful thinking on her part. No, Baxter was clearly serenading her. He had a wonderful voice. He totally relaxed in the moment and held her closer. Carla felt tears threaten to overtake her.

Baxter realized the tears were coming too. He hugged her a little tighter to distract her and halt the waterworks. He didn't want to have to carry her across the dance floor in rescue.

"You okay?" he asked. He knew she wasn't, but she nodded anyway, blinking back tears.

Baxter held her close and continued his serenade, and for a while, nothing else mattered but their melting into each other.

When the song was over, Baxter lifted her chin. "I love you, Carla."

She exhaled. "I love you too."

They kissed in the middle of the dance floor, oblivious to everyone around them.

When it was time to leave, Carla felt exhilarated. She had a wonderful day, and Baxter had finally admitted that he loved her. Carla glowed as she said her farewells to everybody. Jasmine winked at her teasingly. Carla couldn't remember the last time she enjoyed herself so much.

In the garage of Carla's condo, Baxter parked his car next to hers. Neither of them was ready to retire for the night so they had decided to go to the movies. Carla jumped out of her car and ran over to Baxter's. "You can wait here. It'll only take me a few minutes to change," she said breathlessly. She was still excited from the wonderful time they had at the wedding.

"Okay, don't take long," Baxter said. He had already changed. He noted the way the chiffon of her dress caressed her hips. His eyes fastened on her long beautiful legs under the short skirt. "I'll come upstairs with you," he announced.

Carla knew that if he went upstairs with her, they were in for the night, and she was hell bent on hanging out at the movies with her man. She wanted to show him off to the world, especially after he told her that he loved her. She was euphoric. "No, you stay here," Carla laughed. "I'll only be a minute."

But Baxter's eyes penetrated through her dress. He pulled the key out of the ignition. "I'll come up with you."

Carla knew once he stepped out of the car, they could forget about the movies. She stopped him in mid-motion. "If we go to the movies, I'll bring you breakfast in bed tomorrow morning." He wavered. Carla knew she had his attention. "I'll bring you breakfast in this dress . . . and no panties."

He put his keys back in the ignition. His face broke into a grin. "Which movie you want to see?"

Carla kissed him and eluded him with a laugh when he tried to pull her closer. She quickly headed for the elevator while she had the chance. When she turned around, Baxter was already texting on his phone. *He'd better not be texting any of those hussies at the reception,* she thought. But then she smiled and relaxed. She knew he only loved her. It was a good feeling.

CHAPTER 43

Carla grabbed her purse and shawl and ran outside. Baxter was waiting for her. It was Saturday night. Between her schedule and his, a week had passed since she last saw him. They had gone to the movies after the wedding, but after that, they had fallen asleep, bone-tired, at his house. The next morning, when she was ready to bring him breakfast in bed, he flew out of the bedroom fully dressed in his captain's uniform.

"Don't tell me you have to leave," Carla moaned.

Baxter nodded solemnly. "A fire in one of the parks spread to some houses. I have to go in. They may need us."

It took a few moments for acceptance to set in, but once it did, Carla quickly grabbed a pita pocket and slid an omelet and a few sausages inside. She poured Baxter a cup of coffee in a thermos.

"Thanks, baby," he had said and grabbed his meal. He kissed her quickly and managed to feel her butt as he left. "Keep it warm for me."

From the window, Carla had watched in dismay as he pulled off, dismantling her plans for a lazy day of lounging and lovemaking.

Now she felt like a high school kid going on a date. He had sent her a text and told her to be ready. He wanted to take her out to dinner at a small jazz club in Santa Monica, and he had a surprise for her. She refused to speculate on the surprise. Knowing Baxter, it could be anything.

Carla wore the berry red dress again, the one she wore to

the wedding. Baxter had insisted on it. In an effort to pick up where they left off, she wore no panties, but she did wear a strappy lace halter bra. The halter matched the color of the dress. Its skinny straps tied around her neck and back and seemed attached to the dress. She'd keep Baxter guessing about the panties. Inhaling sharply, she imagined his fingers probing beneath her dress. Her insides heated up at the thought. She forced herself to settle down so that she wouldn't mess up the dress.

Outside her condo, Baxter sat grinning in a classic cream-colored Buick Roadmaster. The orange glow of sunset turned the car golden. Carla was absolutely enthralled when he went around to the passenger side and opened the door for her.

He bowed gallantly. "At your service, madam. You know the make and year?"

Carla sucked in her breath and marveled at it. "Don't tell me. Let me guess—a '48 Buick, right?"

Baxter nodded, pleased.

Carla's voice rose with excitement. "It's like the one in my father's toy collection."

"Yep. Thought you'd get a kick out of it."

"Oh, my father would love this car."

Baxter smiled warmly. "That's what I was thinking. Maybe, we can rent it again and take him for a spin."

"Wow! He might like that," Carla said.

"Hop in, young lady," Baxter coaxed. "This is fun. I might want to tinker around with classic cars when I retire."

Carla slid into the front passenger seat. The interior had been redone in tan leather. "Oh, this is heavenly." She looked down at the seat which had been retrofitted with a seat belt. The belt only fastened around her lap, but Carla didn't mind. She figured most classic cars had no seat belt at all. She smiled contentedly and sank back against the leather.

Baxter tried to slide his hand under her dress. "No panties, right?"

Carla pushed his hand away. "Guess."

"Oh, I'll figure it out," he said confidently.

Carla laughed. "I'm sure your x-ray eyes miss nothing. Hope we don't run into anybody from the wedding. They'll see me in this dress twice."

"You look beautiful . . . and sexy."

She smiled. She did feel sexy in the dress and no panties. And the fact that she hadn't sent the dress to the cleaners yet somehow made her feel sexier. She had simply freshened the dress and aired it out. Carla could see a bulge forming in Baxter's trousers. He was dressed in dark slacks and a long-sleeved blue shirt with the cuffs rolled back. The shirt and slacks melted over his taut physique.

He reached down and touched her leg. He fingered the gold and diamond anklet that he had given her. "Glad you wore it," he said.

Carla guided his hand away to control the rising heat between her legs.

"You miss me?" Baxter asked.

"Of course."

He kissed her hand. "I missed you too."

"So you got that fire under control?"

"Which fire?" he grinned.

"The one at the park."

He nodded. "We did good. We got new computers and better software courtesy of—you remember that deputy at the charity ball, the one who was messing with the dancer at the TiTi? He pushed for approval of our budget. I guess I gotta thank him and that young lady."

Carla laughed. "I don't know how much of a lady she is."

"She's okay by me. We didn't expect to get the new computers so soon. That new software helped us map out different scenarios. We came up with a good strategy. I know it's going to take us a while to get some of the other items in our budget. But so far, so good."

"I'm just glad you're safe," Carla said and snuggled cozily into the seat. She liked riding in the antique Buick with Baxter. Because of state law for classic cars, he took the streets, instead of highways. And because he had to handle the car with care, he drove less hurriedly.

* * *

As they ate at the jazz club, Carla allowed Baxter to slide his hand under her dress, but only up to her thighs. She figured she'd keep him in suspense. Her dress worked fine. She hadn't run into anybody they saw at the wedding.

The club was cozy and softly lit, with tables along the walls. The food was good too. Carla ordered grilled trout, while Baxter chose not to eat as healthy and ordered fried catfish. They both enjoyed their meals.

The singer wore an odd zoot suit that was black and gray, pinstriped. It fit right in place once he took the stage and grabbed the mic. He had a raspy voice and smoked e-cigarettes during the performance. He and his band performed a unique blend of jazz and rock music. Carla loved the sound. She and Baxter were having a good time.

On the way home, Carla drove. At first, Baxter balked when she asked him to let her drive. But she insisted that the next time she saw her father, she had to regale him with an account of how she drove the car. Baxter finally gave in. The car didn't handle as smoothly as she imagined. It was stiffer and bigger than her Infiniti, but she adapted quickly. She got a kick out of driving the big Buick, and she enjoyed the attention she got when guys pulled up beside her. A few of the guys definitely appeared as interested in her as the car. Baxter promptly burst their bubbles.

Carla delighted in the attention. She was determined to keep the night going. She didn't want it to end.

Baxter laughed at her. "You're not ready to go in yet?" They were not far from his house in Baldwin Hills and had taken a scenic route. He still wanted to show off the car as much as she did. He had received compliments and inquiries all night.

Under his direction, Carla reached a point in the hills where city lights aligned with the stars, and the tiny crescent of a new moon illumined the sky.

Baxter saw her nipples harden under the dress. He reached

out and touched her breasts, then stopped. "Wait. I know a better place."

Within minutes, he had directed her to a lovers' lane that was part of a spectacular overlook beneath the stars. She parked and turned off the engine. She pushed her breasts against his hands.

Baxter fingered her nipples. "Come on, let's step outside."

"What if someone sees us?"

Baxter chuckled. "It's cool. Cops come up here too."

He got out of the car and opened Carla's door. They kissed passionately, tongues entwining. Carla stood on her toes and opened her legs wider to fuse against the tumescence in his slacks. He untied the halter and, in a single deft move, slid it off. He placed it on the hood of the car. The red lace bra presented a sumptuous contrast against the cream-colored Buick. Carla moaned as he rubbed and stimulated her bare breasts through the dress. Then he reached his hand inside her bodice and continued fondling. He stuck his other hand under her skirt and felt her bare bottom.

"I've been waiting for this all day," he said.

"Me too," Carla breathed against his lips. She pressed deeper against him as he caressed her hips. She grabbed his fingers, slid them along her clit, then into her slippery tunnel. "That feels so good," she panted.

Baxter unzipped his pants and slipped inside her. They stood locked together so that nobody could see him sliding in and out of her. "This what you want?" he asked.

"Oh, yes," she moaned and squeezed tighter around his swollen length. A car came past. Baxter eased out and zipped his pants up. He smeared his fingers all over Carla's butt. She arched against him in response.

He opened the back door, and Carla jumped in. "It's so roomy back here," she breathed huskily as she sank on the seat.

"The better to woo you, my dear," Baxter said with a grin. He dropped down on his knees and put his head under her dress. She began to writhe as he blew lightly on her delicate parts. He licked softly, then harder. He pushed his fingers into her warm, wet softness. Carla gasped and circled his fingers ravenously. She lifted her dress and watched him stimulate her with his tongue. He reached up and stroked her breasts. Carla groaned in ecstasy. She let him play in her lubricated tunnel a little longer, then pushed him away so they could switch places.

She dropped to the floor and buried her head in his lap. He was so hard that she thought he would burst through his zipper. She continued to tease him with her lips and breath.

"Come on, baby. Take it out," he moaned.

Carla finally obliged, massaging his rigid phallus up and down. She twirled her tongue all around the head and stroked his balls. Then she sat beside him and kissed him. He tasted himself on her lips. They were both touching, moaning, probing.

Carla finally climbed on top of Baxter in the back seat, her chiffon skirt encircling their movements. He pulled the top of her dress down so he could play freely with her breasts. Carla cupped them and pushed them into his mouth so that he could suck unimpeded. And he did, as she rode him in the back seat of the car. She slid up and down as he gave her one ecstatic stroke after another. His hands were all over her breasts and butt as she rode harder. Finally, they cried out as their bodies slapped in the throes of wanton passion.

When it was over, Carla laughed weakly. "Now you know what's under the dress."

Baxter's laugh was drained too. "I certainly do."

They huddled quietly in the back seat and beheld a star-studded view of the hilltop as their breathing subsided. Before long, Carla felt the stirrings of arousal again. She slid her dress off and sat totally naked. Baxter stripped too. They found themselves on the floor with Carla lying on top. She popped her breasts into his mouth, then inched down and sucked him. He was rock hard again. She sucked him long and strong, then slid her throbbing canal over the fruits of her labor.

Their bodies coupled this way and that on the floor, with her on top, him on top, creating one delightful thrill after another. He flipped her over and mounted her from the back as he fingered her sex. Carla climaxed several times under the crescent moon and the gleaming stars. Baxter climaxed too. The sultry night had set them ablaze.

CHAPTER 44

Baxter's gleaming red T-Bird knifed through traffic as they rode through the side streets of Hollywood to Atwater Village. Traffic was heavy on Thanksgiving Day as revelers navigated to their dinner destinations. Despite the number of cars, Baxter deftly weaved in and out of the congestion. At a stoplight intersecting Hollywood Boulevard, Carla caught a glimpse of all the hustle and bustle along the street. Tourists and celebrity impersonators, from Marilyn Monroe to Michael Jackson, populated the boulevard. Glittering holiday decorations created additional pizzazz.

Carla gazed pensively out the window, but her attention was elsewhere. Baxter glanced over at her and suppressed a smile. "Why so quiet?"

Carla shrugged.

Baxter burst out laughing. "You wanted this. You've been bugging me for a while."

"I know," Carla said quietly.

He started teasing her and mimicking a woman's voice. "I want to meet your mother. Why haven't I met your mom yet?"

Carla was forced to smile.

"My mom's cool. She won't bite. I'm sure she's just as curious to meet you."

Carla still seemed tense. "I'm not afraid of her. But what if we don't get along?"

Baxter squeezed her hand reassuringly. "She'll love you. I love you."

Carla finally relaxed. "I love you too."

"Good. Happy Thanksgiving."

"Same to you," Carla said.

Baxter noted that she was still more quiet than usual. He put on some party music to elevate her mood. He was still amused. Had he known that all he had to do was threaten to take Carla to meet his mother to shut her up during an argument, he would have introduced them sooner whether his mom liked it or not.

Carla settled deeper into the seat and tried to relish the sights of the holiday season. In record time, they reached Atwater Village where Baxter's mother lived. The neighborhood was both quaint and hip at the same time. Her lawn and hedges were well-manicured. Azalea bushes with a few pink winter blooms brightened the lawn.

Inside the house, the eclectic mix of furniture was somewhat similar to Carla's, but bolder and more of a hodgepodge of furnishings. Carla loved the emerald green couch in the living room. She figured the padded folding chairs stacked in the corner were for occasions when Lillie entertained on a larger scale.

Lillie's boyfriend, Zach, had answered the door. He was a handsome man in his sixties—stocky with a bit of a belly, but in good shape. He appeared trendy in casual slacks and sweater.

Carla liked him immediately. He seemed totally unfazed by the curves beneath her slim black jeans and glittery gold tunic. The jeans were studded along the sides and hung at just the right length over low-heeled booties. The pants were not as tight as some of the others in her closet. She wanted to make a good impression on Baxter's mother.

When Baxter had picked her up and noticed the jeans, he reached out and felt her butt.

Carla had sighed in dismay. "Are they too tight?"

Baxter grinned. "Nothing can hide that butt."

He himself wore jeans and a casual sweater. A sports jacket dressed up his outfit. He had pulled her close and given her a sexy kiss.

Though Carla had felt her body respond, she had ushered him out of the condo so they wouldn't be late. But apparently, Baxter's mom was in no hurry.

Just as Baxter and Carla headed for the kitchen, she finally came out and greeted them. Her eyes narrowed suspiciously at Carla. But Carla barely noticed because her mouth hung open in awe as she stared at Lillie. "You look just like Baxter!" Carla exclaimed. "I've seen pictures of you, but in person . . . ."

Lillie warmed involuntarily. "You mean he looks just like me. Came straight out of my coochie."

"Mom!" Baxter protested.

Carla laughed outright. She was glad Baxter's mother wasn't a prude. Zach simply smiled and shook his head. He had eyes only for Lillie in her black slinky pants, glittery red top, and ballet flats. She was a beautiful woman with ample curves and a full head of hair. Carla wished she had as much hair.

Baxter noted that Lillie seemed to be softening towards Carla. He figured Carla would win his mom over the way she had won him over. But he knew his mom. She was probably going to test Carla in some way.

Carla glanced around the dining room. The table was already set with four place settings in a colorful, informal manner. Carla guessed the dinnerware was disposable and recyclable. It appeared to be made from sugar cane or palm leaves. The fruit cup goblets, however, were real crystal, yet harmonized with the rest of the table. Carla smiled in appreciation at the décor. Her mother would have approved.

"Meet your approval?" Lillie asked.

"Nice," Carla smiled. She no longer felt intimidated by Lillie. She hoped they got along, but she wasn't going to kowtow to Baxter's mother.

"Everything's almost ready. You want to come help me in the kitchen?" Lillie challenged.

"Not really," Carla admitted. "But I will."

Baxter and Zach were already in front of the television watching the football game. Carla longed to join them. "I'll be back," she told them. "I've got to support my Eagles. My father is from Philly," she explained to Lillie.

"Then you might as well join me in the kitchen. You know they're not going to win."

Baxter started laughing. "That's what I told her."

Zach defended Carla. "I got folks in Philly too. The Eagles will win."

"Let's go, girl," Lillie said. "We'll be finished in no time so you can watch them lose."

Inside the kitchen, Lillie pointed to the oven. "The banana pudding is almost ready. Everything else is done." Carla's eyes swept over the foods on top of the stove and counters. There was turkey, dressing, sweet potatoes, baked macaroni, and what looked like a hot kale dish.

"Zach made the mac and cheese and the sweet potatoes," Lillie said.

Carla marveled at the abundance of food. "You could feed an army," she said.

"I like to cook big. You never know."

Carla still thought it was a lot of food. "You made the banana pudding?" she asked, sniffing the pleasant aroma.

Lillie nodded.

Carla arched her brow. "From scratch?"

"From scratch," Lillie answered smugly.

"Wow. I'm impressed. I don't cook, you know, but once upon a time, I could make a mean banana pudding."

"We'll see how yours compares," Lillie said confidently. She pulled out a large glass bowl. "I'll let you make the salad. Everything you need is in the refrigerator or in the cabinets. You don't have to worry about the fruit cup. I bought some ambrosia that I found in one of those health food stores. Baxter says you're all into health."

"I try," Carla responded.

"We can talk while you make the salad."

Carla sensed Lillie trying to goad her.

"Baxter tells me your mom was Missy Etiquette," Lillie started off.

Carla laughed. "I guess. My mom cooked. She cleaned. She came to school meetings. She dressed up for my father. She set a hell of a table. I guess she got it from my grandmother. My mom just loved being a homemaker."

"And you?"

"I thought that's all I ever wanted. But then, I ended up dancing, and time flew by."

"Those stripping days are over, right?" Lillie sought reassurance.

Carla pulled out salad fixings from the refrigerator. "I hope so, but sometimes, I still miss the club life and the dancing." She saw Lillie stiffen. Carla let her stew for a minute. "At my age, though, I realize the strip club is not for me, not even as a manager. Some of the men can be so disrespectful to everybody, but to aging dancers . . . ." Carla's voice trailed off. "I'm trying to set an example for my nieces and a good friend of mine, Mimi. I'm sure Baxter has mentioned her. Don't worry. I'm not going back to my old life. I've got a much better life now." Carla's voice grew steely. "But I make my own decisions."

"Fair enough," Lillie said. Her face was unreadable as she watched Carla prepare the salad. "My son's got a lot going for him. He needs somebody who can complement that."

"I agree."

"He's got money, and I manage his accounts. Did he tell you I went back to school for accounting? I'm retired now, but I handle a lot of his finances."

Carla was prepared to go toe-to-toe with Lillie. "Baxter told me you went back to school—like I'm doing now. He's very proud of you—all your community work, the way you raised him."

"I tried to give my son a good life, that's all. I want him to have the best. I don't want anybody taking advantage of him."

Carla smiled with assurance. "I want him to have the best too. We both love your son. That's what matters. I don't care about his money. I work. I've always supported myself."

"I can see why my son has fallen for you. Did you ever stop to think that you both might be infatuated? I mean, he rescued you from a burning building."

"And I'm forever grateful. But I rescued him too."

"I see you got an answer for everything," Lillie snorted. "You drink?"

"I'm not a heavy drinker."

"Let's see what you're really made of." From the cabinet, Lillie pulled out an old-fashioned glass jar containing a clear liquid. "I got this from my cousins down south." She poured two shot glasses, one for her and one for Carla. "I'm sure you've tasted corn liquor."

Carla nodded. "I've had some before. I'm sure it's strong."

"No. This is the real deal. This separates the women from the girls."

Carla laughed in dread. Lillie downed her shot glass without a wince. Carla downed her glass. Her nostrils flared, and her eyes watered. She coughed. "Damn!" she exclaimed in a hoarse voice.

Lillie chuckled deviously.

"You're right." Carla's voice was still hoarse. "Never tasted anything like it. Did I pass the test?"

Lillie didn't answer. She turned down the oven on the banana pudding while Carla prepared a salad of mixed greens and kale. Carla added some feta cheese she found in the refrigerator and some nuts and raisins she found in the cabinets. She started tossing.

They were both loosening up from the corn liquor. Lillie made one last-ditch effort to rattle Carla. "My son's got a daughter out there somewhere. He's never going to give up on trying to find her."

Carla nodded. "I know."

"That doesn't bother you?"

"If I dwell on it, but I understand why he wants to find her. She's his flesh and blood." Carla paused. "I love your son, Lillie. That's all that matters to me right now."

Lillie sighed. "You know, my son is not the easiest person to get along with. He's got his moods and his ways."

"No shit," Carla responded, pleasantly tipsy.

They both burst out in laughter. Carla felt a barrier crumble between them. Lillie looked Carla up and down admiringly. "Girl, you got a fantastic body. Can you help me get in shape?"

"I sure can," Carla smiled. "Won't take much. You're in pretty good shape already."

Baxter came into the kitchen, curious. "Y'all okay?" He slipped his arm loosely around Carla's waist and glanced directly at Lillie. "You're not trying to scare my girl away, are you?"

Carla smiled at him, pleased at his show of support. She had so much to be grateful for on this Thanksgiving—a new man, a new way of life.

Lillie noted the amorous display of affection between her son and Carla. "Everything's fine," Lillie reassured him.

Baxter kissed his mom on the cheek. "Good." He saw the corn liquor sitting out on the counter. "Good ole cousin Rick," he said and poured himself a shot glass. He gulped it down, then tried to call Zach into the kitchen, but his voice was too hoarse, and his eyes watered.

Lillie laughed and called Zach into the kitchen for him. "We're doing a Thanksgiving toast," she said when Zach entered.

Zach noted Baxter's watery eyes and the empty glasses. "Looks like y'all already finished."

Lillie shook her head. "No. We're just getting started." She poured half shots into Carla's and Baxter's glasses, a full shot into Zach's, and another full shot into hers. Lillie raised her glass. Carla and Baxter raised theirs in toast and in dread. Zach didn't know what to expect as he raised his. Down the hatch, the liquor flowed. At the end of the toast, Lillie's was the only clear voice. They all laughed once their voices returned.

"You want to finish watching the game before we eat?" Lillie asked. "I know you do," she addressed Carla.

No further encouragement was needed. Everybody headed for the living room.

* * *

After Lillie said grace, Thanksgiving dinner started with ambrosia. Lillie passed around a crystal bowl, and everybody spooned the mixture into their goblets. "Everything but the kitchen sink is in there," she said.

Carla smiled. Lillie was right. The ambrosia boasted apples, oranges, bananas, grapes, strawberries, coconut, raisins, and almond slivers. After sparring with Lillie, Carla had worked up an appetite. The juice from the ambrosia was like a heavenly nectar. The crystal goblets sparkled and added an aesthetic touch to the meal. Carla delighted in the myriad of colors reflected in the goblet.

She suddenly became aware of a heavy silence in the room. She looked up and saw Baxter, his mom, and Zach staring at her. They quickly looked away. Carla knew she had good table manners, but was she eating her ambrosia too fast? Did she have something stuck in her teeth? There were no buttons on her blouse, so nothing had popped out. Still, an aura of anxiety permeated the room. Baxter fidgeted and squirmed.

Carla noticed that everybody, except her, seemed to be toying with the ambrosia. Was she indeed eating too quickly? Carla couldn't stand it any longer. She accidentally dropped her spoon on the floor and didn't bother to retrieve it. "What's wrong?"

Then she finally saw something sparkle beside her goblet. At first, she thought her eyes played tricks on her. She wasn't sure if what she saw was simply a reflection from the goblet. But no, her eyes didn't deceive her. She wasn't sure how it got there, but positioned beside her goblet was a beautiful diamond ring that sparkled more than the goblet. Carla picked it up in awe.

Immediately, Baxter ran over to her and dropped to one knee. Hard-assed Lillie smiled with tears in her eyes. Zach grinned, enjoying the momentous occasion.

Baxter breathed nervously. He took the ring from Carla's fingers and held it out. "Will you marry me, Carla? Will you be my wife?"

Carla was astounded for a moment. She was both scared and excited. But above all, she loved him. She regrouped and held her finger out so that Baxter could slip the ring on her finger. She leaned over and kissed him passionately. "Oh, yes. I'd love to marry you," she said.

EPILOGUE

The doorbell rang loudly, but Carla barely heard it. She was so busy beaming and staring at the beautiful ring on her finger. They had finished their ambrosia, but Lillie seemed in no hurry to start the main meal. Baxter got up from the table and answered the door. Moments later, Carla heard all kinds of commotion in the living room. She rose from her chair and followed the noise. Lillie and Zach accompanied her.

Carla's mouth dropped open in astonishment. Lillie's living room was suddenly filled with guests. "Surprise!" everybody exclaimed. Carla's nieces ran over to her in excitement. Carla encircled them in her arms.

"Let's see the ring," they insisted. Stephanie, the pre-teen, held Carla's hand out and marveled at the ring. Brittany and Princess Tiffany giggled in delight.

In amazement, Carla stared at all the other faces in Lillie's living room. Natalie smiled in congratulations. Russell had come with her to celebrate and be with his girls. Carla felt overjoyed at seeing Mimi and Frank. Even Carla's boss, Jasmine, had shown up with her husband, Kenny. Jasmine had also brought along her two nephews. Earl wore a big grin as he stood beside his girlfriend, the young woman he had brought to the charity ball.

Carla couldn't believe it. She felt ecstatic that they had all come to congratulate her. Everybody took turns and gave her a hug. She extended her hand and showed off her ring.

Baxter smiled, pleased. "Now I've got two women in my life." He introduced his mom to everyone who hadn't already met her.

Earl couldn't resist ribbing Baxter. "Now what if Carla had told you, no?"

Baxter hugged Carla playfully. "She better not have. After all that talk about me not wanting any commitment?"

"Kicking and screaming," Earl laughed.

Carla raised an eyebrow at Baxter.

"Nah. He didn't tell me all your business," Earl joked. "Just the kicking and screaming part." Earl reached out and grabbed her finger. "Oh, you fancy, huh?"

Carla's smile said it all. She turned to Mimi and Jasmine. "You two are all lovely and glowing." They both grinned. "Is it okay if I say something?" Carla asked.

Mimi shrugged, and Jasmine didn't protest.

"We need to congratulate them too. They're both pregnant," Carla informed everyone. She realized Baxter and his crew already knew about Mimi.

"You're both pregnant?" Natalie stepped away from them in alarm. Amid raised eyebrows and laughter, Natalie defended herself. "Hey, I want to make sure it's not contagious."

Russell gave her a piercing stare.

"You got a life. So do I," Natalie said. She gathered up her girls. "Y'all stand over on this side of the room with me." Brittany and Princess Tiffany giggled even though they didn't understand what they were giggling about. Stephanie, who had discovered boys, reassured her mother. "I'm good. You don't have to worry about me."

"Good answer," Russell said.

"You get over on that side too, Missy." Earl ushered his girlfriend closer to Natalie and the girls.

Earl's girlfriend started laughing. She looped her arms through Mimi's and Jasmine's. Everybody laughed, except Earl. "I'm just kidding," she said.

Princess Tiffany still had a mild crush on Earl. Her eyes fluttered at him. Earl burst out laughing. "Twenty-two, right? We said twenty-two."

"What's up with twenty-two?" Earl's girlfriend asked.

"Nothing," he said and playfully nudged Tiffany.

She smiled.

"Congratulations," Earl said to Mimi and Jasmine. Mimi and Frank smiled proudly. So did Jasmine and Kenny.

Earl's eyes pierced Jasmine's for a fleeting moment. Then he shook Kenny's hand. He seemed comfortable with Kenny, and he playfully teased Jasmine's nephews the way he had at the barbecue. The boys were about five and six by now, a year younger than Brittany and Tiffany.

Carla still wondered if Earl and Jasmine had gotten intimate after the barbecue that day, but if they had, nobody could detect it now. Fling or no fling, Jasmine's baby was definitely Kenny's. Her glowing confidence dispelled any doubts.

"Well now, if you haven't eaten already, there's plenty of food." Lillie headed for the kitchen to bring out the feast. Baxter and the men opened up the padded folding chairs and placed them throughout the living room and dining room. Zach opened up the patio in case anybody wanted to go outside. Dusk was falling, and the night air held an invigorating chill.

"I wondered why your mom had all these chairs and so much food," Carla said.

Baxter put his arm around Carla and kissed her softly on the lips. "All for you, my dear."

"Where's Percy?" Carla asked.

"With his sons. Said he couldn't make it."

Carla was annoyed that Percy didn't show up. Baxter acted nonchalant, but she knew it bothered him.

"I'm going to tell that Percy off when I see him," Carla said and hugged Baxter supportively.

He smiled in appreciation. "No, don't do that. Let's just enjoy the day."

Carla lightened up and marveled at the family and friends surrounding her on such a happy occasion. She and Natalie linked arms, forging a stronger bond than ever.

"Be nice if dad could have come," Natalie said.

Carla nodded pensively. "Baxter and I are going to see him tomorrow. You want to come with us?"

Natalie's eyes lit up. "That should be fun. We'll take the party to him."

Carla headed over to Mimi who laughed and talked with all the kids. They adored her. Carla nudged Mimi aside.

"You okay?" Carla asked.

Mimi's eyes softened. "I'm fine, chica. Scared, but fine."

"Hope I didn't put you on the spot."

"It's okay, now that Frank knows he's the father," Mimi whispered. "Damn, I was lucky. It's about time."

"How's the baby?"

Mimi crossed her fingers. "So far, the baby seems okay. We'll see."

"Happy Thanksgiving, Mimi. You deserve it."

"We both do. Now if I can just stay out of trouble." Mimi paused. "It's not that hard, knowing I'm carrying a baby inside me, but what happens after the baby is born?"

"One second at a time," Carla said in encouragement. Then she and Mimi were pulled apart by all the fun and activity. In high-spirited camaraderie, Carla joined Jasmine and Earl's girlfriend.

The guys were trying to congregate around another football game, but Lillie wasn't having it. "Let's eat and play some music," she coaxed. The men compromised and left the TV on in the family room so they could sneak back and forth to catch parts of the game.

The doorbell chimed. Earl went to the door. He seemed very comfortable in Lillie's house.

Percy and Teddy walked in. Carla hugged them both, thoroughly delighted to see them. Her eyes narrowed at Percy. "Glad you could make it," she said.

Percy looked a bit sheepish. "You know I had to show up for my boy," he said finally and hugged Baxter. "Congratulations."

Carla sensed that Baxter's night was complete. She held his hand and laughed. "Don't worry. I'll let him out a few nights a year," she teased Percy.

Baxter groaned, and Teddy's face lit up with a smile.

"Girl, how you doing?" Carla said to Teddy. Mimi came over and joined them. All three shared a bond that could never be broken.

Carla's spirits soared as she glanced around at all the loved ones surrounding her. She caught Brittany's eye and hurried over to her nieces so they could share a private moment. She scooped them up in her arms and grinned. "Told you I was going to find you an uncle."

ABOUT THE AUTHOR

A former teacher from the East Coast, N. Kay left teaching and moved to Los Angeles to pursue a career as a screenwriter and film producer. Drawing from experience on numerous independent screen projects and writing collaborations, N. Kay decided to create the ultimate, erotic romance novel.

www.ingramcontent.com/pod-product-compliance
Lightning Source LLC
Chambersburg PA
CBHW030349030726
47497CB00002B/256